ALSO BY MARY SHEEPSHANKS

Picking Up the Pieces
Facing the Music
A Price for Everything

Off Balance

Off Balance

MARY SHEEPSHANKS

THOMAS DUNNE BOOKS ❧ NEW YORK
St. Martin's Press

THOMAS DUNNE BOOKS.
An imprint of St. Martin's Press.

www.stmartins.com

ISBN 0-312-26813-0

First published in the United Kingdom by Century, Random House Group Limited

First U.S. Edition: February 2001

10   9   8   7   6   5   4   3   2   1

ACKNOWLEDGMENTS

The setting and characters in this story are imaginary, but I want to thank all those who have helped me with information and expertise, especially Henrietta and Sebastian Thewes and Lavinia Gordon, who talked to me about 'Music at Blair Atholl' and showed me Strathgarry; Nigel and Malise Forbes Adam for letting me look at the theatre at Skipwith; Mrs P. E. Jones, who allowed me to visit Adelina Patti's theatre at Craig-y-Nos Castle and showed me round herself—special thanks also to Gillie Raikes for arranging this.

My thanks go to Ricky Green, Technical Director of Opera North, and his team for helpful information and for letting me watch scene painting in progress at the Grand Theatre, Leeds; a big thank you to paediatrician Dr Jane Wynne for her generous help and encouragement—any mistakes will be entirely my own. Many friends gave me advice while I was writing this book, particularly David and Squibbs Noble, Charlotte and Tiffy Laing and artist Graham Rust.

My special love goes to my grandson James, who has enriched our lives as a family and taught us all so much about many unexpected things, and I want to take this opportunity to thank everyone at the Camphill School, Aberdeen, who have done so much for him.

Last but not least, my love and gratitude for their patient encouragement go to my wonderful daughters and daughter-in-law, agent Sarah Molloy and editor Kate Parkin.

A Tolerant View

'If a man does not keep pace with his companions, perhaps it is because he hears a different drummer. Let him step to the music which he hears, however measured or far away.'

Henry David Thoreau, 1817–62

One

Glendrochatt stood high on its hill, an ancient house, a house with secrets that represented very different things to different people.

To Giles it was his past and his future: terror and challenge. To Isobel it was a place of warmth and laughter—her children's home. To Lorna it was the elusive goal of her dreams. To Daniel it was an enchantment and a threat. And to Edward and Amy? The house was alive with Amy's music—but who could tell what Edward thought about anything?

When Isobel Grant first heard that her sister was returning home from South Africa, a shadow fell momentarily across her usual sunshine.

Lorna had written that now her divorce was finally through, she wanted to make a fresh start and put the past few years behind her. Could she come and make her base with Isobel and Giles until she got her life sorted out—at any rate until the end of the summer? Might they perhaps have a job for her to do?—naturally she would not want remuneration. As she read the familiar, neat handwriting Isobel knew, with that inner certainty that usually turns out to be deadly accurate, that what Lorna really wanted was not to make a new life but to pick up the threads of an old one—and weave them differently.

Discomfort, like a small but undissolved fish bone, pricked Isobel's throat.

She wondered how her childless sister would feel about the children. More importantly how would they, especially Edward, respond to her? The thought of the effect Edward and Lorna might have on each other made Isobel break out in a sweat. There were so many changes about to take place in the Grants' lives anyway that Isobel wondered how she would cope with trying to fit this new piece of jigsaw into an already complicated puzzle.

Above all, she wondered how Giles would react to his sister-in-law's presence.

They had not seen Lorna since they had last gone to South Africa for a holiday and stayed in Capetown with her and her husband. Despite the lusciousness of the surroundings and the luxury of Lorna's lifestyle, it had been an uneasy time, with tensions never far below the surface. There had been ominous signs of cracks in the Cartwright marriage. John Cartwright, a brilliant eye surgeon, was a highly strung and demanding man, given to occasional outbursts of temper, which left everyone connected with him quaking. Isobel privately thought that Lorna, his second wife, often goaded him deliberately and then enjoyed playing the martyr when he shouted at her. Giles's championship of Lorna, and solicitous sympathy for her, had not endeared him to her difficult husband and Isobel had been thankful when the holiday was over. That had been three years ago.

Giles's first reaction, when Isobel pushed Lorna's letter over to him, seemed straightforward enough—but she had been married to Giles for too long not to know that the feelings he chose to show were by no means always all that were there.

'Oh, great. Good to know she's really shot of that bastard at last,' he had said, flicking through the flimsy airmail pages while he simultaneously fiddled one-handedly with his mobile telephone.

Isobel stared out of the window at the driving Scottish rain that laced the sky to the earth with long diagonal stitches and made the hills temporarily invisible. 'I suppose she'll have to come,' she muttered reluctantly, after a pause, 'though it's not exactly brilliant timing.'

'Oh, I don't know. Might be an excellent moment. You're going to need all the help you can get if this new project takes off—and you know I think you have far too much to do already. Lorna could be extremely useful.'

'It's her usefulness that's always so daunting.' Isobel pulled a face.

'I could find plenty for her to do.'

'How lovely. She might become quite indispensable,' answered Isobel lightly, raising an eyebrow at her husband.

'She might indeed.' Giles let his words fall like carefully measured drops of medicine.

'Right then.' Isobel busied herself gathering up the Lottery Fund Application Pack, together with her notes about a recent meeting of the Glendrochatt Estate Trustees.

After their marriage it would have been too much to expect that Isobel could have remained in ignorance of Giles's old affair with her sister for long: there are always too many people who take pleasure in passing on unpalatable information under the flimsy pretext that they feel the recipient 'ought to know'. Giles had tried to convince her that the relationship had never been serious—boy-and-girl stuff—and assured her that in any case it had been over well before he and Isobel had even met. She had believed him and accepted his version of events, though she had been dismayed all the same; but what her enigmatic sister felt was quite another matter.

Isobel had no intention of telling Giles how threatening she found this new situation, but then she didn't need to. Giles could always pick up the smallest nuance of undercurrent like a magnet attracting pins.

'I know, I know. We can't refuse,' said Isobel, putting up her hands in a mock gesture of defeat. 'I'll write and say we'd be delighted to have her, and that we really could employ her for a bit to give her a start and help us out of a hole too—though I absolutely insist we should pay her properly—but it would have to be on a strictly temporary basis, of course.'

'Of course,' said Giles and he treated his wife to the special smile that used to make her knees tremble when they first met— and still could, on occasion.

'Which of us is going to find time to take Amy for her lesson this afternoon?' he had asked, looking at his watch.

'You know perfectly well I have to take Edward for his check-up this afternoon, o thou lover of snooping in my engagement diary,' said Isobel, laughing at him. 'Sometimes you really are the pits, Giles Grant—you hate not taking Amy yourself. What an old fraud you are—don't dare to deny it.'

Giles flicked her nose. His had been a rhetorical question, a typically Giles way of underlining how much he thought they needed a spare wheel in their lives. He gave his wife a very loving look. People tended to find themselves swept along by the com-bination of Giles's charisma with his organizing tendencies, as though they'd been hit by a tidal wave, but Isobel had never been one of them. He respected her independence of mind, and her capacity to be amused by the ridiculous side of most situations and people—not least himself—was very precious to him. He loved to hear her laugh.

As the day of Lorna's arrival approached, Isobel made special preparations for her sister's comfort. It was a private form of touching wood, a kind of bargaining with fate: if I behave beau-tifully over this and make her really welcome, thought Isobel, perhaps all will go smoothly; perhaps we shall recapture some of the closeness I once thought we had, without the difficulties it brought—but she didn't really believe it. The idea of having Lorna living at Glendrochatt made Isobel's heart sink: Lorna with her paper-thin skin and her private agenda, always so skillfully hidden that very few people knew it was there; Lorna, so helpful, so sympathetic, so dangerously easy to confide in; Lorna, so untrustworthy, such a troublemaker.

The building work, which had thrown the Grants' lives into chaos for months was now almost complete and the opening ceremony for the Glendrochatt Arts Centre was looming. As Giles had pointed out, the arrival of Lorna would save them having to re-advertise for an assistant administrator. There had been quite a big response to their first advertisement, but the replies themselves had been disappointing and the thought of having to spend time on endless possibly fruitless interviews at this particular moment was daunting. To her relief, Giles agreed with Isobel that Lorna must have the proper salary for the job. They knew she didn't need the money because she had received a very generous divorce settlement, but the idea of being beholden to her—a situation she could exploit—was too daunting for Isobel to stomach; put on a professional footing, as an arrangement equally useful to both parties, she felt she could cope with it.

Isobel decided to let Lorna have the first of the new flats that were being converted in the old stables for visiting teachers, performers and staff; it had always been earmarked for the new assistant. With her sister's tastes in mind, she chose a chintz of sprigged lilies of the valley on a pink background, a charming copy of an old Victorian design, for curtains and bedspread, and a dotted Swiss muslin over rose-coloured cotton for the dressing-table. It wasn't what she would have chosen for herself, but pink had always been Lorna's favourite colour, and the room certainly looked very fresh and pretty when it was finished. There was a bathroom in each flat and a sitting area with a breakfast bar dividing it from the small kitchen beyond. Downstairs there was a shared place for the inhabitants to keep boots and waterproofs— essentials for life in Perthshire—and a communal utility room with a washing machine and drying facilities. Isobel knew most people would consider the flats delightful, but she also wondered whether

Lorna would be expecting to live *en famille* with herself and Giles and the children, and braced herself for umbrage.

The garden at Glendrochatt was a paradise for children. Standing outside the south-facing front of the house, before she set out to meet Lorna's flight at Edinburgh airport, Isobel looked down and watched Amy and Edward go through the gate that led from the formal terrace into a wilder area, an open space of couch grass surrounded by birch trees and the species rhododendrons and azaleas which had been collected from the Himalayas by Giles's grandfather. The grounds were famous for them. Clumps of bracken surrounded the clearing and harebells grew among the grass. It was the children's special play area. A cedar, as old as the house above, spread its huge branches, from one of which hung the swing that had been put there when Giles was a child. The ropes had been renewed over the years but the wooden seat was the original one that had been made for him thirty-five years before; here also was the seesaw on which a lonely small Giles had been forced to invent his own games because he so rarely had a playmate to sit on the other end of it. He had shown Amy how to stand in the middle, legs apart, and either tip it dangerously up and down, expertly riding the bumps, or stand absolutely still motionless as a hovering hawk riding the thermals, finding the perfect point of balance. Sometimes Amy played her fiddle standing on the seesaw, relishing the double challenge of keeping the lower half of her body steady while swaying riskily above the waist as she wielded her bow with energetic fervour—although it made Giles furious if he caught her. A few months before she had broken a new half-size violin worth £500 when she had lost her footing and fallen off the seesaw. Luckily it had been possible to have the instrument repaired and it was insured anyway, but Giles had forbidden Amy ever to do such a stupid, irresponsible thing again. Isobel had backed him up, but she thought there was more to his anger than natural anxiety about injury either to Amy or her violin: when she played in this way, like a wild bird singing from the top of a tree, Amy's music escaped from Giles's direction.

Ironic, thought Isobel, watching Amy standing now, brown bare legs effortlessly holding the long plank level despite the wind, her arms linked behind her head, that Giles should have taught Amy about balance when he found it so hard to achieve in his own life. Would Edward, she wondered, ever achieve any point of balance at all, or at least one that anyone else could recognise? But then, of course, Edward could not be judged by anyone else's rules.

On the edge of the clearing was the wooden castle—another legacy from Giles's childhood—in which Amy and Edward had made their headquarters. Edward sat on the drawbridge with the bag of toy snakes and dinosaurs, which he carted around everywhere, fearsome creatures who carried on bloodthirsty battles and fought to the kill under Edward's direction.

'Die, o King of the Dinothaurs,' intoned Edward, who had a lisp. 'Bang! Bang! You're dead. I thlay you with my thord.'

Isobel thought sadly that the plastic creatures were nothing to the strange monsters that writhed around in Edward's mind, but at least today the children were deep in a game together, something that was becoming increasingly rare as their individual paths began to separate. She waved to them, but they were too absorbed to notice and, as she went to get the car, Isobel Grant wished desperately that she could freeze the moment and not face the future.

Two

A long trans-continental flight is as good a time as any to become absorbed in a film, but Lorna Cartwright, unlike the other passengers aboard the flight from Capetown to Heathrow was not glued to the small screen in front of her. Instead, she lay back in her seat, eyes closed beneath the black eyeshades provided for long-haul travellers, and watched the brilliantly clear images flickering across her mind.

With painful clarity Lorna sees a small girl, fair and plump, with big blue eyes and curls in which hair ribbons always stayed put: a solemn child, a solid child, above all a *good* child—no trouble at all, never a bit of bother, she has heard the grown-ups say. Not a child who has tantrums, won't eat, or bites other children; not one who is always calling out for another drink of water after she has been put to bed; not the kind who is afflicted by ogres who hide in cupboards or who keeps subversive imaginary companions invisible to anyone else. It was pleasant being this easy child with whom adults were, if not ecstatic, apparently well satisfied.

At three, Lorna knows all her letters already; she can trace an outline with great care and chalk inside a circle. Well done, Lorna. Yes, that's very nice—now do run along, darling.

At four she can be trusted to feed her hamster without being reminded. She likes looking after things and is conscientious with her dolls. They do not end up hurled naked on the floor and forgotten: they are carefully dressed and undressed, and sleep tucked up in a doll's cot beside her own bed. God Bless Mummy and Daddy and make Lorna a good girl—but he already seems to have done this, so perhaps it is a superfluous request? Goodnight, Lorna, sleep well. The light is switched off, the door closed and there is no fuss.

Something exciting is about to happen. Soon there is going to be a baby in the family—a real one—and Lorna will help care for it, her mother has promised.

The arrival of the baby marks an important moment, for things will never be quite the same again for the heroine of this so far uneventful drama. She is obsessed by the new infant and knows exactly what ought to be done for it. Their father says anyone would think Lorna had read a book on parenting skills. Unfortunately, the baby has not read the same instructions and does not always take kindly to Lorna's ministrations.

'Do leave her *alone*, darling.' Lorna's mother sighs wearily. 'Babies don't *like* being smothered.' Lorna, who regards the new arrival as her private property, is huffed. Later more complicated feelings creep in for the little sister who is so naughty but who makes everyone laugh. Lorna never makes people laugh, yet the curious thing is that when grown-ups comment on the badness, the wilfulness and outrageousness of small Isobel, it always seems to be a compliment.

'Isobel is a little monster,' their mother says proudly and everyone smiles.

Lorna continues to be no trouble, and her school reports on both work and conduct are excellent—so why is there a lack of enthusiasm in people's response to her? Lorna has no idea. She earns the nickname of 'The Perfect' from her contemporaries and it is not one that is kindly given. Later, when Isobel's friends call her Cat, short for Catastrophe, it's an accolade.

When Lorna is fifteen she overhears her mother and a friend discussing Isobel and herself. Lorna is doing her homework at the table in the dining-room of their house in Charlotte Square in Edinburgh, where their father is a solicitor, but the door to the adjoining drawing-room is open. Nobody remembers her presence there.

'In the circumstances I do think it's lucky that Lorna is so pretty,' says the friend.

'I suppose she is.' Lorna's mother sounds surprised. 'I've never really thought about it, but you're right; she's much prettier than Isobel. You couldn't exactly call Isobel *pretty*.'

Teenage Lorna listens entranced, though she does wonder why her mother hasn't thought about it before.

'Oh, Lorna will be extremely good-looking—you'll see: wonderful figure, lovely skin. It's a pity she's not more forthcoming, but then I'm afraid Isobel will always have the shine factor out of those two. Nobody can help loving Isobel.' The friend and Lorna's mother laugh indulgently.

Lorna's throat constricts. To stop herself feeling invisible she picks up the pair of compasses from her geometry set, jabs the point viciously into the dining-room table and makes a deep gouge with it. When her mother finds it later she is horrified—clearly nothing loveable about this particular naughtiness.

'Whatever made you do it? I don't understand. It's so unlike you, darling.' Lorna looks stonily back and neither explains nor says she is sorry. Her mother nervously—and rightly—supposes that Lorna is about to start being difficult; it must be her age, of course.

Lorna appears to cherish her younger sister, but increasingly wishes no one else did. She is always trying to curb Isobel's impetuous behaviour—above all to protect her from overexposure and pull her safely into the shade. If Lorna could cover her sister with total sunblock, she would. Isobel doesn't relish this attempted restraint, but it doesn't worry her too much either, because she loves life in the sunshine and goes her own blithe way. She gives her big sister the spontaneous, demonstrative affection that no one else seems to provide and takes it for granted that Lorna will come to her rescue if she needs help. Later Isobel learns that there is a price to pay for this help, but that is in the future. It is commonly accepted that the sisters are close—sweet the way Lorna looks after Isobel.

Images accelerate to the time when Lorna acquired her first boyfriend. They meet at a party in Edinburgh. Giles Grant, who is easily the best-looking boy present, asks her to dance and after that they sit out together. Giles is nursing a broken heart—or so he tells Lorna, in riveting detail, throughout the rest of the evening. Lorna is outraged at the callousness with which his erstwhile girlfriend has treated him and hangs on his words with a display of sympathy that is balm to his feelings; indignation puts quite a sparkle in her normally rather blank blue eyes. She also learns that Giles's childhood has been haunted by disaster: he has no mother and lives with a difficult, demanding father who doesn't understand him. Lorna vaguely remembers having heard her mother talk about a tragedy involving Giles's famously beautiful actress mother, Atalanta Grant. She is deeply stirred by this drama as it is thrillingly recounted by Giles. Giles has found himself an adoring slave and Lorna has found a cause, a state of affairs that suits them both admirably.

Lorna manages to keep news of this boyfriend away from her family. She has had more than enough over the years of taking friends home, wanting those friends all to herself, only to find them swallowed up by her family, charmed by her pretty mother, fascinated by her clever, witty father and, worst of all, beguiled by her little sister. She has no intention of exposing Giles to Isobel's capacity to amuse. Her parents complain that they never meet any of her friends now.

Later, when she and Giles both attend Bristol University—a comfortably safe distance from Edinburgh—they go round in the same large group of friends, whose interests and activities are mainly instigated by Giles, and it is generally assumed, especially by Lorna, that he and she will probably get engaged one day and end up together for life. It's true that Giles flirts with a great many other girls, but no one takes this seriously; Lorna knows he's devoted to her—absolutely dependent on her, she tells herself—and the fact that he has a connoisseur's eye for the female sex makes his attentions to her all the more flattering; if there were no comparisons and he never looked at any one else it wouldn't be such a compliment to her, would it? There may be a flaw in this argument but Lorna does not explore it. During vacations she goes to stay at Giles's home, Glendrochatt, which she thinks is incredibly glamorous and soon she is deeply in love, not only with Giles himself but with his family house as well. She indulges in fantasies of herself standing at the top of the arch of steps that lead up to the front door receiving guests, a kilted Giles at her side and a brood of incredibly good-looking, well-behaved children ranged around them. She has never been so happy in her life. Giles's scary old father, Hector Grant—with whom Giles really gets on perfectly well—thinks Lorna is dreadfully dull, but supposes he should be thankful that at least she seems fairly harmless. He is wrong.

*A*t this point Lorna Cartwright, now aged thirty-seven, found her fingers gripping the armrests of her seat on the jumbo-jet. The images before her were almost too painful to watch, but Lorna was so hypnotised by her memories that she could not make herself stop.

*L*orna comes down from university with an unexpected 2:1 but Giles, although far brighter than she is, has spent most of his time there either acting or partying and only gets a disappointing third. His father is furious with him, but Lorna makes it clear that she thinks Giles has had exceptionally bad luck—though it's hard to justify this rose-tinted opinion. She confidently expects Giles to propose to her although he shows no sign of doing so. Indeed, he seems unaccountably ungrateful for her loyalty and continued faith in him. In order to wrench some serious commitment out of Giles, but against her own inclination to stick, leach-like, to his physical presence, Lorna acts on the advice of friends and goes off travelling for six months.

'Put some space between you. Play hard to get for a change. He'll be lost without you when you're not always at his beck and call, you'll see,' urge the friends.

Lorna writes Giles excruciatingly detailed letters about her impressions of the places she has visited and the people she has met. These lengthy epistles, accurate to the last war memorial, icon, or battle date—Lorna keeps a conscientious travel diary—fail to capture the atmosphere of time or place, or bring to life the broad sweep of Lorna's new experiences. She receives the occasional postcard from Giles, which brings his disturbing presence strongly to mind and makes her ache for their moment of reunion. What these disappointingly brief communications fail to mention is that something unforeseen has occurred during Lorna's absence: Giles has met Isobel.

Isobel is nineteen and at her parents' insistence is doing a secretarial course in Edinburgh, before taking up a place at drama school. In one of her affectionate, hastily scrawled letters to Lorna, Isobel writes that there are *thrilling* new developments in her life. She is *dying* to tell Lorna all about it when she comes home but must rush now—no time to write more—she sends tons of love and XXXs.

Lorna is aware of the familiar corroding little stab of envy but has no sense of foreboding.

The night Lorna gets back to London, where she has decided to stay for a few days with an old school friend who lives in Battersea, Giles telephones her to make a date for the following night—he has flown south especially to catch her before she goes home to Edinburgh—there is something urgent he needs to tell her. Lorna is blissfully certain her tactics have worked and goes to meet him in a trance of happiness, but instead of producing a ring, Giles explodes a bomb. He has asked her out to dinner to tell her that he is indeed hoping to get married: not to her—not even to some hateful faceless girl but to her own sister. He hopes Lorna can be happy for himself and Isobel, and tells her how much he has always valued her friendship.

Friendship! The word whistles through Lorna like an icy wind. In a voice from Siberia, she asks Giles what Isobel thinks about this. Giles says, 'Oh, I've told her what good chums you and I were at Bristol' and adds shrewdly, 'She seemed very surprised that we'd met. Said she'd never heard you even mention me— not very flattering of you, Lorna!'

Lorna feels a victim of her own secrecy. Giles says he will always be really fond of her, that he's terribly sorry if the news has been a shock, but expects that, like him, she has already real- ised that they have outgrown each other. She was quite right to have gone away when she did, to give them both a chance to grow up and move on.

Lorna wants to scream at him—to beg him to rethink, to tell him that he is making a terrible mistake. She thinks wildly that if she had lost Giles through death she would have been prepared to commit suttee for him, but at the same time, with a desperate sense of déjà vu, she also accepts that she has yet again been found second best to her younger sister.

Somehow she gets through the rest of dinner before creeping back to the friend's flat hardly able to make her legs work, hob- bling along like an old, old woman, to lie awake through the worst night of her life.

Part of her knows that Isobel would never knowingly have stolen her boyfriend, but this is no comfort, rather the reverse— a justifiable grudge would be infinitely preferable—and another, darker part of her longs to inflict as deep a wound on Isobel's heart as the one she feels has been gouged out of her own. Perhaps it is as well that she no longer has geometry compasses to hand when she finally goes home and greets Isobel. Instead, in an immensely painful face-saving effort, she behaves beautifully and pretends to be delighted. Giles, who is inwardly riddled with guilt, though more at his lack of frankness with Isobel than any feeling that he has let Lorna down, is not fooled, but no one else seems to have the faintest idea that behind a bright façade Lorna is bleeding to death.

When Giles and Isobel get married a year later Lorna tells herself they have ruined her life. Though she makes a defiant show of nonchalance at the wedding—and gets uncharacteristically drunk at the party after it—in her heart she does not offer Isobel forgiveness.

As the plane circled over London, Lorna Cartwright was jolted awake by a voice announcing: 'Ladies and Gentlemen, will you please fasten your seat belts, see that your backrest is in the upright position and remain seated while we prepare for our descent to Heathrow.' A voice thanked the passengers for travelling with the airline and hoped everyone had enjoyed their flight. 'Before leaving the aircraft, please check the overhead lockers and ensure that you have all your belongings with you.'

Lorna, whose hand luggage was neat, light and well-organised, but whose emotional baggage was extremely weighty, had no intention of leaving anything behind.

Three

Isobel got to the airport early. The thought that she might be late meeting Lorna's connecting flight and thereby start her visit off on the wrong foot had made her add an extra twenty minutes to the time she normally allowed for driving from home to Edinburgh. Having taken this precaution, of course the traffic was lighter than usual, there were no roadworks and a departing car most conveniently backed out of the first possible slot as she drove into the short-stay car park. Sod's law, thought Isobel. She decided to get a cup of coffee and enjoy a chance to read the paper in peace for a change; it was absurd to feel nervous.

She took her coffee over to an empty table but, instead of devouring the *Daily Mail*, found herself conjuring up scenes from her childhood. She remembered guiltily that life had always seemed more fun when Lorna wasn't there. Lorna too often gave Isobel the uncomfortable feeling of having done her elder sister down in some way, though usually while doing something entirely innocent, pleasurable and actually quite unconnected with Lorna, like climbing trees or laughing at shared jokes with their fun-loving mother on whom the company of Lorna seemed to act like a douche of cold water. She had a vivid picture of Lorna removing her from whatever game she was playing and dragging her along by the hand to tell their nanny that she, Isobel, was about to wet her knickers, had spilled her drink, had fallen in the burn, needed a rest. It seemed as if Lorna was constantly casting her in the role of irresponsible nitwit—dear, hopeless little Izz—and invariably presenting it as an act of kindness. 'Wasn't it lucky that I found her?' Lorna would ask the grown-ups.

Later she had been full of advice about what Isobel should wear—or more likely not wear—and how she should behave at parties. This advice—to which it had to be admitted Isobel paid scant attention—usually had to do with restrictions and dire warnings of the consequences of not heeding them, despite the fact that Isobel, following her own happy star, seemed to get on a lot better than Lorna. Poor Lorna, thought Isobel now, what a thorn in her flesh I must have been, but I don't want to be put under that black cloud of disapproval again. It is years since we have lived under the same roof, she reflected, or even been together for any length of time; we must both have changed to some extent, but how is she going to react now that I no longer fit the role of dizzy, incapable little sister in which she liked to cast me? We are both grown women and I, for one, must remember to behave like one, vowed Isobel to herself: I will not be made to feel apologetic about what I enjoy—and all that I am lucky enough to have.

She finished her coffee just as Lorna's flight was announced and went down to meet her full of good resolutions.

As she scanned the passengers coming through the Arrivals doors she began to wonder if Lorna might have missed her flight from Heathrow, until something familiar about the walk of one made her look again at the elegant figure in the black trouser suit and intimidating hat who was pushing a trolley of expensive-looking luggage.

'Lorna!' shrieked Isobel, waving wildly to attract her attention, and she rushed forward to give her a welcoming hug. 'Oh, Lorna, darling, how good to see you' and to her relief Isobel felt a genuine surge of affection for her sister as they exchanged an embrace. Perhaps all her anxieties had been unnecessary—figments of her imagination? Then she started to laugh. 'Goodness, I hardly recognised you—you look like a film star or something! Is this the new cool single woman's image? You make me feel a real scruff-pot.'

'But I would have recognised you *anywhere*,' said Lorna. 'Still the same little sister I used to look after.'

*T*here was so much to talk about that it was hard to know where to begin.

'Will you miss South Africa terribly?' asked Isobel, after she had collected her car, made a hasty attempt at brushing dog hairs off the front seat and piled Lorna's immaculate luggage into the back. She nosed the car into the stream of traffic outside the airport and accelerated smartly in front of a juggernaut. 'Is that something that will be difficult for you?'

'There's lots I'll miss. It was a great way of life. I loved the climate and the countryside, and all the domestic help—I suppose you could say it was very cushy, except that my marriage was a disaster. Well, you saw that for yourself. I shan't miss John.'

'No. We're so sorry about all you've been through. When did you first realise it wasn't going to work?' asked Isobel curiously. 'We all thought John so charming when you were engaged and he came over to meet us—and later you never let on there was anything wrong.' She remembered vividly her own relief when Lorna, who had gone to South Africa soon after Isobel's and Giles's wedding, had telephoned to announce her engagement. Lorna had sounded triumphant.

'Oh, I knew almost from the word go—though not having children made it worse. I would have given anything for a baby. You don't know how lucky you are, Izzy—we both wanted them so much. But John got increasingly difficult and he was such a big white chief at the hospital that I hadn't a hope of competing with all that adulation.' Isobel couldn't help thinking that adulation had once been Lorna's speciality. 'Then I discovered he was having affairs and not even taking much trouble to hide them from me or anyone else. It became impossible. But I suppose I must take some blame too, because, of course,' said Lorna, carefully taking off her hat, laying it on her lap and not looking at Isobel, 'though he was very attractive, I was never really in love with him and I always knew I'd married him for all the wrong reasons.'

At that moment Isobel had to concentrate on changing lanes to get into the stream of traffic heading for the Forth Bridge. She did not want to go down that particular conversational route with Lorna, and it was not until they had payed the toll, crossed the bridge and were speeding along the M90 towards Perth that Isobel said suddenly, 'There's something different about you, Lorna— it's not just the glamorous clothes—but I can't quite put my finger on what it is.'

Lorna gave her a sideways look. 'I've had my nose fixed, if that's what you mean—but please don't tell the world.'

'You've had your *nose* fixed?' Isobel was astonished. 'It looks the same to me—besides what on earth was wrong with it before—or are you pulling my leg?' Pulling legs seemed almost as unlikely an occupation for Lorna as changing noses.

'No, of course not. I really have. The odd thing is that lots of people have noticed a difference in me but hardly anyone has guessed what it is.'

'I suppose it's like a house. After Hector died we changed all the pictures round in the dining-room at Glendrochatt—Giles had been itching to do it for years—but everyone thought we'd had the walls repainted.'

'Yes, just like that. Which means, of course,' said Lorna 'that no one had really looked at the dining-room—or me—properly before. People are amazingly unobservant.'

'Well, I can't wait to get out of the car and have a closer inspection, but oh, yuk, it makes my toes curl to think of it. I don't know how you could—the pain!' and Isobel put her hand over her own nose as though to protect it from sudden onslaught. 'Was it worth it? You had a perfectly nice nose already.'

'It was worth it to me. *I* like it now—and that's what matters.'

'But one doesn't see one's own nose that much—I can understand it could be nice to feel other people liked it,' objected Isobel, then added hastily, 'Which they did, of course.'

'The really important thing is to be comfortable with your own image, then everyone else will like it too. I've learnt that now.'

'Goodness,' said Isobel, thinking Lorna sounded like an agony aunt in a women's magazine. 'Well, perhaps I should have a leg transplant, then I could wear the slinky clothes I secretly fancy, without looking like a roulade wrapped in clingfilm. But even if you offered me your long, streamlined legs instead of my sturdy numbers I'd never voluntarily face an operation for that. It'd have to be gangrene and ambulance bells screaming to get me under the knife. I'm much too much of a coward—but bully for you if that's what you wanted.'

Isobel sneaked a quick look at her sister's oh-so-perfect profile and wondered what other unsuspected changes lurked behind the façade.

'Tell me about the twins,' said Lorna. 'It's ages since I saw them—not since Mum and Dad finally moved to France, and I came over without John for a holiday and you all came too. I shan't recognise them. How are they?'

'They're fine.' Isobel had unhappy memories of that particular holiday: of Edward, aged two, still unable to sit up unaided, let alone walk or talk; Edward, a prey to sudden terrifying infections, frequently being rushed into various paediatric units, so that holidays away from home were a constant anxiety; Edward not responding much to anyone, absorbed in his own fingers, making weird noises, with a tongue too large for his mouth, skin that always seemed clammy and a nose that was frequently snotty. She remembered Lorna's discernable distaste.

Isobel had overheard her mother remonstrating with Lorna: 'I do think you might make a better effort over Edward, darling—for Isobel's sake' and Lorna's answer: 'I'm sorry, Mum. I do try, but I can hardly bear to touch him.'

'I know, I know,' their mother had said sadly, 'one has this irresistible urge to kiss the back of Amy's neck and one doesn't have it for Edward—but I think you could disguise your feelings a bit better. Pretend—and you may find it comes naturally after a bit.'

Isobel had crept away to shed the anguished private tears that seemed to be squeezed out of her body by an invisible iron hand. She hadn't blamed Lorna; she understood her feelings all too well and was miserably familiar with similar ones herself—she who at the same time had such a passionate protective love for her mysterious little son—but it had hurt, as so many things did hurt nowadays. She sometimes wondered if it was a judgement on her for singing her way through life with such happy heedlessness for her first twenty years. All through our childhood, thought Isobel, I stole Lorna's limelight and then she thought I stole her man. The fact that I didn't to do it intentionally is no help to either of us.

'Amy's making terrific progress with her music,' Isobel volunteered now. 'Giles has got deeply into the whole Suzuki thing. He's taken up the violin again himself and plays with Amy. It's a great bond between them. It all started when we went with some friends to a talk in Edinburgh and people were asked to put up their hands if they regretted never having learnt to play an instrument—or given up learning one—when they were young. I can't tell you how many hands shot up—including Giles's and mine. It's become a big thing in our lives.'

'And what about . . . Edward?' asked Lorna.

Isobel felt the familiar yank from the cruel little hook that was permanently attached to her heartstrings and wished people wouldn't ask after Edward with that special delicate pause. She knew she was being terribly unfair; it was even worse if they studiously avoided all mention of him and didn't ask at all.

'Edward's brilliant,' she said. 'Doing amazing things at school. It's a great bit of luck having such a wonderful special school in the area. He makes us all crack up with laughter—he's terribly funny sometimes.'

'Funny?' Lorna sounded puzzled.

'Yes, funny,' said Isobel fiercely. 'With Edward you either have to laugh or cry. When I can I'd rather laugh.'

There was silence for a moment as each sister remembered uncomfortably how incomprehensible they had always found the other's reactions, then: 'I'm longing to hear all about the new plans,' said Lorna in a neutral voice. 'I always felt there was so much potential at Glendrochatt—the magic of the whole place and that wonderful little theatre. It seemed a waste only to use it for a fortnight in the summer. Do you ever yearn to go back to the stage yourself, Izz?'

'No, not really. I'd only had bit parts and, unlike batty Atalanta, I was never obsessed by it—probably not good enough if I'm honest, and I'd hate to have to keep leaving Giles and the children. I suppose I'm not ambitious enough—but I'm still turned on by the adrenalin of the performance thing, even if I'm not actually taking part myself. A concert, a pageant, a lecture—whatever—I can't resist the lure of the lights. I've been in a few productions at the festival and done occasional poetry readings, but really I just love being involved, which is why I think the Arts Centre will be such fun.' She added, with scrupulous generosity: 'You'll be tremendously useful in helping us get the project off the ground, Lorna.'

'Whose inspiration was it?' Lorna hoped it hadn't been Isobel's.

'Dunno, really. The idea "just growed" like Topsy. We knew we'd have to do something to justify keeping the place financially, getting some return even if we couldn't actually make a profit. From time to time we'd made suggestions to Hector but he simply couldn't face any change. Technically he'd made the whole estate over to Giles ages ago, but it was always agreed that we should carry on as if Hector still owned it. When he died so suddenly all ideas went into the melting pot. Giles is in his element.' Isobel giggled. 'You should see him manoeuvring all the Perthshire ladies on the committee of the new trust—he's got them drooling. He appears to organise their whole lives now and some of them can't make a move without consulting him. I wouldn't put it past him to choose their clothes—which mightn't be a bad idea for one or two of them, come to think of it: not quite so many heather mixture cardies. They're always ringing him up.'

'Don't you mind?' asked Lorna curiously.

'Not at all, I think it's hilarious. Frightfully useful too—they agree to anything he wants.'

Having bypassed Perth and headed north on the A9, Isobel took the turning to Blairalder. She glanced at her sister, wondering what it felt like to come back after so long.

'Oh look, said Lorna. 'There's the house that used to belong to the Carvers. Who owns it now?' Lorna remembered teenage reel parties there. In particular, she thought of the first dance her younger sister had been invited to attend along with Lorna's own older age group. She had tried to persuade her parents that Isobel would be out of her depth. Her father had laughed and said, 'Don't be such a dog in the manger, Lorna—Izzy out of her depth? She'll love every minute of it.' His words had hurt and he'd been proved right, as Lorna had known all along that he would be. Isobel had made an instant hit with everyone. Halfway through the evening Lorna, who had failed to get a partner for 'The Duke of Perth'—she had been thankful that Giles, whom she had recently met, was not among the guests to witness this humiliation—had endured watching her younger sister, curls flying, being whirled down the line by one of Lorna's own contemporaries. Everyone had whooped and laughed indulgently when Isobel and her partner had spun so wildly out of control that they had ended on the floor.

'The house is on the market again,' said Isobel. 'Goodness, we had fun there. I used to adore going to the Carvers, didn't you?'

'Well, sometimes—I was just thinking about that ghastly party when you behaved so badly and had to be fetched home. Do you remember that one?'

Isobel laughed. 'I remember all right—I was having a whale of a time! I was amazed when Dad unexpectedly turned up and dragged me home early—I couldn't think what on earth he'd come for.'

'But you'd drunk too much,' said Lorna, who had telephoned their father to come and collect Isobel. 'I could have died with mortification.'

Isobel—who remembered clearly that she had been lit up by the excitement of the music, the glamour of older dancing partners and her own high spirits, but not by alcohol, which, as she had promised her parents, she had not touched, thought it was better to change the subject: 'Nearly home now. You couldn't have timed your arrival better. We're having a magic spell of weather and the daffodils will soon be at their best—I always love this time of year when everything's so full of promise—the beeches not quite out, primroses on the banks all the way up the drive and all the nesting going on. We're longing to show you everything.'

'I can't wait. What alterations have you actually done so far?'

'Well, the theatre's got completely new lighting. We had a bit of a panic that the rewiring mightn't be finished on time, but it's done now, thank God. The most exciting new development is that a young artist who Giles thinks will have a big future in theatre design is going to come and paint some backdrops—you may remember that there's never been any scenery. Some of our plans for the house will have to wait until the winter because that's inside work, but the flats in the stables are ready and I'm thrilled with them. As a matter of fact,' said Isobel, 'I've decorated the first one specially for you.'

'Oh, but you mustn't waste a brand-new flat on me. I don't mind where I go,' protested Lorna.

'Not wasted at all. You can test it out. Besides, if you're going to spend the summer with us you may be glad of a retreat some-times—we're a pretty chaotic household.'

'Trying to banish me before I've even started?' asked Lorna, making her voice light to indicate that a joke was intended.

'Of course not, *Stoopid*. Anyway, I expect you'll eat with us most of the time,' said Isobel.

As she took the small road signposted to Glendrochatt the house came into view high above them. To locals it was a land-mark—sight Glendrochatt House, with its tall white tower, and you knew you were nearly home. Tourists always enquired about it, greedy for the statutory stories of Grey Ladies, walled-up babies and dark deeds—although most of those tales had originated in the bar of the Glendrochatt Arms.

Lorna caught her breath. 'I always think it looks like a stage set. You don't know how much I've been longing to see that again,' she said. The house went out of sight again as the road wound uphill. When Isobel turned into the drive, under the arch that was partly a gatehouse and the car rattled over the cattle grid, Lorna turned to look at her sister. 'I want you to know that I mean to give you and Giles all the help I can this summer. Not just with administration—though I'm a wizz with computers now—but with the children too, and specially . . . ' Lorna paused impressively ' . . . especially with Edward,' she finished, with the air of someone well aware of her own magnanimity. She patted her immaculately tidy hair, which was done up in a French pleat, and settled her hat back on her head as though she was putting on armour for battle.

Isobel felt as if she had just been challenged to take part in some complicated ritual trial of strength of which she did not know the rules, and her heart sank as she pulled up outside the front door of Glendrochatt and tooted the horn to let Giles know they had arrived.

Four

After Isobel had left to collect Lorna, Giles Grant went to check on the progress of the wall that Mick and Joss were building, using the cobbles which had been dug up from the old yard outside the theatre. This was being transformed into a court-yard garden where Giles and Isobel hoped audiences would be able to wander about during the interval on fine summer eve-nings—should there be any fine evenings, thought Giles wryly. The cobbles—difficult to walk on in high-heeled shoes—had been removed in favour of paving made from the clever new composite concrete slabs, which perfectly mimicked old flag-stones, even down to reproducing the subtle variations in the pinkish-grey local stone. Now the cobbles were making an attractive facing for the inside of the courtyard wall—Mick's brainwave—he was full of good ideas.

He and his friend Joss had turned up at Glendrochatt looking for part-time work to help finance six months travelling round Europe. They were still there a year later, two amiable blond giants who between them could turn their hands to almost any-thing from childminding to masonry, gardening to housework. Joss, in particular, was a spectacular cook, and he and Isobel spent hours discussing recipes.

To start with Mick and Joss had been regarded with suspicion

by the local community who made insinuating remarks about fair-
ies and dubbed them the au pair girls, but the fruitiness of their
language, their ability to down drams and their seemingly unend-
ing capacity for hard work combined with good humour but huge
biceps—especially the biceps, which had once, under extreme
provocation, powered a colossal punch from Mick's meaty fist
into the eye of Angus Johnstone, the estate handyman—had won
them approbation. Angus had gone about with a shiner that took
weeks to fade and when Mick had enquired politely if anyone
else wanted a little medicine from an au pair girl's hand there had
been no takers. Their knowledgeable help with lambing the previous spring had proved how indispensable they were and the two
Kiwis were finally accepted. Now they lived rent free in the old
home-farm house, Mains of Glendrochatt, which in their spare
time—though no one knew how they found any—they were
brilliantly restoring. Sometimes they would disappear to the Con-
tinent for a few weeks of culture, visits to the Louvre, the Sistine
Chapel or the Prado refreshing them for further onslaughts at
building or vacuuming. Giles and Isobel could not imagine how
they would cope without them and dreaded the day when they
might return to their native New Zealand. Amy and Edward
adored them.

After a discussion with Mick about the most suitable height for
the new wall, so that during intervals audiences could enjoy the
arcadian charm of seeing real sheep safely grazing the rough hill-
side grass between listening to Bach cantatas in the theatre, Giles
went to see how Angus was getting on with the installation of a
new lavatory for the disabled. It was part of Giles's perfectionism
that he liked to supervise even the most basic jobs himself, but he
usually managed to do it with such appreciation that it was rare
for anyone to take offence. 'Great work, Angus,' he said. 'Even
that nit-picking inspector should be satisfied with that.' Then he
went into the theatre itself and sat at the back, pondering ideas
for the future and brooding about the past.

The Old Steading Theatre at Glendrochatt was regarded as a

little gem by anyone who had performed in it. It was big enough to seat a hundred and fifty people in comfort—a few more at a push—but small enough to give a feeling of intimacy, and because one could remove chairs and rearrange rows it was also perfectly possible to have an audience of as few as forty people without an embarrassing feeling of emptiness. The acoustics were superb.

Not many aspiring actresses have husbands who can provide them with their own theatre, but it had been typical of his mother, thought Giles, that she had managed to acquire one. Everyone who had seen her perform said she'd had enormous talent, but what she had also possessed in abundance was magnetism. Giles could remember it all too well: it had cast a spell round her, enchanting everyone with whom she came in contact—including her wistful small son—and successfully masking, in the early days, the self-destructive urges to which she was so disastrously prone.

As Giles thought about her, with longing and dread, he was back again under the nursery table, curled into a ball like a hibernating dormouse in an effort to shut down his quivering system and deaden all feeling, poking his fingers deep in his ears to block out the shocking sounds that sometimes reverberated through the house: sounds as out of control as the roar and crackle of a forest fire. Those hysterical screams still returned to him in nightmares, causing him to wake up drenched in sweat and shaking, and the memory of his childish helplessness either to comprehend, or influence, the uncertainties by which he had been surrounded still haunted Giles. After dreams like that, he would turn to Isobel and hold her close, thanking God for her breezy sanity and loving heart.

Overheard voices from the past rang in his ears:

'Dear God! Try to keep the child out of the way. She's back on the bottle again.'

'How she found those pills this time, we'll never know.'

'Well, they've saved her yet again, but—mark my words—one of these days she's going to succeed.'

Again, again, again . . . the words throbbed a terrible drumbeat in Giles's head.

Giles was eleven when Atalanta had finally succeeded.

His father—whom Giles had hitherto admired longingly from afar—told him of her death, searching hopelessly to find the right words. But what are the right words to tell a small boy that his mother has put a gun in her mouth and shot herself? Hector Grant, grieving desperately for the tormented creature he had adored, his cherished, broken-winged bird, was helplessly conscious that the child with whom he should have established a relationship long before was a stranger to him.

Apparently there had been signs of Atalanta's instability early on, but her parents had put them down to artistic sensibility and always tried to shield their daughter from anything that might upset her. They had thoroughly approved of Hector—rich, well-connected, considerably older than their delicate flower child—and desperately in love. All seemed set fair in 1960 when Atalanta floated down the aisle of St Margaret's Westminster on the arm of Hector Grant.

It was not until after the birth of Giles that Atalanta had her first serious breakdown. She recovered—until the next attack—but never forgave her infant son for the damage he had unwittingly inflicted on her and there had not been any question of repeating the experiment of parenthood. Giles remained an only child.

The solid table with the tasselled chenille velvet cover under which a small Giles had taken refuge was still in the nursery, and Amy and Edward frequently made a den under it now. The material had faded to an unappealing shade of khaki, although it had once been a brilliant green; Amy had discovered that you could still see the original colour if you unpicked a bit of the hem where the cloth had been protected from the light. Giles would never contemplate suggestions that it might be discarded in favour of some more cheerful or hygienic covering. The stuffy seclusion to be found under its comforting darkness had represented one of the few securities in his chaotic childhood.

After Hector died, the idea of turning Glendrochatt into an Arts Centre had seemed to Giles and Isobel a logical progression from the fortnight's summer festival, which had started as a vehicle for Atalanta's dramatic ambitions but had grown, over the years, to include concerts and art exhibitions. In theory, a committee had run the festival under the undemocratic chairmanship of Hector, who sabotaged anyone else's suggestions and meddled maddeningly with all arrangements. Since his father's death, Giles had seen how the potential of his inherited property, which included a considerable estate, might be allied to his own theatrical interests and considerable talent for organisation. Unlike Hector, Giles adored committees, although Isobel said his attitude was really quite as cavalier as that of his autocratic parent—just better disguised. He certainly enjoyed wielding influence as much as his father had done, but in a subtler way, manipulating the strings of his marionettes with the delicacy of an expert puppeteer, so that they danced obediently to his tune while giving every appearance of moving under their own volition.

Isobel, however, had never been prepared to act like a puppet—it was part of her charm for Giles, although it didn't stop him trying to organise her too. At the moment he was cross with her: they'd had a confrontation about Amy just before Isobel left for the airport, Isobel insisting that Giles's obsessive supervision of Amy's music was becoming claustrophobic and that he must allow his daughter to develop more on her own. Giles had failed to talk his wife round to his own view—but he didn't intend to change either.

He looked around him with a sense of excitement. Work had been going on for so many months that Giles had begun to wonder if they would ever be free of wires and piping, gaping holes in walls and floors, and the plaster dust that seemed to get everywhere. Now, at last, the structural alterations were nearly finished and by September they should be able to get on with the real work for which the Arts Centre was intended. He imagined how it would feel when, instead of workmen, The Old Steading was full of young artists and performers taking part in various courses and workshops—the whole place humming with creativity. Although he particularly wanted to provide a facility for Scotland, he hoped that eventually people would come from other countries too. He allowed himself to be carried away by his dreams and plans for a few more minutes, then he looked at his watch, gave himself a shake and switched his mind to the present.

He was half dreading, half looking forward to the arrival of Lorna. He recognised the potential for trouble in the situation, but the part of him that enjoyed playing games of emotional Tom Tiddler's Ground with people's relationships was stimulated by the idea of juggling with the possible rivalry between his wife and his ex-mistress. Next week, too, another guest would be arriving to live with them for a few months: the young artist whom the Grants had commissioned to paint a backdrop for the theatre—a bit of an unknown quantity, thought Giles, an interesting wild card in the pack.

Giles had first come across Daniel Hoffman's work on one of his talent-spotting trips looking for young musicians to perform at Glendrochatt. He had gone to a music festival held annually at Nant Dafydd, a Boys' public school in North Wales, which opened its doors during the summer holidays for the festival's use. It had a superb theatre and Giles had attended a performance of Rossini's *Le Comte Ory*. Although the soprano he had gone to hear had proved disappointing and he thought the production pedestrian, what had particularly excited him had been the stage designs. He had subsequently arranged to meet the designer in London—which had proved unexpectedly difficult as Daniel Hoffman was extraordinarily elusive. He apparently had neither permanent address nor agent and depended for contact on his mobile telephone, but never seemed to answer messages. Whereas this might have caused many potential patrons to give up, it had made Giles, who always hated to be thwarted, more interested.

When he finally managed to track Daniel down and actually met him he had liked him enormously and was bowled over by his work.

Isobel had not yet met Daniel, but she had seen photographs of his portfolio and been equally enthusiastic. However, since he had accepted their commission and fixed a date to start work at Glendrochatt, the Grants had been quite unable to contact Daniel and were taking a gamble that the young man would actually turn up on schedule.

What would the conformist, highly organised Lorna make of unconventional Daniel Hoffman, and he of her? wondered Giles. It would be interesting to see.

The summer looked full of promise.

Five

Giles was coming round the corner of the house with the two dogs at his heel as Isobel and Lorna got out of the car. He felt pleased with himself for timing his appearance so perfectly; he knew Isobel would be uneasy about this reunion and thought it would be wise to get the initial encounter over as soon as possible. He was also very keen to satisfy his own curiosity.

He swept off his wide-brimmed blue bush hat, which had a battered elegance that he rightly fancied suited his somewhat raffish good looks, and made a theatrical but slightly mocking bow, clasping the hat to his chest and clicking his heels.

Hats! Oh, *hats*, thought hatless Isobel, looking from her husband to her sister, what useful stage props they are; what messages they give out; how subtly they can add meaning to an unwritten script.

Like Isobel's, Giles's first impression on seeing his sister-in-law was one of surprise. Lorna had always been good-looking and well turned-out, but he was taken aback by her glamour. It was as though he had only seen her before through a blurred lens and she was now in sharp focus. There was a gloss about her that made her both curiously threatening and much more interesting. 'Lorna! Lovely to see you. Welcome to Glendrochatt,' he said, kissing her and then holding her away from him. 'My goodness!

You're a very good advertisement for divorce. You look absolutely wonderful.'

'Thank you,' said Lorna, self-possessed, cool, taking the compliment as her due, with no trace of the spaniel-like desire for approval that had once grown to irritate him so much. 'Good to see you too, Giles. You seem to have worn quite well yourself.'

'Only quite?' said Isobel, laughing. 'He won't like that, will you, darling? Poor old married man. Lorna, come in and have tea and meet the children, and we'll take your things round to the flat later.' As she led the way up the steps to the open front door, each sister was acutely aware of her particular role as hostess or guest, and of how, if things had worked out differently, these might perhaps have been reversed.

Lorna will be on the lookout for every little change at Glendrochatt, thought Isobel, and she won't like any of them on principle out of a feigned loyalty to Giles's father. Hector Grant, who had adored Isobel and allowed her what Giles always said was remarkable licence to tease him and take liberties, had enjoyed pretending to her that he'd secretly admired Lorna as the more beautiful sister—which indeed she was—but Isobel had not been deceived into thinking he had liked her very much. To her irritation, Isobel found the mystery of her husband's relationship with her sister niggling at her again. After the initial surprise of discovering that there had been anything at all between Giles and Lorna, Isobel had been presented over the years with varying impressions of what their relations with each other had really been. Her intuition told her that it had been more than Giles admitted and less than Lorna hinted at.

The children were having tea in front of the television in the big kitchen, supervised by the two New Zealanders. Amy was sitting on a beanbag and Edward was lying on his stomach with his thumb in his mouth, an empty plate beside him on the floor, while Joss and Mick lounged at the table with mugs of tea. They grinned a welcome and got up, as did Amy, standing with a slice of hot buttered toast in her hand.

Edward gave no sign of being aware of anyone.

'Meet Mick and Joss,' said Isobel. 'Part of the family now—Glendrochatt would grind to a halt without them. This is my sister Lorna.'

'Hello there Lorna.' They extended ham-like fists for her to shake and Lorna, smiling graciously, recovered her own soft, manicured hand from their crunching grip with relief, surprised to find no bones broken.

'Amy, I don't suppose you really remember Aunt Lorna, do you, darling? You were only two last time she saw you.'

'And you've certainly changed since then,' said Lorna, bending to kiss her niece. She was presented with a buttery cheek and an appraising look, both of which she found disconcerting.

'Edward!' said Isobel sharply. 'Come and say hello.'

Edward remained glued to the television and gave no sign of having heard. The lenses of his National Health spectacles looked as thick as the bases of glass bottles, but he still sat with his nose almost touching the screen.

'It's his Loch Ness Monster video,' explained Amy.

Lorna wondered whether, on top of his other problems, Edward was also deaf. She seemed to remember that the possibility had been suggested and then proved not to be so. In fact, Edward's hearing was as acute as he wished it to be.

Isobel went and yanked him to his feet and propelled him towards Lorna. 'Say how do you do,' she said sternly and pulled Edward's hand from his mouth.

'It really doesn't matter—please don't bother him.'

'He knows perfectly well that he has to. *Edward.*'

'Hi.' Edward spoke in a breathy staccato, as though he were a pair of bellows and someone had forcibly given him a sharp little puff. He jammed his curiously long thumb straight back in his mouth, effectively preventing any more words from being popped out, and averted his eyes.

Lorna went down on her knees and tried to gather him into what was meant to be a warm, compassionate embrace. He was much smaller than Amy, like a brittle little bird, she thought, but he was surprisingly strong and, struggling frantically out of her grasp, he fled behind one of the curtains at the long windows, which he then wrapped tightly round and round himself as though to ward off contamination.

Amy turned a reproachful face to her aunt. 'Edward can never bear to be held,' she said.

Lorna straightened up, feeling foolish and rebuffed, and two red patches flamed on her cheeks. Giles looked put out and Isobel winced inwardly. She could have kicked herself for having triggered the incident—for having so rashly wanted Edward to show himself to Lorna at his unexpected, remarkable, triumphant best instead of his loopy, uncooperative worst. 'Oh, well,' she said brightly. 'At least he's said hello. Honour is satisfied, I suppose. Sorry, Lorna—all my fault. Give him time.'

'Kettle's just boiled. How about me making a fresh pot of tea and bringing it through to the drawing-room? Treat Lorna like a visitor just for her first day?' Joss, who loved the whole family, but specially Isobel and Edward, was distressed by the little scene and acutely aware of hidden implications. He started getting cups and saucers out of a cupboard, laying them delicately on a tray, using the proper teapot, matching jug and silver teaspoons, instead of the odd mugs, teabags and milk bottle more often in use in the Glendrochatt kitchen. His actions seemed more in keeping with those of a prim, elderly parlourmaid in black dress and white apron than a barefooted modern giant of six foot four, wearing frayed jeans and flip-flops, his open shirt displaying an extremely hairy chest in which a gold medallion was glitteringly tangled.

'Lovely,' said Isobel. 'Thanks. You're a star, Joss. Could one of you possibly take Lorna's stuff over to the flats—then she and I can potter over later?'

'Sure,' said Mick easily, getting to his feet again. 'I need to go there anyway. I forgot to turn on the water.' And he expertly unravelled Edward from his self-imposed winding-sheet, lifting him up by the neck of his shirt as easily as if he were a puppy, and setting him back on his feet.

'See you, then, Lorna. Come on, Edward, let's go feed those darned hens of yours—see if that grumpy one's still broody, huh?'

Isobel blew the two men a grateful kiss, thanking whatever lucky stars had landed them on her doorstep. Edward brightened up immediately. He could not, unaided, fasten or unfasten the door to the hen-run and there was a limit to the number of times a day he could persuade anyone to go there with him. He was obsessed by the hens and would commune happily with them for hours, squatting down among old cabbage stalks and rotting household scraps to carry on far longer conversations with the birds than he was ever prepared to have with fellow humans beings. Isobel thought sadly that not many people would be prepared to crouch in the hens' smelly enclosure for long enough to experience and be astonished by Edward's extraordinary vocabulary, or the unexpected fluency with which he could address his feathered pets.

'I thuthpect thothe feathered gentlemen in pluth-fourth may have attacked each other by now,' she heard him say, referring in his oblique way to the two Silkie cockerels who ruled the roost, as he and Mick collected the hen bucket and set off together. 'They may have pecked each other'th eyeth out,' he added hopefully. Edward adored contemplating disasters, and lived a richly petrifying and gory life of the imagination, but should the most minor accident ever actually occur he would go completely berserk and become uncontrollable with panic and misery—and possibly have one of his fits.

'You've changed the kitchen.' Lorna followed Isobel to the door. 'Surely I remember this room as Hector's billiard room?' The name rolled casually off her tongue, though all those years ago on weekend visits to Glendrochatt she had never addressed Giles's father by his Christian name—nor been invited to do so. She had seldom even entered his private domain from which she only remembered him emerging alarmingly, smelling of expensive cigars and emanating an atmosphere of potential criticism.

'Yes, that's right,' said Isobel. 'Brilliant, isn't it? It was Giles's inspiration. The old kitchen in the basement was miles away and had no view either. We live in here, really. It's bang next door to the dining-room, so it's much more convenient if we ever want to be smart and grown-up and eat in state; this gets all the sun, the stunning view and best of all, I can see who's turning up at the front and take avoiding action if I want to. Vital.' She led the way across the hall to the drawing-room.

'Oh, I'm so glad you've kept those lovely old silk curtains. I remember them so well,' said Lorna, deliberately not commenting on the chair covers and wallpaper, which she wrongly assumed to be new, but which in fact Isobel and Giles had helped Hector choose some years previously. 'This was always my favourite room,' she went on. 'It used to have such a wonderful atmosphere.' Is there an inference that the lovely atmosphere has gone, wondered Isobel, or am I being oversensitive?

'What's happened to the old nursery now?' Lorna continued. 'Has it still got that huge squashy old sofa by the window?' She willed Giles to conjure up the kisses—and sometimes more than kisses—exchanged by them there, in the one room his father never entered.

'Still much the same,' muttered Giles, hearing the ice creak as he skated over it. 'All the children's clobber's there now as mine used to be when I was little. Izzy and I use it as our sitting-room, but today we've lit the fire in here especially to celebrate your arrival.'

'That's touching of you—but I hope I'm not going to be treated as a guest for *too* long,' said Lorna.

'Of course not—but you must let us make today into an occasion.' Giles flashed her his most beguiling smile. 'Besides, Amy and I are going to give you a concert after dinner.'

'Ah—now that I shall enjoy.' Lorna smiled back.

Isobel poured out three cups of tea, concentrating hard so as not to slop any into the saucers because her hand shook a little as she wielded the pot.

*A*fter tea Isobel took Lorna across the courtyard to the flats. Lorna's cases had been carried up by Mick and her coat neatly laid across the bed together with her travelling rug and the bag of books and magazines she had been reading on the plane. The heating and hot water had been turned on. Amy had put a little vase of forget-me-nots and primroses on the dressing-table with a drawing she had done of a rather stumpy-looking bird garlanded by notes of music, with the words 'WELCOME TO GLEN-DROCHATT, AUNT LORNA' coming out of its beak.

'How lovely,' said Lorna, looking around. 'You *have* made it nice.'

'I hoped you'd like it.'

'I do. It's quite delightful. You've been very clever. But—just for the record, Izzy—why have you put me over here? Is it your way of telling me something that I need to know?'

An amber light flashing in her head reminded Isobel that she had already been bounced into being less definite than she intended about eating arrangements. She had expected covert umbrage from Lorna, but not open confrontation. 'I suppose so—in a way,' she answered slowly. 'I thought about it hard and wondered if you'd prefer one of the spare rooms in the house, but if you're going to be here, working with us, for several months we'll all need space occasionally if the plan is to work. For your sake as well as ours.'

'We?' asked Lorna. 'Giles and you, or just you?' There was no mistaking her challenge.

'I organise the domestic arrangements. It was my decision,' admitted Isobel with painful honesty. 'We're often a full house in the summer when we have lots of mates—ours and the children's—to stay. Also we want to be able to put visiting soloists in the house. Then there were other considerations. For instance,' she went on, looking out of the window at the loch and the hills, and thinking that despite the beauty of the view and the comfort of the accommodation it would never satisfy Lorna. 'Mick and Joss work for us too. They're with us a great deal and we all— well, everyone who works for us, like Giles's secretary for ex- ample—have lunch together and that, of course, includes you. We love Mick and Joss to bits but sometimes we want to be on our own in the evenings and they do too. They'll be eating with us tonight, as you will—and on lots of other evenings as well, I hope—but they don't *live* with us. They need to get away from us and lead their own lives.'

'And presumably they always have each other. I imagine they're an item—or am I wrong about them?'

'No, you're right.'

'But I happen to be alone—newly alone.' Lorna's voice was soft. 'I have lost touch with old friends and have no life of my own here. Did that strike you?'

'Oh, Lorna,' said Isobel desperately, 'of course it did, but living in a sort of community—as we've always done during the festi- val—I've already learnt the hard way that it pays to start as you mean to go on. I have to try and be professional about it.'

'Oh,' Lorna commented, 'how wise and clever of you. Nice to know you consider me on a par with your domestic staff.'

'Mick and Joss are not domestic staff—and what if they were?' asked Isobel, feeling her temper rising. 'They're part of the whole Glendrochatt team, as you will be. We're all equal. Oh, do stop this, Lorna—let's not start off with a quarrel.'

'*I'm* not quarrelling.' Lorna raised her eyebrows. 'I just wanted things clear between us. And now they are—thank you. I shall try not to intrude and I do realise you are doing me a favour. I'd like to unpack now. What time shall I come over for dinner?'

Isobel walked back to the house with her heart in her scuffed old loafer shoes, which suddenly seemed extra shabby. She felt her behaviour had been made to appear shabby too and a spark of uncharacteristic resentment flared. Lorna had always had a talent for putting people in the wrong.

*T*o Isobel's relief, supper went well. There was smoked salmon— a fish that had been caught by Giles and sent to the nearby smokery—Joss had cooked a delicious chicken lasagne with spinach, tomato and cheese, which was popular with both grown-ups and children, and earlier that morning Isobel had made lemon ice cream with raspberry sauce. The big kitchen table had a blue and yellow cotton cloth on it and was laid with matching napkins and charming fruit-patterned French china—presents from Isobel's and Lorna's parents who had retired to live in Provence. There were fresh flowers, candles were lit and Giles opened champagne. It was all very civilised and festive. Lorna, wearing a cashmere sweater and black silk trousers, her fair hair loose and held back by a velvet band, was all appreciation and smiles. She was especially affectionate to Isobel. If she harboured resentment about her living quarters, she showed no more sign of it, and tried—not *too* obviously—to avert her eyes from Edward's clumsy eating habits. For her part, Isobel told herself sternly not to let her imagination go into overdrive and took evasive action against potential aggravation by suggesting to Edward, before he'd even started asking, that he should get down early, taking his pudding with him, and go to look at a video. Joss went to set it up for him.

After dinner the rest of them went back to the drawing-room.

'Come on, Amy,' said Giles. 'Aunt Lorna's a good musician too—let's get our violins out and show her what we can do together. What shall we play for her?'

They decided on the first movement of the Bach double violin concerto, with Amy playing the second violin part. 'It comes in the fourth Suzuki book, which is the one Amy's on now, and it's our favourite piece at the moment,' explained Giles. 'We'll play it to the Suzuki backing tape of the orchestra. You'll hear a lot of Suzuki tapes playing while you're here. It's part of the whole idea of getting children to absorb music as naturally as they absorb words when they first learn to speak.'

'Doesn't she mind playing to other people?' asked Lorna as Amy went off to collect the violins.

'Not a bit. Suzuki children are used to performing—it's all part of the system. Amy's been taking part in little concerts since she was four. Actually, you might be very useful to us, Lorna. I can play the fiddle with her but I'm not really a good enough pianist to accompany her for much longer. Have you kept up your piano?'

'Very much so. It was my great solace through all John's and my difficulties. I had a marvellous teacher in South Africa. I'd love to help Amy.'

The enjoyment of father and daughter in each other's playing was obvious, their rapport a lovely thing. Lorna was extremely impressed by Amy's confidence once she picked up her violin, tuned it expertly, looked expectantly at Giles and started to play. Once they'd come to a triumphant finish, there was a moment's silence, then Lorna applauded enthusiastically. 'That was *wonderful*,' she said, meaning it. 'Play me more.'

So they played—some of Amy's studied pieces but also spontaneous fun things, a ragbag of melodies from reel tunes to pop.

'Amy and Giles play in a parents' and children's dance band,' explained Isobel. 'It's brilliant fun.'

'Do you take part?'

'Well, sort of . . . I'm always in demand for catering if not for performing,' said Isobel, laughing.

'Don't you feel left out of the music?'

'I never have done so far.'

'Well, I think that's very generous of you,' said Lorna.

Isobel got up. 'Come on, Amy, darling. Bed now.'

'Oh, Mum! We're just getting warmed up. Can't we go on a bit longer? It is Saturday tomorrow after all.'

'Absolutely not. You're late already. Go and collect Edward

and I'll be up in a quarter of an hour. Say goodnight to Aunt Lorna.'

'Daddy? Please?' Amy wheedled her father.

'No. Enough. You heard what Mummy said, but thank you, darling. Well done—we're a great team, aren't we?' Giles put his arm proudly round his daughter and kissed the top of her head. When Isobel went upstairs she heard peals of laughter coming from Edward's bedroom. Amy was sitting on the bed, helpless with giggles, while Edward, looking thoroughly manic, appeared to be searching through her hair like a monkey.

'What *are* you doing?'

'He's inspecting me for body lice. He's got this book from school on common household pests.'

'You're a pair of household pests yourselves. Have you done your teeth yet?' asked Isobel.

She sat on the end of Edward's bed. 'You let me down badly this afternoon, Edward,' she said. Edward pressed his nose into his book and peered at a particularly unpleasant picture of a much magnified house-flea. Isobel whisked the book away. 'You were very rude to Aunt Lorna. You're a big boy now—you don't need to go behind the curtain any more when someone kisses you.' Edward pulled the invisible shutters over his eyes that could make them look completely blank, like the kind of dark glasses that enable people to see out but not in, and gazed at the wall.

'Edward, I'm talking to you. You made me very sad.'

He rolled into a tight ball and clutched his head. 'Trouble? trouble?' he asked from inside the ball, muffled, trying to be invisible.

'Don't be cross with him, Mum,' begged Amy.

Isobel sighed. 'Not trouble this time, but don't do it again. Tomorrow you must show Aunt Lorna that you can be friendly too.'

'You mean that long-legged black thpider lady,' said Edward, uncurling himself cautiously. He had an aversion to calling people or things by their usual names and was endlessly inventive.

'I mean *Aunt Lorna*.'

'Perhapth the long-legged black thpider lady'th got body lithe. I may inthpect her tomorrow,' said Edward, making concessions.

'Perhaps if she's a spider she has hairy legs as well as long black ones.' Amy giggled.

'I doubt it,' said Isobel. 'She's far too well-groomed.'

The dimples that always melted Isobel's heart suddenly hollowed the cheeks of Edward's funny, pale, blobby little face. 'Perhapth if the long-legged black thpider lady'th a horth ath well,' he suggested, 'I could groom her.'

'*Hurry up!*' said Isobel, trying not to laugh.

She took Edward's face in her hands, a nightly ritual, as vital a practising of a difficult skill for him as Amy's violin sessions were for her.

'Look at me, Edward.' Reluctantly he looked into her face. 'Take your thumb out. Now kiss me—right here on my cheek. No, not like that—properly.' He gave her the quick, wet peck that meant he had done his best. 'Well done,' said Isobel, her heart giving its habitual, sad little lurch. 'Goodnight, my darling. Sleep tight. Come on, Amy.' Edward curled under his duvet, plugging his thumb back in his mouth.

Amy cartwheeled out of the door, then took a flying leap on to her bed in the next-door room; impossible not to compare her easy grace and physical perfection with the lopsided little body and uncoordinated, lumbering movements of her twin. Amy twined her arms round Isobel's neck. 'One more kiss? One more hug?' Her nightly ritual could hardly have been more different from his.

Isobel hugged her daughter, so quick, so bright, so talented— so unlike her twin. 'You played beautifully tonight, darling. I was so proud of you. Night-night.'

'Mum?'

'Yes?'

'Edward doesn't like Aunt Lorna.'

'Rubbish. You know what he can be like with strangers. He hasn't got to know her yet, that's all.'

'But Mum?'

'Don't procrastinate, Amy. Tuck down.'

'I don't think I like her either,' said Amy, diving under the bedclothes when Isobel turned out the light.

*A*s she went slowly downstairs she could hear music coming from the drawing-room. Giles and Lorna were playing duets, seated together at the old Steinway grand piano that had belonged to Giles's mother. They stopped playing when she came in. 'Oh, don't stop,' she said, but Giles got up.

'I'm thankful to have an excuse. Goodness but Lorna shows me up! I hadn't realised how out of practice I was—dreadfully humiliating,' he said. 'Do you remember that ghastly old honky-tonk upright we used hammer away on at Bristol, Lorna? Which was the note that always stuck?'

'It was G,' Lorna answered. 'How long-suffering our friends must have been.' She closed the piano and stood up. 'I think I need an early night. Thank you both for a lovely evening.'

Giles offered to escort her over to the flat. 'Just to make sure you're all right and know where all the light switches are.' Lorna hesitated for a moment, glancing questioningly at her sister.

'Good idea,' said Isobel. 'Do walk over with her, darling—and don't forget to give her a key to the front door and show her the alarm code in case she wants to come over here for anything. The security lights come on automatically, Lorna, so you won't need a torch.'

'Oh, well, that will be lovely. I'll accept gratefully then.' Lorna kissed Isobel affectionately. 'Goodnight, Izzy. Thank you for meeting me. It's great to be here again.'

'See you in the morning—don't hurry. Have a lie-in. Hope you've got all you want. Tell Giles if there's anything missing.'

———————

Isobel was standing by the window brushing her hair and gazing out at the garden when Giles came up to bed some time later. She went to lean against him. 'Do you love me?' she asked.

'Little Izz—you know I do.' Giles put his arms round her and rocked her gently.

'Yes,' she agreed. 'I know you do. But I also know how much you like manipulating people . . . like *meddling*,' said Isobel, looking up at him. 'And how you can't resist taking risks even with things that are really important to you.'

He stroked her hair, strangely disturbed by the expression in the grey-green eyes that were her best feature. He felt sliced in half by the truth behind her words, his light and shade uncomfortably divided and exposed, the haunting uncontrollable screams from his childhood, that he was always seeking to exorcise, ringing in his ears—the ears of a little boy who had constantly been hustled out of the way, hurried along without having his questions answered; a child who secretly studied people; who had learnt to amuse himself by outwitting the grown-ups; who invented his own dangerous games of chance.

'Don't tell me you never enjoyed risks too,' he said guiltily, aware that he was trying to duck the real issue. 'Where's that dashing skier I married—the girl who went hang-gliding and raced downhill? The girl who used to laugh if a sudden storm blew up when we sailed across the loch—who always charged at life with such abandon?' He took her face in his hands, just as she had held their son's a little earlier, only unlike Edward she gazed back at him and her eyes held his. He smoothed her cheekbones with his thumbs. 'Where is that girl now, Izzy?' he asked softly.

'Gone,' Isobel replied sadly. 'Part of that girl evaporated for ever after Edward was born. Now there seem to be too many unexpected hurts waiting to pounce without going courting risks for fun.'

They stood together in silence, both afraid of saying too much or too little.

'Love me, Giles,' she said. 'Prove to me that you do.'

'Come to bed and I'll show you,' he whispered, his mouth close to hers and her body melting towards his.

But pleasurable though it was, they both knew this was not the kind of reassurance she had really been seeking.

Six

The weekend passed without incident and everyone was on their best behaviour. On Saturday morning Giles invited Lorna to come and sit in on Amy's violin lesson with her teacher, Valerie Benson, who lived about forty minutes away at Bridge-of-Cullen.

'Won't Amy mind?'

'Of course not. There's often someone else there.'

'Do you always take her yourself?'

'Nearly always. It's part of the system. I take notes of all Valerie's points during the lesson, then I can make sure Amy concentrates on them when we practise.'

'It must be a terrible tie for you.'

'It's a complete commitment—not a tie. I absolutely love it,' said Giles truthfully.

Lorna, who had been about to tell him how wonderful she thought he was and to hint that she would have expected Isobel to help him out a bit more in this direction, felt she had narrowly escaped saying something alienating.

As it turned out she was impressed with the lesson: with the spontaneous hug with which Amy greeted Mrs Benson and the easy relationship they appeared to have. It was clear that Amy enjoyed every moment of her playing. She was working on the first movement of Vivaldi's A minor concerto. 'Well done, Amy!' said Valerie. 'You got the fingering right that time. Now shall we try that bit again, keeping the semiquavers quieter than the rest of the bar, and make it even better?' Amy nodded enthusiastically. Lorna thought Valerie had just the sort of friendship with Amy that she herself would like to achieve.

Giles sat quietly in the background, scribbling down any comments Valerie made. Lorna was surprised that he made no attempt to take charge of the lesson. Later she remarked on this to Isobel. 'Poor Giles. I did admire him, just sitting there, not really taking part when I'm sure he was longing to.'

Isobel laughed. 'Valerie'd have him out on his ear if he started to get too bossy. Being Giles, he did of course try to interfere when Valerie first took Amy on—but he soon got his come-uppance because you either fall in with Suzuki or it's no good.' She added, 'Giles and I don't always agree about Amy's music.'

As soon as the words were out of her mouth, Isobel regretted them. Lorna looked like a cat licking its chops in anticipation, after spotting a particularly promising-looking mouse that might be pounced on when the moment was right.

*O*n Sunday afternoon they piled dogs and children into the boat and took a picnic tea to the island in the middle of the loch. Edward, who drove them all crazy on the way there by asking the same question twenty-five times, had taken his bag of monsters to play with once they arrived; he became totally absorbed, happily putting them through blood-curdling adventures while he paddled about in the shallow water at the edge of a bay; as always, if he was near any water, Isobel made him keep his life jacket on even when he was not in the boat. So far no one had been able to teach Edward to swim.

Isobel and Lorna collected sticks and made a fire on which to cook sausages and boil a kettle to make lovely smoky-tasting tea. Amy went off in the boat again with Giles, and later they returned triumphantly with two good trout.

'This is fun—quite like old times,' said Lorna. 'Remember all our picnics on Mull when we were little, Izzy?' Isobel nodded. Perhaps Lorna will be all right after all, she thought with relief. Perhaps she was just tired yesterday—edgy after her long journey and all the trauma she's been through. She smiled at her sister. 'Good to have you here,' she said.

*W*eekday mornings at Glendrochatt started early and were always hectic.

Amy did an hour's violin practice with Giles before breakfast, which meant starting at half past six. Over the years, other times had been tried, but at the end of the day she had homework to do, and was tired and less likely to be co-operative.

Up until now, Isobel had marvelled at how little fuss ten-year-old Amy created about the demands made upon her; Amy's enjoyment of both lessons and practice was certainly partly a tribute to Valerie Benson, but was also very much due to Giles. He was a hard taskmaster, never accepting second best and totally committed to the Suzuki method of parental involvement in which he believed so passionately. Although occasionally stormy, practice sessions were more often hugely exhilarating and fun for them both.

Giles had always possessed the capacity to generate excitement; Isobel was often ignited by his enthusiasms herself and was used to watching him fire the most unlikely people with his ideas—it was why so many of his schemes came to fruition—but recently his obsessive involvement in Amy's music had started to worry Isobel. It was not so much for Amy that she felt uneasy, though anxiety about her certainly came into it, it was more for Giles himself. Under a veneer of laid-back ease he was so extreme, thought Isobel; the word diplomacy certainly came into his vocabulary of what was acceptable—as a means of getting his own way—but failure did not. He played to win in everything he did and the most taxing competition came from inside himself. All the helpless, bitter disappointment he had felt over his son's un-expected handicaps now fuelled his obsession with his daughter's talent and it worried Isobel to see how dangerously he had over-filled this particular basket of eggs. It had not occurred to Giles that there might come a time when Amy would cease to welcome his participation in her every musical moment, but Isobel saw a straw spinning in the wind and wondered which way the wind would blow in future.

There was no time to brood about such things this morning, however. The minibus that collected Edward to take him to his school usually arrived about eight, but as it catered for a large catchment area, the timing could vary wildly and this morning it was late. Getting Edward ready for anything was time-consuming enough: the unreliable message transmitters that scrambled round his brain had such tenuous and faulty links with his limbs, in particular with his hands, that the temptation to do everything for him rather than watch him struggle unwillingly and slowly—oh, so slowly—with armholes, or putting the correct foot into its corresponding shoe, was frequently overwhelming if time was short. Keeping Edward ready was sometimes even more difficult. He hated feeling restricted and the Velcro fastenings on all his shoes and clothes, which made it so much simpler for him to cope with putting them on, also made it easier for him to rip them off. It was vital that someone should keep a very open eye on him until he was safely on the bus, to make sure he didn't vanish completely just as it came up the drive. Retrieving Edward what he called 'bare-naked' from outside the hen-run in pouring rain while everyone on the bus was kept waiting was never a great start to the day. It was a relief—but one about which Isobel felt a twinge of guilt—when the white vehicle bearing the logo of *Greenyfordham School for Children with Special Needs* disappeared from view with Edward fully clothed and safely on board.

Although Isobel shared Amy's school run with two other families, it still meant someone driving every morning as far as the garage outside Blairalder, which was their nearest meeting point.

'*Hurry up*, Amy!' she nagged now, yelling up the stairs. 'Have you remembered it's swimming today?'

'Can't find my towel.'

'Well, get another one, then.' Isobel hated the fishwife screech in her own voice, but this morning she felt unusually frayed at the edges, as though one extra tweak might unravel her into a tangled heap of loose threads. She had just got Amy, plus swimming things and satchel, into the car and switched on the ignition when Lorna appeared across the courtyard looking elegant but workmanlike, her hair tied back in a scrunchy, a crisp cotton shirt tucked into jeans that had sharp and purposeful-looking creases pressed into them. She looked ready for anything—anything that wouldn't rumple her too much, thought Isobel feeling thoroughly rumpled herself.

'I've come to get my orders for the day,' said Lorna, smiling brightly through the car window.

'Did you sleep all right?'

'I was fine, thank you.' Lorna did not tell Isobel that she had lain awake for most of the night.

She had half hoped, half feared that her feelings for Giles might have altered during her long absence and that she would at last find herself cured of a destructive addiction—like being a recovered alcoholic, she supposed, suddenly finding oneself able to think about brandy without a violent longing to consume it. After three days she now knew that her malaise was worse than ever. Actually seeing Isobel in her role as Giles's wife, the mother of his children and the chatelaine of Glendrochatt was even more painful in reality than it had been in her frequent imaginings. The question was, how was she going to tackle the problem now? Lorna had not yet decided—she only knew that she was not going back to South Africa.

A spurt of hurt anger flared when she thought about the children. She had wanted babies so desperately herself—a physical longing that was one of the motives that had driven her to a difficult and loveless marriage; a family seemed one more coveted thing that Isobel possessed and she did not. Recently she had imagined herself at Glendrochatt in the role of a specially adored aunt, a magnet to Giles's children. She had fully intended to try to overcome her fear and distaste for Edward, genuinely ashamed of her feelings of repugnance, but she had not bargained for such a wounding and public rebuff from him on arrival. And what about Amy, wondered Lorna, Amy who was clearly fiercely protective of her twin? Remembering her niece's accusing expression, she felt their relationship had kicked off to a bad start and had the uncomfortable feeling that as far as Amy was concerned she was not only very much on trial, but constantly in the beam of a searchlight.

How was I to know Edward hated to be held and why do I always get everything wrong? she asked herself miserably, as she lay sleepless in the immaculate flat to which she felt she had been deliberately banished by Isobel. Why must I always be the outsider with my nose pressed longingly against the window of someone else's life? She had hoped to win Giles's approbation by developing a friendship with his handicapped son, but perhaps it was Amy rather than Edward whom she should try to cultivate?

At four o'clock, just as she was beginning to hope she might drop off to sleep, Edward's cockerels had started crowing, greeting the dawn with a dreadful repetitive persistence as though they were practising one difficult bar of music before a major concert. Lorna—poised, controlled Lorna, in her silk crêpe de Chine nightdress, her dressing-gown, its sash ends exactly level, hanging tidily from the hook on the back of the door, her clothes folded and put away—had beaten the pillow furiously with her fists before burying her face in it and moaning.

'Where are you off to?' she asked Isobel now, no trace of the sleepless night showing on her perfectly made-up face.

'I'm off to drop Amy—then I have to go on to the supermarket,' Isobel answered. 'But I shouldn't be long. Do please make yourself at home. Giles is knocking about somewhere. Joss will know where he is.'

'Please don't worry, I'll track him down. He said he'd show me the office set-up this morning, then I'll be able to make myself really useful. Unless it would be more help if I came with you?' There was an edge to Lorna's voice as sharp as the knife-edge creases in her trousers.

This is weird, thought Isobel, we're talking like polite strangers. She felt a stab of disappointment that the rapport she had hoped they were achieving the day before did not seem to have lasted. 'No, no,' she said, conscious of her wild hair and a hole in the sleeve of her jersey that would not normally have bothered her at all. 'Thanks all the same, Lorna. Must rush. See you later.'

' 'Bye then—please don't hurry back on my account. I'll be fine.'

Lorna watched the car roar off down the drive, the door at the back, which had been left open, banging up and down, while Flapper, Isobel's black-and-white springer spaniel, tore joyfully along behind, ears streaming out like windsocks. As the drive was nearly a mile long it was a wonderful way to give the energetic little dog a morning run. When Isobel slowed down as she approached the cattle grid at the end, Flapper would leap in and Amy would hang over the back seat to pull the door shut with a string. Lorna reflected that such a haphazard arrangement—but one which actually worked—was typical of Isobel, and she walked up the steps and back into the house, not at all anxious for her sister to hurry home.

As Isobel drove into the forecourt of the garage outside Blairalder she could see that the Fortescues and the Murrays were already there. It was Grizelda Murray's turn to do the full run— all ten miles of it—and her own two boys, plus Emily and Mungo

Fortescue, were already strapped into the back seats and ready to go.

'Quicksticks, darling—I'm afraid we're a bit late,' said Isobel, trying to prevent Flapper from leaping out of the car while Amy dragged her school bag out of the back.

'Oh, sugar!' Amy pulled a face. 'Now I shall have to sit in front with Mrs Murray.'

'So? What's wrong with that?'

'I'll be interrogated, that's what. Mrs Murray's always trying to analyse us. Anyway it's much more fun sitting in the back with the others. Then we can swap our stickers or do arm wrestling.'

'Well, tough.' Isobel knew Amy was one of those lucky children who act as a magnet to their school friends so she never had to worry about her being left out—unlike poor Mungo Fortescue from whom tears dripped so easily that he had earned himself the unfortunate nickname of 'Tap'. The other children considered him too wet for words but Isobel had a particularly soft spot for the little boy and owed him a debt of gratitude because of his devotion to Edward. Though Mungo was four years younger than Edward, they played together wonderfully well and Mungo was able to enter the strange world of Edward's imagination as no other child could. He was really Edward's only friend. Isobel dreaded the moment—which she knew must come soon—when Mungo overtook and outgrew Edward as so many other children had already done.

'You be nice to Mungo,' she warned Amy now. 'You know what I said about teasing last week.'

'Yeah, yeah, yeah.' Amy rolled her eyes and grinned at her mother. 'Don't fuss. I'll be Miss Perfect.' She wasn't really an unkind child and would have died in defence of her twin, but she had a quick tongue and the other children's tendency to think that everything she said was utterly hilarious acted as a dangerous intoxicant.

When Grizelda Murray had driven off, Fiona Fortescue came

and leant on the bonnet of Isobel's car. They had been friends since their schooldays and there was not much they did not know about each other's lives.

'Are you in a rush?' asked Fiona.

'I ought to be. I've got to do a big, boring shop, and Lorna only arrived on Friday and I've hardly seen her this morning.'

'I'm dying to hear about her. Shall we go and have a quick sinful together?'

'Oh, why not? Do us both good. Let's go to the caff, then.'

A 'sinful' meant snatching a gossip, when there were more pressing things that needed to be done, and the Bide-a-Wee café just beyond the garage provided a convenient setting where they could dissect their own lives and those of their friends as well.

Though the Bide-a-Wee opened early all through the summer, there were no other customers yet. The café had a gift shop extension, which did a roaring trade later in the season selling such covetable items as grouse's claw brooches, kilted Rob Roy dolls and Robert the Bruce spiders to tourists for whose benefit the whole place was swathed in tartan. Mrs Mackenzie, the owner who was well known locally for her excellent shortbread and home-baked bread, also produced surprisingly good coffee.

'I didn't have time for breakfast this morning and I bet you didn't either. I think we owe it to ourselves to have croissants as well, don't you?' asked Fiona. 'You look a bit down in the mouth, Izzy. Is life at the Arts Centre hotting up or is it the effect of your sister already? Hey there,' she went on in a more serious voice, disturbed by the daunted expression on Isobel's usually cheerful face, 'is my godson all right? Not in trouble, are you?'

'No—bless you—Edward's fine. Rather too fine, in fact—he didn't exactly kick off to a good start with Lorna and it wasn't her fault.' Though Isobel snorted at the memory and made Fiona laugh over her account of Edward wrapping himself in the curtains, Fiona could tell it hadn't seemed funny at the time.

'So what about Lorna? Still the noble martyr: all sighs, sweetness and sensible examples like when we were growing up? I bet nothing's changed there.'

'Well, you're wrong. She has changed. You'll goggle when you see her. She's absolutely *stunning* now.' Isobel longed to tell Fiona about Lorna's plastic surgery, but scrupulously resisted the urge. She went on, 'I can't explain precisely why, but she makes me uneasy. I have the most disconcerting feeling . . .' she paused to search for the right words ' . . . that she's . . . she's come home to declare war on me.'

'You're joking!' said Fiona, but could see that she wasn't. 'Lorna can't seriously expect to win Giles from you after all this time? She wouldn't have a hope in hell anyway.'

'I don't know what she expects. Perhaps she doesn't know herself. I only know she's set to cause trouble.'

'Have you talked to Giles about it?'

'I tried to on her first night—but I wished I hadn't afterwards. You know what ostriches men can be. They pretend a difficulty's not there and then—hey-presto!—because they don't look, they really can't see it. Think how long Giles managed to con himself that there was nothing seriously wrong with Edward—ages after I'd accepted it and long after he knew it in his heart of hearts. Anyway, it was very stupid of me to draw attention to Lorna's feelings for him, because though he denied it, in a way I think he finds the whole scenario quite titillating.'

Fiona's heart sank. Over the years she had watched with an-guished admiration the battles Isobel had waged on behalf of her puzzling, often heartbreaking little son. Fiona had frequently kept Isobel company during interminable waits in the paediatric de-partments of various hospitals in order that yet another eminent professor should see this interesting specimen—whose condition, after ten years, had still not acquired a specific label. And a good job too, thought Fiona, remembering Isobel's despair at the med-ical enthusiasm when yet another horrendous-sounding syndrome had been mooted as a possibility.

'Why don't you just put him in a chloroform jar and pin him out on a board so you can all take a jolly good look?' Isobel had once demanded passionately of a zealous but not very sensitive young houseman, who in her presence—but with scant regard to it—had demanded excitedly of his boss: 'Do you think we might possibly be able to turn this one into a Prader-Willi case, sir?' Edward had been nearly three at the time, a should-be toddler whose floppy legs showed no signs of toddling, and who was unable to use his finger and thumb in the required pincer movement, while his twin sister was already picking up a violin and getting notes out of it. It had been a relief when that particularly daunting condition had been ruled out.

In those days Isobel had always been bracing herself to face shattering possibilities. Now, infinitely more medically knowledgeable, she was constantly thanking her stars for the things Edward *didn't* have. The perimeters of her expectations had changed and the acute stage of diagnostic snark-hunting had modified. If his peculiarities had no definitive name, Isobel had come to take comfort from the fact that neither could there be any absolute ceiling to what he might achieve. Dr Connor, the wise and compassionate paediatrician who was now in overall charge of Edward's case, said he must possess an astonishingly strong life force to have weathered all the many crises of his early years; even with the aid of modern drugs and medical expertise it was still remarkable that he'd survived. Edward's small spark had simply refused to be snuffed out. The fact that he was now capable of doing so many things that had once been deemed impossible for him— walking and talking, for instance—was, in Dr Connor's view, not only due to his mother's effort and determination, but also partly to a persistent quality in Edward himself. His tenacity, along with his various obsessions, was one of the things that made him so tiring to deal with: Edward could wear you out. But Isobel had fought for him along every painful inch of his uncertain life, even when she had been inwardly screaming tortured questions to herself about its value.

Fiona admired her friend's courage with all her heart, but she and her husband Duncan, an accountant who was one of the Glendrochatt Estate trustees, were also very fond of Giles and sometimes felt for him when Isobel, unintentionally, shut him out of Edward's battles. In order to modify his bizarre behaviour and try to make him socially acceptable, it was often necessary to be tough with Edward. Fiona knew how painful Isobel found this, but was also aware that if Giles tried to back her up and discipline Edward himself, Isobel nearly always flew protectively to her son's defence. She reminded Fiona of a little pied flycatcher she had once watched darting desperately to and fro to feed the bafflingly different, time-consuming chick that she had unexpectedly hatched—literally a cuckoo in the nest. Fiona could quite see why Giles concentrated on Amy.

Despite these difficulties, which had frequently put their marriage under strain, Fiona thought Giles and Isobel still had one of the strongest relationships of any of their friends. They might drive each other crazy sometimes—and often did—but they could still stimulate and amuse each other. Their marriage was full of laughter.

'Stiffen your sinews, Mrs Grant,' she said bracingly, now. 'If Lorna thinks she can upset your applecart she's forgotten about your band of devoted chums. We'll soon see her off. What we need is some really dishy man—other than your husband or mine—for her to fall in love with. Whom can we conjure up?'

'Neil Dunbarnock?' suggested Isobel and they fell about with laughter.

Lord Dunbarnock was the local eccentric. In his youth, for a bet, he had agreed not to shave or cut his hair for a whole year and somehow the habit had stuck. He strode about in Highland dress, looking like a mobile cartoon of a bewhiskered Scotsman. It was hard to tell where his beard ended and his sporran began, and his hair usually billowed out in the wind like a grizzled shawl, though on Sundays, if he was reading the lesson in church, he sometimes wore it in a pigtail as a special concession to God.

Despite this wild-man-of-the-woods disguise, he was in fact extremely erudite, but years of living under the petrifying eye of his old gorgon of a mother—who had recently died aged ninety-two—had made him so inhibited that social chit-chat was difficult. His hirsute appearance had been his one act of defiance and then, Samson-like, he had feared his strength might vanish altogether if he visited a barber. Giles was one of the few people who could manage to talk normally to him for any length of time and Lord Dunbarnock, who was not only immensely rich but extremely generous, was a great supporter of the Glendrochatt musical events.

'Brilliant idea,' said Fiona. 'We'll work on it. Lorna will be the ideal Lady Dunbarnock. God! Izzy! Look at the *time*. Ring me with every latest development about her.'

'Had you forgotten you're supposed to be bringing your mother-in-law to the committee meeting tomorrow—you can see Lorna for yourself.'

'Oh, good, so I can.' Fiona raised her cup and drank the last dregs of her coffee. 'To Lorna, the future Lady Dunbarnock of that ILK,' she said.

Isobel drove to Tesco's feeling much cheered by Fiona's company.

Seven

By the time Isobel got back to Glendrochatt it was nearly
one. She drove round the side of the house to the kitchen
entrance and went to find Joss to help her unload the groceries.
They would be providing lunch for the Friends of Glendrochatt
committee meeting the following day, so the car was loaded with
boxes and carrier bags bulging with supplies. Often she and Joss
did the shopping together, but this morning he had wanted to get
ahead with the cooking.

'Hi there. Sorry I've been such ages, but I'd forgotten I had to
pick up the salmon, so I had to go all the way round by Inverbeith, and the road was up by the bridge and there was a horren-
dous tailback. Hope Lorna's all right. Have you seen her?'

'Oh, yes—very busy, she is. I gather she's totally reorganising
the office. Mrs Shepherd rang to say she couldn't get in this morning—she's unexpectedly had to go to see her mother in hospital—
but she's going to get quite a little surprise when she comes in
tomorrow. Interesting situation.' Joss sounded amused.

Sheila Shepherd was Giles's secretary and had worked for his
father before him. Though most of her work was concerned with
the running of the estate, she had always dealt with the June
festival as well. Because the Arts Centre would now involve them
all in so much more work, it had been at her request that Giles

and Isobel had advertised for extra help. Between them they had hit on the title of Assistant Administrator, which they thought sounded attractive without being specific. As Sheila had said: ' "Competent dogsbody required" doesn't have quite the right ring to it.' When the suggestion of temporary help from Lorna had been mooted, after the original advertisement had failed to produce the right person, Sheila had been very enthusiastic, but she certainly hadn't envisaged a takeover operation.

'Oh, dear,' said Isobel. 'Perhaps I should go and try my hand at a bit of diplomacy?'

'You can always try,' said Joss. He winked at Isobel. 'Powerful lady, your sister. You go and have your little talk with her and I'll deal with putting away the shopping. Glad you got the fish. I'll get them cooked straight away.'

'Where's Giles?'

Joss roared with laughter. 'If you ask me, I think he's beaten a rapid retreat. He got me and Mick to help shift some furniture to suit your sister's wishes, then he went down to the theatre with Mick to get it cleared up for this artist bloke who's arriving to-morrow.'

'Oh, Lord—I'd quite forgotten about him; that's all I need. I'd better go down to the office and calm Lorna's ideas down a bit. Thanks, Joss.'

The office was in the basement in the room that Lorna had remembered as the old kitchen. It made an ideal business head-quarters—a large, long room with windows looking out on to flower beds in the sunken area at the front of the house, below the arch of steps, which led up to the front door. Because there was separate access from the courtyard at the back it was not necessary for anyone coming to the office to go through the main part of the house. Unusually, the door was closed. Isobel flung it open and looked about her, stunned.

The whole layout had been altered. Mrs Shepherd's office desk had been moved up to the far end of the room and the one Giles used to the other. In the centre, Lorna was sitting behind the imposing mahogany kneehole desk that had belonged to Hector Grant, which had been carried down to the basement and stored, ever since the old billiard room had been turned into the new kitchen.

She looked up and gave Isobel a pleasant smile. 'Surprised? What do you think? A great improvement, isn't it—or at least a good start?'

'Oh, Lorna, what have you done? Sheila's going to be incandescent.'

Lorna raised her eyebrows. 'Surely not. It will make life much easier for her. She can deal with all the estate business down there and keep it quite separate. I can take over all the concert stuff and be easily available here to man the telephone or answer any queries in person—and Giles still has his own desk near both of us.' It was not lost on Isobel that Giles's desk was much closer to Lorna's than to Mrs Shepherd's. She stared at Lorna, temporarily speechless with dismay.

'I've been going through the files on the computer,' said Lorna. 'I must say Mrs Shepherd seems very efficient, but Giles agrees with me that we'll need another machine now and I'll transfer all the relevant data on to it. I thought I'd go into either Perth or Edinburgh and fix that up right away. I'm going to buy myself a car some time, but Giles thinks we shall need an extra one for the centre anyway so he says he'll get hold of a second-hand one this week. Meanwhile, is it OK for me to borrow yours this afternoon?'

'Lorna—just hang on.' Isobel sat down in the chair that Lorna had placed in front of the desk and felt as if she were being interviewed for a job herself. 'I'm sorry to be a wet blanket, but you really can't do this. This is Sheila Shepherd's office.'

'I know—and I don't mind sharing it with her at all,' said Lorna. 'She can stick to the estate work and I'll administer the Arts Centre. That is what you've asked me to do after all, isn't it?'

'No,' said Isobel desperately. 'We've asked you to be temporary assistant administrator—assistant to Giles and me *and* Sheila.'

'Look, Izzy . . .' Lorna's voice, full of calm capability, but with just a touch of underlying menace for those who could discern it, took Isobel right back to the old nursery pecking order when the sensible older sister had so often tried to put the brakes on the giddy irresponsible younger one. 'You have so much to do already with the children—and the domestic arrangements. This is a burden I really can take off your shoulders. Why don't you just leave it to me? Goodness, but you haven't changed—still the same impulsive Isobel. You do jump to conclusions, don't you? I think you'll find I can deal very tactfully with Sheila. It's unfortunate that she couldn't come in today because of *course* I would have consulted her if only she'd been here—actually, I thought you'd be back much sooner too. As it is I went and got the go-ahead from Giles. There's only six weeks before your opening concert, you know, and there's an awful lot to be done, but if you don't think we can work together, well . . .' Lorna shrugged and spread her hands. She leant back in her chair and smiled at Isobel—sweetly reasonable, but unmistakably throwing down a gauntlet.

How strange, thought Isobel, we have both changed so much in so many ways and yet the dialogue between us hasn't really altered at all. It's as though we are acting archetypal roles in an ancient, universal drama in which we have both taken part many times before. This time the translation may be slightly different but the real meaning of the play never changes.

She picked up the gauntlet. 'Fine.' She got to her feet and looked down at her much taller sister. 'We do need help. You do want a job. I'm sure you can be invaluable and this is only a teething trouble—just so long as we understand each other in future. None of this is a burden to me. The idea of the centre is very much my baby, so please consult me before you make any alterations another time, even if it means waiting. Meanwhile I'll go and talk things over with Giles and let you know what we decide. It would be too awful to lose Sheila Shepherd and Giles would be the first person to be appalled. I don't suppose he realised quite what you intended to do. You're not in South Africa now,' Isobel added pointedly. She had hated the aloof and high-handed way in which Lorna had dealt with her considerable household staff when they had stayed with her in Capetown. 'Do come up and have a scratch lunch in the kitchen when you're ready.' And Isobel walked out of the office.

Each sister knew that battle lines had been drawn up.

Lorna watched Isobel go. Throughout their childhood she had always been conscious of competing with her sister, whereas Isobel had not. Now both were engaged in a struggle and Lorna felt, with a little frisson of excitement, that by picking up her own implicit challenge, then issuing one herself, Isobel had suddenly flung open a window and released something. She's set my conscience free, thought Lorna. It's been like a trapped bird beating its wings against a pane of glass for years. Now, at last, it can fly away because Isobel has given permission for an open contest between us. But for what? Lorna asked herself. For dominance, for position, for revenge—or simply for possession of Giles?

If Isobel had been there to see her sister's expression she might have felt a chill. As it was, she stormed upstairs, red-hot, in search of her husband. Cool calculation had never been a weapon in her armoury.

'So how was diplomacy, then?' asked Joss as Isobel stomped through the kitchen, Flapper pattering along beside her, rear end rotating like a chorus girl's.

'Useless—it's unsheathed knives now.'

'Oh, well, keep the blood out of the kitchen,' said Joss equably, 'or I might have a funny turn.'

'I'll try.' In spite of herself Isobel laughed. 'Is Giles still down in the theatre?'

'Far as I know.'

'Right,' said Isobel. 'I'll go and carve him up there, then.'

*G*iles was sitting on the edge of the stage, his long legs dangling, talking into his mobile telephone. Isobel always thought he had that cat-like quality of being able to look completely relaxed and comfortable wherever he placed himself. He acknowledged her entrance by blowing a kiss from the end of one finger; his rough-haired German pointer, Wotan, got up and came to give her a condescending greeting before flopping back at Giles's feet. Wotan, who had dauntingly perfect manners, loved and protected the children but only tolerated Isobel and Flapper.

'I'm just so sorry,' Isobel heard Giles say. 'How *awful* for you. Yes, of course I understand. We'll manage somehow. Yes, it is indeed a bit of luck that she's arrived, so don't you worry about a thing. Hope your ma gets better very soon. Give me a call later with the telephone number of her house, then I can ring and ask you any queries and keep you up to date with things here—oh, and Isobel has just come in and I know she'll be sending you her love. Bye then—good luck.' He clicked off the telephone and held out his hand. 'Hello, my sweet.'

'And who am I sending my love to?' asked Isobel, though with a mixture of rage and relief she could guess.

'That was Sheila. Her mother was taken to hospital this morning and now it looks as if the old bird's had a minor stroke. They're sending her home tomorrow but Sheila will have to go to look after her for a bit. Looks as if she won't be back for several weeks. Bloody nuisance, actually. Good thing we've got Lorna or we would be in the soup. Lunch now, do you think?'

'It's Lorna I've come to talk about.' Isobel pointedly ignored his outstretched hand.

'Aha,' said Giles. 'I rather thought it might be. The moment I saw your stroppy walk and the sparks coming out of your ears I guessed there was trouble—but I think since this telephone call we've got an unexpected reprieve.'

'A completely undeserved one, then. You do have the devil's own luck, Giles.'

He glinted at her, not pretending to misunderstand. 'I do, don't

I? I take it Lorna's gone a bit over the top? Perhaps I could have said to Sheila, "Oh, well, your mother's stroke might be quite a stroke of luck for me because it'll delay you discovering that I've let my sister-in-law loose in your office and Isobel is just about to eat me up because of it." ' He cocked his head on one side and looked consideringly at his wife. 'Have I ever told you how pretty you look when you're really cross?'

'Often,' Isobel replied. 'And it doesn't get you anywhere.'

'Oh, but I think it does.'

'For someone who's supposed to be so clever and who fancies himself as sensitive you really are incredibly stupid sometimes, Giles,' she said furiously. 'You must have known Sheila would be mortally hurt if you let Lorna rearrange everything like that—and don't say you didn't guess what she was up to because I'm dead sure you did. You can jolly well sort it out yourself because I'm certainly not going to. If Sheila had come back tomorrow and given notice I wouldn't have blamed her but I'd have killed you— with relish.'

'Poor Izzy! Thwarted of your prey—another bit of luck for me, then. I'll take all the blame and think of a wonderful justification for the changes by the time Sheila returns. How's that?'

'Very second best. You may enjoy getting away with things but why do you always have to stir? I warned you not to meddle. I think you're monstrous.'

'The Unjust having the Just's umbrella again?'

'Exactly.'

'Much more fun living with the Unjust, though. The Just are always so dreadfully dull. Think how you'd hate to be married to worthy old Frank Murray—you'd be bored out of your mind. No wonder poor Grizelda turns to alternative therapies—all those infallible elixirs of squashed newts' tails that she sells. What's her latest panacea?' Unlike a lot of men, Giles adored hearing the gossip about his wife's friends.

'Don't try to sidetrack me,' Isobel said. 'This may give you time to think of a way of mollifying Sheila, but Lorna's going to gloat over me so intolerably that I'm really not sure I can bear it.'

A tremor in her voice made Giles look at her sharply. He saw that she was not just in a rage but genuinely upset. He was immediately contrite. 'Oh, Izz, darling, I'm truly sorry. I was quite out of order—some demon possessed me. Would it help if I tell Lorna you were absolutely right to be cross and make it plain to her how important Sheila is to both of us?'

'It might—a bit.'

'Leave it to me. All shall be sweetness and light, I promise. Kiss?'

'You're impossible,' said Isobel, but she let him kiss her.

'All the same,' she said as they walked back to the house hand in hand like a pair of teenagers, 'I'm warning you, Giles, and I'm deadly serious. I've watched Lorna making trouble all my life. Don't let her do it between you and me.'

'Would I?' asked Giles.

'I don't know,' said Isobel. 'I really do not know.'

Eight

The meeting was due to begin at eleven thirty, but people started to arrive well before this, knowing that Isobel always provided coffee and home-made biscuits first to get everyone in a cheerful frame of mind. Most of the members regarded Friends' gatherings as a good day out, certain there would be an excellent lunch, interesting wine, old friends and—equally enjoyable to some perhaps—a few old enemies; there would be stimulating ideas floating about, but hot air was usually cut to a minimum by Giles's skilful chairmanship.

The Friends of Glendrochatt had been founded by Hector Grant as a means of drumming up attendance at the June festival, but now they had a far more crucial role to play. Major fund-raising had been involved recently and sponsorship was vital to the success of the venture. Today, lunch was to be held for the first time in the newly converted premises, which had been built out of the old farm buildings adjoining the original theatre. These consisted of a small but extremely well-equipped kitchen, a bar and a reception room. A considerable transformation had taken place, and Giles and Isobel were dying to show it off to the members of the committee, most of whom had approved the original plans, but not many of whom had seen the finished product in all its glory of pale polished wood and spacious lightness, partly achieved by clever artificial lighting but also by Velux windows in the roof. It had been Isobel's bright idea to move some of the antlers from the old billiard room—legacies of Giles's sporting forebears—and place them round the bar, inviting anyone who contributed to sponsoring a concert to donate a hat to hang from them. She had already been presented with an amazing collection, from a John Boyd number that had been worn at a royal wedding to a wartime ARP warden's helmet; from deerstalkers and Glengarry bonnets to sombreros and panama sunhats. The key to the success of this idea, of course, was that each hat was clearly labelled with the donor's name. Giles, who usually had most of the best ideas himself, was generous about other people's brainwaves and had been very pleased with Isobel about this one.

The main area was designed to be used not only for intervals during performances, but also as an attractive gallery, which could be used independently from the actual theatre for exhibitions, seminars, or any functions connected with the arts; the walls would be hung with paintings, all of them for sale, by contemporary Scottish artists.

Everything had at last been approved for Fire, Health and Safety regulations, and though there had been some nightmarish moments during the early stages, the final result was a triumph. Between them, Giles and the architect—but mostly, it had to be said, Giles himself—had managed to preserve the charm and character of the old buildings while making them practical and comfortable.

The meeting itself was to take place in the diningroom in the main house; Mick and Joss had put all the leaves in the big mahogany table and Isobel had covered it with a large baize tablecloth. Lorna, in her element, put fresh notepads and newly sharpened pencils by each place and had suggested that, in the absence of Mrs Shepherd, she should sit next to Giles and take the minutes. Isobel had a small inward struggle over this, but as she loathed doing it herself and her secretarial skills were not only poor in the first place but extremely rusty, she knew her reasons for refusing Lorna's offer would have been pure dog-in-the-manger ones. All the same, she intended to keep a sharp eye on the manger, ready to leap into it, growling, if necessity arose.

Fiona, avid for a glimpse of Lorna, was the first to arrive, chauffeuring her formidable mother-in-law, Lady Fortescue, a renowned judge of Highland ponies and other people's morals. Violet Fortescue's face was always carefully coated in a sweet expression and a great deal of make-up, both of which she applied first thing in the morning and touched up at frequent intervals during the day. No one had ever seen Violet with either a shiny nose or a disagreeable countenance; she was fond of announcing that she had been brought up to believe that if you could not find anything nice to say, then it was better to say nothing at all—an utterance which was frequently followed by an eloquently chilling silence. Even strong men had been known to quail when shaking Lady Fortescue's velvet-gloved hand. Fiona had a theory that all her mother-in-law's four sons (of whom her husband Duncan was the youngest) had been conceived by remote control and were a triumph of Violet Fortescue's mind over matter, though Fiona conceded that since Violet was among that fortunate band of people who believe they have a direct line through to their Lord—no mucking about with intermediaries for Lady Fortescue—it was possible that she'd called on the Holy Ghost for help. Violet was constantly on the receiving end of guidance, or so she said, though it was noticeable that the advice she received usually seemed to be more of an endorsement of her own strong opinions than an unpalatable edict from on high. Though not without its element of risk, her presence on any committee was a guarantee of respect from less socially secure souls. Giles adored bending her subtly to his will, much as Uri Geller might bend a silver spoon with no apparent force, and bore the distinction of being on the select list of people of whom Lady Fortescue thoroughly approved. Isobel told him this was monstrously unfair as it probably meant his name was photocopied angelically and sent on to God for recommendation like a mail-shot. Isobel herself, on the other hand, was certainly not among Lady Fortescue's approved élite—suspected of being prone to frivolity, given to inappropriate displays of affection or hilarity and not above taking pot-shots at Lady Fortescue's prize herd of sacred cows.

Giles and Isobel had been watching from the kitchen to see who would arrive first. 'Oh, good, here comes Fiona with old Touch-me-not. Better go and do your stuff with her, darling,' said Isobel to Giles, and she flung the front door open and ran down the steps to greet the Fortescues.

Violet inclined a guarded cheek in her direction, keeping a good three inches clear of actual contact—no hugs from Lady Fortescue. Fiona caught Isobel's eye as Giles, a suitably dignified Wotan at his heels, followed at a more circumspect pace and extended both hands to Lady Fortescue, thus skilfully avoiding the question of to kiss or not to kiss.

'Violet! How absolutely *wonderful* of you to come,' he said, giving Fiona a conspiratorial wink. 'I was so hoping you'd manage it because there are a lot of things I want to pick your brains about: if you're here I know we'll have a good meeting. Hi there, Fiona, lovely to see you too.' Fiona tried not to laugh and muttered 'Creep!' in his ear as she kissed him hello.

A noise like the sound of a runaway concrete mixer heralded the arrival of Lord Dunbarnock in one of his fleet of vintage cars—this time a 1937 Lagonda V12, which had been sprayed a particularly virulent shade of yellow. He was wearing an old leather flying helmet that had belonged to his father and his hair was tied back in a ponytail in deference to the meeting.

'Hello, Neil,' said Giles. 'Good to see you. Think I'd put your roof up if I were you—might be a shower. Would you like Mick to do it for you?' Mick, who was supervising the parking, was only too keen to get his hands on the Lagonda. He shared Lord Dunbarnock's passion for tinkering with cars without suffering from the same inconvenient desire to wash his hands every five minutes. It was bad luck for Neil Dunbarnock that he should be at his happiest and most confident draining sumps, tuning throttles and repairing exhausts while his other great obsession in life was hygiene—a legacy from an overzealous Nanny in his childhood. The awful threat of GERMS haunted him, though he waged relentless war on them, keeping a sachet of antiseptic wipes in his sporran and refusing wine at Holy Communion between October and May, lest dangerous contact between lordly lip and chalice should cause him to pick up a cold. Lately he had transformed his spiritual life by taking his own little packet of cut-down straws to church.

'Oh, thank you most awfully, Giles—that would be a huge relief to me,' he said now, sounding as though he'd been saved from an overwhelming burden of indecision and incidentally making Mick's day because it was a mark of great trust if Neil Dunbarnock allowed anyone to touch one of his cars. All the same, making frantic soaping motions with his hands and glancing round nervously in case anyone might overhear such an intimate request, he murmured in a low voice to Giles, 'I wonder if I could possibly just have a quick—you know—er, *wash* before we start the proceedings?' He'd only driven five miles but you never knew what sinister bacteria might have landed on the steering wheel in that distance. He'd tried wearing surgical rubber gloves for driving, but then read that they could cause a dangerous allergic reaction.

'Of course,' said Giles. 'You know the geography—do go on in.' Lord Dunbarnock bolted thankfully for the haven of the Glendrochatt downstairs loo where Joss, knowing he was coming, had made sure there were enough clean towels and a clinical bottle of anti-bacterial wash to keep him calm all day.

Isobel tried to introduce Lorna to people as they arrived—a few of whom, like Fiona Fortescue, remembered her from her Edinburgh youth. She was looking very attractive in a navy-blue silk shirt and short red linen skirt, which showed off her wonderful legs to perfection. She was charming, friendly and welcoming, and seemed totally at home at Glendrochatt—a second hostess. Isobel could see what a very favourable impression Lorna was making and wished she could summon up the generosity to feel really pleased about this. Normally she loved the meetings but the presence of Lorna put her off her stroke to a quite unforeseen and extraordinary degree, making her feel unwontedly nervous and uneasy. Isobel had never suffered the pangs of jealousy before and it was not a welcome sensation. How the tables have been turned on me, she thought ruefully. Perhaps it's poetic justice; I suppose this is what I did to Lorna in our childhood.

When the full complement of Friends had arrived and were seated round the dining-room table, Giles made a short welcoming speech and called everyone's attention to the copies of the agenda beside each place. Then, indicating Lorna beside him, he went on, 'For those of you who haven't yet met her, it gives me great pleasure to introduce you all to a new member of our team—someone who is already a very important part of our family—my sister-in-law, Lorna Cartwright. It's marvellous for Isobel and me that Lorna, who has just returned home to Scotland after living in South Africa, has agreed to help us start off our new venture. Lorna's a good musician herself and besides being wonderful company to us all she's also quite remarkably efficient. She's going to bring a little much needed sanity and organisation into our general family chaos . . .' finished Giles, smiling at Lorna to affectionate laughter from the Friends.

'Like hell,' muttered Isobel to Fiona Fortescue.

Lorna stood up briefly, smiling and making vague, polite disclaimers, and looking charmingly modest.

'We have wonderful things ahead of us,' Giles went on. 'I want to discuss our forthcoming programme with you all, including, of course, arrangements for our Gala Evening and opening concert in September. Then I have an announcement to make, which gives me enormous pleasure. Even in my mother's day there was never any scenery at the Old Steading Theatre and we've always relied for effect on a few props, wonderful acting and the imagination of our audience, but some of you may know that Isobel and I have commissioned an exciting young artist, Daniel Hoffman, to paint a backcloth for the stage. This is our personal contribution to mark the opening of Glendrochatt as an arts centre. We felt we could only run to one—but with his usual amazing generosity, Neil Dunbarnock has offered to commission a second alternative backdrop as well, so now we can ask Daniel Hoffman to do both an outdoor and an indoor set for us . . .' Giles paused for the clapping that followed and Neil Dunbarnock studied his beard in an agony of pleased shyness.

Lady Fortescue did not applaud. She did not care for Lord Dunbarnock and found eccentricity distasteful.

'Now,' said Giles, 'let me run through our programme of events. First our Gala concert for which tickets are already sold out. We've been lucky enough to get flautist Flavia Cameron and harpist Megan Davies to come for this, which is particularly suitable because of Flavia's local connections—as many of you know, she's Colin Cameron's niece. Both Colin and Elizabeth have sent their apologies today as they're away, but of course they'll be bringing a party to support Flavia for the performance.'

Colin and Elizabeth Cameron, who were much loved and respected, lived in a vast Victorian pile a few miles from Glendrochatt, and many locals had heard Flavia Cameron performing at charity concerts for her aunt and uncle before she became well-known. She had first rocketed to wider attention by winning the Young Musician of the Year Award, then by collapsing while performing at a major concert in the Festival Hall conducted by the flamboyant French conductor Antoine du Fosset, with whom she was having a well-publicised affair at the time. He had dropped her, with even more publicity, both as a lover and a musician, as soon as ill health had struck and the press had enjoyed a field day of speculation about them both. Flavia had temporarily given up her promising career in favour of a disastrous marriage to the headmaster of a boys' preparatory school who was twenty-five years her senior and had then speedily hit the headlines again by running off with the father of one of the boys in her husband's school. She had now resumed her career and married her lover— though the wedding had not taken place until a year after she had given birth to a baby girl, thus providing further cause for malicious tongues' to wag. Giles and Isobel were very fond of both Flavia and her husband, Alistair Forbes—indeed Isobel was godmother to their two-year-old daughter Dulcie—but Giles had known what he was doing when he'd managed to get Flavia to play for their Gala concert, because she was one of those people—like her or loathe her—who can't help attracting attention. Lady Fortescue's silence factor with regard to Flavia was almost tangible, but as she was both an old friend of the Camerons and a tremendous snob, Giles was confident that what she considered to be a lapse of judgement on his part would not cause her to withdraw support. Lady Fortescue's God, who seemed to have a firm grip on social niceties, would, he felt sure, guide her to overcome moral scruples and attend the concert: Christian forgiveness can have its uses.

'Not so many of you will have heard Megan Davies,' Giles went on, 'the young harpist with whom Flavia has recently teamed up so successfully. I heard them play together at the Wigmore Hall together last autumn and I promise you you've got a treat in store. I knew they'd be right for Glendrochatt. The Gala concert will be the prelude to a week of music making. Flavia has agreed to stay on and teach master classes for aspiring flautists and to take seminars for young musicians. Valerie Benson, who is a Suzuki violin teacher—and incidently instructs our daughter Amy—is also donating her services, as is Donald McClean the celebrated organist from St Mungo's University. It should be very exciting. As you all know the Gala is on the Friday evening. On the Saturday and Sunday we're going to have two days of informal music making, jointly organised with the trust for Young Musicians in Scottish Schools—or YMISS—which you mustn't miss. Several youth orchestras, choirs and children's groups are taking part, and we've been thrilled with the response. Please come along and bring your friends, plus your own picnic lunches. Of course, we're hoping for fine weather, but with these new rooms, the Old Steading Theatre and various rooms at the house available as well, we hope we can cope if it's wet. It doesn't look as if my family and I are going to have anywhere to eat and sleep ourselves that week,' he added, laughing, 'but it's all in a very good cause.' As usual, Isobel could see that Giles's enthusiasm was carrying his audience along with him.

'You'll find all the details in the notes you've been given, but of course I shall welcome suggestions for improvements if anyone wants to make any,' continued Giles, who had no intention of allowing the Friends to have a free-for-all discussion or make any changes. 'As you know, we are dedicated to giving a chance to young talent and next year we are hoping to put on an opera— a first for Glendrochatt. We hope it will provide an opportunity for aspiring young singers to tackle operatic roles they want to include in their repertoire but might not yet get the chance to perform—we won't be ready to do that this year but we are having a concert performance of *La Traviata*, which should be a delight. We are also going to have a children's theatre weekend— actually copying something my parents once did years ago. I be- lieve I was six at the time and naturally gave a star performance! Local children will partly invent and then perform a play for us under professional direction. It should be fun. I'm afraid we're going to have to be very strict about age and numbers are limited. There's already a waiting list and a rumour has reached me that some would-be Mrs Worthingtons are preparing to sabotage each other's children by devious means. More details later. Now that's more than enough from me,' finished Giles. 'We must hurry on, so please will you all look at the second item on your agenda.' He could see that corpulent Mr McMichael, who owned the local printing press and was extremely helpful about programmes and brochures, as well as being a valuable supporter financially, looked ominously pregnant with a speech. Mr McMichael, who consid- ered himself to be musically inclined and played the pipes with the local band, was a good deal stronger on breath control than word control and, once launched into an opinion, could be dread- fully long-winded; luckily you could usually see him filling up with hot air first, so it was sometimes possible to forestall him.

The meeting continued smoothly. Besides taking the minutes, Lorna occasionally scribbled little notes, which she passed to Giles and, from her seat at the other end of the table, Isobel could see him nodding appreciatively and assumed that, as usual, Lorna would be making relevant and competent suggestions.

At exactly quarter to one Giles, having managed to get all the people he wanted to volunteer to help with various duties, gained approval for a small sub-committee of his own choosing to make final decisions without the necessity to call another full meeting of Friends. He then dealt with the last item on the agenda, brought the meeting to a close and announced lunch.

'Thank you all so much for your support and enthusiasm.' Giles was careful not to look at Mr McMichael, who was having a comfortable snooze. 'Now if you could make your way over to the Steading you'll find lunch. Do take the chance to have a good look around at all the improvements, and come and find either me or Isobel or Lorna if you have any suggestions to make.'

Joss had produced a wonderful buffet of cold salmon with a yoghurt and dill sauce, chicken chaudfroid, various delicious vegetarian quiches and salad. He had gone to town with irresistibly wicked puddings, which were guaranteed to set various weight watchers' ambitions back by several pounds. Lorna, who had taken an instant dislike to Joss and Matt, had to admit to herself that they were exceptionally good at all the very varied jobs they seemed prepared to turn their hands to—which in no way lessened her resolve to try to discredit them. Their devotion to Giles and Isobel was obvious, but they treated Lorna with a kind of mocking deference that not only made her uncomfortable but beneath which she detected a distinct hostility. It was as though they could somehow read some of the hidden desires that Lorna hardly even admitted to herself.

$\mathcal{F}$iona and her mother-in-law were the first to leave because Fiona had to do the school run and had promised to keep Amy for tea so that Isobel could pick her up later.

'Thank you so much for a delightful lunch,' said Lady Fortescue as she made her farewells to Isobel. 'How absolutely charming your sister is. She's been telling me that she has come over from South Africa especially to help relieve you of some of your burdens. I do think that's touching. She's been telling me some of her ideas and I can see she will be a great asset to the Arts Centre. I hope you'll spare her to come over to have dinner with me one evening.'

'I'm sure that would be lovely for her. Thank you.' Isobel was half amused half outraged at the line Lorna had obviously chosen to shoot, but determined not to be inveigled into this subtle guerrilla warfare herself. Fiona rolled her eyes behind Violet's back. ' 'Bye, Izz. Super lunch as usual. I'll give Amy tea. I'll see you when you come to collect her,' she said pointedly, obviously bursting to discuss the Lorna situation. 'When does this artist—Daniel Whatsit—arrive? I'm dying to meet him.'

'Hoffman,' Isobel stated. 'Daniel Hoffman. Well, in theory he's supposed to turn up some time this evening, but I don't think he's a great communicator. We haven't heard a squeak from him since Giles first made the arrangement. I'm beginning to doubt that he actually exists.'

'You mean you haven't met him? I thought you said you were mad about him.'

'Mad about his work, yes; but it was Giles who went to meet him, after first seeing some things of his in Wales. I've had a look at his portfolio and then Giles and I both went to a production of *Cenerentola* at the Wexford Festival where he'd done the sets—which I absolutely adored. Brilliant. I'm dying to meet him, though he sounds a bit eccentric. Hope he turns up, otherwise we shall be in the soup.'

————

*T*here was still no sign of Daniel Hoffman after the last of the Friends had departed and the Greenyfordham minibus had delivered Edward home from school. Isobel waited as long as she could in the hope that he might turn up before she went to collect Amy, conscious that while it wouldn't have worried her not to be there provided Giles was present to greet their new visitor— or even Joss and Mick—she did not at all want Lorna to receive him and do the honours in her absence.

I am getting petty and obsessive, she told herself. I must stop this, but all the same she suggested to Lorna that she might like to go and collect Amy.

'I would, of course, any other time,' said Lorna. 'But I've just promised Giles I'll type up the minutes for him. I'll go later if it can wait a bit,' which of course she knew perfectly well it could not. Isobel was in a half a mind to call her bluff and ring Fiona to ask her to keep Amy for an extra half-hour, but knew Amy would be tired and Fiona had her own children to get to bed. 'Oh, don't worry. I'll go.' She ran down the steps and opened the car door. 'I expect by the time I've been waylaid by Fiona I'll be about an hour. Get in, Flapper. Hup!' Isobel drove off, unaware that Lorna had omitted to tell her that she had just answered the telephone to Daniel Hoffman, who had said he'd got lost and had just reached Blairalder for the second time. She had given him competent directions, told him they would expect him in less than ten minutes and, having seen Isobel disappear safely down the drive, went to tell Giles that his artist had just rung and was about to arrive.

Nine

Daniel Hoffman had driven peacefully past Glendrochatt several times before he resorted to his mobile telephone. He was in no great hurry and, as always, rather dreaded arriving to stay with unknown people—the polite exchange of banalities, the false chat and the effort of starting new relationships.

He had, of course, noticed the house on the hill—harled white and with its romantic-looking tower dominating the skyline it was difficult to miss—but he had been looking for some long, low, farm-type building in pinkish-grey sandstone that fitted the photograph of the Old Steading Theatre on the brochure Giles had given him. Giles had described the theatre and all the work they had done on it so vividly that it had not occurred to him that this spectacular ancestral-looking building—almost a castle, Daniel decided gloomily—was his destination. Better get it over with, he had admonished himself, and pulled into a lay-by just short of Blairalder to dial the Grants' number.

Chilly-sounding woman on the telephone, he thought—he'd take a bet she'd turn out to be the kind of snooty, class-conscious type he most disliked. He assumed she was Giles's wife. He'd asked to speak to either Mr or Mrs Grant and the female voice that answered said, 'Yes—Lorna speaking.' He'd been tempted to suggest she should spit out her mouthful of marbles before she gave him fresh directions, but had resisted. From the way she kept asking 'Have you got that now?' he was left in no doubt that she considered him extremely inefficient to have got lost in the first place. He regretted having accepted the invitation to stay with the Grants and wished he'd insisted they should put him up at some nearby campsite where he would have been completely independent. He'd suggested this originally but Giles wouldn't hear of it and at the time Daniel couldn't be bothered to argue. He was prepared to sleep almost anywhere so long as it was reasonably clean, only his freedom was important.

He got out of the car to stretch his legs and have a cigarette. Because he spent so much time up a ladder painting stage scenery or murals in people's houses, he often got awful cramp in the muscles of his calves. The bossy-sounding female had implied that he was late and would do well to get a move on, but Daniel, who was by no means as vague as it often suited him to let people think he was, knew perfectly well that he had only agreed on a date, not a time, of arrival.

Before he met Giles Grant, Daniel had wrapped all his preconceived prejudices against wealthy patrons—crucial as they often were to his livelihood—carefully round him like a protective garment. On first appearance Giles epitomised everything Daniel most distrusted—smooth appearance, toffee-nosed vowels and the kind of expensive, elegantly casual-looking shoes that were such a trade mark of his species—but in fact they had got on very well. Daniel was impressed by Giles's understanding of the technology of stage design, his obvious passion for the theatre and patent knowledge of music. He might have been born with a silver spoon *in situ* but it was obvious he knew his stuff and was no mere dilettante. Of course, Daniel admitted wryly to himself, there is always the flattery factor to be taken into account but Giles's enthusiasm for Daniel's work was clearly genuine.

Daniel Hoffman was looking forward to the new commission—especially now that the order for one backcloth had been doubled.

He had submitted rough designs to Giles, but knew that these would inevitably change once he got the feeling and atmosphere of the place under his skin. His inner-city childhood and globe-trotting student years had given him a delight in contrasts and a passion for new experiences, and the scenery here was stunning. Daniel had never been to Scotland before and he had relished the last part of the drive north, his eyes straying dangerously from the road to the countryside beyond it; impossible not to watch the shadows moving across the hills—driving with Daniel could be an exciting experience for anyone rash enough to risk it.

Latterly the road had wound along by a river and those trees that were not yet in full leaf looked as if stage smoke had been puffed through them—wonderful scenery for a grand opera, or perhaps a ballet with dryads and oreads darting in and out, and a hairy-legged Pan lolling on a boulder at the foot of a rowan. The larch trees, swaying in the wind, had made Daniel think of a troupe of chorus girls; he half expected to see them pick up their light-green skirts and dance away—Birnam Wood, charlestoning all the way to Dunsinane—and had been sharply brought out of his romantic reverie by the screaming horn and violent flashing of a car approaching from the opposite direction, just as he was about to overtake a juggernaut behind which he had been stuck for too long. Daniel had hastily tucked in behind the lorry again, happily exchanging rude signs with the other car driver as they missed each other by a whisker. He had driven along in a more circumspect fashion after that, though he could feel new ideas for the Glendrochatt backdrop bubbling away in his head. It was his favourite feeling, this moment of conception just before he started on a new project, worth all the other times of despair and anxiety when he was afraid he would never come up with fresh inspiration again.

He got back into his car, started the engine and did a U-turn to retrace his tracks towards Glendrochatt. He had gone about three miles when the car suddenly started to drift; he changed gear and put his foot down hard on the accelerator, but there was no power and all he could do was steer it into the side of the road.

'Shit,' said Daniel to himself. He got out, opened the bonnet and peered inside, not because he had the slightest confidence that he would achieve anything, but because it seemed the right thing to do; it didn't give him any clues. He gave the car a kick, got back in and turned on the ignition. It started all right, but when he tried to drive it, nothing happened. There were no houses in sight. He felt singularly loath to ring Glendrochatt again and confess to this further sign of incompetence, but supposed he would have to—not a great start to his visit. He picked up his mobile and was about to punch in the number, hoping very much that he would get Giles this time and not the superior-sounding wife, when he saw a car in the distance coming towards him from the other direction. He stepped out into the road and signalled hopefully. Isobel, singing to herself as she drove to the Fortescues to collect Amy, had the windows down and the sunshine roof open; her hair was blowing round her face and Flapper, who was standing on the passenger seat with her nose poking out of the window, had her ears blown back too.

Isobel saw a young man standing by the side of the road waving at her. She slowed down and stopped when she was level with his battered-looking old car. He looked scruffy. He was wearing a frayed pair of denim shorts, a tattered T-shirt and walking boots; his dark hair was cut very short, but he clearly hadn't shaved for a few days; he had numerous gold hoops in his ears and there was a tattoo on his right arm. There was something slightly foreign about him; he certainly didn't look local. A student, perhaps, thought Isobel, or an early holiday-maker—possibly a gypsy? Later in the season there were always a lot of them about, looking for casual work, but it was too early in the year for the berry pickers to have descended on the area. She might have hesitated to stop on such an isolated stretch of road, but despite his rag-tag appearance she didn't think he looked at all threatening.

'You in trouble?' she called out of the window. 'Can I help at all?'

He came across the road. 'My old banger seems to have conked out. D'you happen to know where the nearest garage is?'

He spoke with a south London accent. At close quarters she could see that his eyes were so dark they looked almost black.

'There's a service station at Blairalder, but I don't think they do repairs. There's Bruce Johnstone who's a brilliant mechanic at Drochatt. He might come out if you can get hold of him. I'll ring him for you if you like. Where are you trying to get to?'

'I'm trying to find a house called Glendrochatt—belongs to people called Grant.' He pulled a wry face. 'But I'm not doing too well about getting there. I've already had to ring for directions and I got the big freeze from the lady of the house.' He grinned. 'Don't you worry—nice of you to stop. I'd better ring them again.'

'You're never Daniel Hoffman?' asked Isobel.

He looked surprised. 'That's me. Do you know the Grants, then?'

'I'm Isobel Grant—Giles's wife.'

'Well, what do you know?' Daniel put his thumb against the side of his head, stuck his tongue in his cheek and rolled his eyes. 'Looks like I really blotted my copy book now, doesn't it? You sound a lot less scary in the flesh.'

'Well, thank you for that, but I haven't actually spoken to you before,' said Isobel. 'I think you must have got my sister Lorna on the telephone. She's so wonderfully efficient herself she's got a sort of built-in map of the world in her head. How lucky I've found you now. I'm so sorry you've had such a hassle. Giles usually sends out frightfully competent directions.'

'My fault entirely. Hard to send directions to people who don't have an address I'm afraid.' He gave her an apologetic grin.

'Well, yes.' She laughed up at him. 'I had gathered you're a bit hard to pin down. Must be tricky for getting trade. How do you manage?'

'I don't deserve it, but I usually seem to get away with it and strike lucky.'

'You should get on well with Giles, then. I always tell him he has a lot of undeserved luck. Oh, help.' She looked at her watch. 'I'm on my way to collect my daughter from a friend and I'm going to be late. Look, why don't you jump in my car, and we can ring Giles as we go along and get him to see if Bruce could come out. Then we can meet them on the way home. Would you mind a bit of a detour?'

'Fine by me,' said Daniel. He thought he could get on well with this open-faced, cheerful young woman. 'I must just lock the car. It's got all my paints in the back.'

His car was a very ancient Volvo. Several rusted dents bore witness to a hard life—it looked an obvious candidate for a break-down. From his appearance, Isobel wondered if its owner was struggling to make ends meet—a penniless young artist—though Giles had told her Daniel was beginning to get himself a big reputation and his quotation for the backcloth had certainly reflected this. 'If we don't get him to do it soon, he'll be far too expensive for us and too booked up in advance as well,' Giles had said. As it was, they had only managed to get him this summer because another commission had unexpectedly fallen through. Daniel Hoffman was not at all what Isobel had expected, but she thought he was intriguing. He had a way of putting his head on one side and cocking an eyebrow that made him look as if he found life permanently amusing.

He rescued his mobile and locked his car. Isobel shooed Flapper into the back.

'You don't need to do that—I like dogs.'

'Oh, Flapper's only allowed in front when we're alone together—then it's her special perk. She's my permanent shadow.'

'Lucky Flapper.'

'Will you dial the number for me?' asked Isobel as she started the car and they shot off down the narrow road.

Giles answered almost immediately and Daniel handed the telephone to Isobel, who tucked it under her chin and explained what had happened.

'Brilliant. Right—see you, then. 'Bye, darling.' She rang off. 'Giles will try to get hold of Bruce Johnstone so they'll either meet us at your car on our way back, or if they're not there we can go home first and take you out to it later. This will give you a chance to admire our local scenery.'

'I've been doing that all the way. Thanks. You're very kind.'

'Not kind at all: it's entirely self-interest. We want you to do our backcloth for us,' she said and added, 'Do you really not have a home address?'

'Nope. I really don't.'

'But it must be so difficult.' She shot him a curious glance. He was smiling at her, looking amused again. 'What happens if someone needs to get hold of you urgently?'

'There are several people who know my mobile number.'

'*We* knew your mobile number, but it didn't do us much good,' she retorted. 'And where do you keep your things, for instance? You must have some base.'

'I don't have many things—apart from my paints, that is—and I usually have most of them with me.'

'But you must have *some* things,' she persisted. 'One gathers possessions over the years.'

'Gathering possessions is not my thing,' he said, then added, rather reluctantly, she thought, 'I rent a garage off some mates and I suppose there are one or two things stored in my mother's garden shed.'

'So you *do* have a home.'

'No.' His voice was rebuffing. 'I have a parent. I haven't had a home for years.'

There was a short silence, then: 'I'm sorry,' said Isobel. 'I really didn't mean to be nosy. It's just that I can't imagine not having a home myself—and I'm always so interested in people that I want to know all about everyone. But my daughter Amy—whom you're just about to meet—complains that I interrogate people. I shouldn't have done that to you.'

'That's OK. I can have a turn now. Why is your base so terribly important to you?'

Isobel considered this seriously. 'I suppose it's because it's my nest,' she said. 'I have children, you see. That alters everything. I take it you don't?'

'No, I don't have children. But that doesn't mean I don't like kids—and women,' he added, giving her another amused look, mocking her slightly. 'How many children do you have, then?'

'Only two—they're twins.'

'Twins must be a handful. Are they identical?'

'No. One of each sex—Amy and Edward. But Edward,' Isobel went on, 'is not quite like other people.' She felt surprised at herself. She didn't usually tell people about Edward until she knew them better.

'Good for Edward. Who wants to be like other people?'

'*I* want him to be like other people,' she said.

'Yes,' he answered seriously, not at all embarrassed by the conversation. 'Yes, I can imagine that as a parent one would. Perhaps that's one of the reasons why I don't want to be one. He must be interesting, though—a challenge?'

'Oh, Edward's interesting all right, heartbreaking sometimes, but never dull—and Amy's a ball of fire.'

'I'll look forward to meeting them both,' said Daniel.

They had reached Blairalder, which made for a natural change of conversation. Isobel gave him a running commentary about the neighbourhood for the rest of the way. She couldn't help hoping that Lady Fortescue would not still be with Fiona when they got there; she didn't think, from his appearance, that Daniel would be her type.

———

$\mathcal{T}$he Fortescues lived in the kind of grey stone house Daniel had been expecting Glendrochatt to be. There was an old pony in the field next to the drive and when they got to the front door they were greeted by two black labradors and a very noisy Jack Russell terrier. 'Come on in, Daniel, and meet the Fortescues. They're great friends of ours and they've heard lots about you,' said Isobel, getting out of the car. 'Shut up, dogs. Down, Piper—this is a friend.' The Jack Russell was somehow managing to give Isobel an ecstatic welcome while still throwing a few threatening barks in Daniel's direction. Flapper, who was clearly on cordial terms with the host dogs, had leapt out of the back of the car and was soon engaged in a dizzy game with the noisy Piper, tearing round the lawn and crashing through the flower beds. Isobel made no attempt to call her back. There was a children's slide on the not very newly mown grass and an overturned toy tractor; several abandoned bits of clothing lay strewn about. Clearly not a formal set-up, thought Daniel with relief. He followed Isobel through the open front door into a hall, where a sixteenth-century oak chest gleamed with the patina of years of loving polish, but was casually covered with children's riding hats, a pair of garden se-cateurs and several anoraks.

Isobel led the way down a passage. 'Fiona?' she yelled. 'Fee? Are you there?'

'In the kitchen,' came an answering shout.

Fiona was peeling potatoes at the sink and had changed out of the tidy clothes she had worn for the Friends' meeting into jeans and cotton polo-neck. She was one of those lucky women who look equally good dressed for a party or in working clothes— something to do with well-behaved hair more than anything else. Daniel saw a woman in her early thirties with reddish-fair hair tied back from her face. She was taller than Isobel.

'Hi there,' said Isobel, exchanging a kiss. 'This is Daniel Hoff-man—our artist for the theatre, no less. Guess what? I found him languishing at the side of the road with a broken-down car. Wasn't that a bit of luck?'

'How d'you do, Daniel. Welcome to Scotland. Sorry I can't shake hands.' Fiona indicated her dripping hands and gave him a friendly smile. 'Do you mean lucky you found him, Izz, or lucky the car broke down?'

'Both—certainly lucky about the car, judging by its appearance,' said Isobel, laughing. 'I can't feel it's got a very long life ahead of it. It looked terminally sick to me.'

'I won't have you knocking my car—we've been through a lot of adventures together. It's got years of life in it yet,' protested Daniel, thinking he might have been premature in writing the Grants off as a lot of stuffed shirts.

'Where's Amy?' asked Isobel.

'She and Emily are upstairs dressing up. They found my old evening dresses in the spare-room cupboard and now they're experimenting with my make-up. God knows what the mess will be like. It's unnerving how like you Amy looks in a bit of war paint, Izzy.'

'I who wear make-up so often.' Isobel made a rueful face. 'Wouldn't Giles love it if I did. Can you give them a shout?'

'I hoped you might stay for a drink and have a postmortem on the meeting and hear my impressions of your sister. Now *she* really does know how to put on make-up.'

'Thanks for the comparison.' Isobel laughed. 'I told you she'd metamorphosed into something extraordinary. She's already frightened the life out of Daniel just on the telephone,' she continued. 'But I'm afraid we must go because Giles and the garage chap may be waiting by Daniel's car and they can't do anything about it until we get there.'

'Pity—Duncan will be back soon and he'd love to meet Daniel. Still, I do see. I'll go and chivvy up the girls, then.'

Two visions of beauty—in their own opinion—came mincing down the stairs, walking gingerly in Fiona's high-heeled shoes, their feet looking like those of Minnie Mouse.

'Goodness,' said Isobel. 'Could we have royalty in our midst?

Darlings, say how do you do to Mr Hoffman and then I'm afraid we must fly.'

Amy and Emily, their arms and fingers covered in bracelets and rings saved from old Christmas crackers, extended languid hands. Daniel, rising to the occasion with great aplomb, bowed low and kissed their fingers reverently, murmuring 'Your Royal Highnesses' in a most satisfactory way. Clearly used to little girls, thought Isobel, however cagey he might be about his family.

'Mum, can't Amy stay the night? We're in the middle of an absolutely brill game,' asked Emily.

'Well, she can as far as I'm concerned, but I rather think Isobel wants her home.' Fiona looked questioningly at Isobel.

'Oh, darlings, I'm sorry, but definitely not tonight. We must rush because poor Mr Hoffman's car has broken down and he wants to get back and minister to it—and anyway Amy must practise in the morning.'

'Oh, Mum! One practice wouldn't matter. It's not fair. Nobody else has to slave like I do.' Amy stopped looking aloof and royal, and changed back into a rebellious child.

'No, I'm really sorry, darling. Another day. How about Emily and Mungo coming to us on Saturday for the day? Edward would love that too.'

'We shall have completely lost the game by then,' said Amy tragically. 'Games are never the same once they've gone cold.' But she could tell that Isobel was not in the right frame of mind to be talked round and besides, there was the visitor to be investigated, and afterwards discussed with Mick and Joss, so she gave way with only a token show of resentment and it was agreed that the two Fortescue children should come to Glendrochatt at the weekend.

'Make yourself at home, Daniel,' said Fiona. 'Help yourself to a drink while we get these two royal ladies divested of their robes' and she and Isobel disappeared upstairs leaving Daniel to look at the collection of early Victorian watercolours in the drawing-

room. He thought them quite delightful and surprisingly vigor-
ous—several cuts above the wishy-washy efforts that sometimes
adorned the walls of country houses. These had been beautifully
framed and carefully hung, and he noted approvingly that each
had a protective blind above it, which could be pulled down to
shield it from bright light.

'Lovely pictures you've got—unusual. I hope you don't mind
but I've been admiring them,' he said when they all returned.

Fiona looked pleased. 'Oh, thank you. I'm so glad you like
them because I've always thought they were special. We found
them in an old trunk when Duncan's grandmother died and we
had them framed. They were done by his great-great-
grandmother. Her husband was in the Indian Army and she
painted wherever they were posted. Nowadays I'm sure she would
have been professional. When we found them I was stunned by
the colours—I don't think they'd been exposed to the light since
they were painted.'

Thank yous were duly said. Flapper, panting and covered with
burs, was whistled up out of the garden, and the Glendrochatt
contingent piled into Isobel's car and drove off.

$\mathcal{W}$ ell, what do you know? I've met the famous artist,' said Fiona
to Duncan when he got home from work.

'What was he like? Flowing locks and long white fingers? All
Francesca di Rimini, mimini pimini?'

'Absolutely not. Voice: London cabby; appearance: a cross between hiker and lager lout.'

'Doesn't sound Giles's cup of tea at all.'

'Um—no. That's what I thought. Isobel was thankful your ma
wasn't still here, but I'd love to have seen her face if she'd met
him. Wonder how God would have told her to react? Still—there
was something engaging about him all the same,' Fiona decided.
'He was nice to the children and he smiled with his eyes when
he said hello. I really liked him.'

'Well, I'll take your word for it. You women have the most unaccountable tastes.'

'I know,' Fiona acknowledged. 'After all, I chose you, didn't I?' They walked arm in arm into the house.

So how was your day, darling?' Isobel asked Amy.

'OK. Me and Emily had to go and stand in the hall for talking in Assembly, so then we did deaf and dumb and missed half Arithmetic. It was cool. Mrs Murray got awfully worked up in the car on the way to school because Christopher threw Jamie's cap out of the window, and then the boys had a fight and we all joined in. It was great.'

'You're a lot of horrors. You know Grizelda hates it when you riot—you wouldn't do it with me or Fiona.'

'No, but honestly, Mum, she is barmy. She said we all ought to shut our eyes and visualise pale blue to counteract our aggressive urges, and then she put on this tape of soothing dolphin noises to calm our vibes. It sounded like a series of farts and we all got hysterics.'

'So the dolphin noises worked?' suggested Daniel.

'How d'you mean?'

'Well, if you all got hysterics together you must have stopped fighting.'

Amy considered this novel interpretation. 'Well, yes—but it wasn't how she *meant* it to work.'

'Sounds like one up to the dolphins to me,' said Daniel and added, 'I went swimming with dolphins last year.'

Amy was immediately interested. 'What was it like?'

'Bloody cold.'

'You must tell Edward,' said Isobel. 'That's the sort of thing he loves hearing about—that is if you're prepared to tell him the story over and over again.'

'Oh, I think I'd manage that. I never get tired of hearing my own stories.'

'You will,' promised Isobel. 'Believe me, once you've met Edward you'll think twice before telling him any story.'

'He sounds like my ideal audience,' said Daniel and Isobel thought their new guest might prove to be an asset quite apart from his painting.

At this moment they reached Daniel's car and saw that Mick was there with Bruce Johnstone.

'Hello there, Isobel. How are you the day?' enquired Bruce.

'I'm fine, thanks, but our guest's car isn't so well. Can you help?'

'Family heirloom, is it?' asked Bruce, looking at the Volvo with amusement. He said he would tow it back to his garage and see what could be done.

Isobel left Daniel to transfer everything into Mick's Land Rover. He might travel light from a sartorial point of view, but there seemed no end to his painting paraphernalia.

'We'll see you later, then,' said Isobel. 'Come on, Amy.'

'Do I really have to call him Mr Hoffman?' asked Amy, waving out of the window as they drove off. 'He doesn't seem like a "mister" kind of person, d'you think?'

'No,' Isobel agreed. 'I'm sure it would be all right for you to call him Daniel—though it's always polite to ask first. Did you like him?'

'He's cool,' said Amy. 'I'm going to play for him and he says I can help him paint' and she added, 'Edward will like him too.'

Isobel felt absurdly pleased that her sometimes rather critical daughter had given Daniel such a seal of approval.

I wonder, she thought, whether or not I had already left for the Fortescues when Lorna answered the telephone to Daniel? And she knew with a flash of certainty that the call must have come while she was still at home and was the real reason for Lorna refusing to do the school run for her.

But I have met him first after all, thought Isobel, and she felt, with what she knew was most unworthy satisfaction, as though she had somehow stolen a march on both Lorna and Giles.

She also felt as if she had known Daniel Hoffman for longer than just one hour.

Ten

While Bruce Johnstone hitched Daniel's car to his truck, Daniel and Mick carefully reloaded all the paint into the back of the van. Daniel might appear casual but he was meticulous about anything to do with his painting so it took some time.

'Sorry about this,' he apologised to Mick, conscious that in about five minutes it would all have to be unloaded again.

'No worries,' said Mick. It took a lot to worry Mick.

'Which part of New Zealand you from?' asked Daniel, heaving a large pot of paint out of his car.

'South Island—near Christchurch.'

'I spent six months painting there a couple of years ago. Stunning scenery—not unlike this, really. You been with the Grants long?' asked Daniel.

Mick grinned. 'They're a great family to be with, if that's what you're asking. They've got terrific kids, too. You'd better be warned about Edward—that's Amy's twin—he's handicapped. Isobel and Giles do a fine job there.'

'Yes,' said Daniel, 'she told me about Edward. What's his trouble?'

'Don't think anyone quite knows. He's a bit autistic, bit this and that. I'd just say there's a few screws not quite tightened up and a few scrambled phone lines—but once you get to know him he's great. He's actually got quite a fascinating mind if you can tune in to his wavelength—and get him off the subject of chickens.' Mick laughed good-naturedly, and shook his head. 'Is that child obsessed with hens! Yeah,' he went on, 'work permits permitting, me and my mate Joss wouldn't mind settling here. Still, we don't have to worry about permits yet; we've got a bit of time left. How long d'you reckon your painting will take?'

Daniel laughed and shrugged. 'If I knew that, mate, my life— and no doubt the plans of those who commission me to paint— would be a whole lot easier. It's like how long's a bit of string once I get started on something. I guess I'll be around for most of the summer, on and off. In theory I'm booked to start a mural in the States in September. I spend my time panicking about meeting deadlines.'

'Rrright ye are, then,' said Bruce, rolling his 'R's like a rattle to scare the birds, as Mick and Daniel finally slammed the doors at the back of the van shut. 'I'll be hitting the road. I'll give you a ring in the morning and let you know what the damage would be to salvage this lot.' He winked at Mick. 'Reckon if I can fix the old warrior at all, it could be flogged to Lord Dunbarnock for a handsome profit. I'll be seeing ye, then' and he swung himself up into his van.

'Who's Lord Dunbarnock?' asked Daniel.

'Local weirdo.' Mick grinned. 'He collects vintage cars.'

'What's Isobel Grant's sister like?' Daniel was curious about the owner of the voice. 'She sounded like one of those high-speed dentist's drills that spray cold water through your teeth.'

If Mick thought this was rather an accurate description of Lorna, he wasn't going to admit it to the newcomer, nor was he going to tell Daniel that he and Joss had conceived a deep mistrust of her. He reckoned the artist could judge for himself. 'She's only been here a short time. She had a marriage break-up or something—but she's efficient all right. Busy reorganising the office. Well, here we are then,' he said, as they turned in at the gates and added as they rattled up the drive, 'Joss and me—we expected

Snow White and the seven dwarfs to appear when we first came here.'

*I*sobel had got home twenty minutes earlier to find Lorna and Giles pouring over three huge charts, which Lorna had made to go round the walls of the office on new notice boards. One was primarily concerned with fixtures, showing all the concerts and events that had been arranged for the rest of the summer; one was about personnel, including all the members of the Grant family; another concerned accommodation, so that you could, in theory, discover immediately who was staying, for how long and what rooms they had been allocated. It was a dream—or a nightmare, depending on your point of view—of cross-referencing, colour codes and huge pins, representing various individuals, which could be moved about like pawns on a chessboard. Giles, who had al- ways considered himself an ace chart producer, was clearly en- chanted and was paying the homage due from one serious timetable buff to another. At the moment it was all laid out on the big table at the far end of the kitchen.

'Lorna, you're a genius!' Isobel heard Giles say. 'I couldn't have done better myself and they exchanged a connoisseur's look of delight. Isobel had never been able to share Giles's passion for timetables, graphs and lists. Early in their marriage it had been a joke between them that the sight of Giles bearing down on her, diary in hand, had always sent her running for cover and her inability—in his view—to keep him au fait with every small up- date about her own movements had become an occasional source of friction. Isobel was brilliant at carrying everyone's engagements in her head—less good at committing them to paper. Giles was a meticulous keeper of the diary, but hopeless unless he had a piece of paper to consult. Up to now it had always seemed as if they complemented each other in a Jack Sprattish arrangement, which was highly satisfactory.

Joss, who was patiently waiting to lay supper on the table, was good-naturedly filling in time by looking at a book on prehistoric monsters with Edward. He shot Isobel a commiserating look as he saw her expression. 'Don't you worry—won't take long to bugger up their system,' he said cheerfully. 'Leave it to me.'

Edward sounded like an old-fashioned record playing at too slow a speed: 'Tyrannothauruth recth, ichthyothauruth, plethiothaur, diplodocuth, pterodactyl,' he droned. 'How long can a diplodocuth grow, Joss?'

'You know how long they are—you just told me three times, Edward—twenty-seven metres.'

'You tell me. *How long are they? What do they eat?* Tell me, Joss, tell me.'

Edward could go on asking the same question almost indefinitely and greatly preferred to have the answer couched in exactly the same words that had been used before. It had nothing to do with acquiring fresh knowledge, since he only asked questions to which he already knew the answers. It was one of his rituals, deeply reassuring to him but capable of driving the other participant almost insane with boredom.

'No way.' Joss's voice was firm. 'That's enough, now. You say hi to your mum and then it's bath time or the hot water'll run out later.'

'Thanks, Joss,' said Isobel gratefully. 'You're a star. Ed, darling, if you go up now, I'll read you that chapter again later when you're in bed.' She walked over to the table. 'Hi there, you two. Don't I get a greeting?'

Giles looked up at once and gave her his usual brilliant smile, his eyes crinkling at the corners in the way she loved. 'Hello, my Izz, I didn't hear you come in.' He reached up a hand to touch her cheek and Lorna, looking up too, felt sick with jealousy. 'Just come and look at this, darling. See what your brilliant sister has done—not that it's quite your sort of thing.'

'Isobel will absolutely hate them,' Lorna agreed, laughing,

though her laugh had an edge, sharp as a newly creased paper dart. 'Never mind, Izz, I'm sure I can explain them to you. The whole idea is that they should be user friendly.'

'Well, I can see it's all a great work of art.' Isobel inspected the charts, running her eye over the various squares and columns. 'Are these rough drafts, then?'

'Rough drafts?' exclaimed Giles. 'I should think not! We're just about to go and put them up. They're practically worth an unveiling ceremony in their own right.'

'Then perhaps you should make a few changes first—but I'm afraid you'll have to move it all off here for now. Poor Joss has been waiting to lay the table and Daniel and Mick should be here any minute.' Lorna, seething inwardly, thought Isobel sounded as if she were telling Amy and Edward to clear up one of their games.

'Daniel!' said Giles, instantly diverted. 'Oh, my God, yes—I was so absorbed in these I'd almost forgotten. What a bit of luck you found him, darling—and what did you think of him?'

'Not what I expected but I thought he was fun and . . . nice.'

'I thought you'd be interested.' Giles looked pleased with himself. He loved leaving people in the dark and then springing surprises, and had deliberately not described Daniel to Isobel.

'What changes did you mean, Izzy?' Lorna asked, looking hard at her sister, but trying to keep her voice neutral.

'Oh, not many,' Isobel replied. 'It's just that there are one or two mistakes—nothing I'm sure you can't easily put right.'

'Like what, for instance?'

'Like the date for the opera group that's coming to give a concert performance of La Traviata—that's actually in November, not October,' said Isobel coolly. 'And the string quartet cancelled and we've got two marvellous young Irish singers instead. Then Megan Davies and Flavia Cameron won't actually be staying here because Flavia wants to stay at Duntroon with Colin and Elizabeth, and has asked Tara to go there too, so that they can practise together. There may be other things, but that's just off the top of my head. Otherwise', Isobel continued, 'it all looks quite wonderful. But I like to allocate rooms myself—so it would be easier if you don't fill those in without asking me first.'

Giles gave a shout of laughter. 'You two! Talk about battling with old nursery pecking orders. But honours are even now. Clever Izz to pick this up—not just a pretty face, are you, darling?—but it shows how brilliant Lorna's charts are, that you could see all that at one glance.'

Perhaps it was as well that at this moment Mick drove up with Daniel.

They all three went through into the hall and on to the steps outside the front door.

'Daniel! My dear chap how good to see you again. Welcome to Glendrochatt. What adventures you've been having. I'm so sorry about your car.' Giles ran down the steps, hand extended. 'I don't need to introduce you to Isobel after all—your rescuer—but let me introduce my sister-in-law, Lorna Cartwright.'

Giles loved welcoming new guests to Glendrochatt and was at his best putting people at their ease, organising the disposal of their luggage and making them feel they were the one person he really wanted to see. Daniel envied Giles his instant ease in any company, his charm and apparently genuine warmth—his absolute social confidence. He thought these were gifts he himself did not possess. Any sense of his own self-worth was entirely centred round his painting and, though this was usually strong enough to enable him to conceal his natural shyness, he was stuck with a lurking sense of social inadequacy for which he despised himself. He hid behind a jester's cap and bells for protection and no one who didn't know him well—and there were not many who did—had any idea what an effort it was for him to be plunged into a completely new setting every time he started a job.

He nodded rather stiffly at Isobel, feeling unsure, after their easy camaraderie in the car, how to start off again without seeming overfamiliar. Isobel, who had been ready to give him an enthusiastic greeting, felt slightly rebuffed.

Lorna, on the other hand, though dismayed at what she fastidiously considered to be Daniel's yobbish appearance, was determined to reverse the bad start she knew she had made with this important new player on Giles's stage. She gave Daniel a particularly warm smile and decided to launch a charm offensive.

Daniel, prepared for a tweedy harridan, looked at Lorna with his artist's eye and quite simply thought she was one of the most beautiful women he had ever seen.

Eleven

It was Amy, hurtling round the corner of the house on her bicycle, who rescued Daniel from the slight awkwardness of his arrival. 'Daniel!' she shrieked, skiddering to a halt, gravel churning. Flinging down the bike and abandoning it on the drive with pedals spinning, she rushed to greet him as if he were a favourite uncle who had turned up unexpectedly.

Lorna looked at Amy with disapproval. She couldn't help contrasting this meeting with the restrained welcome she had received from her on her own arrival—not to mention Edward's less than enthusiastic reaction. She supposed one had to make allowances for him, but found her niece's demonstrative enthusiasm for this scruffy stranger not only thoroughly over the top, but unnervingly reminiscent of how Isobel might have behaved at the same age.

A painful recollection, long buried, reared its ugly little head out of her weedy patch of memories: Lorna was thirteen, hovering awkwardly between childhood and adolescence, disturbingly aware of her changing body and feeling wrong in whatever role she tried to play. Her mother's godfather, a recently widowed High Court judge, an aloof and alarming figure to the children, had joined them for an annual fishing holiday on Mull. For the first three days the rain had sheeted down remorselessly, every burn was in spate and a gale, which made casting virtually impossible, had whipped the loch to such a frenzy that Donald-John, the old gillie, had refused to take the boat out, preferring instead to keep a pressing appointment with a bottle of whisky in his croft. Even Lorna's and Isobel's father, famously impervious to the weather—one of those admirable but heart-sinking men who insist on continuing with whatever outdoor ploy is supposedly being enjoyed long after everyone else is praying to give up—had admitted defeat and allowed the family to return to the house after a bone-chilling picnic lunch when they had gobbled soggy sandwiches while huddling under a boulder. After they had trudged home, changed their sodden clothes and lit the fire in the sittingroom, their mother had suggested the judge should read aloud to them all, as he had apparently done in her own childhood. 'Oh, Frank, couldn't you light some fires in the children's minds as you used to do for me,' she had asked persuasively.

Amazingly, her godfather's crab shell had suddenly cracked open to reveal someone capable of great humour and emotion. The children had listened entranced while he had read Hilaire Belloc and W. S. Gilbert; Hardy and D. H. Lawrence—and then he read them Tennyson, transporting them to a world of chivalry and romance, and filling the shabby old sitting-room with the music of words. Lorna had been astounded to see a tear trickling down his cheek at one moment. Isobel, curled beside him on the sagging old sofa, utterly absorbed, had unselfconsciously cuddled up to him, resting her cheek against his rough tweed jacket. Afterwards she had flung her arms round his neck. 'I shall never forget that—never,' she had said and Lorna, smouldering inwardly like a silent volcano, had wished passionately that she had been the one to say it. She had just been about to make a little speech of thanks that would have revealed her understanding and appreciation of all the finer points, but as usual her younger sister had taken a short cut and got there first.

Isobel had become the old man's shadow for the rest of the fortnight, skipping along beside him and prattling away about everything under the newly emerged sun.

'So touching to watch old Frank thawing out,' Lorna had heard her father say to their mother and they had exchanged pleased smiles. Lorna, trying desperately to achieve the same effect, had started hanging on the judge's arm, leaning against him, stroking his sleeve and even attempting to sit on his knee, although, being tall for her age, she was almost the same height as he was. This time she had had the mortification of hearing her father saying to her mother: 'Darling, you really must try to stop Lorna pawing at Frank like that. It's becoming positively embarrassing' and her mother had sighed and said, 'I know, I know—but you know what Lorna is; it is so very difficult.'

Now, nearly twenty-five years later, as the old, familiar, jealous pain gimleted into Lorna, she asked herself, as she had so many times throughout her life, what is it that other people have and I do not? But, as always, the answer eluded her.

She gave herself a fierce mental shake. Stop this, admonished the new Lorna Cartwright, things are different now. In her head she heard the voice of the therapist who had helped her so much in her efforts to change her self-image: concentrate on your strengths, her therapist had taught her, believe in yourself. I know I am glamorous, recited Lorna to Lorna like a well-learnt litany; I am more beautiful than ever before in my life; I am a desirable woman. I left my husband of my own free will. I am a talented achiever; I am exceptionally competent; if I set my mind to anything, I can do it; I have re-invented myself. She thought her younger sister had let her looks go to a foolish degree—it was one thing to get away with looking careless and uncontrived at eighteen, quite another at thirty-three. That young artist might have struck up an instant surface friendship with Isobel, but his look of admiration at her own cool elegance had not been lost on Lorna. He might not be to her own taste—besides being far too young—but she thought that if he were taken in hand he might polish up surprisingly well, with his interesting, bony face and enigmatic dark eyes. She decided Daniel might have his uses in more ways than one. Giles needs me, thought Lorna, but he does not yet realise how much. I shall make myself indispensable to him—but it might help if there were a rival for his attention.'

Daniel couldn't help being flattered at Amy's greeting. He smiled at Isobel over the top of Amy's head, cocking his in his questioning way and making the amused, self-deprecating face she had noticed before.

'There's decorum for you,' said Giles, laughing at Amy and gently tugging at her ponytail. 'I can see you've made a hit already, Daniel—but I have to warn you that my daughter is enormously susceptible to male charm, so watch out.' He didn't say anything about his wife or his sister-in-law. 'Come along in,' he went on. 'You must be ready for a stiff drink after all your adventures and it's a great occasion to get you here. Let's hope you and the Old Steading at Glendrochatt will be an inspired partnership—all my inspiration, of course. I mean to go down in history as one of your early patrons. Mick will take your kit up to your room.'

'Poor Mick,' said Daniel. 'He'll be fed up with my clobber already, but I'd like to help him unload my painting stuff myself. Perhaps that should go straight to wherever it is you want me to work? Would you like me to do that first?'

'No, no, definitely not. Drink first. We'll all have one. Come on, Mick, you probably need one too.'

Giles led the way into the kitchen, and while he was getting Daniel's choice of beer out of the fridge and introducing him to Joss, Lorna said to Isobel, 'I take it Daniel's having the flat next to mine?'

'No,' Isobel answered. 'I want to keep that free because we're going to need it for various other people. Daniel might have to move later if we put him there because I gather he'll be coming and going quite a lot. I'm putting him in the old single spare room on the top floor. Then he can leave his stuff there if he goes away and the flat won't be tied up.'

'Do you really think that's a good idea? I'd got him down as occupying the second flat, which would be nearer the theatre and, as you pointed out to me, more independent,' said Lorna in the kind of reasonable but controlled voice one might use to a tire-some teenager who needs firm but tactful handling. 'Besides, I'd have to change it all on the plan.'

'Joss and I discussed it weeks ago—long before you arrived. It can't make any difference to you where Daniel sleeps,' said Isobel. 'The room's ready and all you'll have to do is move one of your fat red pins, representing Daniel, from one square to another, much easier than making up different beds.' She knew she sounded unwontedly sharp. 'Lorna—darling Lorna—please don't look like that,' she pleaded. 'Don't let's fall out over something so petty. I really can't stand it.'

Isobel felt the whole summer would be a nightmare of irritation if every little decision was going to become an excuse for con-frontation. Once she would have laughed it off and let Lorna have her way, but now the old saying about inches and miles seemed dangerously relevant. How exhausting, how unnecessary, thought Isobel, then with a flash of insight: Lorna hopes she will wear me down because this is not at all the sort of issue that I would once have given two hoots about; she will expect me to get bored with all this detail soon, shrug it off and let her take over everything—including, perhaps, Giles?

While they were having a drink Edward, freshly bathed but wearing a tracksuit over his pyjamas, came in with Joss. Because Giles was able to introduce them both jointly to Daniel and Ed-ward did not feel singled out by the threatening spotlight of direct attention, this passed off without any curtain-hiding incident. Daniel gave them both a friendly nod and said 'Hi'. Lorna looked sharply at Isobel to see if she was going to force Edward to shake hands, but Isobel pretended not to notice.

'Right,' said Giles, when they'd finished their drinks. 'Let's go down to the Steading, show Daniel the theatre and help decant all his stuff. Would you like to pull out any of your personal stuff that you want here first?'

Daniel yanked out a battered bag, a backpack and then, more carefully, an accordion.

'What's that?' asked Amy.

'My squeeze-box,' Daniel replied, giving it an affectionate pat like a trusted old dog. 'Some people call them the clown's instrument. I hear you're a bit of a whizz on the violin yourself. Perhaps we could play together? Go busking in Perth and earn a few pence?'

'Oh, yes,' breathed Amy, entranced at the thought.

'Over my dead body,' said Giles, laughing. 'But we might all have a jazz session together some time.' He did not relish the idea of Amy playing with anyone else unless he was there too.

'You go with them, Joss,' said Isobel, 'and I'll finish getting supper—we've got so many leftovers from lunch there's really nothing to do. You'll be more help heaving things about and after all the cooking and clearing up you've done already today you deserve a break from the kitchen. I know you and Mick want to go off to the Highland dancing tonight. Mind you don't break anyone's arm doing "The Duke of Perth".'

'Fine,' said Joss.

'Can me and Edward go and help too?' asked Amy.

'All right—then supper and bed, and no argy-bargy. Don't let Edward get filthy again.'

Mick drove the van down and Giles led the way along the paved path from the house, with Amy skipping along beside him humming a tune and Edward, with his awkward shambling gait, keeping up a barrage of questions concerning the eating habits of hens. Giles answered patiently, managing to give the impression that he was as interested in this limited topic of conversation as if he'd been discussing a vital concert performance. Lorna fell into step beside Daniel. There was absolutely no need for her to help, but it seemed a perfect opportunity, with Isobel out of earshot, to establish herself in Daniel's mind as Giles's right-hand woman and prove to him how warm and approachable she could be. She regretted her earlier impatience on the telephone.

'You must feel free to ask me for anything you want,' she told Daniel now. 'I expect there'll be lots of things you may need, which we won't have thought of providing for you. Please remember that's what I'm here for—so you only have to tell me. Giles doesn't like Isobel to be bothered over minor details concerning the theatre. She's always so busy with the children and gets tired easily. Giles is touchingly protective of her.' Both Isobel and Giles would have been astonished at this picture of their life.

'I'll try not to bother her. Thank you,' said Daniel, surprised. Isobel had not struck him as someone who was either frail or short of energy. 'Perhaps you can tell me something, then . . . I'm assuming the special canvas and stuff I ordered has arrived? *Brodie and Middleton*, the theatrical suppliers in Drury Lane, confirmed that they'd sent it off and they're usually very reliable.' This was awkward; Lorna hadn't the faintest idea what the answer was and didn't know whether to be relieved or annoyed when Joss, who had come up behind them, chipped in and said, 'Oh, a great load of stuff came weeks ago and we stored everything in the stables. Isobel got me and Mick to take it all over to the theatre last week, once the electricians had moved out and there was no fear of anything getting damaged.'

Lorna wondered if Joss had heard the whole conversation, or only Daniel's question. She did not at all want to encourage any friendship between the young artist and the two New Zealanders. 'Thank you, Joss,' she said and added graciously for Daniel's benefit, 'I don't know where we'd all be without Joss and Mick sometimes.'

She did not see the ironic look and amused wink that Joss gave Daniel.

As they arrived at the Old Steading, Mick was already opening the back of the van. Giles unlocked the side door that led directly into the theatre. 'Take a look, Daniel. This is where you're going to work your magic.' Giles watched with satisfaction the look on the younger man's face.

Daniel could feel the rush of adrenalin that came when something about a new setting started to fire his imagination. 'What a thing to have in your family,' he said. 'I don't wonder you want to make more use of it. I can't wait to get going.'

Giles grinned at him. 'Then let's get cracking with getting the paint in here for a start. Where do you want everything put?'

'It's a question of whether you actually want me to work in here—it all looks so very smart—or whether you've got some large empty building where it wouldn't matter how much mess I made?'

'Oh, dear, not really. I suppose I should have thought of that.' Giles rubbed his chin thoughtfully. 'I know you want some sort of frame fixing up, and I've arranged for Mick and Angus Johnstone, our estate handyman—brother of Bruce, the chap who's got your car—to come and concoct what you want tomorrow. But we haven't really got a suitable empty weatherproof building free. We're very much a working farm as well as a concert venue.'

'Oh, well, don't worry, I'll just have to be specially careful,' said Daniel cheerfully. 'Probably best to put everything on the stage itself? Less chance of anyone kicking any paint over—which is the story of my life.'

'Can we help carry things out?' asked Amy.

'Sure,' Daniel replied. 'You're going to be my chief assistant, aren't you? We agreed that in the car. Come and grab some buckets and pots of paint. They're not heavy but some of the lids may not be too secure, so better not drop one.'

'Is it wise to let the children touch anything?' asked Lorna, but no one paid any attention.

'There's several big sheets of polythene and some huge old dust sheets somewhere in your van,' Daniel told Mick. 'I'm afraid everything's got so mixed up it may be at the bottom now, but I'm going to need them to protect your floor—and we'd better put the paint pots on old newspapers, if you've got some?'

'No worry—we've loads of those. I'll get a pile.' Mick was delving in the back of the van and starting to pass things out to Joss.

Daniel handed Amy a pot of paint. 'Crimson lake,' she read as she put it carefully into the garden trolley, which Joss had brought with him. 'How funny. You'd think it would be blue for a lake, wouldn't you?'

'Oh, I don't know. What about the Red Sea?'

Amy giggled. 'How many other colours have you got?'

'Lots. I usually have about seventeen basic ones with me—and of course I mix colours too.' Amy looked at the names. 'Cadmium yellow, Naples yellow, raw umber, burnt umber, viridian, vermilion,' she read. 'They sound like the words of a song.'

'Perhaps you could compose one for me and play it on your fiddle? After all, there are hunting songs and marching songs, lullabies and love songs. Why not a painting song? Then I could sing it while I work.'

Amy beamed. 'Could we, Dad?'

'I don't see why not,' said Giles. Edward watched from a distance, thumb in mouth, scuffing the ground with his shoe, wary as a wild animal that might scuttle away into the undergrowth at any moment and be lost to view.

'What can Edward carry?' asked Amy, able to pick up her twin's transmissions when no one else could receive the signals he was giving out.

'How about this?' Daniel held out a stick.

'What's that for?' asked Amy.

'It's called a mahlstick. See, it has a little blob of wood on the end covered with leather? Well if you're working up a ladder—say on a big mural—and you want to paint a bit of detail very carefully and need your hand to be extra sure, you sometimes want to steady yourself by putting your left arm on the wall but if you did that you might smudge things. So you put your left hand on this stick and the little blob holds the rest of it away from the paint. Perhaps Edward would take that in for me?' Daniel tossed out the question, addressing no one in particular, and Edward came and took the stick from him, and carefully carried it inside and laid it on the floor at the foot of the stage.

Then he came back. 'What elth?' he asked.

'How about carrying one of my paint kettles?'

'Do you make tea in them?'

'No. They're just called that, I don't know why.' Daniel smiled at Edward. 'I mostly keep my brushes in them, but sometimes if I'm painting a big area of background I might mix paint in them.'

'I don't think Edward should touch *anything*,' said Lorna but at this moment Giles's mobile rang in his pocket. 'Yes?' he said. 'Oh, right, darling. I'll come straight up and speak to him. Ask him to hang on.' He put the telephone back in his pocket. 'Sorry, chaps. I'll have to skive the unloading—there's a call I have to take up at the house. Lorna, perhaps you'd bring Daniel back whenever he's ready? No hurry, Daniel. Dinner's a totally flexible feast—and quite informal.' And whistling to Wotan, he strode back towards the house. Daniel thought man and dog looked as if they had been specially designed to go with their setting, with their distinctive, long, elegant lines and easy self-assurance. He resolved to follow an old artistic tradition and put them both in the scenery he was about to paint: he liked having his patron's likeness somewhere in a commission. Often they didn't even notice.

Lorna was pleased to have been left, as she considered it, in charge. She didn't feel there was any occasion for her to offer to help with manual work herself, so she perched on the edge of the stage and supervised, while the others heaved things out of the van, the children carrying the lighter items and placing them where Daniel directed.

All was going well with so many willing hands and they had nearly finished unloading when Lorna realised that Edward was staggering along with two pots of paint clutched to his chest. 'Edward!' she said sharply. 'Put those down *at once.*'

Edward, who was just about to place them on the stage with the other things, immediately did as he was told and dropped them as if they were contaminated and his life depended on it.

There was a crash and a splash as cobalt blue spilt over the floor-boards.

'Wet cloths—quick,' said Daniel. Matt and Joss rushed into the adjoining kitchen and reappeared with old tea towels and buckets of water.

Lorna took Edward by the elbow and yanked him away from the spreading pool at his feet. 'You naughty boy!' she said, giving his arm a vicious little shake. 'See what you've done! I told you not to touch the paints.'

Edward twisted frantically to get away from Lorna's angry clutch. Then there was a sharp crack as he trod backwards on the mahlstick and it snapped in two.

Amy turned on her aunt, her face white with passion. 'How could you? How could you say that to Edward? It's not his fault—it's yours, all yours,' she spat out furiously, looking like a little cat protecting its kitten. 'You're horrid. I hate you, Aunt Lorna.'

'Hey—steady on there, Amy.' Joss gave her a warning look, though he wanted to wring Lorna's neck himself. He and Mick and Daniel were already cleaning up, mopping up the blue mess, which seemed to have spattered everywhere, with the wet rags and a shovel.

Lorna picked up the bits of mahlstick. 'I'm *so* sorry, Daniel. I should have stopped Edward from touching *any* of this.' She widened her blue eyes at him, wanting him to feel on her side, willing him to see her in a good light.

'Heavens—the stick couldn't matter less.' Daniel felt deeply embarrassed and upset by the little scene, sensing something darker and deeper going on than the spilling of paint warranted. 'Anyway, I only use it on a hard surface like a wall for painting murals. If I leant on the canvas I'd probably put my arm through. I don't think the floor will be marked—luckily the paint's water-based and Mick was so quick with the rags. It wasn't Edward's fault—it would never have happened if my crock car hadn't broken down and caused all this trouble. It won't be the first pot of paint that's got spilt and I don't suppose it'll be the last, but look—I don't think it's going to show at all.'

Edward now stood, quivering, at the far side of the room facing the wall, his right thumb jammed in his mouth and his left arm clutched over his head. Anyone who didn't know might have been pardoned for thinking he was attempting to ward off expected blows. Actually, he was trying to make himself invisible like a small child using the ostrich principle by hiding its head in a cushion. His eyes were blank with fright.

Joss walked over to him, picked him up and sat on the stage with him. 'It's OK, Ed,' he said. 'It's quite OK. Nobody's cross. Amy, run and get your mum. Ask her to bring one of Edward's shots just in case.'

'Oh, surely there's no need for that.' Lorna's colour was heightened. 'I think you're overreacting, Joss.'

'We keep his Valium in the kitchen fridge and we always have it on us if we take him out anywhere—Isobel or Giles or me. If Edward has a fit we need to get it into him quick.' Joss's face was expressionless.

Amy raced out of the theatre.

'Isobel told me he hadn't had a fit for ages,' challenged Lorna.

'He hasn't. But a big upset could bring one on.'

'Personally I think Edward has too much medication,' said Lorna in a knowledgeable voice, though she was uncomfortably aware that she had no idea whether Joss was deliberately winding her up, or if the situation might really be serious. She did not wish to appear as either ignorant or unfeeling before Daniel.

She turned to him and shrugged apologetically. 'Please don't give the mess another thought, Daniel,' she said. 'I'll order another mahlstick if you tell me where to get it. Edward's clumsiness is one of the hazards we're used to in the family and I blame myself. I shouldn't have allowed him to touch anything that matters. He can't help it, of course—he's retarded as you've no doubt gathered. I'll take full responsibility about the paint—it was my fault.'

'Yeah, too right, Lorna. It *was* your fault. You told him to put it down immediately so that's exactly what he did. I'd say he reacted pretty damn quick—and he's not deaf either,' said Mick pointedly. 'No slouch, are you, Ed?' He ruffled Edward's hair as he went past him to fetch in the last things from the van and cast Lorna a look of undisguised dislike. Watching him go, Lorna resolved that somehow she must try to get rid of the New Zealanders. She would never be comfortable while they were around with their hostile attitude and what she considered their over-familiarity to their employers.

*W*ell, I think we've about finished in here now,' she said to Daniel, ignoring Mick. 'Joss can look after Edward. Let me take you up to the house. I expect you'd like to see your room, get your personal things unpacked and perhaps have a bath before dinner? You've had a long drive. You must be tired.'

'Thanks, but I think I'll just get a few last things organised here,' said Daniel, wondering what was behind all the animosity he sensed—the atmosphere seemed electric with ill feeling. 'It's very kind of you, but you go on ahead and I'll make my own way up. I'll be fine.'

'Oh, very well—if you're sure. I have actually got quite a lot to do.' Lorna didn't like leaving Daniel with Joss and Mick, but neither did she want to be there when Isobel appeared. The possibility of being reproached, and further humiliated, by her younger sister in front of the new arrival was too much.

When she had gone, Daniel went and sat beside Joss and the still huddled Edward. He felt in his pocket for a pencil and the small sketch pad he always carried on him. 'I hear Edward keeps hens,' he said to Joss, bypassing an approach to Edward himself. 'I wonder what kind they are?'

'Well, some of them are Silkies, there's a few Marrans and a Light Sussex—and then there's some bantams—but most of them are a bit of a mix-up, aren't they, Edward?' said Joss. There was no response.

'I wonder if any of them look like this?' Daniel started to draw. 'These two cockerels are fighting over the same bit of bacon-rind,' he said conversationally, 'but neither of them can swallow it because if either of them opens his beak for a second the other one will pull it away and gobble it up.'

'Hey! That looks just like Pecker and Claws having a battle,' said Joss, giving Daniel an encouraging nod. After a bit, Edward cautiously took his arm away from his head and glanced sideways. Daniel went on drawing. Edward peered at the paper. He took his thumb out of his mouth and Joss automatically mopped the dribble that escaped down his chin.

'Pecker and Clawth have feathered legth,' said Edward.

'More like this?' asked Daniel.

'Pecker'th legs are very, *very* feathered. He ith the motht feathery cockerel in the whole of the north.'

'So more like this, then?'

Edward nodded.

*I*sobel had been in the kitchen, listening to Mozart while turning the remains of cold salmon into kedgeree. She had carefully removed all skin and bone, and flaked up the fish—a job she detested because it always made her fingers itch—had finished cooking and draining rice and hard-boiling eggs, and was just sweating chopped onion in butter with a dash of curry powder, happily humming along to *'Voi che sapete'*, when Amy had burst into the kitchen.

'Come quick, Mum—it's Edward.' Urgent explanations tumbled out of her; she was fizzing with indignation like an ignited sparkler. As soon as she heard what had happened, Isobel grabbed Edward's emergency kit and ran down the path to the theatre. By the time she and Amy rushed in Daniel, under instruction from Edward, was busy drawing a scene that might have been a rough sketch for a barnyard painting by Edgar Hunt.

Isobel could see at a glance that no diazepam would be needed.

She stopped in the doorway and shot Joss an enquiring look. He nodded reassuringly and made a thumbs-up sign. Relief flooded through Isobel, as always, trouble averted bringing her nearer to tears than crisis itself. She waited for the choky feeling in her throat to return to normal and watched the little scene, not wanting to break it up. I will remember this moment, she thought.

Amy went over to inspect the drawing. 'That's wicked!' she said admiringly.

Edward looked up. 'The paint got thpilt,' he said to his mother.

'I know, darling. Amy said it wasn't your fault but thank you for telling me—that's brave.'

'But the long-legged thpider lady ith very, very angry with me.' Edward looked at the floor.

'I expect she got a fright—that makes people sound cross. She won't be cross now.'

'Will it be forgotten?'

'Yes, darling. All forgotten.' But as she said it Isobel wished this were true, knowing that Lorna's memory was singularly retentive and that if, after their unfortunate start, there were any small amount of goodwill in Edward's account with her it would certainly be gone from now on. 'Everything all right now, Joss?' she asked.

'No worries,' Joss replied, standing up and smiling reassuringly down at her. 'But you have Daniel here to thank more than me. Mick and I'll be out of here now, then. Night all. See you in the morning.'

'Thank you, Daniel,' said Isobel, her voice shaking a little. 'Thank you very, very much. Now come and have some supper.'

As he followed Isobel and the children back to the house, Daniel thought he would be happy to have done far more than draw a few chickens to earn the look of gratitude in his hostess's eyes.

Twelve

Lorna had not gone straight back to the house when she left the theatre. She went over to her flat first in order to avoid meeting Isobel. One of the sitting-room windows looked over the courtyard, and from it she had watched Isobel and Amy rushing up the path to the theatre. Lorna waited until they disappeared inside the building, then went in search of Giles. She found him emerging from the door that led down to the cellars, a couple of bottles of Chablis under his arm. 'I must speak to you, Giles,' she said.

'You look very solemn. Let me just put these in the fridge and we'll go and have a peaceful drink in the drawing-room. I was really pleased with the way the meeting went this morning—you were a wonderful help. Let's have a post-mortem and pool ideas about anything that came up. So . . . what would you like now? White wine as usual?'

'I think I'd rather have whisky this evening, please.'

'You must be in a bad way.'

'I am.' She waited until they were in the drawing-room, then closed the door.

'Right,' said Giles, handing her a glass of whisky and water, and looking out at the familiar view of which he never tired. 'You look positively pregnant with doom. So fire ahead, then—tell me what's bothering you. I'm all yours.'

I wish you were, thought Lorna, oh, I wish you were. She took a swig of her drink; then put down her glass and came and stood beside him in the window, close, but not quite touching. 'I've done something awful. I have to tell you about it. I've had an upset with Edward, and everyone is blaming me. Izzy will kill me.'

'Is Edward all right?'

'Oh, I think so . . . I hope so, but Joss insisted on sending Amy to get Izzy, though I don't think it was really necessary . . . I clearly wasn't wanted. That was made quite plain.'

'Oh, well, if Joss and Izz are both with him I'm sure there's nothing you can do,' said Giles soothingly, though Lorna could see he was bothered. 'Joss has become so good at coping with Ed that both Izzy and I have complete faith in him.'

This, however, was not at all what Lorna wanted to hear. 'But I feel so awful about what happened—responsible in a way, though I really don't think I could have helped it.'

'I'm sure you couldn't,' said Giles, wondering what on earth was coming. 'So what did happen?'

'After you'd gone, Edward kept wanting to fiddle with things and I tried to stop him touching anything, but he wouldn't listen. Izzy has always told me she has to be extra firm with him to make him behave, so for his own sake I started to get a bit cross with him—but obviously not cross enough,' said Lorna, conveniently changing the order of events, 'because he then went and got hold of a jar of paint and deliberately dropped it on the floor, and there was paint everywhere. Then, of course, he did get upset, and Joss said he might be going to have a fit and Mick actually said it was all my fault. Luckily I don't think the floor is marked because Daniel was so quick at clearing it up. I wasn't impressed with Daniel at first sight, you know, but I must say I've revised my opinion. It was highly embarrassing for him—an awful start to his first evening.'

'Oh, I'm sure it'll all be all right,' said Giles, though he didn't feel certain at all. 'Someone would have come for me by now if there were a real problem with Edward, but I think I'd better go and check. Ed wouldn't have dropped anything on purpose, you know—that would be quite out of character. But don't worry; we know people find him baffling to start with.'

He turned to go, but Lorna put a delaying hand on his arm. 'Oh, Giles, I've made such a bad start here. I so badly want to help you and Izzy—to have some purpose in my life again—but everything I do seems wrong. Izz has changed so much, and . . . and there's so much resentment around I'm not sure how much more I can take. I know Izzy thinks the world of Mick and Joss but there are things about them that I don't quite like, things that perhaps you and Izz don't realise—they treat me like an intruder and can be quite unpleasant. Amy actually says she hates me to my face and I'm sure that's due to them. I don't know what to do. I think it was a mistake to come. Perhaps I ought to leave— but I don't know where to go. I suppose I could go to Ma and Pa in France for a bit . . . but they didn't think I should have come here in the first place so I suppose I don't want to admit they were right and I was wrong. Please help me.'

She looked up at Giles with brimming eyes. It was easier to cry at will than Lorna had imagined. It was like having a tap, which had tremendous water pressure behind it and the reservoir that fed the system was deep and full—a build-up of all her pent-up miseries and jealousies. She gave the tap a cautious quarter turn—she didn't want a gushing flood—and the tears came instantly with just the right controlled trickle.

Giles felt a surge of pity for her. He put a comforting, brotherly arm round her and she turned into him and leant her head against his chest, quivering with a few well-orchestrated sobs. It was per-haps unfortunate that Isobel should have chosen this moment to open the drawing-room door.

Having finished the clearing up and pushed Mick and Joss off to the Drochatt Arms, Isobel had walked back from the theatre with Daniel and the children. She had then sent Amy upstairs with Daniel, instructing her to show him his room. 'You can be a grown-up hostess for me, darling,' she had said. 'Make sure Daniel has all he wants, knows where his bathroom is and where the landing lights switches are, then after you've had a quick bath yourself, you can come down in your dressing-gown.' Amy had whisked off happily, feeling important, and Isobel could hear her chatting away to Daniel as he followed her up the graceful staircase that curved up from the hall. When Isobel had settled Edward in the nursery with a video, she finished making a salad to go with the kedgeree and went to look for Giles, needing to tell him what had happened and hoping to have him to herself for a little.

Given Lorna's obvious tears, the incident she witnessed might have passed off without much significance had Lorna not leapt ostentatiously away from Giles with a guilty little gasp, put her hand up to her mouth and rushed dramatically out of the room, leaving husband and wife to confront each other.

'Oh, very cosy,' said Isobel. 'Sorry to interrupt.'

'Don't be silly, darling. Lorna's in a state because she seems to think she accidentally upset Edward. I was just trying to smooth her down.'

'So I saw. How nice for you both.'

'Is Edward all right?' asked Giles, anxious to know, but also wanting to divert Isobel's attention.

'Luckily yes—but no thanks to Lorna. Joss said she terrorised him. He genuinely thought we might be in for trouble. I won't have her upsetting Ed. How dare she?' asked Isobel furiously. 'Joss and Mick were both there to look after him—it was none of Lorna's business. Edward's calmed down now, thank goodness. Apparently Daniel was brilliant with him. It's amazing; he seems to know instinctively just how to treat Edward. He must be a natural with children. Amy thinks he's wonderful too.'

'Daniel seems to have made a big hit with all the women in my family,' said Giles drily. 'I gather Amy has been very rude to Lorna, though. That we can't have. I'll have a word with her myself in the morning.'

'I've already talked to Amy about it. Just keep out of it for once,' said Isobel unfairly, because she had actually intended to ask Giles to speak to Amy. 'And keep your hands off my sister in future too,' she added fiercely.

'Jealous?' teased Giles.

'Should I be?'

'No, of course not, you goose. Friends again?' But Isobel did not feel ready to be won over as easily as usual and did not take his proffered hand.

'I might quite like you to be a little jealous, you know,' Giles raised an eyebrow at her. 'It could be rewarding.' Then, catching her expression, he continued in a different voice, 'Don't pretend, Izz—you're really much more concerned about Edward and Lorna than about Lorna and me. Perhaps I'll try comforting Lorna a bit more.'

'Then you'll be playing with fire,' she flashed, though the grain of truth in his words left a disquieting little feeling in her mind. Fiona was always warning her about the perils of being too much the mother, not quite enough the wife and girlfriend, though coming from Fiona, Isobel thought this was a fine case of pots calling kettles black. She also knew that however obsessed Giles might be with Amy and her music, he could never have been accused of making his wife feel a poor second to their daughter. She still ignored his outstretched hand but said more calmly, 'I warned you, Giles. Lorna makes trouble. Watch how you go. I came to tell you supper was ready. Let's go and have it now. I'll go and give Daniel a shout' and Isobel walked out of the drawing-room.

Giles looked thoughtfully after her. Holding Lorna in his arms, he had been aware of a pleasurable frisson of excitement.

Isobel half expected that Lorna would not appear for supper and might stay in her room in a martyred huff, waiting for someone to be worried about her absence, but she was in the kitchen, methodically drying and putting away the things that Isobel, who never quite managed to finish clearing up, had left to drain on the rack by the sink.

'Izz! Let me explain. What you saw in the drawing-room wasn't what you thought,' said Lorna.

'Oh, I think it was. You were upset and went and had a little cry on Giles's shoulder that's all,' said Isobel lightly. 'That's what brothers-in-law are for. Don't worry. I know Giles too well to suspect anything more sinister.'

'Yes—well. Good. So long as you understand . . .' but Lorna sounded more dissatisfied than relieved. 'Anyway I'm sorry. And I'm sorry about Edward too, because all I wanted was to help you with him.'

'Ah. Now that's another matter. Look, I know he's difficult and I'm sure you meant well,' lied Isobel, who didn't think anything of the sort, 'but it would be easier for everyone if you left him to Joss and Mick if I'm not there—at least until you know him better,' she added, relenting a little.

'If that's what you want, Izzy.' Lorna had on the hurt face that Isobel remembered so well from their childhood. It could hang about for days like fog. It could also blow away remarkably quickly if it suited Lorna's purpose, as it did now when Daniel walked in.

'Am I late or early?' he asked diffidently, hesitating in the doorway.

'Neither,' said Isobel. 'You almost can't be either late or early for meals in this house, because we never know ourselves when we're going to eat. But—amazingly—supper is ready, so sit down and have a drink while I dish up. It's only the four of us this evening. The children are having theirs in front of the telly and I was just going to offer Lorna a glass of wine and have one myself. Would you like one too?'

'Yeah. Thanks. That would be great.'

Daniel had showered and shaved, and was wearing a clean

white T-shirt and dark-blue jeans. Both Isobel and Lorna were struck by the transformation and thought with a jolt of surprise that he was actually quite good-looking.

Both sisters were also aware how very much they wanted him to like them.

Thirteen

Daniel started work the next morning. There was much preliminary preparation to be done and once the special scenic canvas, weighted with a chain along the bottom, was unfolded, Angus Johnstone and Mick set about making a wooden paint frame to Daniel's specification.

'My brother thinks you must be on the breadline,' said Angus, shoving the old cap he always wore back to front even further back on his head by way of greeting when Giles introduced him to Daniel. 'I gather yon car of yours is no in a verra good condition. Bruce hopes to sell you a new one.'

'Don't raise his hopes, then. You ask him to patch the old warrior up,' said Daniel, laughing.

'Not much the Johnstone brothers can't mend,' said Giles. 'I'll leave you in good hands. Just tell these two what you want.'

Daniel explained what he had in mind. 'And we'll need some cross struts for extra strength,' he said, 'otherwise the canvas will be too heavy for the frame, but don't actually fix it to those—it must only be nailed round the outside edge. As soon as we've got it up, I'll have to size-prime the canvas to stiffen and tighten it up before I can start painting. I'm afraid I shall stink you out when I boil up the size because it makes the most bloody awful smell. Lucky I've brought my own metal buckets and electric ring.' He grinned. 'Isobel and I certainly wouldn't welcome that pong in the kitchen.'

Mick and Angus were full of helpful suggestions and the little theatre became a hive of activity; Angus produced the trestles and planks, which were used for any household decorating required on the estate. They were not ideal but better than just a stepladder, thought Daniel, and anyway he had resigned himself to the extra physical effort that would be involved in doing without the facilities of a professional theatre before accepting the commission. It would be a challenge, he thought. He envisaged the final result as a sort of cross between a mural and stage scenery, knowing that because of the small scale of the stage and the close-quarters inspection to which the backcloth would be subjected, Giles wanted greater detail and something more intimate than would normally be necessary to make a theatrical effect. Because there was no fly tower at the Old Steading, and in order that the backcloth could be moved backwards or forwards to suit the sort of performance involved, it would have to be hung by web ties from flying bars above the stage. Luckily the bars had been installed when the theatre was first made, though they had never been put to use. Giles knew from his father that it had originally been Atalanta's wish to have scenery, but her will to live had run out before that ambition was realised. After her death Hector had lost the incentive to make new additions.

Once the canvas was up and had been primed with size and whiting, Daniel started to mark out a large grid of squares in willow charcoal, so that he could scale up the outlines from detailed small designs. The powdery black lines could then be rubbed out before making the outlines of the whole scene more permanent with the red ochre paint traditionally used in fresco painting. He liked the feeling he was following an old and venerated custom, even if the paint he used now was based on acrylic.

He and Giles had sat up late the previous evening discussing the designs and sparking ideas off each other. Giles, who would never have been satisfied with any project in which he had not had considerable input, was in his element, though Daniel hoped he had not got himself an interfering patron who would always be wanting to make last-minute changes. Giles had been particularly enthusiastic about Daniel's latest idea that the whole family should appear in the picture.

'But I'd have to do drawings of you first, which will take a bit longer, and add on to the time,' Daniel warned.

'That doesn't matter, it would be fun. In fact, I was going to ask you if you ever did portraits. I've wanted to have Isobel painted for a long time, but she's not keen and always makes excuses. So far I've never managed to pin her down, but with the artist actually staying in the house, we might trap her. I don't remember seeing any portraits in your portfolio, though?' He raised an eyebrow.

Daniel grinned. 'You don't remember them because they weren't there. The trouble is, if you get yourself known for one particular thing—and are lucky enough to keep on getting work—you tend to get a bit trapped in the system. Like an actor getting typecast, I suppose. But I've always had a yen to do portraits. Catching the essence of a person—seeing through the outer shell and revealing the hidden person inside—now that would be rewarding. I've painted a few mates of mine, bribed a few unlikely people to sit for me, but no serious commissions have come my way so far. I wouldn't want you to think I've got a name for it.'

'I like blazing trails, not following them,' Giles told him. 'I'd love to feel you were branching into something new because of us. Start doing the drawings you need for the backdrop, then paint a proper portrait of Izzy for me. She's a very special lady, my wife, and she's wonderfully unaware that just by being herself and living here she's changed what was once a rather gloomy and oppressive atmosphere into one where people seem to feel light-hearted—and welcome. Lots of people have remarked on it. There ought to be a picture of her here now. The house demands one.'

'Hmm—*The Mistress of Glendrochatt*, but not done in conventional ancestral style? Something a bit more casual perhaps? By the way, the woman over the fireplace in the drawing-room, was she Isobel's predecessor?' asked Daniel. 'She must have been quite something.'

'Yes, that's my mother. She was indeed a famous beauty. My father built the theatre for her, so you could say she was the original inspiration behind our venture—but hers is the ghost that Isobel has partly laid to rest. She was beautiful and talented but . . . terribly flawed. An emerald who cracked.'

Giles waited for Daniel to question him, but no question was forthcoming. 'When I was a young boy she shot herself in the head,' he went on, watching Daniel, deliberately trying to disconcert his guest. He felt he needed to establish dominance over this young man, who seemed tantalisingly enigmatic—so diffident in one way, so self-assured in another—and who, more important to Giles, appeared to have made such a hit, not only with the children but with Isobel and Lorna too. Naturally he was pleased they all liked Daniel, but there were limits and they needed to be set, thought Giles possessively. He occasionally enjoyed seeing what effect bald announcements about his mother made on people, though he knew Isobel considered he only used it as a form of social bullying and disapproved.

'Really?' Daniel sounded unimpressed by this stirring tale. 'We have something in common, then. My father committed suicide when I was fourteen.' He looked back at Giles and something unfathomable in his expression made Giles feel not only ashamed of himself but unexpectedly threatened. 'It's not something I often talk about—I find it can embarrass people,' said Daniel.

'Touché. I deserved that.' Giles acknowledged the thrust—so this was not a man to be easily intimidated. It made him more interesting, more of a challenge. 'We must compare notes on our damaged childhood some time,' he said lightly. 'But if you painted Isobel, I'd only want the portrait if it was *my* Isobel who emerged. Would you be prepared to risk the fact that I might not like the picture enough to hang it?'

'Of course.' Daniel shrugged and nodded, well aware that Giles was testing him out in some way. He thought they were like two dogs sniffing round each other, not actually wanting to fight, but circling, stiff-legged—marking territories. Daniel felt surprised at himself. Marking territory was not usually his thing at all. Territory, emotional or physical, was something he eschewed. 'You'd still have to pay me,' he said, 'whatever you thought of the finished result and that would be your risk. Or I suppose I might agree to scrub the fee and keep the picture myself to exhibit or sell elsewhere—if I was specially pleased with it but you didn't want it.' Giles wasn't sure he liked this idea. 'Either way,' Daniel went on, 'I'll have to paint the person *I* see, not just try to please you. That never works. If it turned out that I'd managed to capture your vision of your wife, that would be great. But I wouldn't let you inspect it until it was nearly complete. Take it or leave it.'

Giles digested this. 'You don't like being pushed around, do you?' he asked.

'No,' Daniel replied.

'OK. You're on.' Giles nodded after a slight pause, and he gave Daniel an amused, appraising look. 'But I may have to work on Izzy to get her to agree.'

'Fine,' said Daniel. He added more diffidently, 'I'd also like to try to paint your sister-in-law while I'm here—if she'll sit for me, that is. I thought of it the moment I saw her. I'd do that in my own time, of course, but would you mind if I asked her?'

'What a splendid idea.' Giles was immediately intrigued by the possibilities of this and what effect it might have on the relationship between the sisters. 'Two very different personalities. It will be fascinating to see what you make of them both.'

*G*iles gave Isobel an edited version of this conversation when he went to bed that night. Because she was still feeling annoyed with him—and even more furious with Lorna—Isobel had pretended to be asleep when he came up, though in fact her brain was in too irritable a state of activity for sleep.

Giles was not deceived. 'Oh, what a huffy back,' he whispered, running his finger down the curve of her spine as he slid in beside her. 'It's unlike you to keep such a grump going. And I've just been talking about you—saying such nice things, too.'

Isobel pulled away from his stroking hand and jerked an unfriendly shoulder.

'Want to know what I said?' he asked.

'No, I don't. For goodness sake get off and let me go to sleep.' Isobel sounded cross, but Giles could tell she didn't really mean it.

'I've just given our artist another commission.'

'Oh, yes?' In spite of herself Isobel was curious.

'I've asked him to paint your picture. You know how badly I want one and he's keen to start doing portraits, but hasn't got any takers yet—too successful at stage design and decorative art, and locked into it. Would you sit for him? To please me and to help him make his name?'

'I suppose I might.' Though Isobel was used to Giles's wily methods of getting his own way, she couldn't help feeling mollified; she thought it might be fun to sit for Daniel: legitimate time out from more serious commitments; a chance to get to know him better—she knew she would enjoy that. All the same, she had no intention of committing herself. 'I'll think about it,' was all she would say.

Giles started to kiss the back of her neck.

Later, just as she was really drifting off to sleep, Giles said, 'Oh, and I forgot to tell you: Daniel is absolutely dying to paint Lorna too—but that's entirely his own idea.' And he left his wife to make her own interpretation of this.

Fourteen

During the following weeks the two most recent arrivals at Glendrochatt started to shake down in their new setting and become absorbed into the household.

After the scene over the paint pots, Lorna reviewed her situation and decided she needed to behave with greater discretion. Despite her obsessive preoccupation with Giles, she still wanted to retain her sister's love. She treated Isobel with an ostentatious display of affection and made a show of deferring to her over important issues, while being seen, most touchingly she hoped, to try to smooth her path over smaller details. Outwardly, she appeared to have accepted her younger sister's more authoritative position in the pecking order of things—although Isobel, who marked the shift but did not trust it for a moment, thought sadly that nobody had cared two hoots about pecking orders before Lorna's arrival.

Lorna also went out of her way to be helpful to Daniel—something both Giles and Isobel noticed, as indeed they were intended to do—and anything he asked for was organised immediately. She managed to be polite—though only just—to the two New Zealanders and was circumspect about giving them direct requests. For their part they made it clear they had no intention of discussing their work with anyone other than Isobel or

Giles; they referred to Lorna behind her back as Miss Mona Bloody Lisa.

Lorna's efficiency ran like a well-tuned engine. Giles began to wonder how they had managed without her, though he was too perspicacious not to notice that some of the carefree feeling of Glendrochatt—which he had told Daniel, with such pride, was due to Isobel—was in danger of leaking away. 'It's just that, inevitably, we're becoming more professional now,' he explained to Isobel, justifying the situation to himself, when she commented on this change of atmosphere one day. 'I think you're being a bit ungenerous, Izz, in laying all the blame at Lorna's door. We needed to smarten up our act.'

She was silenced, knowing there was some truth in his accusation. She felt she should be pleased that Giles's dream for Glendrochatt—*our* dream, she reminded herself—was unfolding so well, but a possessive bit of her, which she had not hitherto been aware of, couldn't help resenting her sister's meticulous oiling of Giles's ego. She still felt cross with them both.

Despite Lorna's efforts to ingratiate herself with them, the children were not won over by their aunt's overtures. Edward was terrified of her. If Lorna addressed him he would only answer her questions—if at all—with unwilling monosyllables, not looking at her, and in her presence always appeared at his most goofy—head down, mouth ajar, dribble escaping. The engaging, funny Edward—the Edward who sometimes made bizarre, but often surprisingly perceptive observations and who talked in an original sort of code, the Edward who, despite his scrambled system, struggled so bravely to make sense of a world that was alien to him—was always missing when his aunt was there.

Isobel could hardly bear it. There had been enough truth to be uncomfortable in Giles's observation that she was more concerned about the relationship between Lorna and Edward than about Lorna and himself. However cross the latter situation made her, she hoped—she thought—that their marriage was strong enough to cope with it; the former filled her with sadness and despair, and activated the inner panic that underpinned her whole existence. Despite the enormous and unexpected achievements he had made, Edward's future was a huge unanswered query and the incident with Lorna emphasised how easily he could be set back and how heavily dependent he was on his mother. Sometimes Isobel felt as though she carried a heavy rock about inside her located somewhere in her chest.

Amy, having received a sharp reprimand from her father regarding her attitude towards her aunt, now sailed as close to the wind of impertinence to Lorna as she dared, guessing that her mother might turn a more short-sighted eye to such behaviour than was usual, and knowing that Mick and Joss derived positive amusement from it. Giles, accustomed to being Amy's idol, whose approval was her sunshine but whose disapproval was usually enough to throw her into a storm of tears, had been disconcerted to find himself confronted, not with a deluge, but with a closed, mutinous face as Amy had listened resentfully to his strictures after her violin practice.

'I won't have you being rude to Aunt Lorna, do you understand, Amy? It was monstrous to tell her you hated her. That's not the way we treat guests in our house,' Giles had said. 'She's very upset.'

'Then she shouldn't have tried to bully Edward.'

'She didn't *mean* to bully Edward.'

'Oh, but she did,' Amy had stated, jutting her chin at him. 'She *did* mean to and she was gross to him. You weren't there, Daddy, so you didn't see, but I watched her face. Ask Mick and Joss—they'll tell you. Anyway,' she had added relentlessly, 'Aunt Lorna says she doesn't want to be treated like a guest—she's always telling me I mustn't make her feel like one. She says she wants to be ab-so-lootely part of our little family now.' Amy's sharp ear, Suzuki-trained to listen, had picked up Lorna's honeyed tones and she reproduced them so perfectly that Giles found it difficult not to laugh. He had received an account of the scene from Joss, couched in colourful language, and was more disturbed by the incident than he liked to admit. He got the feeling that Amy had a good deal of right on her side, and thought that it would be wise to keep contact between Lorna and Edward to a minimum.

'Well, don't let me hear any more complaints or you'll be in deep trouble.' He sounded stern but prudently decided not to discuss the matter any further with his daughter. She threw him a scathing look and stalked out of the room, her head held at a defiant angle and—unprecedented occurrence—without putting away her violin.

Giles felt he ought to call her back, but guilt at his own disconcertingly ambivalent feelings for Lorna prevented him. Normally he would have discussed Amy's behaviour with Isobel, but somehow he didn't feel inclined to do that either.

Daniel observed them all and kept his own council.

Everybody liked Daniel. Even shrewd little Mrs Johnstone, wife of Angus, who came in to help with the cleaning, approved of him. Usually her pointed little nose could sniff out flaws in visitors to Glendrochatt like a ferret scenting fresh rabbit droppings. Her nostrils twitched suspiciously whenever she saw Lorna, but Daniel seemed to get the thumbs up and could do no wrong. She didn't care for his earrings, she told her husband, but supposed it was due to him going in for ART. Daniel teased her, which was more than her husband dared to do, and she admiringly pronounced him to be an 'awfie laddie'—a rare compliment—and plied him with cups of tea. She even tolerated the fact that he smoked, although luckily not too heavily; Mrs Johnstone would not have put up with that without waging guerrilla warfare. Mick and Joss had become Daniel's firm friends and the children rushed to find him as soon as they got home from school, insisting on inspecting what progress he had made with his painting.

Once the grid had been marked out, the outline for the background went on astonishingly fast.

'You've nearly finished,' said Amy in disgust. 'I don't want you to go away when you've only just come—Daddy said you'd be here most of the summer.'

'I've hardly begun.' Daniel laughed at her. 'This is the easy bit. The detail takes ages. Don't worry, you'll be stuck with me for a long time yet. By the way, I want to draw you soon—OK? D'you think you would sit for me?'

'Could I talk while I sat?'

'I doubt if anything could stop you,' he teased.

'Would I have to sit very still? What would happen if I got a desperate itch?'

'Oh, I think I'd allow you to have a good scratch.'

'I thought you had to sit *absolutely* like a statue for hours on end.'

'Some artists like their models to hold a position, but I quite like people to move about. I wouldn't want my portraits to look like statues. Ever heard of Velasquez?'

'I think so. Isn't he Spanish?'

'He is—do you do History of Art at school, then?'

'No, but Daddy's invented this game with postcards. You have to collect sets of pictures by famous artists and you play it sort of like *Happy Families*. It's cool. Isn't he the one who painted the goofy king of Spain with the long lip and the little girl with the long hair and all those dwarves?'

'Spot on. Clever Daddy—I'm impressed. Well, when Velasquez painted portraits he liked people to roam around his studio. He thought he caught a better likeness that way—and his portraits are among the greatest in the world. He's an artist's artist—we'd all like to achieve his special wizardry.'

He considered her for a moment. 'Actually, I've had a good idea. I think I'd like to draw you playing your fiddle. Would you do that for me?'

'Would I be playing it in the picture?'

'That's the idea: standing under a tree, or up on the hill in the heather perhaps, with notes of music coming out of your violin. You could be Euterpe, the muse of lyric poetry and music.'

Amy was enchanted. 'Who could Edward be? He'd have to be in the picture too.'

'How about Puck—Robin Goodfellow?'

'Could he be holding a hen?'

'I don't see why not. Sure.'

'What about putting in a dinosaur or the Loch Ness Monster for Edward? He'd like that.'

'Yeah, I think we could manage that. We might put the monster's head and a couple of its humps coming out of the water of the loch to remind people we're in Scotland and perhaps have a dinosaur lurking in the woods to show that the picture is timeless, down the ages. Or what about a pterodactyl flying above the tower of the house? A bit spooky, like a huge bat—a touch of menace is always interesting in a picture. Would that do?'

'Cool,' said Amy.

It had been decided that the backcloth should be based on Glendrochatt, a composite of all seasons and all views, with the house in the distance, the hills, the loch and of course the Old Steading Theatre, not to mention members of the family, friends and dogs . . . the list grew daily. Daniel moaned every time anyone produced a new idea. A vignette of Lord Dunbarnock driving one of his vintage racing cars, with his hair and beard streaming in the wind, had proved an irresistible suggestion of Isobel's.

'Brilliant,' said Giles. 'Our rich patron.'

Lorna disagreed. 'He might be offended,' she protested, 'and then he might withdraw financial support. Had you thought of that?'

'Oh, I don't think he'd do that,' said Giles. 'He's actually got a good sense of humour once you dig it out. It's just got rusty because no one greases it for him.'

'I didn't think the painting was supposed to be *funny*,' objected Lorna, making it sound like a dirty word.

'Not funny, exactly—witty, perhaps?' Giles suggested.

'I could make him reasonably small,' said Daniel persuasively. Lorna looked unconvinced and made a disapproving mouth.

'Oh, do lighten up, Lorna!' Isobel rolled her eyes, as she doled out chicken fricassee for the children's lunch. 'Think of the fun of the wonderful stage sets Osbert Lancaster did at Glyndebourne. We must have a few visual jokes.'

'You could make the number plate on Lord Dunbarnock's car "I GERM",' suggested Amy, and she and Emily Fortescue were convulsed with giggles.

Emily and Mungo had come over to spend the day with the Grant children, and their parents were invited to have family supper at Glendrochatt when they came to collect them. After lunch Edward and Mungo became completely absorbed in a game, dashing about the garden slaying imaginary monsters with wooden swords, capes made from old curtains tied round their shoulders. Their games were always horrendously bloodthirsty, yet they blossomed in each other's company: Edward able to take the lead and dictate the game, as he could do with no other child, and the oversensitive, lachrymose Mungo for once unafraid of incurring the derision of his peers. It was not only mentally that they were on a par: despite the five years dividing them, Mungo was nearly as tall as Edward and much more sturdily built. Isobel often thought it was only when she heard the two of them playing together that she got any clear idea of Edward's mental progress. He had an almost encyclopaedic memory, a large vocabulary which—if he chose—he could use correctly, though often in unusual ways, and a capacity for absorbing information about topics that interested him that was like a sponge sucking up moisture. The heartbreaking thing was that unlike a sponge it was often impossible to squeeze anything out of him afterwards. He could read, but not write; take in, but not give back and direct questions seldom produced any answer. You had to approach Edward's mind sideways like his own slanted, crab-like gait.

His educational psychologist had taught Isobel the trick. 'Don't ask Edward if it's raining,' she had once explained to her. 'Look out of the window and say you *wonder* if it's raining. Then he might tell you.' It had been a vital clue to dealing with him. Up till then, though he would often sit peering short-sightedly at a book, apparently absorbed, they had never been sure how much sense he could draw from it, or whether he was only studying the pictures. Attempts to get him to read aloud were fruitless until Isobel, experimenting with this new idea, had said to no one in particular, 'I do wish I knew what gorillas feed on.' To her astonishment Edward had turned to the back of his favourite book on animals, had run his finger down the index, found the relevant page and announced, 'Gorillath eat leaveth.'

Giles and Isobel had clutched each other with tears in their eyes. It had been a day to remember.

$\mathcal{I}$t was fun having the Fortescues for supper. Isobel and Fiona bathed Mungo with Edward and put him to sleep on the spare bed in Edward's room, while Edward came downstairs again to watch his inevitable video. Though Mungo objected tearfully to being tucked down before Edward, he was dropping with exhaustion after so much rushing about and crashed out the moment his head hit the pillow. Fiona and Duncan could scoop him up later, as they had done many times before, and he would hardly stir when they carried him out to their car.

Lorna, somewhat reluctantly, had gone for the night to see an old school friend and Isobel was conscious of a feeling of relief. Lorna's insistence that she would have no life of her own apart from Glendrochatt was not quite honest; she had, after all, been brought up in Scotland and, though she pretended to have lost touch with most of her old friends, quite a number of them were starting to come out of the woodwork. Isobel hadn't dared remind Lorna that this particular one, Daphne Crawford, had always been referred to by their father as Dismal Daphers the Do-Gooder. Daphne, together with an equally worthy friend called Susan McQueen, had set up a centre for alternative therapies in her own house near Edinburgh. Lorna secretly intended to pick their brains about Edward.

After supper the Grants and the Fortescues had played Hassock Polo in the hall, a vicious Glendrochatt game, which usually involved a lot of noise and some very dirty play—not a pastime for those with weak nerves or bad backs. The participants peddled about the polished floor on battered old kneelers, which had once been used for family prayers in the God-fearing days of Giles's forebears; a beanbag made an ideal puck, rolled up newspapers were used as sticks and the doors at either end were the goalposts. Daniel proved an enthusiastic novice, more wild than wily, and Mick and Joss took it in turns to referee or play for the Fortescues' team. Amy and Emily got thoroughly overexcited, Giles and Duncan argued about the rules like two small boys and a happy time was had by all.

'God, but my hamstrings are murder after that. I can hardly walk,' moaned Fiona, as she and Isobel, both breathless and scarlet in the face, went upstairs to collect Mungo. 'By the way, I think your artist fancies you something rotten. I can tell by the way he looks at you when he doesn't think anyone's watching.'

'Rubbish,' said Isobel. 'It's Lorna he's keen on. He can't take his eyes off her—I suspect he thinks she's like the Botticelli Venus and he's longing to immortalise her on canvas. Rising starkers out of the loch on a sprig of heather perhaps.'

'Who's talking? Giles told me at supper that Daniel's going to paint your portrait too,' Fiona retorted.

'Ye-es . . . but that's only because Giles asked him to.'

'Better watch out all the same,' teased Fiona. 'I think Daniel's frightfully sexy. Giles might get jealous.'

'Serve him right if he did. Giles is being a real pain at the moment—but though I like Daniel very much, luckily,' she said loftily, 'I don't find him attractive in that kind of way.'

Fiona raised a sceptical eyebrow.

*T*he next week Isobel decided to drop in on Sheila Shepherd after she had done the school run, to enquire after her mother and take them both some flowers. She was surprised to discover that Lorna had been to visit them before her.

Sheila was delighted to see Isobel, kissed her fondly and pressed her to come in for a cup of coffee. 'Mother's doing just fine,' she said. 'She's really grand now. I'm hoping to come back to work part-time in a couple of weeks. I did think it was nice of your sister to come to visit me and introduce herself—I really appreciated the gesture. She was telling me she's changed the office round a wee bit so that she can take most of the concert work off me, which in the circumstances will be a blessing. I shan't be nearly so worried about letting you and Giles down. She seems a very efficient lady.'

'Oh, Lorna's wonderfully efficient.' Isobel tried to keep the edge from her voice. 'But she could never replace you. We're all longing to see you back.' 'Did you know Lorna had been to see Sheila?' Isobel asked Giles, when she got home. He was in the hall looking through the post, which had just arrived.

'Yes. As a matter of fact I suggested it.' Giles looked pleased with himself. 'I've still got the scar from that great strip you tore off me when Sheila's mum first went sick and I thought it might be diplomatic. So do I get Brownie points this time, o Critical One?'

'It was obviously a good idea but I felt a bit silly not knowing about it. You might have told me, Giles.'

'Oh, we are getting touchy, aren't we?' he mocked. 'You look just like one of Ed's broody bantams when it's been turfed off the nest—all your little feathers ruffled up.'

'Don't be so bloody condescending,' said Isobel and added, 'I certainly didn't imagine Lorna would have thought of anything so tactful herself—she's always been practically autistic about other people's feelings. Perhaps that's where Edward gets it from.'

'Izzy! That's the first time I've ever heard you be genuinely bitchy.' Giles looked at his wife with surprise and interest.

'I feel bitchy,' muttered Isobel miserably, hating herself.

The night before, just as she had been about to switch off Amy's light, Amy had said, 'Mum, why does Aunt Lorna always have to sit in on my practices now? I *hate* it.' Isobel, who had not realised this was happening, had been taken aback.

'She's always with Dad now. She discusses my playing with him and it's none of her business,' said Amy fiercely. 'I used to love practising with Dad but now I'd rather do it on my own. I'm quite old enough—next time I have a lesson I'm going to ask Valerie if I can.'

'Oh, darling, I think Dad might be rather hurt. He's always been involved in your music.'

'Well, *I'm* hurt too. He asks her what she thinks all the time and then tells me to do it her way. Aunt Lorna doesn't give a stuff about my playing really—she just wants to suck up to Daddy,' said Amy shrewdly and Isobel had not known what to say. She too felt Lorna was monopolising Giles. They always seemed to be in the office together, brooding over charts and sharing ideas; sometimes when she went in they broke off their conversation in a way that made her feel an intruder.

She longed for Giles to take her in his arms, to kiss her and coax her as he usually did when she was upset, so that she could say she was sorry, and tell him how much she hated doubting him and feeling grudging and suspicious about her sister—but he did not do so.

'Oh, and by the way,' he said. 'I meant to tell you yesterday but I forgot—Lorna took a call in the office from Flavia. Apparently she and Alistair and the children are coming up to stay at Duntroon with Colin and Liz for the May Bank Holiday and she wants to come over and inspect the theatre—suss out the acoustics for the concert and talk about the programme for the Gala.'

'Oh, wonderful.' Isobel was distracted from her irritable mood; she loved the Forbeses. Though Flavia was several years younger than Isobel they had become friends during Flavia's many visits to her aunt and uncle, and Isobel had given her moral support during the breakup of Flavia's first marriage when she had brought down a flood of disapproval on her head and a few censorious souls like Lady Fortescue had actually cut her in public. 'I'll ring and see if they can all come over for lunch on the Saturday. I'm dying to see my god-daughter again and I'd love to have a gas with Flavia. You and Alistair could take Ben fishing or play golf.'

'Good. I thought that's what you'd say, so actually I got Lorna to ring and suggest it. She says they'd love to come.'

There was a pause. 'Oh . . . right. All nicely arranged, then. Great.' Isobel's voice was light, but her heart was dark with hurt and resentment.

'So—do you want to come with me now and look through the latest bookings, and talk about one or two ideas I've had for next year?' asked Giles, offering the twig of an olive branch.

Isobel flipped through the letters on the table and found one with a French postmark addressed in her mother's writing. She tore it open and started to read it with apparent concentration. 'Umm—no thanks, not at the moment,' she said absently, deliberately using the voice she employed to ward off the children when she was busy. 'Actually, I'm just off to have a first sitting with Daniel. He's starting on my portrait today.'

'He didn't tell me that.' It was Giles's turn to feel put out.

'Oh, didn't he?' Isobel hoped she sounded suitably offhand, and headed towards the theatre, very much hoping Daniel would be there and that her impromptu bending of the truth would not be exposed.

Fifteen

Daniel was painting background when Isobel came into the theatre, whistling away to himself, totally absorbed.

The work was going well and he was enjoying being at Glendrochatt more than he would have thought possible. He was used to working in isolation without much interruption, but here someone was always dropping in to have a look, to fetch something or just for a chat. Usually he would have found this infuriating, but he found himself relishing the company, entertained by the gossip and goings-on at Glendrochatt and enjoying the outspoken feedback on his progress. He had always been an amused observer on the sidelines of life and was intrigued by the power struggles going on in the community in which he found himself. But I mustn't let myself get beguiled by them, thought Daniel. He realised with surprise that he would find it all too easy to become involved with their lives and a warning amber light flashed in his head; he vowed he would not break his strict, self-imposed rule: no commitments, other than professional; no binding attachments to people, possessions or places—and above all not to people. This was Daniel's code for survival and if it was sometimes a lonely one, that was a price he felt he had to pay for the protection it gave to his peace of mind—and to his heart.

It seemed appropriate that the Grants were the owners of a

theatre, thought Daniel, mentally reviewing the cast of players in their family drama. First there was Giles, the director, who clearly also cast himself in the starring role: the hero with the interesting past, always exorcising inner demons, testing himself and those he loved to a risky limit. It had not been lost on Daniel that Giles had been put out to discover that his guest had an equally disturbing family background, though it was to his credit that he had made a graceful recovery from his first churlish reaction. Giles's sense of humour was a very redeeming feature, thought Daniel, a counter-balance to any impression of arrogance he might give. Then there was Amy, so talented, so vital, so passionately loyal to her difficult twin. Daniel had become very fond of Amy and guessed she would survive the pressure to succeed, which her father constantly put on her—but he wondered how Giles would cope when his precious nestling turned into a fledgling bird. He thought there were signs that she was already flapping experimentally on the edge of her branch, not yet sure in which direction to fly. And what about Edward? Daniel wondered what Edward might have been like if some unaccountable accident of birth had not knotted his talents like a tangled skein of silk. Perhaps his unusual use of words and his flair for imagery might have made him a poet? Possibly, with his passion for facts and phenomenal memory, he could have been a historian? When Daniel considered Edward—that changeling child—a stab of unwelcome involvement went through him, stirring private memories that were safer buried.

The beautiful Lorna was the joker in the pack, he thought. Who could guess what effect she might have on all the others? As an artist, Daniel enjoyed looking at her and studying her physical perfection; as a male animal he couldn't help feeling challenged by her; as an observer he speculated—was she an iceberg, or an inferno? Did she really love Giles or was she merely acquisitive? Did she simply wish to score points off a younger sister? Daniel was intrigued.

And then, of course, there was Isobel. . . . At the thought of

Isobel Daniel deliberately switched his mind into another gear and tried to concentrate on Birnam Wood.

*I*sobel, Flapper in attendance, came in through the side door to the theatre, closed it quietly, and stood watching Daniel's deft and rapid wielding of his brush. He had not heard her come in, and the little curves and splashes of green paint, which at close quarters looked no more than that, sprang to life and turned into convincing trees, when seen from where she stood. It was like seeing magic at work.

It was not until Daniel came down from the plank between his trestles to stand back and view what he had done that he became aware of her presence. 'Hi,' he said, more pleased to see her than he wanted to admit to himself. 'How long have you been there?'

'About five minutes.'

'I'm sorry. I didn't hear you come in.'

'I know. I love watching you work. Besides, I didn't like to interrupt.'

'You could never do that,' he said. 'Were you looking for me for something special, or have you just come to inspect progress?'

'Progress looks terrific, but it wasn't that. I just wondered . . .' Isobel hesitated, already regretting the impulse that had made her come and feeling uncharacteristically self-conscious. She looked so embarrassed that Daniel wondered what on earth could be coming.

'The thing is,' she said, seeming reluctant to come to the point, 'I happen to have quite a free morning . . . unusually so.' She paused again.

'And?'

'And I just wondered if you wanted to start on this portrait of me that Giles seems so set on. But you probably don't want to break off what you're doing now . . . and it could hardly be less important.'

'Of course it's important. I was really chuffed when Giles asked me to paint you—besides,' he said, looking down at her, the expression of uncertainty on her face moving him strangely, 'I want to do it for myself anyhow.'

When he had first met Isobel she had struck him as a carefree extrovert, comfortable in her own skin, secure in her marriage. Now he suddenly thought she looked unhappy—and not just about Edward. 'As a matter of fact,' he added, 'I've already done a few preliminary drawings of you—just rough sketches, nothing much.'

'Goodness! But when? I've never seen you doing that.'

He laughed at her surprise. 'Oh, off and on. I have a useful gift for invisibility.'

'I don't think you have—I always notice if you're there or not.' Isobel, caught off guard, blurted this out, then felt her colour rising.

'And I, you,' said Daniel quietly and held her gaze. She looked away first, and found herself suddenly breathless as though she had fallen from a great height and been winded.

Daniel, who had not had much occasion in his life for trusting either people or events, thought he had met someone who was remarkably lacking in guile. What you saw with Isobel was what you got—and what he was getting was something that warmed him through to his carefully insulated heart. He said, 'People often don't notice if I sketch them because they're so used to seeing me scratching away. I'm always drawing something.'

'Like Ed's chickens?'

'Like Edward's chickens—only you're a bit more of a challenge than them. They don't have very expressive faces. Look, I'll show you.' She followed him on to the stage and he opened a flat wooden box.

'Ed keeps your drawings blue-tacked over his bed,' said Isobel. 'They're very precious to him.' She laughed. 'Flattering to know I've joined Claws and Pecker as one of your models.'

She was suddenly at ease again—her usual self.

Daniel drew out some sheets of paper and handed them to Isobel.

He had caught her in several different moods and different settings, and there was a strength and immediacy about the drawings that was arresting: there was one sketch of Isobel curled up on the sofa, deep in a book; another showed her in her tattered old jeans carrying the hen bucket with Edward beside her; there was Isobel holding Flapper and leaning over the bow of the boat, hair blowing in the wind—a stiff breeze seemed to blow through the whole picture.

Even Isobel herself could see the likenesses were remarkable. 'You must have done that one when we took you to the island. I had no idea. So few lines—and yet there I am. You have an extraordinary gift, Daniel.'

He handed her another sketch. This time she studied it for a long time in silence, while Daniel scanned her face, his own expression inscrutable. When she looked up her eyes were full of tears.

It was a pencil drawing with a sepia wash on it, a picture of Edward standing in the hen-run. There was no attempt at flattery—no pretence: Edward was wearing his pebble-thick glasses; his hunched shoulder and crooked stance, his awkward hands with their very long thumbs, his uneven, slightly lumpy features were all there, but Daniel had also caught the look of delight which could illuminate his whole face and give it—for those with eyes to see—its own special beauty when something amused or particularly pleased him. It was Edward at his very best.

'Oh, Daniel,' whispered Isobel. 'I don't know what to say . . .' But her face said it all.

'It's for you. If you'd like it, that is. I thought nothing less than honesty would ever do for you, but I still wasn't sure it would be right . . .'

It would have been entirely natural for Isobel to fling her arms round Daniel and give him a spontaneous hug. She did not do so. Instead, they stood looking at each other, about a yard apart, neither of them attempting to make physical contact and yet they might as well have been locked in a close embrace, so concentrated were they on each other.

If I can catch the look on her face now, thought Daniel, I will have done something to be proud of; I will have stopped sheltering behind the decorative arts and taken a courageous leap. But he knew that for him it would be a very big risk indeed. Whether he captured it on canvas or not, he was certain Isobel's face at this moment would be ingrained in his memory for the rest of his life. He thought that, unlike Lorna, Isobel had the sort of looks that did not strike you as beautiful at first meeting—it was her warmth and vitality that made the first impression, not her features—but Daniel also thought that once you had glimpsed beauty in her face you would never see it any other way and must always wonder why you had not been dazzled the first time you saw her.

Isobel felt as though a spell had been put on her. She was quite unable to move.

'Give me back the drawing for now,' Daniel said at last. 'I'd like to frame it for you.' He took it from her and their hands just touched as he did so. He hesitated for a moment, then, 'Right,' he said quite brusquely. 'You said you'd come to sit for me this morning, so that's exactly what we'll do now.'

He turned away from her abruptly, fetched an easel, which was propped against the back wall of the stage, brought it down the steps and set it up. Then he collected a canvas and put it on the easel. It was quite large and Daniel had fixed a sheet of light cotton along the top, which covered it.

When he folded the material back, Isobel saw that the outline of a portrait had already been started. 'Is that me?' she asked.

'It will be.'

'Can I look?'

'No—definitely not.' Daniel was emphatic, but he smiled at her with his eyes.

'Which of the drawings will you use?'

'Probably all of them. I have something in mind. You'll see when I'm ready. Now if I spread out this old rug here,' he said, throwing one down on the edge of the stage, 'and we add a couple of cushions for comfort, could you go and sit up there on the floor?'

'I'm not used to posing. I feel a bit silly. How do you want me to sit?'

'Whatever way is comfortable. Imagine you've thrown yourself down in the heather as you did on the picnic the other day—or I may eventually have you perching on a wall with your legs dangling down, or curled up in the way you so often are. It doesn't really matter for now. Chat away to me. I like to be entertained.'

She sat on the rug, her hands clasped round her knees, looking at him, with Flapper curled up beside her. 'I feel you know so much about us,' she said. 'We're all so garrulous. We must be an open book to you—a book I know you read. But you . . . we know practically nothing about you.'

'What do you want to know?'

'Everything.'

'Oh, no,' he protested. 'No one should know *everything* about anyone else.'

'Well, perhaps not everything—but friends should know lots about each other, otherwise how can they ever get really close?'

'I've never wanted to be close.'

'I don't believe you. *Never?*'

'Not for a very, very long time.'

'I bet that's not true,' said Isobel. 'I bet you're just afraid of it. What I'd like to know is why?'

Daniel did not answer. He painted with great concentration, occasionally looking at her through narrowed eyes, so that she had a sensation of being transparent.

'It's not fair, Daniel Hoffman.' She laughed at him suddenly. 'Placing me under your personal microscope like this. You have to yield up your secrets as well, you know.'

He gave a non-committal smile but went on painting.

'Giles said your father committed suicide too,' she persisted. 'He told me you made him feel like a cheap exhibitionist because he boasted about his awful mother to you. I hate it when he does that—but I think this Mr Mystery act of yours is just as much bravado as his particular way of trailing his coat and possibly more pusillanimous.'

'Ouch!' said Daniel. He was surprised, not that Giles should have told Isobel about his father, but that he had admitted to her his own part in their conversation—one of which Isobel obviously did not approve. He felt a bleak little stab of envy at the thought of such trusting intimacy between husband and wife. 'All right,' he said at last, still studying her, still painting. 'Fire your questions at me, then. I don't guarantee to answer, but I suppose it's a fair request.'

He smiled at her and a shiver of excitement ran through Isobel. What am I getting myself into, she asked herself. It had never before crossed her mind in twelve years of marriage that she might even be tempted by any man other than Giles. It must be because of Lorna, she thought, it's all because I'm hurt and not used to feeling jealous . . . but she didn't entirely convince herself. She knew there was something more at work. It's like yeast, she thought, you don't notice anything's started happening and then suddenly a potent force has caused an insignificant possibility to grow larger than you'd believe possible. 'Tell me about your family—your childhood,' she said. 'I read somewhere that if you know what someone's very first recollection is you have an important clue to that person. Quick now! Don't stop to think . . . what's your very first memory?'

'Listening to my father singing the Yiddish songs he'd learnt from his own father as a little boy,' Daniel replied instantly. 'I'm lying in bed upstairs and I creep out on to the landing to hear him. I sit halfway down the stairs in my pyjamas and listen spellbound. He's accompanying himself on his old fiddle and the songs are sad and haunting; they fill me with a feeling of nostalgia for some place I've never been to, some people I've never known. That's my first memory. It's as clear as yesterday.'

'How old were you?'

'Oh, I dunno—about three? Certainly not more. He didn't sing those songs often, but when he did it sometimes used to make him cry. It was addictive and disturbing.'

'Why was he so sad?'

'Just before the war my grandmother brought my father to England on a visit to her brother. My uncle was a child psychiatrist who worked with Karl König, the physician and educator who started the first Camphill school in 1940, based on Rudolph Steiner's teaching. My grandfather, also a doctor, was supposed to join them, but he never made it. Grandfather Hoffman must have known all too well what might happen and sent his wife and child to safety. They never saw him again. Most of his family disappeared in the Holocaust.'

'Oh, Daniel!' Isobel's expressive eyes looked dark with distress. 'Tell about your own parents. Were they happy? Did you have brothers and sisters?'

'No brothers or sisters. My father was a lovely man: gentle, impractical, idealistic—though he could be hilariously funny too. I suppose he was a bit barmy, actually—he suffered from terrible bouts of depression. His family were middle-class, intellectual Jews in Poland—teachers and doctors mostly—but of course my grandmother landed up here with no money and no possessions. She wasn't even able to speak more than a few words of English at the time. She was an artist—mainly self-taught but good—so I suppose I have her to thank for the painting gene in me. Anyway, she stayed on to help in the community where her brother worked, in exchange for free board and lodging for herself and her child—so my father was brought up there. Eventually he qualified as a Camphill teacher himself—it may seem surprising to our generation, but when the movement was first started, Karl König's vision of a therapeutic residential community where mentally handicapped children could live and share with normal people in a family environment was considered quite revolutionary. I was born in one of the Camphill communities.'

'Ah,' said Isobel. 'That explains why you understand Ed so well. I *knew* there had to be something. I know all about Camphill.'

Daniel did not volunteer anything more and went on painting in silence. Isobel felt as if she was having to drag information from him. 'What was your mother like? You haven't mentioned her. Were you brought up in a Camphill school?'

'Partly, when I was little, but my mother couldn't stand the communal lifestyle or what she considered to be the weirdos to whom they devoted their lives. There could never have been a greater mismatch than my parents. I still go back to the community where my father worked and help out there occasionally. I suppose it's as near to a home for me as anywhere.'

'So what did your mum do?'

'She disappeared when I was four. My grandmother helped my father look after me.'

'You must have been devastated.'

'I don't remember missing her at all—but my father was gutted.'

'Awful for you too, even if you didn't realise it.' Isobel thought she was beginning to understand a few things about Daniel. 'Did you know why she'd gone?'

'Not at the time. Nobody talked about her much, but children pick up more than grown-ups think. I do remember once sitting under the kitchen table hearing my grandmother talking about her and using words I didn't understand, but which made me feel sick all the same.'

'It may have been pretty tough for your mum, you know,' Isobel suggested. 'It takes a special person to live and work in a community for handicapped children. I know from Edward's school—I know from myself. Most of us just aren't equipped to do anything so altruistic. Don't judge her too hard. She probably couldn't cope.'

'You cope with Edward.'

'That's different. There's no credit attached. I cope with Edward because I love him. And I cope because—luckily—for me there's no choice.'

'There's always a choice—that's what life's about. But as you say, you do love Edward and that makes a big difference.'

'It's felt like, a very mixed love sometimes,' Isobel admitted sadly. 'Sometimes there are great dollops of self-pity and resentment mixed in with it. I couldn't do what I do for Ed for anyone else's child. That takes love of a much higher order.'

'Not *higher*,' he said. 'Different, more impersonal, yes—but being impersonal, less acutely painful too. Your kind of love accepts terrible wounds.'

'I'm like the man in the nursery rhyme,' said Isobel. 'The one who found a crooked sixpence against a crooked stile. Edward is my crooked sixpence.'

'And now, because of him, you walk a crooked mile?'

'I suppose so. But I wouldn't have it otherwise.'

'No?'

'Oh, if I could have Edward as he ought to be—as sometimes he so tantalisingly nearly is—then *of course* I'd want that, *of course* I would,' she said passionately. 'But if I were offered my life over again and had the choice of Ed as he is now, or not having Ed at all, then I know I'd choose to have him. You can't know how much he's given me—even when I haven't always wanted it—so much, much more than I've given him.'

'Perhaps,' he told her, 'but you can't help giving—it's how you are.'

Something in the way he looked at her and in the expression of his dark eyes made Isobel feel as though she was running over a conversational bog: if she chose the wrong tussock to jump on she might not recover her footing. 'Carry on about you,' she said, changing tack and carefully unmatting the tangles behind one of Flapper's ears. 'So off goes your mum, you're happy with your father and grandmother—then what?'

Daniel longed to put out a hand and touch Isobel's face. He thought talking about Edward gave her a look of such vulnerability that it hit him like a physical pain. He did not want to be made to venture back into these areas of his past, but neither did he want to risk breaking the cobweb thread of intimacy that stretched between them. 'Well,' he said, his voice deliberately matter-of-fact, 'when I was seven my mother reappeared. She turned up one day without warning.'

'Had you had any contact with her in the interval?'

'Absolutely none—but I recognised her instantly. I remembered her delicious smell.'

'That says a lot about the feelings of a little boy who'd been abandoned by his mum.' Isobel pictured a small Daniel, and imagined his muddled emotions of love and guilt, longing and betrayal.

'Um, well . . .' Daniel was painting with great concentration. 'Anyway she didn't take long to create havoc in the community.' He rolled his eyes and laughed, though Isobel didn't think it was with much amusement. 'Bit of a nympho, my mum,' he added lightly. 'She was like a well-fed cat who catches mice for fun— and she brought her mice inside so that she could play with them right under my father's nose. He had a breakdown.'

He stood back with his head on one side, considering Isobel's face intently, looking from her to his canvas. He picked up a pencil, held it out at arm's length, closed one eye and ran his thumb up the length of the pencil to check the space between Isobel's eyes with the measurement on the portrait.

'Go on,' she prodded.

'Not much to tell. My mother eventually took off back to London—only this time she took me with her. I was frightfully excited. I thought we were going on a trip to the zoo.' He pulled a wry face. 'Big disappointment, that was.'

'So then?'

'My mother filed for divorce on the grounds of my father's mental state and persuaded a judge he was unfit to look after me.

She got custody—my father got limited access. I shuttled to and
fro. End of story.'

'Not quite,' she said, 'but don't tell me if you'd rather not. . . .
Did your father kill himself in a fit of depression?'

'Yeah, I suppose so. I was living with my mother and her latest
man, and going to a school in London that I loved—loved the
school, I mean. Then my grandmother died of cancer.'

'Were you very sad?'

'I wasn't exactly thrilled.' Isobel winced.

'I'm sorry,' he said quickly. 'Don't look like that—it wasn't
meant to be a put-down. I'm not being a very satisfactory witness,
am I? I'm no good at this sort of conversation.'

'It's me that should be sorry. You must think me dreadfully
nosy. I didn't mean to put you through an inquisition.'

Daniel laughed at her, this time with genuine amusement. 'Yes,
you did,' he mocked her gently. 'Regular little pumping station,
you are—but it's OK. And yes, I minded like hell. My grandmother had always been great. I owe her a lot. I bunked off school
to go to her funeral. I'd never been to one before and I couldn't
stop thinking about her body shut in that box. She'd always been
such fun—so alive. They didn't let me see her—no doubt with
the best motives—but I don't think it's the sight of a dead body
that's scary to children so much as their own lurid imaginings of
the unknown. Afterwards I couldn't wait to get away from my
father's terrible gloom. I nagged him to put me on the train back
to London, even though I knew he wanted me to stay. I never
saw him again: two days later he hanged himself.'

And you've been blaming yourself ever since, thought Isobel.
She also thought how sheltered her own life had been compared
with his, how much she had always both expected and received
love. She said, 'He was ill. He couldn't help it, any more than I
suppose Giles's mother could—though I've always resented her
for what she did to him and my father-in-law. It wasn't your
fault, Daniel.'

He shrugged. 'Maybe not, but what you know with your mind doesn't necessarily convince your heart.' He added abruptly, 'You were on the button when you said I was pusillanimous. I take care never to let myself get emotionally involved with anything or anyone.'

'Of all the sad things you've told me, I think that's the saddest so far,' said Isobel. 'What about being in love?'

'I've never been in love. I've had sex, of course.'

'*You* may not have been in love, but I bet people have been in love with you.' She couldn't help wanting to know if there was a particular woman in his life, though she felt ashamed of herself for her curiosity.

'If I thought there were a danger of anyone really loving me I'd take care to back off,' he said.

'That's a terrible attitude,' said Isobel, 'and anyway I don't believe you.'

They gazed at each other. Daniel opened his mouth to reply but before he could say anything the door opened and Lorna came into the theatre.

Sixteen

I'm sorry to interrupt you both.' Lorna was at her most sugary. 'But you're wanted on the telephone, Izz.'

'Oh, damn. Wouldn't they leave a message? Who is it?'

'A Mrs Duff-Farquharson—something to do with the children and a party? I know you don't like me to make decisions and Giles said I'd find you here.'

Lorna had been distinctly put out to discover from Giles that Daniel had started on Isobel's portrait before her own and also thought Giles seemed slightly surprised himself. She had perceived a small shoot of possible dissatisfaction in him, which she might profitably cultivate. 'I think it's a bit off that he didn't consult you first. You might have wanted him to finish the backcloth before he started on anything else.'

'Oh, well—I did ask him to do the portrait in the first place.'

Lorna had given him an admiring look. 'You're so wonderfully tolerant, Giles. I don't think I'd be very pleased in your shoes . . . for various reasons.' The telephone call had been a timely excuse to come and see what was going on and interrupt it—whatever it was.

'I don't know any Mrs Duff-Farquharson,' Isobel replied. 'Could you say I'll get back to her later if she leaves her number?'

'She insisted on holding on—something about needing to

know about numbers for the party and having to go out soon,' improvised Lorna, who had no intention of revealing that Mrs Duff-Farquharson had offered to ring back later.

Daniel, who had covered the portrait the moment Lorna came in, started to pack up his paints and brushes. 'A good moment to have a break,' he said easily.

'Won't the paint smudge if you cover it up like that?' asked Lorna.

He gave her a look of sardonic amusement. 'No, don't worry. I've fixed something to keep the material off the canvas—but it wouldn't matter much anyway at this stage.' Lorna made up her mind to take a secret look at his handiwork at the first opportune moment.

'OK,' said Isobel. 'I suppose I'd better see who she is and what she wants.' The interruption was most unwelcome, but she was not going to give her sister the satisfaction of seeing how annoyed she was. 'Thanks, Lorna—sorry you've had to rush down. Come on then, Flapper, we'd better scoot. See you both at lunch.'

Lorna marvelled that Isobel should have been prepared to sit for Daniel looking such a mess. She would not have dreamt of allowing herself to be snapped for a family photograph, let alone posed for her portrait, without full warpaint, carefully applied. When people looked at Lorna she was used to seeing admiration in their expression and yet, and yet . . . the old pain stabbed her: When people looked at Isobel something in their eyes softened. Lorna realised that Isobel, without appearing to make the least effort, achieved relationships that quite eluded Lorna herself no matter how hard she tried—and she tried very hard indeed. Though Daniel had had his back to her as she came in, and she had not overheard anything Isobel and he were saying to each other, Lorna felt quite certain she had interrupted something between them. She glanced towards Daniel and met a cool, appraising gaze that disconcerted her. Like Isobel, earlier on, she felt transparent before the artist's analysing eyes; Lorna did not at all want Daniel Hoffman to glimpse what was going on in her mind.

As so often happened at this time of year, Scotland seemed to have forgotten that spring was supposed to have arrived and reverted to winter. Isobel walked briskly back towards the house, her hands shoved deep in the pockets of the old green cashmere cardigan she frequently wore; it had once belonged to her father-in-law and had definitely seen better days, but Isobel loved it and could never be prevailed upon to downgrade it to floor-polishing duties, though Mrs Johnstone had made several attempts to commandeer it. 'Ye look a reet tink in that auld garment,' she often said reproachfully. Flapper, her ears flying out in a delirium of happy expectation, went bounding ahead of her mistress, rushing to check the shrubs round the courtyard for any incoming messages that might have been left for her by Angus Johnstone's collie, but Isobel's shoulders were hunched against the sharp little wind that blew from the east, her heart seethed with complicated emotions and her mind was full of uncomfortable questions.

The caller turned out to be the mother of a new school friend of Amy's.

'Hello, I'm Jilly Duff-Farquharson. You won't know who I am but we were once in the same party as your charming husband, years ago, at the Black Watch Ball before he was married and I've never forgotten what fun he was. Lately I've heard so much about *you* that I feel I know you already, even though we haven't actually met.'

Isobel could tell that this comfortable state was not going to last much longer. Mrs Duff-Farquharson's voice sounded relentlessly bossy. 'We're hoping to get up a little party for the Pony Club hop in June and I know Tara would be thrilled if Amy could come too.'

'I should think she'd love to—can I check with her and ring you this evening?' said Isobel cautiously. She was conscientious about consulting Amy before accepting invitations on her behalf.

'Oh, *do*. Emily Fortescue's coming and the two Murray boys.

They're all quite a little gang together, aren't they? We only moved up here in March after Plum—my old man—left the army, but we know Grizelda and Frank Murray well. Plum and Frank were in the Regiment together and have been friends for years.'

Isobel felt condolences might be in order on that count: Frank Murray, an unlikely choice of mate for the whimsy Grizelda, was a man of unimpeachable rectitude, narrow vision and extreme dullness, who always sucked her good intentions not to argue with his pedantic views out of Isobel like a powerful vacuum cleaner. Giles, who enjoyed their encounters as a spectator sport, always said that in Frank's presence Isobel became a ragingly left-wing, agnostic agitator.

'Plum's going to be Neil Dunbarnock's new factor when old Mr Crombie retires, so we're going to be neighbours,' Mrs Duff-Farquharson went on chattily, clearly establishing credentials. 'Tara tells me Amy has a brother but I gather he goes to a different school? Our sons are all much older than Tara—she's our little afterthought—so we're a bit short of boys for this party—not that it matters *too* much at this age—but we'd love it if your son would like to come too? I've seen Amy at the Pony Club, but I don't think your son belongs?'

'It's very kind of you,' said Isobel 'but I'm afraid dancing reels isn't quite Edward's scene.'

'Oh, we'd soon jolly him into it,' said Mrs Duff-Farquharson firmly. 'Nobody's allowed to stand on the sidelines with us. One of my boys used to be frightfully shy, but I always made him go to parties wherever we happened to be stationed. Plum used to wonder if I was too tough with Rob, but Rob's grateful to me now, I can tell you. I think it's so important for the young to *mix* and make the right sort of friends early on, don't you? Now tell me, where does your Edward go to school?'

Isobel conceived an instant dislike of Mrs Duff-Farquharson. 'He goes to Greenyfordham. And it's *really* kind of you but actually I know reels are just not for him. Amy's very sociable, though, and loves dancing. I expect she'd love to come.'

'Greenyfordham?' Isobel could imagine Mrs Duff-Farquharson riffling through her mental directory of socially acceptable schools. 'I wonder who else goes there that we might know? That's not a school I've come across yet.'

'No, well I don't suppose you would have done.' Isobel wished she'd come clean about Edward straight away; sometimes she did, but sometimes, like this morning, she evaded the issue because certain people seemed to find it so difficult to know how to react. 'Edward has problems,' she explained now, 'and Greenyfordham is the wonderful local school for children with special needs.'

'Oh, *poor you*. Trust me to put my foot in it!' Jilly Duff-Farquharson's laugh caused Isobel to move the receiver several inches away from her ear. She crashed on, 'But don't worry—my lot have always been brought up to help the less fortunate; let him come all the same and we'll see he has a super time. I do Riding for the Disabled so I absolutely know the form. Now don't say no because I insist.'

'Thank you so much,' said Isobel, feeling as if she'd tangled with a metal-crushing machine, 'but actually Edward simply wouldn't cope.' It was clearly a well-intentioned offer, and at least there had been no embarrassed pause—one up to jovial Jilly, she thought with grudging approval—but the idea of Edward being jollied along to dance reels made her cringe. Memories of parties when the twins were small flooded in: of Amy, bright as a military button, throwing her heart into musical bumps while Edward was still unable to walk; of being asked 'How old is your little one?' and seeing the look of disconcerted disbelief when she explained that Amy and Edward were twins. I ought to be used to it by now, she told herself. The fact was that Edward adored the occasions when the Greenyfordham children went to Riding for the Disabled; for a magical hour it seemed as if his physical disabilities became of no account. I must be impossible to please, thought Isobel guiltily. Jilly Duff-Farquharson probably drips with the milk of human kindness, but oh, dear. She floundered about, trying desperately to stall without actually resorting to rudeness, and eventually extricated herself from the metal cruncher with difficulty and promises to ring back.

'Who was that?' Giles, who had come quietly into the kitchen at the end of the conversation and was standing behind her, made her jump. He picked up a lock of her hair and curled it round his finger.

Isobel jerked her head away. 'Some beefy chum of Frank's and Grizelda's whose husband seems to be called after a pudding. She wants the children to go to the Pony Club hop.'

'You didn't sound your usual friendly self. Not pleased at being disturbed during your sitting perhaps?' asked Giles, who had a deadly aim for hitting nails in the right place.

'As it happens, no, I wasn't at all pleased,' said Isobel frostily, 'and it must have been maddening for Daniel. I expect Amy'll want to go to the party, though—Emily's going, apparently, and Christopher and Jamie. I refused for Ed of course.' She wondered if she would ever be able to turn down this kind of ordinary invitation for Edward without an inner pang for might have beens.

'I rather think the band is playing for that party,' said Giles, 'so Amy could do a bit of reeling as well as fiddling. Why don't you suggest we join forces?'

Isobel pulled a disparaging face and Giles gave her a sharp look. It was just the sort of invitation she normally loved best—an all-ages occasion for dancing, with Giles' and Amy's band providing the music. Luckily there were usually enough members in the band to enable everyone to take to the dance floor for part of the time.

'We could take Daniel along too and show him a bit of Scottish life—if that would gild the pill for you.' Giles's voice was silky as he raised an eyebrow at her. 'And Lorna too, of course. She used to be such a marvellous dancer. I expect she'd love it.'

The temperature between them, chilly to start with, dropped several more degrees.

'Fine,' said Isobel. 'I'll ring plummy Mrs Plum Duff and suggest it, then. She's clearly dying to meet *you* again—she made that quite plain.'

'You do that, o Huffy One. I vaguely remember Old Plum from my childhood although he was older than me so I didn't know him that well. I think he's a retired general now, no less, but even as a boy he looked as if he'd been born wearing knife-edged khaki shorts and a pith helmet—a touch pompous but perfectly harmless as far as I recall. I'd heard they'd bought the Old Manse at Largan. Might become subscribers to the theatre—if we don't offend them by being stand-offish.'

'Oh, *well*, by all means do let's get our priorities right.' Isobel's voice was bright and brittle. 'If they could be *useful*, of course that's another matter. Perhaps it would be better if you asked Lorna to ring them?'

They eyed each other. Then Giles suddenly laughed and held up both hands in a gesture of appeasement. 'Pax, Izz . . . we can do better than this. I'm sorry.'

Isobel came and stood beside him, and rubbed her cheek against his arm. 'I'm sorry too,' she whispered. There was no need for explanations between them: Daniel and Lorna, in very different ways, might both have experienced envy at husband's and wife's instant understanding of each other.

Giles and Isobel felt as though they had been walking too close to an unknown cliff edge and had taken—for the time being—a step back to a well-trodden and safer path.

Seventeen

There was a constrained feeling at lunch, as though everyone suddenly felt the need to be on their best behaviour.

'I hope it's OK with you, Giles, that I started on Isobel's portrait this morning,' Daniel said, doling out a large bowl of Joss's delicious home-made soup for himself and carrying it back to the table together with a hunk of hot bread. Kitchen lunch at Glendrochatt was always an any-old-time, help-yourself affair. 'I find it's quite good to take a break and work on something different now and then, but I'm sorry if I've jumped the gun from your point of view—Lorna tells me you wanted me to finish the backcloth first.'

Lorna had opened her mouth to contradict this statement but, conscious of Daniel's quizzical eyes on her, closed it again; she had a feeling it would be unwise to challenge him. Despite his gentle banter and diffident-seeming manner she suspected Daniel could be a formidable adversary, if he so chose. Anyway, she would prefer him to be an admiring slave rather than an antagonist, although so far that didn't seem to be working out quite as she had planned.

'Of course it's all right—you do anything you like, my dear chap. Absolutely.' Giles sounded a little over-hearty in his reassurance, thought Daniel, and noted that Giles, Isobel and Lorna all seemed to be avoiding eye contact with each other. After Isobel left the theatre, Lorna had made a point of asking Daniel when he intended to start on her own portrait, and he'd replied, with an amused look that she found disconcerting, that any time out of his normal working hours would suit him. He would leave it to her to suggest one.

That evening, for the first time since his arrival, Daniel absented himself from supper and went off drinking with Mick and Joss. 'What's the local nightlife like?' he asked when he'd finished work for the day.

'There's the bar at the Drochatt Arms, that's not bad—or you could always go to the clubby with all the old choochters,' said Joss.

'What the hell are "choochters at the clubby" when they're at home?' asked Daniel.

Mick grinned. 'Joss fancies himself at picking up the local jargon,' he said. 'To the likes of you and me, mate, it's the Bowling Club at Blairalder with all the old fogies like Bruce and Angus Johnstone, and that old windbag McMichael who's on the committee.'

In the end the three of them went to the Drochatt Arms where they all consumed a great deal of beer and whisky. Mick had suggested Daniel should take his accordion along with him and his playing was greatly appreciated. As they staggered out to the car park, singing, none of them in any fit state to drive, Daniel thought he hadn't been so drunk for ages and next morning had a hangover to prove it, though Mick and Joss seemed quite unaffected. The throbbing in Daniel's head helped to block out other feelings. Lorna also took herself out for the evening and went to see her friend Daphne Crawford again, with whom she enjoyed discussing herbal remedies and the shortcomings of her sister.

Isobel thought the words 'Daphne says' were beginning to crop up with tedious frequency in Lorna's conversation, but it now transpired that Grizelda Murray belonged to the same meditation group as Daphne and would also be having supper at her house that night. Up to now, Isobel had deliberately avoided introducing Lorna and Grizelda because she trembled to think what might happen if they started swapping remedies, but the image of the three of them together brought the weird sisters in *Macbeth* irresistibly to mind. 'I suppose Dismal Daphers will be the self-appointed head witch, but I bet their cauldrons will be bubbling away like mad tonight, casting spells on us all,' she predicted darkly. It amused Isobel that Grizelda and Lorna were so totally convinced of the success of their pet panaceas, though there the similarity between the two women ended. Lorna, blessed from birth with a gold-plated constitution, now gave the credit for her radiant health to the mineral supplements with which, since she had renewed her friendship with Daphne, she had started fortifying herself, conveniently forgetting the healthy years she had enjoyed previously. Grizelda, on the other hand, while happily in thrall to an ever-changing variety of interesting ailments, remained equally certain that her cure of the moment was proving amazingly efficacious despite what her sceptical friends considered evidence to the contrary. One morning she had forced Isobel to sample her latest discovery, a noxious-tasting tea made from a mix of herbs, pumpkin seeds and the pulverised bark of monkey puzzle trees instead of the coffee Grizelda eschewed. Despite the reassuring information on the label that the brew was guaranteed to contain no arsenic, Isobel had expected to have her socks blown off, so alarming was the taste. Grizelda had tried to persuade her that this life-enhancing beverage would transform the quality of Edward's life, if only Isobel would allow him to try it.

'It doesn't seem to be doing *you* much good,' Isobel had been goaded into saying, to which Grizelda unanswerably replied, 'But you don't know how much worse I might be without it.'

Though relieved that Lorna was meeting friends, Isobel had tried to pretend to herself that she did not miss Daniel's presence. Despite the amnesty with Giles she felt an unwelcome twinge of disappointment when Joss, chatting away while he made a chicken casserole, had told her Daniel would be joining Mick and himself for a night out and would therefore not be in for dinner after all.

'Well, it seems our visitors have deserted us.' Giles had stretched out his long legs in front of the fire that was still necessary in the evenings and smiled at her winningly. 'Just the two of us for once, isn't this good, darling?' A few weeks earlier Isobel would have agreed with him wholeheartedly.

Stay away from the cliff edge, she warned herself sternly.

A few days later Lorna, finding Edward standing outside the hen-run one evening, nose uncomfortably pressed against the wire netting, decided to take a hand in his education. 'What is it you want, Edward?'

'The heh . . .'

'The what?'

'The chi . . .' said Edward who, if he wasn't talking in his own peculiar code, often refused to complete words.

'Do you mean the chickens?'

Edward nodded.

'Then say so. Say please, Aunt Lorna, can I go in and see the chickens.'

Silence. 'Edward? I shan't let you in unless you ask me properly.' She had often heard Isobel making similar conditions, but to Edward Lorna's voice held more than a hint of menace and he started to walk away without even looking at her.

Lorna tried another tack. 'If I help you, Edward, would you like to open the door yourself?'

Edward looked round cautiously. He was absolutely forbidden to fiddle with the fastening on the door. 'Not allowed,' he muttered.

'You are if I say so,' said Lorna firmly. 'Would you like to learn to do it? I'm sure you could manage it and I'll help you. It'll be quite all right, I promise.'

Edward brightened up at once.

'Say yes, please, Aunt Lorna, then.'

Though Edward's eyes sparkled he wasn't going to let the spider lady have everything her own way. 'Plea . . .' he mumbled through his thumb.

Lorna decided to let this go. 'Look. First you take hold of the bolt and push this bit up like this. Now you do that.' After several attempts Edward managed it. 'Now with that bit sticking out towards you, slide the whole thing back.' They practised several times. 'There now,' said Lorna. 'It's easy, really. I knew you could do it. Now push the door open.'

Edward hesitated. 'Tell Mum?' he asked.

'Not yet,' answered Lorna. 'It'll be our special secret. Tomorrow we'll try shutting the door, then we'll practise some more and it will be a lovely surprise for Mummy and Daddy.' She allowed herself a fantasy in which Isobel looked first disbelieving, then put out, but Giles gazed at Lorna in wondering admiration as she proved she had been able to teach Edward a new skill. 'It was really nothing . . . it just took a little patience and perseverance,' she would say modestly.

Over the next few days, under her secret tuition, Edward managed to open and close the door—not always, but often. Lorna hadn't quite bargained for his unpredictability—there were many moments when her patience and perseverance were tried to the limit and she felt like screaming at her nephew—but on the whole she was pleased with their progress. She managed not to let her irritation with him show sufficiently to scare him off, but had to admit to herself that she would not voluntarily want to try teaching him anything again. Lorna felt a grudging admiration for her sister who coped with the undoubted irritations of dealing with Edward and still managed to be amused by him. It was an admiration, however, which Lorna kept sternly under control. Analysing her own motives was not one of her hobbies, though she spent a lot of time suspecting those of other people.

Somewhat to her surprise, Edward appeared to have no difficulty in keeping the secret of their assignations. She had been afraid he might spoil the surprise by blurting it out to Joss or Amy, if not to his parents, but as far as she knew he had told no one.

Daniel, passing the chicken run one day and seeing Lorna and Edward in there together, wondered if he had maligned Lorna. Perhaps she was not as self-centred a character as he had thought? He must keep an open mind, he thought, and promised himself he'd start on her portrait at the weekend. He longed to ask Isobel for another sitting, but avoided doing so, hoping she might suggest it herself.

For her part Isobel tried to carry on with life as normal and thrust away any treacherous, encroaching thoughts. Giles appeared to be his usual affectionate self, and if he and Lorna found rather a lot of time to play duets together in the evenings, Isobel told herself it was petty and churlish to feel resentment, especially when she had so many of the things that her sister longed for and lacked.

Everyone was looking forward to seeing the Forbeses at the weekend. They had been persuaded to extend their visit and spend the night as well as the day at Glendrochatt. Alistair and Giles intended to play some golf, Isobel was looking forward to gossiping with Flavia and in the evening Giles thought they would test the acoustics in the theatre with an impromptu concert of light-hearted music.

Partly so that they could meet the Forbeses, who were old acquaintances, and partly to provide an audience, Isobel and Giles had asked the Fortescues and Murrays to dinner on Saturday night. Flavia would of course provide the star attraction for the concert—with Lorna as accompanist—but Giles and Amy, who had been practising madly for the occasion, would perform too; they hoped Alistair, a gifted amateur pianist, and Alistair's son, Ben, who played the trumpet, might then be prevailed on to play some jazz with Flavia—one of those lucky performers able to switch from her classical repertoire to wild improvisation—and anyone else who cared to take part. Isobel had hoped Daniel would join in with his squeeze-box, but Daniel suddenly announced that he would be going away for a few days. He neither offered any explanation nor volunteered information about his prospective whereabouts. Isobel felt absurdly disappointed. 'I do think it's a bit casual,' she complained to Giles. 'He might at least have let me know sooner—what with all the meals to be thought of and the Forbeses coming and everything. And suppose we want to get hold of him urgently?'

Giles raised his eyebrows. 'Daniel's perfectly entitled to go away,' he said reasonably. 'He always told us that he'd have to fit other things in while he was working for us. Anyway, what could we possibly want him for urgently? And since when have you ever been fazed by unexpected numbers for meals I'd like to know?'

Isobel was annoyed to find herself flushing. Giles gave her a penetrating look. 'You sound like Lorna does when there's a change of plan—you must be more alike than I realised,' he said, deliberately provocative.

'Well, that should suit you just fine then,' Isobel retorted, rising to the bait, then feeling furious with herself.

'So you really *are* miffed about Daniel.' Giles was triumphant at scoring a bull's-eye, but he did not look pleased that Isobel should be so put out.

No more was said, and Isobel was careful not to bring up the subject again. Everyone hoped that the chilly grey spell of weather might improve before the weekend.

Eighteen

The weather at the weekend proved to be perfect.

After the dismal chill of the last week, the sun blazed in a cloudless sky and on Saturday morning, as Isobel took Flapper for an early-morning run while Amy did her practice with Giles, the garden and its surrounding woods had been transformed into a medieval pageant of colour.

A pair of red squirrels, skiddering up a tree, tantalisingly out of Flapper's range, reminded Isobel that she wanted Daniel to include one in his painting—a sign to future generations that the indigenous reds were still to be found in Perthshire pre the millennium, despite the recent unwelcome appearance of grey squirrels north of the Tay. She could hear a roe deer barking somewhere above her.

At about midday the Forbes family arrived, with much tooting of horns as they drove up to the house.

'Fantastic to see you again,' said Isobel exchanging hugs with Flavia and Alistair. 'Hi Ben. Great to see you too.' Ben, whose own mother had died when he was nine, was Alistair's son by his first marriage. At fifteen he was already slightly taller than his father, with feet that foretold more height still to come. He had the loosely threaded look some boys get while going through a phase of rapid growth, as though he might come unstrung at any moment and shed an arm or a leg.

'How many other people do you expect to get inside your trousers with you—or have you borrowed them from a Sumo wrestler?' asked Isobel, gazing at the incredibly voluminous jeans in which Ben's thin frame appeared lost. 'You look like Charlie Chaplin.'

'Oh, *Mummy*!' Amy was mortified by her mother's lack of fashion know-how. 'Can't you see they're *"Baggies"*?'

Ben grinned. 'Cool, aren't they?' he asked. 'Dad hates them— "not what we wore in the SAS", are they, Dad? Glad someone appreciates them, though.' Ben nodded approvingly at Amy, who blushed scarlet with pleasure.

'I think they're perfectly frightful,' agreed Alistair equably. 'I keep hoping he'll grow out of them—mentally rather than physically, that is.'

'I must see my god-daughter. Where is she?' asked Isobel, peering through the car window, then: 'Goodness! Has Flavia had anything at all to do with that child, Alistair? It's ridiculous—she looks more like you than ever.'

Dulcie Forbes, named after the eminent pianist who had been Flavia's godmother, benefactress and a huge influence on her life and career, was sitting in her car seat at the back. She had a mop of red curls and gazed at the world through the piercing, rather fierce-looking blue eyes that her father and brother also shared. Alistair laughed. 'Oh, don't be deceived by appearances, there's plenty of Flavia in Dulcie too. She's got all her mother's temperament—a performer if ever there was one.'

'Well, thanks,' said Flavia, pulling a face at her husband. 'I must admit she runs rings round me, though—she's an absolute tiger, we have the most frightful battles. Ben and Alistair are the only people who can cope with her at all. She's even got my mother stitched up. Imagine that! Do get her out, Ben—with any luck she mightn't scream if you do it.'

Ben, who was clearly his small half-sister's devoted slave, unstrapped her and set her down carefully on the gravel.

'Oh isn't she just *adorable?*' Lorna, who had come to join them, swooped down intending to pick Dulcie up.

Dulcie scowled at her, her small hand gesturing dismissal like a royal wave in reverse. 'Away, away. Back, lady, back,' she commanded imperiously. Everyone laughed but the expression on Lorna's face made Isobel's heart bleed—Lorna had gauged her approach wrongly yet again and been made to feel a fool. It was such a tiny incident—most people would not have minded a rebuff from so small a child—but Isobel knew that Lorna would be mortified. Amy smothered a giggle and Isobel shot her a quelling look.

'Oh, dear, I'm sorry, Lorna,' said Flavia, not sounding at all concerned. 'Dulcie's developed this awful glare lately, like a particularly nasty gargoyle. Take no notice of her. She'll be all over you if she thinks you're not interested.'

'Dulcie go with boy,' Dulcie announced, suddenly turning her blue gaze on Edward, who as usual was standing on the sidelines watching everyone else.

Isobel nodded encouragingly at Edward. 'Take her hand, darling,' she said. '*That's right*, help her up the steps. Well done. You go with them Amy—get Joss to give Dulcie some juice if she wants it and find the old box of toys in the nursery.' As Isobel saw the look of pride on Edward's face, she felt as if her small god-daughter had given her a marvellous, unexpected present.

'Can we let our dogs out?' asked Ben. 'Will yours mind?'

'Lord, no. Flapper's the original sycophant and Wotan doesn't actually know he's a dog—despite his German origins he thinks he's a member of the Scottish aristocracy and has lairdish notions of his own importance. But don't worry, he practises condescending manners to lesser mortals. Oh, I remember Wellington of old, but who's the newcomer?'

Wellington was the huge black mongrel, rumoured to be a St Bernard crossed with Aberdeen Angus, who had been Ben's inseparable companion since he was a small boy. During her short but disastrous marriage to the headmaster of Ben's prep school, Flavia had looked after Wellington for a spell and claimed that he'd had a considerable paw in getting her and Alistair together.

Alistair rolled his eyes as a squirming ball of energy, covered in wire wool, hurled itself out of the car and started rushing round in circles, churning up the gravel and barking madly. 'This is my wife's latest folly,' he said. 'So practical to embark on another puppy when you live in London and are frequently away on tour yourself. We're going to have to employ two nannies now: one for Dulcie and one for Flavia's dog.'

'What rubbish,' said Flavia. 'You know you love him just as much as I do. Battersea Dogs Home's very best—name of Brillo. Isn't he heaven, Izzy?'

'If that's your idea of it,' laughed Isobel. 'They say we all get the heaven we deserve. Can we leave him to hurroosh about out here, though? Giles will go spare if he comes in the house and puddles everywhere, won't you, darling?'

'Dulcie makes more puddles than Brillo.'

'I'm prepared to take a risk with Dulcie, but it's my golden rule: no visiting dogs allowed inside,' said Giles firmly. 'He won't come to any harm here unless he's learnt how to cross cattle grids. Come on, now, I want to show you the revamped theatre. Have you brought your flute, Flavia?'

'Of course. We've brought everything you can think of: flutes, golf clubs, fishing rods, twenty-five spare pairs of knickers for Dulcie, dog food—it was like equipping an army for a long campaign. Alistair loved packing up the car, though—didn't you, darling?—made him feel all military again.' After a distinguished career in the army, Alistair was now a partner in a firm specialising in security.

Despite the disapproval Flavia's defection from her first husband had caused, and many dark forebodings that her passionate affair with Alistair wouldn't last, Isobel could see that, behind the teasing, the Forbeses were as much in love as ever. It was lovely to

be with them—that's how Giles and I have always been, she reminded herself, and felt forlorn.

Ben, who clearly didn't trust Amy and Edward to look after
his little sister, followed the children into the house while the
others walked down to the theatre. Alistair had never seen it before but Flavia had performed there several times. 'But it's totally
transformed!' she said. 'How brilliant to give it such a facelift and
still keep its charm. Oh, and *wow!* Just look at this!' She gazed at
the half-finished backcloth in admiration. 'It's Glendrochatt in all
its aspects. Fantastic. Who's doing it?'

Giles explained about Daniel. 'Sadly he's away at the moment.
I'd have liked you both to meet him, but I think you'll just miss
him. He said he might be back tomorrow evening but he's a bit
of a law unto himself. Interesting chap.'

After a full tour of all the alterations and improvements, about
which the Forbeses were gratifyingly enthusiastic, they all had an
early lunch before Giles took Alistair and Ben off to play golf.
Amy, who had conceived a tremendous crush on Ben, was put
out at not being invited on this all-male outing, until Joss suggested that he and Mick might take them to the safari park at
Inverbeith. 'All the world and his wife will be there on a fine
Saturday afternoon,' warned Isobel, 'but Edward does adore it—
if you can face it.'

'No worries,' said Mick. 'We'll pick the kids up at two, then
you and Flavia can have a peaceful afternoon. See ya' and he went
off whistling.

'Can we take Dulcie too?' asked Amy, brightening up; she had
put on a bored, grown-up face to indicate to Ben that she was
really too old for such babyish amusements as safari parks, though
secretly she always enjoyed it.

'Oh, yes, do take her,' said Flavia.

'Perhaps I ought to go too, then?' said Lorna. 'I hardly think
Joss and Mick should take Dulcie on their own.'

'Why ever not?' demanded Amy, who realised that her aunt's
presence would be guaranteed to ruin any outing.

'It wouldn't be suitable,' said Lorna primly.

'Oh, come off it, Lorna. Joss is brilliant with small children,' said Isobel.

Lorna raised her eyebrows and gave a disapproving little shrug. 'Well, I wouldn't allow it myself—but then it's not up to me. Anyway, I have a date with Daphne this afternoon, so it wouldn't really have been at all convenient. I just thought I'd better offer . . .'

Isobel felt intensely irritated by Lorna's look of huffy martyr- dom, but decided this was not the moment to have something out with her sister that had been hanging in the air for some time. It was not the first time Lorna had made veiled but un- pleasant insinuations about Joss and Mick doing things for the children. 'Would Dulcie be prepared to go without you, Flavia?' she asked.

'Heavens, yes. She has a strong preference for male company,' said Flavia easily. 'She only wants me when she's ill—which luck- ily is practically never. She'd love it. I brought her buggy, so they can push her round in that, if they don't mind coping with her. She'll probably frighten all the animals into fits.'

'We'll take ourselves off, then. See you all later—have fun,' said Giles, noticing but not reacting to the tension between his wife and his sister-in-law.

*W*hile Isobel put on the kettle to make coffee, Flavia made polite enquiries about Lorna's life. 'I gather you're being marvel- lous in getting the centre started,' she said. 'What will you do once it's up and running? Will you stay in Scotland?' This was a question Isobel had longed to ask herself but had so far not dared to broach.

'I may join two friends of mine in an alternative therapy clinic—the ones I'm going to see this afternoon—and run the business side for them,' Lorna was pleased at the surprise on her sister's face. 'They've asked me to go in with them.' This was news to Isobel: good news insofar as it indicated that Lorna was planning a future away from Glendrochatt, not such good news in that she clearly intended to stay within close range.

Some demon made Isobel say, 'You mean Dismal Daphers has offered you a job? Rather you than me.'

'She'd hardly be likely to offer you one since you're not qualified in any way,' said Lorna, crushing Isobel underfoot like a beetle. She added to Flavia, 'Daphne feels this is the way health care will go in the future. I wouldn't be directly involved with the therapy side of things but I'd love to help with the organisation. She and Ruby McQueen have got a marvellous set-up going.'

'Oh, I know the place,' said Flavia. 'I think Aunt Liz goes there to have her back tweaked. Daphne's a brilliant chiropractor. I thought her partner was called *Susan* McQueen though?'

'She says she's never felt comfortable with the name Susan,' Lorna told her. 'She wants to be called Ruby now.'

'Goodness,' said Flavia, 'why does she suddenly feel comfortable as a Ruby one wonders?' Lorna had wondered this herself, but wasn't going to admit it to the likes of Flavia.

'Ruby's what Giles calls a TDD name,' said Isobel.

'What on earth's a TDD name?' asked Flavia.

'Tarts, Dowagers or Dogs.'

Lorna gave her sister a quelling look.

'Wasn't she *christened* Ruby, then?' asked Amy with interest.

'I've no idea,' Lorna answered coldly.

'I don't suppose she was actually *christened* at all,' said Isobel. 'I expect she and Dismal invented a deeply significant vegan ceremony of their own, with stones and shells and blessings from Gaea the Earth Mother; extra virgin olive oil from Sainsbury's for the anointing, of course, and pure spring water from a sacred site— ready bottled by some entrepreneurial company and widely available at major health food stores.'

'What about a robe?' asked Amy. 'Smelly old goatskins?'

'Vegans wouldn't have goatskins,' objected Flavia. 'Not unless the goats were known to have died from natural causes and one wouldn't fancy that much. More likely hand-woven hemp, coloured with their own veggie dyes.'

'Poor Ruby. Bit scratchy.' Amy giggled.

'Ruby made Grizelda Murray have a special ceremony before her hysterectomy to say farewell to her uterus,' said Isobel. 'A healing ritual.'

'You're not serious?'

'I promise you. Grizelda invited me and Fiona, but we didn't dare go together because we knew we'd laugh too much and spoil it, so we tossed for it and Fee won.'

'Mum!' Amy was riveted. 'That's spooky. You never told me. Wish you'd gone.'

Lorna got up. 'I can see you think you're screamingly funny,' she said. 'But I really must get going to Edinburgh or Daphne will wonder where I've go to. I'll leave you to it' and she swept out of the room, leaving her coffee untouched.

'Oh, dear,' said Isobel. 'That was rather awful of me, to tease her so much—I suppose I'd better go after her and apologise.'

'Oh, for goodness sake,' said Flavia, 'she shouldn't take herself so seriously.'

'She always has. That's what's so difficult about Lorna. The maddening thing is that I'm interested in complementary medicine myself—though I wish people wouldn't call it *alternative*, as if one couldn't have the orthodox kind as well—but Grizelda and some of her chums are so fanatical they put one off—and I can't resist baiting them.'

'Grizelda's always been wildly tiresome. No wonder poor old Frank drives about on dipped headlights, like a glow-worm without the glow,' said Flavia. 'What's her latest food fad?'

Isobel giggled. 'It varies, but her food's always disgusting whatever it is. She gave the children what she said were quorn fritters the other day—she didn't think it at all funny when I asked if they were made from fox—and when we went for Sunday lunch the other day she produced the most terrible overcooked chicken you've ever seen. Giles said it was like a very old tart lying on its back with a flabby white breast and its legs falling open.'

*A*fter they had waved off the expedition to the safari park Isobel and Flavia went for a walk along the loch. Bluebells were out in the woods above them and birch trees trailed silver fingers in the water. The sun pretended it was looking down at the Mediterranean.

'Shall we take Brillo?' asked Isobel. 'Flapper's sure to swim so I hope you don't mind if he gets wet too.'

'I think Alistair must have taken our dogs with him,' Flavia replied, looking around vaguely. 'They don't seem to be about and Wellington's always glued to Ben. Let's go.'

Privately Isobel didn't think the Blairalder golf club would be all that entranced with Brillo, but she reckoned Alistair could be counted on to keep control.

'How's Amy's music?' asked Flavia. 'I'm looking forward to hearing her play when we have some music making this evening. Giles says she's really talented.'

'Yes, I think she is, but it worries me sometimes that Giles pushes her so hard. We're hoping she'll get a music scholarship next year, but I dread to think what Giles will do if she goes away to school.'

'Might be a good thing,' said Flavia. 'My mother was far too involved with my career. She wanted me to fulfil all her own thwarted ambitions. It fact, it nearly ruined everything for both of us.'

'Do talk to him if you get a chance,' Isobel begged. 'You might be able to say things I no longer can. It's become rather a touchy subject between us. At the next Bank Holiday weekend he and Amy are going to go to a workshop and orchestral weekend in Northumberland for parents and children. I'm going too, for once, because Giles wants me to hear a young cellist who's giving a concert in Newcastle the night after. Should be fun.'

It was so hot that before they had walked very far they flopped down by the water's edge, kicked off their shoes and dabbled their feet in the icy water while they gossiped. There was much catching up to do.

'Now you've got Dulcie, do you find it difficult to cope with your concerts?' asked Isobel.

'It's a bit hairy sometimes. Luckily I've got wonderful help, but I do get torn. I hate going abroad now. But after I was ill for that year and dropped out of the musical scene I had to work so hard to get my career back on course—and then there was all the drama of my marriage to Gervaise busting up—that I don't want to let it go just when it's taken off again. It's great having found Megan Davies. I love playing with her, and flute and harp are a great combination. I think you'll enjoy our performance together—hope so, anyway. Oh, I do feel so blessed, Izz, now I've got Alistair and Dulcie, and my music too—more than I deserve.'

'Do you still feel guilty about leaving Gervaise?'

'I feel guilty for having *married* him. I should never, never have done that, but Alistair and I are so blissful together, it has to be right. I'd die if anything happened to Alistair.'

'Did Gervaise ever marry that matron at the school? I know you hoped he would.' Isobel knew all about Flavia's first marriage and wanted an update.

'Oh, dear, poor Meg. Not so far. Gervaise is a lovely man, but he's an awful old slow top. I think marrying me must have been the only wild impulse he ever had in his life—and a disastrous one at that. Meg ought to leave Winsleyhurst and give him a shock, that might galvanise him into action. I *do* feel bad about her, but I only hear news of them through Mum and Dad. I'm not exactly flavour of the month at Winsleyhurst.'

Flavia's father was headmaster of the boys' public school Ben now attended and to which Gervaise Henderson's prep school, Winsleyhurst, sent most of its boys.

'Ben seems fine now,' suggested Isobel.

'Yes—that's great again. We had a tricky patch with him when Alistair and I first lived together, but Dulcie's arrival has helped, and I'm careful to see that he and Alistair have time together without me—they've always been so close. But what about you, Izz? It must be a real pain having Lorna around all the time.'

Isobel carefully selected a flat stone suitable for ducks-and-drakes and sent it skimming across the surface of the loch. 'I dreaded her coming but it's even worse than I thought. She's in love with Giles, you see, and . . .' Isobel's voice suddenly became choked.

Flavia shot her an anxious look. 'But surely Giles isn't interested in her?'

'I'm not sure. I think he may be.'

'Rubbish,' said Flavia bracingly, though her heart sank; she thought she had detected uneasy undercurrents between Giles and Isobel but had hoped she was wrong. 'Giles has always been an awful old flirt,' she said. 'It's part of his charm, but no one ever doubts that he adores you. You're his linchpin, Izz.'

'It can get a bit exhausting being a linchpin. Perhaps like Meg I ought to give him a shock. I might just do that.' Isobel sent a second stone across the water.

'Oh, Izzy, don't take risks. It's too important.'

'You're a fine one to talk.'

'No.' Flavia shook her head emphatically. 'I got something terribly wrong, I didn't take a risk with what was right. That's different. And don't tell me you've fallen for someone else? I wouldn't believe you.'

'N-no. Not exactly.' Isobel sounded a little uncertain, Flavia thought, and looked as if she might have said more but had suddenly changed her mind.

'Oh, well, all marriages have their ups and downs I suppose,' Flavia said lightly, dying of curiosity but not liking to probe. With hindsight, it struck her that Daniel Hoffman's name seemed to have cropped up rather a lot in their conversation that afternoon, but then the new painting was a very exciting project and one that Giles was clearly thrilled about too.

Isobel got up and slipped her feet into her shoes again. She said, 'Well, it sure as hell doesn't help our marriage having Lorna breathing down our necks, that's for certain. Come on, let's wander back. The children will be home soon.'

The trip to the safari park was a great success. Edward had been in seventh heaven, Amy had quite forgotten that it wasn't cool to be enthusiastic about such a childish expedition, Dulcie had apparently nodded off and had a refreshing nap in her buggy, and they'd all stuffed themselves with ices and Coke. Mick and Joss said a good time had been had by everyone including themselves.

'Well, you're a pair of angels,' said Isobel.

'Any time. No problems.' The angels sloped off back to their own house.

'What an unlikely pair of nannies. They're heaven,' said Flavia. 'I'd pinch them off you any day.'

'Don't you dare!'

After Isobel and Flavia had given the children tea, Isobel suggested that Dulcie might like to feed the hens and see if their were any eggs to collect.

Amy groaned. 'Do I *have* to go too?' she asked. 'I'm fed up with the chickens.'

'Oh, please, darling. I know it's a bore, but just go and do the door for Ed and make sure the hens don't get out. I'm only going to put the plates in the dishwasher and then we'll come along too. I swear I won't be long.'

'Don't they look sweet together?' said Flavia watching as the three children went off down the path, Dulcie in the middle holding Amy's and Edward's hands. 'How wonderfully Edward has come on since I last saw him, Izz. Amy's very good with him, isn't she? Must be quite hard for her as she gets older, though.'

'I know,' said Isobel. 'I sometimes wonder if I expect too much of her.'

At that moment a white-faced Amy came hurtling back into the kitchen, so out of breath she could hardly get her words out. 'Mum, come quick,' she gasped. 'Something terrible's happened. The hens are all dead.'

Nineteen

A terrible scene of slaughter met the eyes of Isobel and Flavia as they dashed out to the hen-run, the door of *which* swung ominously open. There were feathers and blood everywhere.

Dulcie was standing alone in the path, happily crooning to herself and stroking the lifeless body of one of the Pekin bantams. 'Lubbly fedders, Mummy,' she said brightly, beaming at her mother. 'Dulcie take them home.'

'Ed? Ed? Where are you, darling?' Isobel rushed to the hen house in the middle of the run. Just outside it the mangled corpse of Pecker—best-beloved of the pair of swaggering, parade-ground-shouting cocks—lay at her feet. Summer guests at Glendrochatt, unlucky enough to be allocated a bedroom on the west side of the house who had been roused at dawn by Pecker's remorseless reveille, had frequently begged Giles and Isobel: 'For God's sake ring that bloody cockerel's neck.' Now, had it been possible, Isobel would gladly have given him the kiss of life.

She wrenched open the hen house door—but there was no sign of Edward. 'Amy, where's Edward?' she asked urgently.

'I don't know,' wailed Amy. 'I left him here with Dulcie—I thought I'd better come and get you quick. Oh, Mum, Ed's hens!' Amy could hardly speak. Tears poured down her face. 'I should have stayed with him. I didn't know what to do.'

'No, no, you did just right. Of course you had to come for me' Isobel tried to sound calm. 'But think, Amy. Where will he have gone?'

'To the castle?'

'Good idea. You scoot down there quick and if you find Ed for heaven's sake shout—but stay with him. I'll search the bushes here first, then I'll ring Mick and Joss. I'll come on down to you.' Amy flew off.

Flavia squatted down by Dulcie and tried unsuccessfully to re-move the body from her daughter's vice-like grip. 'Dulcie, do you know where Edward went—the big boy?'

'Boy gone,' said Dulcie, clutching the lifeless bantam to her chest, the spark of battle in her eye.

'Which way did he go? Show Mummy like a clever girl—point where he went,' coaxed Flavia.

But Dulcie wasn't going to be fooled into letting go of her prey. 'Boy just runned,' she said firmly.

'He'll have gone to ground somewhere,' Isobel moaned. 'But he'll be in a terrible state.'

They hunted through the shrubs, calling reassuringly all the time, but to no avail. A squawking from one of the rhododen-drons at least proved that not all the hens had been massacred: a few of them—mostly minus tail feathers—were sitting glumly in the branches of various bushes.

'I can't understand how they could have got out,' said Isobel, as they searched for Edward in the outbuildings where rolls of spare wire netting and the hens' corn were kept. 'No one ever leaves the door of the run open, in case of foxes or stray dogs. That's why Edward's never allowed to go in by himself . . . oh, shush! Listen!'

There were shouts of 'Mumm-ee! Mumm-ee! I've found him!' and it was with huge relief that they heard Amy's voice yelling from the direction of the children's play area below the front of the house.

'You go on quick,' said Flavia and Isobel was off like a bullet, leaving Flavia and Dulcie to follow. At the mention of stray dogs a terrible suspicion had occurred to Flavia. The hen house was raised slightly off the ground. Flavia got down on all fours and peered underneath; the smell of rotting cabbage was over-powering, but she could see something else, which made her fear the worst. She put her arm in and touched a cold nose. With a sinking heart she felt for a collar and, after getting a stranglehold on it and tugging hard, eventually managed to drag out a filthy and resisting puppy, round whose mouth tell-tale feathers, adhering to clotted blood, looked like a grizzled beard and gave him an unnerving resemblance to Lord Dunbarnock. Brillo had clearly not been part of the golfing expedition after all. He looked strangely swollen, like a python that has swallowed a pig and set-tled down to do some serious digesting.

'Brillo likes fedders too,' said Dulcie beadily.

Flavia sat in the hen-run, contemplating dog and daughter with disfavour. A wrestling match ensued as she tried to hang on to the struggling puppy while wrenching the remains of one of his victims away from Dulcie. By the time she had dragged them both back to the house, respectively yelping and screaming, she felt as if she'd taken part in the London Marathon. Edward was crouched in a corner of the wooden castle, curled up in a tight little ball, his arms over his head.

'Oh, Mum, he won't even speak to me,' said Amy, much ag-itated.

Isobel wound herself round Edward and rocked him to and fro. Edward, who hardly ever cried, was shaking with sobs. Isobel thought *wryly* that perhaps she ought to be pleased: it had been one of the many worries when he was little that he seemed unable to cry like a normal baby. He had often mewed continuously like a sick kitten—fourteen hours non-stop had been one of the worst records—but never bawled or screamed. At one time Isobel had wondered if he could actually feel pain at all. She remembered Edward at two—exactly Dulcie's age now, she thought, making sad comparisons—falling out of his high chair and hitting the floor with a tremendous thwack, and not reacting at all. Showing emotion still came hard to him, which made his delighted laughter special, an unsolicited gesture of affection a jewel, his tears a terrible torment. Knowing how difficult he found physical contact, she had been thrilled earlier in the day that he had voluntarily taken Dulcie's hand—another reminder of what huge milestones the simplest things could be: things which in a normal child would seem insignificant.

'It's all right, darling, it's *all right*,' she whispered over and over again. She knew it was no good questioning him while he was in this state. Amy hovered anxiously.

Gradually the sobs subsided. 'Was it my fault, was it my fault?' he whispered frantically, clutching at Isobel's arm.

'Of course not, darling,' she said reassuringly. She knew he would go on asking her the same question obsessively for days now.

'What will the spider lady say? Will she be angry?'

'Of course not,' said Isobel again. 'It's got nothing to do with her.'

Eventually they got him to his feet and led him back to the house. Isobel was in two minds as to whether to give him a precautionary shot of diazepam, but decided to watch him carefully and see how he was later on.

*T*he golfing party had returned to find Flavia, looking extremely hot and bothered, trying to shut Brillo in the back of the car while Dulcie enthusiastically carried on with her tantrum, legs going like piston rods, her small red shoes drumming a beat on the gravel that would have done credit to a student of African tribal dance.

'Oh, thank God you're all back. There've been awful disasters here and it's all my fault. Giles, you're never going to want me to stay again,' Flavia wailed. She told them what had happened. 'I really thought Brillo was with you. I'm just so sorry.'

'The hens are normally shut up—I'm sure you couldn't have

helped it.' Giles, whose social graces seldom deserted him, shot into the house.

Alistair put his arm round his wife. 'Cheer up, darling, don't look so dismal. They did say it was safe to leave him loose and we'll buy Edward lots of new bantams as a small atonement. I'm afraid I never thought of taking Brillo with us—he'd have been an awful liability on a golf course.' He refrained from saying that it was Flavia who had insisted on bringing him to Glendrochatt at all. 'Ben, do go and forage around, and see if you can get hold of some old newspapers to protect the back of the car. That puppy looks as if it might have the most appalling explosion.' Ben grinned and went off to see what he could find.

Alistair turned his attention to his daughter. 'Dulcie, stop that noise *this minute* or you'll go straight to bed with no story,' he said sternly. Amazingly, Dulcie stopped as suddenly as though a burglar alarm had been switched off. She gave her father a radiant smile and held up her arms for him to pick her up.

'She is the absolute limit,' said Flavia indignantly. 'Why doesn't she do that for me?'

'Because she knows I mean business and you don't. You either laugh or lose your temper—two equally gratifying reactions.' He gave his wife an amused and loving look. 'Come on, buck up, darling, we'd better go and face the family and see how Edward is.'

*G*iles found his family in the kitchen sitting on the sofa. Edward was wedged between his mother and his twin, thumb plugged in mouth, while they struggled to make some sense for him of the loss of his beloved hens. Amy had rashly told him that the hens were no longer inside the mangled bodies he had seen with such horror, but had gone to heaven.

'But can I go and see them?' Edward asked.

'No, I'm afraid you can't because it's too far and we don't know the way there,' said Isobel firmly. She had learnt that explanations needed to be short and unequivocal. Edward's grip on abstract ideas was tenuous at the best of times: he was bothered that people did not exist if he couldn't see them. Where, for instance, were Isobel, Giles and Amy when Edward was at school, or Joss and Mick when not at Glendrochatt? Edward appeared to have no idea. Ronald Knox's limerick querying whether 'a tree as a tree, simply ceases to be, if no one's about in the Quad' might have been written for Edward; it was certainly no good embarking on discussions on life's great mysteries with him. If forced to look at his watch—a gadget he hated—he could accurately read the hour, but had no idea how to apply this skill to his life; no conception, yet, of the meaning of time. It drove everybody crazy. Isobel hoped it would come to him in the end, as so many of the other things of which they had once despaired had done.

'Is he OK?' asked Giles.

Isobel nodded. 'I think so—so far.'

'That bloody dog! Whatever can have possessed you to allow Flavia to let it loose all day?' shouted Giles, relief at seeing Edward was all right making him aggressive with the wrong person.

'That's not fair! It was you just as much as me.' Isobel was outraged. 'But go on, Mr Marvellous, do blame someone else. What I want to know is how the hell the hens got out.' They glared at each other, pent-up emotion bubbling over.

Lorna arrived in the kitchen at the same moment as the Forbes family. She had seen the golfers return and the sight of Giles had, as usual, acted on her like a magnet. When she heard what had happened, Lorna felt furiously disappointed that her plan had gone so awry, rather than disturbed by the incident itself. She looked accusingly at Edward, who shrank back and clutched his head. 'Oh, Edward, you *have* let me down,' she said sharply. 'You managed that door perfectly well yesterday. Now you've completely spoilt our surprise for Mummy and Daddy. How could you be so stupid?' The moment the words were out she realised that she would have done much better to say nothing, but it was too late.

Edward made a strangled noise and disappeared under the table.

'What on earth are you talking about, Lorna?' asked Isobel, her voice dangerously quiet.

Lorna gave an exaggerated sigh. 'Only that I'd been planning to give you all a really nice surprise, that's all. Edward and I have been practising on that door for days. He can do it perfectly well—if he wants.'

'How dared you do that?' Isobel, white with fury, had never felt more angry. 'How could you, Lorna?'

'I might have guessed that nothing I did would be right for you,' said Lorna bitterly. 'You're obsessed with that child. No one else is allowed to try to help him, even Giles.'

There was complete silence from everyone. The ticking of the old-fashioned kitchen clock, which normally no one even noticed, seemed suddenly deafening.

Amy started to cry hysterically. The Forbes family looked acutely uncomfortable.

'Oh, come on, Lorna, I'm sure you meant to be really kind and it's bad luck about the hens—but that's certainly not true.' Giles looked uncomfortably from his wife to his sister-in-law.

'It is true,' said Lorna recklessly. 'You were complaining about it yourself only the other day.'

Giles got up. 'We're getting everything quite out of proportion. Let's all calm down.' He lifted the tablecloth and looked underneath. 'Edward, that's enough now. Come out from under there.' He bent down to move his son, but Edward, back arched, arms and legs jerking convulsively, could not hear him.

It was only a matter of moments before Isobel and Giles had checked that Edward's airways were clear, put him on his side and administered his diazepam. Isobel sat with him on the sofa, waiting for the convulsions to subside.

'Can we do anything useful?' asked Alistair.

'Not really, thanks all the same. Sorry about this,' said Giles, with an attempt at ease.

'Then we'll get out of your hair for the moment and go and put Dulcie to bed. Give us a shout if there's anything at all we can do—anything. Come on, Flavia. Ben, you come too.'

Alistair scooped up his daughter and firmly shepherded his family out of the kitchen. Flavia gave Isobel a quick hug as she followed her husband.

Lorna sat at the table with an expressionless face. She looked as cold and pointed as an icicle, but inside her emotions were in turmoil.

Amy, her face blotchy with tears, clutched at Giles's hand. He gave hers a reassuring squeeze, though he felt far from reassured himself. 'It's all right, Amy,' he said, his eyes on Isobel and Edward. They waited in silence.

'Will you carry Ed upstairs now please, Giles? I think the worst is over.' Isobel felt as though she were speaking from the other end of a tunnel. It was a surprise that when it came out, her voice actually sounded quite normal.

'Can I come too?' asked Amy.

Giles started to say yes, but Isobel said no. 'Not at the moment, darling, you can come up later. Please go and see if there's anything Flavia wants for Dulcie. Tell them we won't eat before eight at the very earliest, so there's no sort of hurry.' Amy looked from her father to her mother and hesitated. 'Please do as I ask Amy.' It was rare for Isobel to use that cold tone. Amy went, slamming the kitchen door behind her as hard as she could.

Giles picked up Edward, by now as floppy as a rag doll, Isobel opened the door and they headed upstairs. Despite being a dead weight, Edward's body felt so insubstantial in his arms—like a brittle bundle of bones—that it turned Giles's heart over. It would have been a very different matter to carry Amy, he thought.

When they reached Edward's room, Isobel went and pulled back the duvet and Giles laid Edward carefully on his bed. Together they managed to undress him and get him into his pyjamas. Then Isobel tucked the duvet round him and sat down on the edge of the bed. Her legs were shaking.

'Shall you call Dr Nichol?'

'I'll give him a quick ring and let him know, just to be on the safe side, though there's not much he can do now. It's lucky Ed's having his annual assessment with Dr Connor at school next week anyway. She'll be disappointed to hear about this,' said Isobel. There was silence between them.

Giles stood looking at her. 'Izz?' he began tentatively.

'Did you really complain about me to Lorna?' Isobel's voice sounded almost casual, so calm and flat a glass of water might have balanced on it with no drop spilled.

'It wasn't like that.'

'What was it like, then?'

Giles, guiltily aware that Lorna's insidious mix of admiration and commiseration often caused him to say far more to her than he intended, struggled between the wish to appease Isobel, a scrupulous desire for honesty—they had always tried to be honest with each other—but also, at some level, a longing to make her understand how deeply he minded what he thought of as his own failure to be of help to his difficult disappointment of a son. How could he explain to Isobel that Lorna made it so easy to confide in her that her sympathy was becoming an irresistible luxury? 'I suppose I may have mentioned something about it,' he admitted at last, but it didn't come out as he intended; it sounded defensive and sulky, even to his own ears.

'How dare you discuss me with Lorna,' she said, suddenly passionate again, the deceptive calm all gone. 'I can't bear that, Giles. I *won't* bear it.'

'Oh, come off it, I know very well you discuss all my shortcomings with Fee or Flavia if it suits you.' He meant to make a joke of it, but again it didn't sound like one—and the arrow struck home.

'Oh, so it's my *shortcomings* you talk about with Lorna? How loyal!' she flashed, infuriated by the truth of his words.

'Stop sounding such a bloody prig,' said Giles angrily. 'Think what it must be like for Lorna if she feels this whole episode is her fault when she genuinely wanted to do something helpful for Edward.'

'If you believe that you'll believe anything.'

Both of them, in their hurt and rage with each other, had momentarily forgotten the small figure in the bed. Edward, heavily sedated, started to snore, reminding his parents of why they were there.

Isobel suddenly felt deadly tired. 'Please go,' she said. 'I can't leave Edward yet and I really don't want to talk about it any more. Luckily Mick and Joss wanted to do some overtime, so Joss is coming to cook supper. I shan't be needed. Go down and cope with our guests. I'll sleep in here tonight. But you might ask Joss to come up and have a word with me.' To Giles this was the last straw: Joss is more use to Isobel over Edward than I am, he thought.

He turned on his heel and walked out without saying another word.

*A*my had been allowed to come in to visit her twin and Isobel had assured her that he would be all right.

Trying to put life back on a more comfortingly mundane level, she had told Amy what to wear for supper and how late she could stay up. 'Make yourself look respectable for once. There may not be enough hot water for you to have a bath before supper if all the Forbeses have had one, but do *wash*, darling. Come and show me when you're ready and I'll tie your hair up for you. And you can have a good sleep-in tomorrow. No early practice. Tell Dad I said so.'

'Won't you be able to hear us play, then?'

'Oh, Amy, sweetheart, I'm afraid not. I'm dreadfully disappointed too.'

'Mum?'

'Yes?'

'Are you still cross with Daddy? I hate it when you are.'

'No, of course not,' lied Isobel, a choky feeling in her throat

as Amy twined her arms round her neck. 'We just got a fright
and it made us both snappy.'

This was something Amy completely understood, so she allowed herself to be half convinced. 'But Mum?'

'Yes, Amy?'

'Aunt Lorna is a real pain, isn't she?'

'*Yes,*' said Isobel, hugging her daughter. 'Yes, darling, just between you and me I really think she is.'

Amy went off feeling much cheered up.

$\mathscr{L}$ ater, Flavia had poked her head round the door. Edward was
crashed out, making a noise like a simmering kettle. Isobel was
lying on the spare bed. A book was open on her knees but she
was not reading it. Flavia thought she looked awful.

'Giles says you want to stay with Edward but I wondered if
you'd let me sit with him while you go down and have dinner?
I promise I'd come for you if he even moved.'

'You're a love, but no, thank you. I'm pretty sure he won't
wake but if he does I'd rather be here. Joss is going to bring me
up a tray. The best thing you can do for me is to go and make
music in the theatre as planned—take everyone's mind off all this
and have fun. Chat up Neil Dunbarnock. Check that all our alterations to the building haven't ruined the acoustics or anything.
See what you really think of Amy's playing. Honest opinions,
please.'

'OK, if that's what you want. Look, I won't go on about it,
Izzy, but I am just *so* sorry for my part in all this. If it's any comfort
to you Brillo was frightfully sick in the car.'

'Well, I'll bet it wasn't you who cleared it up,' said Isobel,
laughing.

'No,' admitted Flavia, one of that lucky band of women for
whom other people always do things, 'it wasn't.'

'Well, we know now that it was Lorna's fault, not yours. Please don't let your visit be spoilt by this—I really couldn't bear that. Ed will be fine tomorrow, Mrs Johnstone's coming to help wash up and I had arranged for her to babysit for Dulcie and Edward so that Mick and Joss can come and hear you all play, but she needn't stay on now, as I've got to be here anyway.'

'You're a star. Luckily Dulcie practically never wakes.' As Flavia went downstairs, she thought that though Edward, thank goodness, might be fine, his parents had a problem with each other. She could not bring herself to like Lorna and yet, and yet . . . Flavia, who had always been the star in her own family, a spoilt younger sister herself, had been made to feel sorry for the older woman. As Alistair had pointed out when they were changing for dinner and she was angrily expounding on the awfulness of Lorna, it can't have been much of a picnic for her to grow up in the shadow of the attraction that Isobel, less talented, less beautiful, but much funnier and more loveable, undoubtedly possessed.

$\mathcal{F}$lavia had resolved to be nice to Lorna for the rest of the evening, but it had been a struggle. There was something so triumphant in the way Lorna acted as hostess in Isobel's absence, graciously greeting the Murrays and Fortescues—both of whom were actually more familiar with the house than she was herself—explaining that Edward was unwell and making Isobel's apologies; deferring so charmingly to Lord Dunbarnock, and immediately noticing that his glass had a thumb print on it and asking Joss to get him a clean one. Lord Dunbarnock looked quite bewitched by her, but Flavia did not think it was an accident that Joss had splashed grease on Lorna's aquamarine silk trousers when he was handing her the gravy boat.

Towards the end of dinner Fiona insisted on collecting Isobel's tray, so that she could report how Edward was before they all went down to the theatre.

Isobel was thrilled to see her. 'Oh, Fee, how lovely. I hoped you might come up. Is everything all right? I *hate* not being with you but I couldn't leave Ed—you do see? Are you having fun?' she asked.

'Not as much fun as if you were there too, but yes, we're fine. Poor you, what a bummer! Alistair's been telling me all your dramas over dinner—now there's a charmer for you, lucky Flavia. Scrummy food, Izz. You and Joss have excelled yourselves and Giles has produced marvellous wine as usual. Duncan's well away. I only hope he doesn't drop off to sleep and snore during the concert. Not much doubt about which of us will be driving home tonight. The children are having a ball too. My ma-in-law wouldn't come when she heard Flavia was staying with you—said she was far too busy.'

'Doing what?'

'Oh, I don't know. Probably something life-enhancing like polishing the chains on her evening bags.'

'How's worthy old Frank—scintillating for Scotland?'

Fiona giggled. 'You should have seen Flavia switch to automatic pilot while he told her exactly how his new wind-powered generator works in the lambing sheds, while he chomped his way through lamb noisettes. I don't believe she heard a single word—sonatas were floating above her head in a great big "thinks" bubble—but she fooled Frank into imagining she was utterly fascinated.'

'So tell what Grizelda's wearing?' Grizelda's clothes were a constant source of fascination to Fiona and Isobel. Could she really think them becoming? Did Frank find them attractive?

'The most extraordinary long, clingy garment—green, naturally, to tone with her politics, which makes her look like a prize cucumber—absolutely straight all the way down, except for two little pimples at the top indicating what Emily calls ENS—Erect Nipple Syndrome. Maybe she fancies Alistair too.'

Though she had succeeded in making Isobel laugh, Fiona gave her an anxious look. 'Why don't I stay with you, Izz, and let the others get on with the concert?' she urged. 'We could have a gorgeous gas.'

But Isobel wouldn't hear of it. 'Absolutely not. Giles and Amy will be dreadfully disappointed if you're not there. Besides, you're my spy. You can ring and tell me all about it tomorrow. Honestly, I'll be fine.'

'Shall I ask Giles to come up?'

'No, thanks. Just tell him Edward's OK but that I'm going to go to try to go to sleep early. I feel wrung out. Night, Fee, bless you for coming.'

Rather reluctantly Fiona left her.

*D*espite her brave words Isobel felt desolate after Fiona went downstairs. When misery attacked her—luckily not something that happened often—her usual comfort habit was to immerse herself simultaneously in a gripping book and a deep, boiling-hot bath. Isobel had never agreed with the Revd Sidney Smith's bracing advice to Lady Georgiana Morpeth on how to fight 'Low Spirits' by going 'into the shower-bath with a small quantity of water at a temperature low enough to give you a slight sensation of cold'. However, this evening she wanted to keep her ear cocked for Edward, so she decided on a quick bath and no book, and went down the passage to her own and Giles's bathroom. Normally she hated sleeping apart from Giles if one of the children as ill. Tonight she told herself she was relieved. Nevertheless, despite the fact that she had instructed Giles to go away, she was surprised that he had not been up. Flavia had come, and Fiona, but not Giles . . . oh, not Giles.

When she returned to Edward's room, ready for bed and having collected what she wanted for the night, she paused on the landing. The sound of voices and laughter floated up the stairs from the hall as the party got ready to go down to the theatre. She could hear Lorna's voice, organising everyone. She waited to hear Giles's familiar step, expecting him to dash up to check if she was OK, taking the stairs two at a time as he usually did, but he did not come. Then the front door closed and the house went quiet.

Isobel went into Edward's room and shut the door. It was that rarity in Scotland, a really warm evening; earlier she had flung open the bottom of the big sash window. She propped her elbows on the sill and leant out, smelling the luxurious scents of the azaleas and Pheasant's Eye narcissi which grew in beds in the sunken garden that surrounded the house—scents evocative of spring and happiness, of sweetness and love. She thought about her unknown mother-in-law—who she had always considered must have been spoilt and selfish to an inexcusable degree—of whom she had often felt resentful, despising her for inflicting such wounds on her young son that the scars still remained, puckered and angry, albeit usually concealed, on the grown man. She had seldom thought about Atalanta's own tormented unhappiness. Had Atalanta gazed out of the Glendrochatt windows, as Isobel was doing now, seen all the beauty and charm of her surroundings, known herself to be loved and lucky—and been unable to take comfort from any of it?

The silence of the house vibrated round Isobel. She shivered.

From Edward's room it was just possible to see the roof of the Old Steading. Through the Velux windows in the ceiling of the auditorium she saw the lights go on and her pent-up feelings throbbed until she felt she might burst. She flung herself down on the spare bed and the tears, which she had kept at bay all evening, started to flow.

Twenty

For four days Daniel had been on the run—from Glendrochatt, from Isobel and from himself. He had been taken aback
at how disappointed Isobel had looked when he'd announced, so
suddenly, that he was going away.

'But you'll miss the Forbeses,' she had said, 'and I so badly
wanted you to meet them. And you could have been one of the
first people to play in the theatre on Saturday evening—that
would have made it perfect.' Her disappointment had caused him
enchanted surprise and alarm in about equal measure. It had also
hardened his determination to put space between himself and her
as quickly as possible, while he inspected some escaped emotions
and tried to force them back into their cage.

He had not, in fact, gone south to London to fulfil any other
commissions or see to his business affairs and, though he'd not in
any way pretended this was the case, he knew it was what Giles
and Isobel assumed. Daniel had long ago armoured himself against
the urge to explain his actions to other people and thereby expose
himself to their opinions, but despite his supposed self-sufficiency,
the reason Daniel had actually left Glendrochatt was to seek out
an old mentor of his, who had played a part in his turbulent
childhood and whose influence still flickered in his consciousness
like a distant guiding star.

Dr Carl Goldsmith, eminent psychiatrist and homespun philosopher, had been a friend of his grandmother's. 'What would Carl think?' was a question Daniel still occasionally asked himself when he needed some sort of yardstick, although he by no means necessarily acted on the answers the question triggered. He wasn't looking for *answers* now, he told himself, and in any case it would be out of character for Carl—the least didactic of men—to offer anything so predigested as an instant solution to anyone else's problem.

Was it three or four years since he'd last seen Carl? Daniel was all too aware that he'd been meaning—and failing—to visit the old man for far too long; ever since he'd heard that Carl had officially retired from his consultancy and gone to live on a Hebridean island to concentrate on writing academic books and was now something of a recluse; ever since Carl had left London and was no longer easily available, thought Daniel uncomfortably. It would have been nice to imagine he was going now for purely altruistic reasons, but he was too honest to allow himself the luxury of pretending this was the case. Daniel, who prided himself on having achieved a workable balance in his life—not of course a perfect one, but one that enabled him to live without emotional upheavals—had been tipped out of kilter. Carl might help him regain his equilibrium; the fact that Carl would be delighted to see him was just an added bonus.

For the first time for ages Daniel had looked at himself through someone else's eyes and found the experience disconcerting in the extreme. Just before Lorna had made her unwelcome entrance into the theatre and interrupted their conversation, he had been shown a glimpse of himself by Isobel. It was as though they had gazed together at his reflection in a millpond and he had not liked what he saw.

'That is a terrible attitude,' Isobel had said to him as he'd expounded his philosophy of self-protection and her words had been as hard to shake from his mind as grit from a bathing towel on a sandy beach.

He had tossed his old backpack into the recently mended Volvo, together with paints, sketchbooks, his squeeze-box and—a last-minute decision—the half-finished portrait of Isobel, and headed towards Oban. If Carl was not at home on the island of Iona, well, decided Daniel, I will at least have made the effort and who knows what benefits may stem from any journey? The pilgrimage itself, he thought, is often the important thing.

He left Glendrochatt very early in the morning, before anyone was about, expecting to feel a sense of release as he temporarily turned his back on the pitfalls with which he felt himself surrounded. There was hardly any traffic yet and the scenery along Loch Tay was wonderful, but somehow Daniel lacked the happy sense of freedom that driving alone in wild and unfamiliar countryside usually gave him.

He stopped for petrol at Crianlarich, checked his route on the map and continued on the A85 along the top of Loch Awe to the west coast. Coming down the hill into Oban itself he experienced a lightening of the spirits. Perhaps it was the sight of the sea that did it: the seaweedy, slightly fishy smell of the place, the sound of gulls crying and the boats in the harbour all gave him a sense of freedom—it certainly wasn't the shops full of tartan hats, reproductions of Celtic crosses and pastel-coloured mohair scarves.

He followed the signs to the car ferry, which took him to the far side of the town, past the railway station.

He wondered if he ought to have made a reservation on the Caledonian MacBrayne ferry to Mull, but it was early enough in the season for it not to be a problem. He bought a return ticket for the 10.30 a.m. sailing for Craignure, left the Volvo in the line of cars queuing to be driven on board and went in search of a cup of coffee.

There is something romantic in going westwards. When he was a little boy, his father used to recite a poem by Patrick Chalmers about Mull that had captured his childish imagination, and a verse floated into his head now:

There's a Western Isle I know
Where the lost land merges
In the grey and outer seas,
Southwards of the Hebrides,
And through old sea-caverns go
Old Atlantic dirges.

Some words carry a powerful magic all their own, he thought, and Hebrides is one of them. His parents had spent their honeymoon on the island—he must actually have been conceived there, he realised. It was hard to imagine a more disastrous choice of place for his father to have taken his urban, party-loving mother, Daniel thought. He dedicated his trip across the Firth of Lorn to his father, about whom Isobel had succeeded in stirring up a great many memories, which he normally kept securely buried. It was as if an echoing space had been hollowed out inside him.

Daniel would have given a great deal to have Isobel by his side now, acting as his guide and interpreter, not just to these islands where he knew she had so often been herself, but to a quite different sort of territory, one where he had never so far dared to go exploring.

After he had driven on to the ferry he went up on deck. He stood gazing at the spectacular backdrop of hills, making a quick sketch of their outlines against the sky, and wishing there were some way of reproducing the taste of salt on his lips and the feel of the breeze on his face. Someone on board was playing the 'Eriskay Love Lilt' on a mouth-organ. The half-hour crossing went too quickly and Daniel's was one of the first cars off; it all seemed very easy. Once disembarked, he turned left and followed the sign to Fionnphort, terminus for the sacred Isle of Iona. He dawdled along, once or twice pulling into one of the regular passing places on the road to make way for an oncoming car, but there were very few. He stopped to pick a piece of bog myrtle and stuck it on the driving mirror, remembering how his father had said he always did that for the aromatic smell and for luck.

It hadn't occurred to Daniel that vehicles, except for those belonging to residents of the island, were not allowed on Iona; it would mean leaving Isobel's portrait behind, and not only had he hoped he might work on it in the peace and privacy of Carl's house, but he had been loath to part company with it, not trusting Lorna's prying eyes if he left it at Glendrochatt. He concealed the canvas under an old rug and reassured himself that the battered old Volvo would hardly be first choice for anyone thinking of stealing a car—it didn't seem a likely spot for joyriders anyhow. He heaved his backpack out, his old bed-roll strapped to the top of it, locked the car and went to sit on a wall at the side of the concrete ramp, waiting for the small ferry to return across the narrow strip of water dividing Iona from Mull.

He thought his first sight of Iona disappointing. He had expected it to look more dramatic than the flat outcrop of rock and grass, with the row of small stone houses and a jetty, which was all it appeared to consist of—though he could see the square tower of the abbey up to the right. Still, the scenery of Mull had been spectacular enough for anyone, he supposed. Two bus-loads of tourists arrived, on a day trip from the mainland and Daniel, who had imagined splendid solitude, felt rather resentful.

Once the ferry arrived and everybody had crowded on, the crossing only took a couple of minutes. The bearded ferryman knew exactly where Carl's house was—he clearly knew everything about everyone. 'You'll be meaning the foreign doctor that bought old Mhairi's house? Carry on up the hill, past the school and it's on the way to the Machair. Ask anyone—you'll not miss it,' he said. Rather surprisingly, he proved to be right. The choice was hardly enormous.

It was a small white cottage of no great architectural merit, surrounded by a dilapidated fence and a vegetable garden. Larks sang a repetitive plainsong overhead and on a rough patch of grass, from which speedwells reflected the brilliantly blue sky, stood a couple of beehives. A sign nailed on the gate guardedly announced:

'Honey—sometimes. Please enquire if you would like some.' This has to be the right house, thought Daniel. It was such a Carl-ish sort of notice: cautiously optimistic, but giving no guarantees; courteous and friendly, but not pressing. He knocked on the door.

He waited a couple of minutes and was just about to go round the back to see if there was another entrance, when the door opened and Carl stood there. He had aged since Daniel had last seen him. His ring of white hair still stood slightly on end, as it always had, his face was a little more creased and certainly a good deal thinner, but its expression was as serene as Daniel remembered and he wore his eighty-five years lightly.

'My dear boy, what a pleasant surprise,' said Carl, beaming a welcome but not looking particularly surprised. 'I always knew you'd turn up some time.'

Daniel laughed. 'I don't know whether to apologise for poling up unannounced or for not coming to see you sooner. Or for both?'

'Why apologise at all? You know I'm always pleased to see you. Time's got nothing to do with it. Come on in.'

The house was splendidly untidy and strewn with books, which sat about in teetering piles on every possible surface, though Daniel knew Carl would immediately be able to put his hand on any one he wanted.

They sat in the garden, ate bread and rather stale cheese, drank beer and exchanged news.

'And how is your mother at the moment?' asked Carl.

'I've no idea,' said Daniel, which wasn't strictly true. He looked at Carl, a gently mocking challenge in his eyes, trawling a line, but Carl's face wore his professional look of polite non-judgemental acceptance which Daniel remembered of old—and which could be infuriating.

————

*F*or three days they enjoyed each other's company; Daniel painted while Carl was working, then Carl showed Daniel the island. They walked up Dun-I, Iona's one pimple of a hill, and on to the North Bay where Viking invaders had massacred so many monks that the white sands were said to have turned scarlet with blood; they visited the lovingly restored abbey with its beautiful modern carvings on the pillars of the cloisters and went inside the little chapel of St Oran in the abbey's ancient burial ground— an oasis of quiet, where even the most garrulous sightseers usually kept silence, said Carl, but which had wonderful acoustics. 'If you sing in here,' he said, 'it's as flattering as singing in the bath. Even I sound like Pavarotti.'

They had walked to St Columba's Bay and searched fruitlessly for one of the translucent green stones supposed to be the petrified tears shed by St Columba on arrival, homesick for Ireland. Over the hill and to the right of the Machair—that stretch of sandy grass so typical of the west Highlands—Carl showed him the remains of the cell where the saint withdrew to meditate, just a ring of stones now.

'I should think he needed to get away from his fellow monks,' suggested Daniel.

He collected pocketfuls of cowrie shells to take back to Amy and Edward, and one morning did a watercolour for Isobel of the tiny snails that clung to the black rocks below the abbey—red, black, orange and green, like jewels encrusting an ancient sword-hilt, he thought, and hoped she would prefer it to a conventional landscape.

The sheep grazing everywhere were so unfazed by people that they never even bothered to move out of the way. It was incredibly peaceful.

'But don't you get fed up with so many tourists on such a small island—all those questing feet tramping everywhere?' Daniel asked.

'No. Why should I? I couldn't have been more pleased to see you and after all, you're one yourself.'

'Funny how that's an unwelcome thought, like being outraged if someone else fancies one's favourite picnic spot. I like to think of *other* people as tourists.' Daniel grinned. 'I think I'd rather fancy myself as a pilgrim.'

'Not much difference—pilgrims and tourists are both looking for something. Neither may find what they expect, or each may find something surprising. I'm sure the pilgrims of the *Canterbury Tales* must have been like any typical package-tour coach-load today.'

After two days, Daniel told Carl he had begun to appreciate a different Iona from the one that had, at first, disappointed him. 'It's being *on* the island and looking *out* that's so beautiful and the ever-changing light. I didn't see the charm to start with. It's a bit like those plates of coloured dots where you're supposed to be able to pick out a rabbit or a bird if you look long enough, but you can't see anything to start with except the dots, then suddenly, for no particular reason—bingo!—you've got it.'

He remembered the moment when he had suddenly seen the beauty in Isobel's face—and perhaps recently, he thought, a lack of it in Lorna's.

'Ah, yes,' said Carl, nodding. 'Lots of people come here expecting an instant spiritual high and feel let down when they don't get it. They've read that the veil between our world and the next seems thinner here, and they imagine the "Cloud of Unknowing" will miraculously dissolve—then they're annoyed to be stuck in the same old fog. But you're right: Iona's not a place of outstanding beauty in itself, it's more an eye through which one begins to see other things—looking outward, as you say, certainly,' agreed Carl. 'Or . . .' he paused ' . . . or, of course, looking inwards, as the case may be' and he looked thoughtfully at Daniel.

It had struck him how much the would-be detached Daniel talked about this family with whom he was staying at the moment, as though they constantly filled his mind. 'What made you come to see me at this particular time?' he asked.

It was the topic that Daniel had been both avoiding and longing to discuss.

He found himself telling Carl about Isobel.

'Are you afraid of breaking up her marriage? Is that the trouble?'

Daniel looked horrified. 'Oh, I'm sure I could never do that—I certainly wouldn't want to even if I could.'

'Then you are afraid of being wounded yourself?'

'I suppose so,' Daniel admitted. 'Whatever happened I couldn't bear to hurt her—I know that for certain—but yes, if I'm honest I'm very afraid of exposing myself to hurt. Part of me wants to run away.'

'Only you can decide whether someone is worth loving whatever the risk,' said Carl, who thought it extremely naïve of Daniel not to think Isobel might get hurt too. 'But this wife—this woman—whom you clearly think about so much.' He deliberately made it sound slightly derogatory. 'She may well not be worth the risk of such love.'

'Of course she's worth it,' said Daniel angrily, before he could stop himself.

'Then you have answered your own question. But real loving can be very costly' and Carl looked at Daniel with concern.

*D*aniel had not intended to return to Glendrochatt until after the weekend, but it turned out that Carl himself was going away on the Saturday to give a lecture tour in the States. 'But you are welcome to stay here on your own as long as you like,' he said.

'I need to get on with my commission at Glendrochatt. I'll go back on Saturday too, but thank you, Carl, thank you for everything. May I come again?'

'Don't leave it so long next time,' said the old man lightly—but he did not share with Daniel a medical prognosis about himself that made him wonder privately whether he would still be there to see the younger man another time.

*W*hen Daniel got back to Glendrochatt on Saturday evening it was nearly ten o'clock, though it was still quite light. He drove round to the rear of the house and let himself in at the back door. He had seen the lights in the theatre but decided he could not face meeting a whole lot of strange people or being pressed to take part in any music making. He went upstairs.

Daniel's bedroom was on the top floor, but as he went along the passage to get to the stairs leading to the upper landing he saw a crack of light under Edward's door. Then he stopped and listened. He could hear muffled sobs coming from inside the room, but he didn't think it sounded like Edward. Surely it couldn't be Amy? Very softly he opened the door and looked in.

The far bedside light was on. Edward, fast asleep, was in his own bed, nearest the door, but in the other, crying as though her heart would break, was Isobel.

Daniel stood looking at her, his heart hammering. Isobel, hearing the door open, suddenly sat bolt upright and stared at him in astonishment, too startled to try to hide her tears. She looked absurdly young and exactly like her daughter.

'Daniel! Whatever are you doing here? I didn't know you were coming back today.'

In a second Daniel was kneeling by the bed. He took both her hands in his and held them tight, looking at her swollen, blotchy face with great distress. Then he gathered her into his arms, holding her and comforting her as if she were a small child. 'Want to tell me what's the trouble?' he asked, his cheek against her rumpled hair.

Twenty-one

Isobel poured out the story of the chicken disaster, of Edward's distress and subsequent seizure and of Lorna's part in everything. She even managed to laugh as she described the Forbeses' delinquent dog. She did not mention Giles at all.

'I'm so angry with Lorna that it physically hurts. I get a lump here' and she banged the top of her chest with her fist. 'It feels like a sharp stone when I even think about her. It hurts so much I can't swallow. It's horrible—I hate myself for feeling like this but I can't help it.'

'I saw her in the hen-run with Edward several times lately. I was rather impressed. Are you quite sure she wasn't actually trying to help him?' asked Daniel.

'Oh, I'm sure all right—but I wish I weren't. She may have been trying to *achieve* something with him and get some Brownie points for herself, but she doesn't give a stuff about Ed as a person. It's so terribly disappointing because I really thought he might have grown out of these fits at last. He hasn't had one for ages and I was hoping we might be able to start cutting down his pills. I was going to ask the paediatrician about it next week. Now I don't suppose she'll let him and I don't know how much this whole episode will set him back either. I could kill Lorna,' she said fiercely and added in a whisper, 'There's only one thing

Lorna's interested in and it's not either of my children.'

Daniel didn't know what to say, although he was well aware of her meaning. He just sat on the bed, listening and letting her talk it all out, occasionally rocking her gently while she leant against him.

Isobel suddenly gave herself a little shake, and gently detached herself from his arms. 'Oh, Daniel I'm so sorry,' she said. 'I shouldn't be burdening you with any of this. What will you think of me? Could you chuck me my dressing-gown from that chair?' She suddenly felt very conscious that she was only wearing a flimsy lawn nightdress and a host of disturbing feelings flooded through her that had nothing to do with Lorna.

Daniel got off the bed, passed her dressing-gown without looking at her and went to lean out of the window, as Isobel herself had done earlier that evening. She slipped her arms into the sleeves of the robe and tied it tightly round her, as though by making a knot in the sash she was making a reassuring statement to herself. She went to check on Edward, who appeared to be sleeping normally. She placed her hand on his forehead, testing its temperature, but it felt perfectly cool. She stroked his cheek gently and went to join Daniel in the window.

'Tell me what you've been doing,' she said, kneeling beside him, her arms also on the sill. 'I've talked more than enough about us.' So he told her about his trip to Iona and how he had gone to visit Carl—although he did not tell her what had sent him there in the first place. They talked about the island and she told him about her many childhood holidays on the west coast, and he found himself telling her about his link with Mull through his parents, and it was as easy and companionable as if they had known each other for ever. Neither had any idea how long they talked for, watching dusk steal over the garden as swifts shrieked and swooped for evening midges; as it grew darker, bats took over night patrol from the swifts, fluttering spookily against the sky— and still Isobel and Daniel talked. Then they heard the sound of

doors opening and voices coming from the direction of the theatre.

'I think I should go,' said Daniel. 'Will you be all right?'

'I'll be fine now,' she replied. She walked with him to the door
and out on to the landing. 'Thank you for coming in—it was a
lifeline. Goodnight, Daniel.' She lifted up her face and kissed him
goodnight, and it seemed the most natural thing in the world.
Daniel walked upstairs with wings on his old trainers and Isobel
went back into Edward's room. She debated whether she should
go downstairs, greet the performers and hear how everything had
gone—bury a few hatchets, she thought wryly. Meanwhile she
climbed back into bed just to give the Murrays and Fortescues
time to depart, listening as car doors were slammed and goodnights were called. But before she had time to come to any decision she was asleep, utterly exhausted by the emotions of the
day.

What neither Daniel nor Isobel knew was that Lorna had left
the theatre earlier than everyone else, intending to come over to
the house before the others and try to make some sort of peace
with her sister. Although Lorna was an expert at justifying her
own actions to herself, this time she was deeply ashamed of the
trouble she had caused and felt very afraid that Edward's seizure
might have done him lasting harm. Outwardly she could pretend
that her motive in trying to help him fasten the door to the hen-
run had been altruistic, but inwardly she knew she had only been
hoping to win favour with Giles, and she felt a grudging admiration for the courage and humour with which Isobel coped with
her difficult son. I will tell Izzy I am sorry, vowed Lorna. As she
walked across the garden she gazed up, thinking how romantic the
house looked with the floodlights on, though wishing, as always,
that it were hers—and then she had seen Isobel and Daniel, shoulder to shoulder, leaning out of an upstairs window and talking.

She had heard them both laugh. They looked . . . happy, she thought, with a sense of outrage and went rigid with suspicion; all her good intentions galloped away like stampeding horses. Was the fuss about Edward much less serious than her sister had made it out to be? Had Isobel, all the time, known Daniel was coming back that night? Was this in fact why Isobel had really chosen to stay with Edward? In her heart Lorna knew this last idea, at least, could not be true, but it suited her to give it credence.

Lorna stood in the shadow of a tree watching and listening, though try as she might, she could not hear what they were saying.

She was well aware that Daniel had been attracted by her at first meeting and she had intended him to fall, just a little, in love with her—not enough to cause serious complications, but enough for him to act as a 'teaser' for Giles; enough, perhaps, for a pleasurable little interlude together.

Was Isobel always to be the loved and chosen one?

Lorna went back to her flat, a whole series of new images running through her head like a strip cartoon. She decided to hoard the knowledge of what she had just seen as ammunition for the future, as a poacher might put a cartridge in the barrel of his gun ready for use in case of sudden opportunity. Misery and self-pity, not unmixed with self-dislike, washed over her. Sometimes she felt she would drown in her own feelings.

The concert had been a huge success. The invited audience, made up of several supportive locals and workers from the estate, as well as Lord Dunbarnock and the Fortescue and Murray families, were extremely enthusiastic. Flavia, accompanied by Lorna, enchanted everyone just as Giles had hoped she would and it was with some trepidation that he and Amy followed her on to the platform to play Bach, as they had done for Lorna on her first evening at Glendrochatt. After that, Alistair took over from Lorna at the piano—she gave up her place somewhat grudgingly, Flavia noticed with amusement—and he, Flavia and Ben had launched into jazz, soon to be joined by Giles and Amy. Amy, who had never improvised like this before, was lit up like a sparkler, fizzing with excitement. She was thrilled when her aunt departed and she had her father's attention to herself again. The musicians had ended the evening by playing an Eightsome: everyone had pushed the chairs to one side and all the audience took to the floor to dance.

After sitting still for what was, to them, a long time, Christopher and Jamie Murray became thoroughly out of hand, showing off in order to impress the older Ben and competing with each other to see which of them could do the most press-ups when it was their turn to dance in the middle of the set. Frank had been quite unable to control his sons and Grizelda wondered nervously whether they might be becoming hyperactive. She worried constantly in case their unruly behaviour might be due, not to her own limp parenting, but to some imbalance in their diet. She didn't think Isobel took such matters seriously enough. She had watched all the children devouring praline ice cream at supper and thought the choice of menu unwise. What if they developed a reaction to nuts?

I shall watch Amy's future career with interest,' said Flavia to Giles as they walked back to the house. 'I'm very impressed. That daughter of yours has *real* talent—but do be cautious how you handle it.'

'You've been talking to Isobel.' Giles gave her a sharp look.

'Well, perhaps,' she admitted. 'But I know what I'm talking about, none better. I had a terrible struggle to fight free from my mother's all-pervasive influence over my music. You've given Amy a brilliant start—just be aware that a time will come when you need to back-off a little. And I think the theatre's a dream,' she went on hastily before she could get into an argument with Giles. 'The sound in there is fine and I'm greatly looking forward to the Gala evening. That painting will be enchanting when it's finished. I do wish we could have met the artist.'

'Well, it looks as if you may do so after all,' said Giles. 'He must be back—that's his car.'

*C*an I go and see Mum?' asked Amy, as soon as they got in.

'Not tonight,' Giles replied. 'Mum said she was going to get an early night and she's in with Edward. You can tell her all about it in the morning.'

'That's not fair.' Amy, tired and suffering from reaction to applause and adulation on top of all the dramas of the day, contemplated mutiny. 'I'm sure she won't be asleep yet. Why can't I just look and see?'

'Because I said *no*,' Giles himself was in a very uncertain mood. 'Say goodnight to everyone and off to bed. I'll come and tuck you down in ten minutes.'

Amy kicked at the floor and took as long as possible over her goodnights, which were less than gracious.

'Isn't it a horrid let-down when a performance is over?' whispered Flavia tactfully, giving Amy a hug. 'But we did well together, didn't we? I'll come up with you if I may—I want to check on Dulcie—then I'm going to bed too.'

*A*fter he had seen off all his guests, Giles let the dogs out and locked up. Then he went slowly upstairs, undecided whether to look in on Isobel or not. His better nature won. Very quietly, so as not to disturb Edward, he opened the door, expecting, despite what he had said to Amy, that Isobel would be wide awake. The bedside light was still on, but mother and son were asleep. For a moment it occurred to him that Isobel might be pretending, but after watching her for a while he decided she was genuinely out for the count. He looked down at Edward with love and sadness. Earlier that day, when he had played golf with Alistair and Ben, he had experienced a moment of acute envy at the easy banter between father and son, their many shared interests, their obvious enjoyment of each other's company.

I must support Isobel better, he thought, she carries more of this burden than I do, and he felt a pang of self-loathing at the feckless, reckless game of playing one sister off against the other with which he had been amusing himself. A wave of love for his wife washed over him and he was ashamed of his anger with her earlier. Then something in the room—the very faintest whiff— made him pause and freeze, like a setter pointing when it scents a bird.

Someone who smoked had been in this room. Mick smoked, but Joss who had been up to see Isobel earlier did not and anyway they had both been at the performance. Giles suddenly remembered the Volvo parked at the back of the house and he knew with absolute certainty that Daniel had been in here, had been talking to Isobel, perhaps keeping her company while he, Giles, had thought she was alone and unhappy.

He walked away from Edward's room with an ice pack round his heart.

Twenty-two

On Sunday morning Edward seemed back to his usual self, obsessively lining up stones to his own mysterious formula, although his constant repetitive questions about the whereabouts of the hens drove everyone mad. Giles and Isobel treated each other with unnatural politeness, and conversed in the stilted manner of two people practising a foreign language.

Giles, at his smoothest but with a dangerous glitter in his eye, was particularly attentive to his sister-in-law and charming to Daniel, whom he kept under surveillance with all the outward nonchalance but secret diligence of an undercover agent.

Isobel and Daniel, while trying not to look at one another, seemed unable to avoid catching each other's glance. Giles watched them.

Lorna, apparently groomed for the catwalk rather than informal Sunday breakfast, might have been dipped in sugar frosting but Amy, who had slept late, came down at ten o'clock in her dressing-gown and a grumpy mood. She had big rings round her eyes. 'So what are we going to do today?' she asked, yawning, but nothing anyone suggested was right. 'Boring, boring, boring.'

'If you go on whingeing like that, Amy, you'd better go back to bed,' said Isobel, uncharacteristically snappy. 'You're clearly not

grown-up enough to cope with compliments and late nights.'
Amy flounced out of the kitchen.

*T*he Forbeses left before lunch.

'Oh, dear, what an atmosphere this morning,' said Flavia as
they drove away. 'How sad. I've never, ever, been pleased to leave
Glendrochatt before. I hope they'll have recovered before the
opening concert. And ghastly though it was, I don't think the hen
drama is responsible for all that's wrong with the Grant family.
D'you think Giles and Isobel will be all right, Alistair?'

'Oh, Lord, yes,' said Alistair with more optimism than he felt.
'I've always thought they had a cast-iron marriage—although it
seems to have a bit of metal fatigue at the moment. But they need
to get shot of Lorna, that's for sure. She's trouble.' He grinned at
Flavia. 'Funny, when we were young I remember thinking her
amazing to look at but pretty damn boring—certainly not the fire-
and-ice number she is now. If you were Izzy I don't think you'd
like having her around too much.'

'And Daniel Hoffman? I'm glad we met him after all. I thought
he was delightful, but what about him and Izzy? Did you like
him?'

'He's OK—not quite my type, but yes, I did like him. I can't
believe he'd be a serious threat, though.' Alistair looked surprised
at the idea. 'Well,' he qualified, 'I can see perhaps he may have
taken a shine to Isobel, but I certainly can't see there's anything
the other way round.'

'Then I think you're very unobservant,' said his wife.

*A*fter the Forbeses had gone, everyone dispersed. Joss and Mick
had promised to take Daniel on an expedition to a favourite view-
point up the hill so Daniel put his sketchpad in his pocket and
went to meet them at their house, glad of an excuse to leave the

Grants to their own devices and inspect his thoughts. Giles took Edward and Amy out in the boat, and Isobel took Flapper for a run in the woods. She thought about the night before and in particular she thought about Daniel. It was something of a relief to know he was out for the day, thus freeing her from either the hope or fear that she might find herself alone with him again. On an impulse she picked a bunch of bluebells to put in his room.

When she got back to the house she went into the old butler's pantry where the vases where kept, but couldn't find one that looked right. Then she opened the baize-lined silver cupboard, which smelt faintly musty, and got out a Victorian silver mug with *'Isobel Mary Forsyth'* engraved on it in italic script inside a Rococo scroll; it was inscribed with the date of her birth. She filled it with water, carefully spreading the flowers out over the rim so that there was a purple reflection in the silver, then carried the mug upstairs and left it on the chest of drawers in Daniel's room. She hoped he would realise it was intended as a thank you for his understanding the night before—and for what she knew had been his forbearance. She stood in the middle of the room for a moment, tempted to linger, to touch Daniel's things, see what he was reading—a book lay open on the bed—but she forced herself to leave and shut the door quietly behind her.

On her way down from the top landing she met Lorna, apparently about to come up. The sisters eyed each other in surprise.

'I've been putting some music on Amy's bed—Giles wanted her to have it,' said Lorna defensively, feeling she had been caught out of bounds. 'I heard footsteps and as I thought you were all out I felt I'd better see who it was.'

'How wise of you,' said Isobel.

Lorna raised her eyebrows. 'Is Daniel all right?' she asked pointedly. 'Is he sick or anything?'

'As far as I know he's absolutely fine.' Isobel looked at Lorna, outwardly unconcerned, inwardly furiously aware of the insinuation behind the enquiry. Let her guess whatever she likes, she thought.

She made a gesture with her hand for Lorna to go on down before her. 'After you,' she said coolly, 'unless, that is, there's anything else you want up here?'

Lorna hesitated for a moment, then turned and went on downstairs in front of Isobel. She would have given anything to know whether Daniel was in his room, but she felt she had just been presented with another useful cartridge to put in her belt all the same.

$\mathcal{T}$he ordinary routine of life gradually took over again.

'You have got Thursday down in your diary, haven't you, Giles?' asked Isobel.

'Thursday? What's happening on Thursday?'

Isobel rolled her eyes. 'Oh, really, Giles! Only Ed's Annual Review, that's what. I told you *ages* ago.' Every year she dreaded the review—so much hinged on it. For weeks beforehand she got an anxious feeling in the pit of her stomach when she thought about it. Would the local authority still agree to fund Edward at Greenyfordham? He would drown in a mainstream school but she was always terrified it might be suggested. There were so many imponderables about Edward's future and the Annual Review brought all the hidden worries to the surface. 'You know how important it is.'

'If you told me I'll have put it in my diary,' said Giles, who had forgotten all about it. He, who had always been so meticulous about dates and engagements—provided they were written down—had recently got into the habit of relying on Lorna to tell him each morning what was on the agenda. So far she and Sheila Shepherd seemed to be dovetailing his various appointments between the estate and the Arts Festival in a most amicable and satisfactory way. It was the overlap with his personal life that was proving more tricky.

'I have a nasty feeling that Paul Donaldson—that artist who wants us to hold an exhibition of his paintings—is coming to see me some time on Thursday. Remind me of the Greenyfordham timing again.'

'I suppose you could miss the first bit if you have to. I can see Ed's physiotherapist without you at ten, but you promised you'd meet me at the school at twelve to see Dr Connor and Peter Ramsay.' Peter Ramsay was the Educational Psychologist and much depended on his recommendations. 'And I do think you should be at the final meeting of everybody.'

'Then naturally I shall be there.' Giles sounded as courteous as if Isobel were a new business acquaintance.

*F*or God's sake don't let me forget Edward's appointment on Thursday,' he said to Lorna. 'Isobel would kill me if I didn't turn up. Did you extract it from my diary?'

'Surely you don't have to spend the whole day at Greenyfordham? It does seem a waste for you and Izzy both to go when there's so much to do here.'

'I must at least try to see Dr Connor and the psychologist chap, but I don't have to be there for the early bit.'

'You've got that artist coming to see you. Poor you, it will be a bit hectic, but I'll put Edward's date down on the chart,' said Lorna. 'I do think you're a marvellous father, Giles. I hope Izzy knows how lucky she is.'

Isobel felt as though there were a sheet of glass separating her from Giles, as though they could observe each other's every move, but neither hear nor touch each other. Over the years their marriage had frequently been stormy, but it had never before lost its intimacy. She felt a terrible sense of isolation.

*N*ot many of Amy's friends understood the total commitment that was required for her to stick to the rigid daily discipline of early morning practice sessions—and sometimes another shorter practice in the evening too. It often meant she had to refuse invitations to stay overnight with friends or go to parties after school. On Thursday morning Giles—with Lorna in attendance—supervised Amy's practice as usual.

They were concentrating at the moment on two particular pieces for the Suzuki course: the *'Allegro' by Fiocco*, which had been chosen as the piece to be played by the orchestral group to which she had been assigned, and *Massenet's 'Meditation from Thaïs'* for her individual tutorial.

'That's a tricky bit, isn't it?' said Giles, stopping her after a few moments. 'Shall we do those few bars again—let's say . . . five times if you get it right, ten if you don't?' Amy started even more, and looked questioningly at her father, but his mind seemed to have wandered and he was looking at Lorna.

At breakfast, Giles and Lorna discussed Amy's bowing technique while they drank their coffee, but Giles said nothing about Greenyfordham. Angry pride prevented Isobel from reminding him again—which she would normally have done—and Amy, pushing her porridge round her plate in bolshy silence, cast looks of deep resentment at her aunt.

At eight o'clock Edward went off on the school bus as usual.

Isobel arrived at Greenyfordham for the first appointment at ten thirty. From the outside the school resembled many others, except there were ramps rather than steps, all doors were extra wide and there was an unusually high ratio of staff to pupils. As always, Isobel thought the thing that struck you most forcibly was the atmosphere of calm cheerfulness in the school. Whenever she saw some of the brave but heartbreaking children who were Edward's friends, she thought humbly that she and Giles had got off pretty lightly compared with some others. It was contrasting Edward with normal children that flipped her trip switch.

At the end of the previous autumn term Isobel had attended two performances of *The Nutcracker* in one week, but apart from Tchaikovsky's romantic music the two productions had little in common. The first was a traditional performance of grace and magic, given by the Royal Ballet's Touring Company at Edinburgh's Festival Theatre. She and Fiona had taken Amy and Emily as a pre-Christmas treat. After each curtain call the girls had applauded until the palms of their hands were scarlet and afterwards had pirouetted and twirled their way down the Royal Mile, two potential Darcey Bussells—at any rate in their own estimation. The second performance had been at Greenyfordham. The Sugar-Plum Fairy, her face radiant with triumph, had managed to achieve a series of spins in her wheelchair, which she could only manipulate by a system of sucking and blowing. Clara, proudly wielding new crutches, her uncooperative legs supported by callipers, had won all hearts. Edward had been given the part of Franz and apparently had been brilliant in rehearsal, but on the actual day he had become quite unable to look at the faces in front of him and, to Isobel's desperate disappointment, would only perform with his back to the audience. He had then become so hyped up and uncontrollable that for the safety of the unsteady Clara he had to be removed. Isobel had found the sight of him, nose pressed forlornly to the glass doors of the hall, longing—too late—to participate again, almost more than she could bear. She had gone home and wept all over Giles.

Today, however, the physiotherapist was pleased with Edward. He was making progress with the use of his hands and his balance was improving. They were going to try to teach him to ride a bicycle soon, though it would take time.

Isobel thought this sounded wildly overoptimistic. 'How long?'

'As long as it takes . . . six months? Probably a year?'

Mrs Leslie, the headmistress, told Isobel that an art therapist had been seeing Edward recently. Because he was not himself capable of drawing, Edward had to tell the therapist what he wanted and she drew pictures to his instructions; she then tried to interpret his ideas. Isobel thought Daniel, who often drew for Edward, would be interested in this.

'But recently we've been puzzled by his terrible phobia about insects. This is quite new. Have you had problems with it at home?'

Isobel looked blank. 'Edward's always been mad about insects. He's absolutely hooked on his "bug box" with the magnifying-glass top. I'm always having to catch bluebottles and things so that he can study them. He looks at them for hours.'

'But what about spiders?' asked Mrs Leslie.

'He loves spiders—ugh!—which is more than I do,' she answered, laughing, 'but I've schooled myself to pick them up for Ed.' Then an unwelcome thought struck her 'What are you suggesting?' she asked.

'Well, he keeps asking her to draw big black spiders with long legs, then he wants her to rub them out and becomes extremely anxious and upset. He tore the picture into shreds the other day, and went and hid himself in a cupboard. We wondered if you could throw any light on this?'

Isobel put her head in her hands. 'Oh, dear. Yes, I think I do know what that's about. Mrs Leslie, will you do me a favour? My husband's coming to join me any minute. Could . . . could you tell him about this yourself when he arrives?'

'Yes, if you want me to. Of course.' Mrs Leslie looked a little surprised.

'Thank you,' said Isobel. 'I'd like to hear what Giles makes of it.' She most desperately did not want to lay herself open to the charge of sniping at Lorna, so she just prayed Giles would arrive in time to talk to Mrs Leslie before the other appointments, but by twelve o'clock there was still no sign of him. She managed to swap her slot with the parents who were after her on the list and sat in the waiting-room in a state of seething disappointment. Miserable memories of Edward's early years flooded through her. Giles, who had longed for a boy before the twins were born, had taken much longer to accept their son's limitations than she had. Then there had been many times when she had sat alone in doctors' consulting rooms, but it was a long time since Giles had found excuses for not accompanying her to medical appointments. Isobel admired the way he had battled so hard with his disappointment and gradually learnt to love Edward as he was. She knew his involvement in Amy's music had undoubtedly helped and had recently felt they were at last achieving some sort of equilibrium in their commitment to their two very different children—until, that is, she thought miserably, the arrival of Lorna had thrown everything out of sync.

*G*iles had spent a busy morning at Glendrochatt. He'd had a long discussion with Paul Donaldson, whose abstract paintings he had liked, then taken him down to the Old Steading to see where his pictures could be exhibited. He had introduced him to Daniel and though the two artists' styles could hardly have been more different, they appreciated each other's work. Daniel suggested they should go off to the Drochatt Arms for a drink and a sandwich together, and Giles had gone back to the office to deal with correspondence.

'Time for a break, d'you think?' he asked Lorna after they'd sorted through the day's mail. 'Glass of sherry before lunch?'

'Lovely,' said Lorna. This was beginning to be a daily ritual between her and Giles, and it was rapidly becoming the highlight of her routine.

'Oh, by the way,' she added casually as they went upstairs to have their drink and see what Joss had left out for them to eat, 'before I forget, you asked me to remind you about an appointment at Greenyfordham.'

'Oh, my God! What time is it?' Giles shot out his wrist to look at his watch. It was after one o'clock.

'But I'm too late already.' He looked at her in horror. 'The appointment was for twelve.'

'There wasn't a definite time in your diary but I got the impression it was during the afternoon.' The first part of this statement was true at least: the entry in Giles's diary had just said *'Ed's review'*, heavily boxed in with double lines. 'Oh, Giles, I'm so sorry,' said Lorna. She was somewhat shaken at how distraught he looked and felt uneasily ashamed of herself. She had known perfectly well what time the appointment was. 'Izz will think I let you skip it on purpose.' She looked up at Giles, blue eyes wide with convincing anxiety.

'Of course she won't. It's not your fault, but she will think it's mine and she'll be right.' Giles banged one fist angrily against the palm of his other hand. 'How could I have been such a bloody fool?'

'Look, these appointments nearly always run late. I'll ring to say you've been delayed. After all, Paul Donaldson stayed for ages and you *had* to see him. He'd come all the way from Aberdeen.'

'I should have put him off. Edward is much more important.'

'Well, but Izzy will have seen everyone. Honestly, Giles, Izz could easily have reminded you—or me—this morning, but she's terribly possessive about Edward and then she's been so contrary lately. Are you sure she didn't half mean you to forget?'

'Of course she didn't,' said Giles—but the seed of doubt had been sown. 'I'll drive there like a bat out of hell—and you let them know I'm on my way. Say I'm most dreadfully sorry an see if by any chance you can get the appointment postponed

'Let me ring first. There's no earthly point in you going if it's too late already.'

Against his better judgement Giles, who had left h downstairs, agreed and Lorna ran down to the office a she came back she said, 'No luck, I'm afraid. Izz with Dr Connor, but the headmistress was very didn't matter and she quite understood.'

But it wasn't the headmistress that Giles w at

rval

nuine

*D*r Connor had been reassuring abou a little his fit on Saturday was disappointin without any similar incidents, bu trauma to account for it. She su longer before trying to cut down on his regular medication, but was full of praise for all that his parents and his school were jointly achieving.

Isobel always felt better after a session with Dr Connor who had that healing gift of making each patient she saw feel he or she was of special importance to her. 'Just keep on as you are,' she said to Isobel. 'You are doing wonderful things for Edward.'

Peter Ramsay had said he would be recommending to the Local Authority that Edward should continue at Greenyfordham, at any rate for the time being, and Isobel felt a huge sense of relief. All the same, she drove home with her mind in turmoil. She should have been sharing this moment with Giles, talking about it together on the way home. She could not believe that he had let her and Edward down so badly.

She came to a decision in the car. She would stay at Glendro- the following weekend and not go to Northumberland with nd Amy. She trusted Joss absolutely to care for Edward, 'd not trust her sister not to interfere with Joss's authority. would be a recipe for disaster to leave them together herself or Giles in charge and she had been badly about the spider pictures—she wished Mrs Leslie daulk to Giles about this and did not look forward in th though she supposed she would have to do rappor lf that it would be good for father and beginnin er, as they had so often enjoyed doing Amy and them a chance to recover their old Giles could en herself and Giles that Lorna was and angry sta ought Isobel sadly, but between offering him an promising young cellist, well, to Daphne Crawf bout that. Isobel, in her hurt ing time at home w iles, had no intention of several uninterrupted na could take herself off rd could have a calm- could give Daniel

Giles, who had braced himself for a furious scene with his wife when she got home, was prepared to try to win her round with a mixture of charm, sex and genuine contrition. What he was not expecting was to be met with a wall of apparent indifference that blocked off all his approaches. His apologies were scornfully cast aside, leaving him feeling both wrongful and wronged—a dangerous combination. All Giles's old insecurities about the trustworthiness of women made a perfectly prepared trench to receive the rich mulch of Lorna's flattery.

When Isobel told Amy about her decision, Amy expressed token umbrage that her mother would not be there to listen to the orchestra, but accepted that, at the moment, her twin's need for their mother was greater than hers; she also looked forward to having her father to herself for a whole weekend.

What neither mother nor daughter bargained for was that Giles should immediately invite Lorna to go to Northumberland in Isobel's stead.

Twenty-three

Lorna felt as if she had thrown a double six; she had not expected to reap such a bonus from her devious behaviour over the appointment at Edward's school and a surge of confidence shot through her like an electric current. It was as if she had landed on a lucky square in the dice game she was playing with her sister and was about to swarm up a particularly long ladder while her younger sister slid down a wriggly little snake. She almost felt sorry for her, but not quite. She thought Isobel had made a wonderfully opportune error of judgement and a very surprising one unless, that is, it actually suited Isobel to stay at Glendrochatt as much as it suited Lorna to go to Northumberland with Giles? Could Isobel secretly welcome the opportunity to spend the weekend with Daniel without the inhibiting presence of her husband? Lorna wasn't sure. Well let her try it and risk the consequences, she thought, reassuring herself that this would certainly release her from any pangs of conscience she herself might feel.

Because the Bank Holiday weekend coincided with half-term, Giles and Isobel had planned to drive Amy to stay with acquaintances who lived near the school where the Suzuki gathering was to take place. They had met Jim and Linda Broughton at a musical event the previous year and the Broughtons had pressed the Grants to come and stay if they ever wanted a halfway stop between Scotland and the south. This seemed the ideal occasion to take them up on their offer.

The alterations that had gone on at Glendrochatt all winter meant that Giles and Isobel felt unable to go, as originally planned, on a skiing holiday with the Fortescues. Giles, conscious that they both badly needed a break, had hoped that once the workshop weekend was over, he and Isobel could enjoy a couple of romantic nights in a country house hotel and combine this with some talent-spotting for the next season at Glendrochatt. Amy could be given a lift home by Valerie Benson, who would be taking classes at the weekend course, though she would not be teaching Amy—part of the idea of the Suzuki weekend was that children should be exposed to new ideas and different teaching methods, as well as having the chance to play in a group.

Though Giles intended the trip to be a special treat for Isobel, Lorna had actually made all the arrangements. More and more she was taking over as Giles's personal assistant and, since Sheila Shepherd had never had a hand in organising anything to do with his private life, this caused no conflict with her. Somehow it would have been easier for Isobel to accept if it had.

'You had better ring Gattersburn Park and see if you can change the booking from a double to two single rooms,' he said to Lorna in Isobel's hearing. 'Since my wife has stood me up, perhaps you could do with a nice break yourself—you've worked so hard since you came here—and I would value your opinion on the cellist. I'm sure the Broughtons will love to have you for the weekend, and I think you'll enjoy attending all the teaching sessions and the concert. These affairs are always the greatest fun.'

*I*sobel endured a very tearful session with Amy who had been looking forward to the weekend for months; she had been learning the music that all the children would play together at the final concert on Sunday afternoon as well as a piece for her individual lesson.

'Aunt Lorna will spoil everything if she comes,' Amy moaned. 'You don't know what she's like with Dad when you're not there, Mum. They talk *about* me and discuss my playing, but they don't talk *to* me,' she complained and added devastatingly, 'They're really just using me to talk to each other—I might as well not be there.'

'Oh, darling, I'm so sorry.'

'Do you know what she's done?' Amy looked outraged.

'No, but I can see you're going to tell me.'

'She's put down all my practice times on her beastly charts, in what she calls Dad's special colour code—*and hers* too. It's got nothing to do with her. Dad doesn't need her to tell him when my practice is,' said Amy fiercely.

'Oh, dear, that does seem over the top.' Isobel knew just how Amy felt. Only the other day she had told Giles crossly that she resented being reduced to the status of a coloured pin in her own house, to be moved about at Lorna's will.

He had roared with laughter. 'Jealous?' he had asked maddeningly.

'Just between you and me, darling, I hate those charts too,' she told Amy now.

'I understand why you have to stay behind with Ed, and I don't really mind that because it's Dad's and my special thing anyway, but I don't see why Aunt Lorna has to barge her way in. Can't you stop her, Mummy? Tell Dad she can't come.'

But Isobel didn't feel she could, even for Amy. She was tugged in different directions. That morning she had received a letter from Valerie Benson. She had been surprised, because it was normally Giles who dealt with anything to do with Amy's music.

'I thought you had better see this. I am not sure what I ought to do about it,' Valerie had written and suggested Isobel should ring her.

She had enclosed a letter, which she said Amy had left on her hall table after their last lesson. Isobel read it with a sinking heart:

> *Dear Val,*
>
> *Please will you tell Daddy not to let Aunt Lorna come to my practices and anyway I think I am quite old enuff to practise on my own now but he wont beleeve me unless you tell him.*
>
> *Love from Amy XXX*
>
> *PS This is VERY URGENT.*

Isobel thought Valerie was not the only one with doubts: she had no idea what she ought to do about the letter either. She had so far felt quite unable to tell Giles what Mrs Leslie had said about Edward's fearful new obsession with spiders, but she rang Valerie Benson about Amy's letter. Lorna had twice gone with Giles to sit in on Amy's lesson so she and Valerie had already met. They had not taken to each other and Valerie was not pleased to hear from Isobel that Lorna would now be accompanying Giles to Northumberland. 'Is that a good thing, in the circumstances?' she asked on the telephone.

'Not really, no. But I don't think there's much I can do about it.'

'I see,' said Valerie, who hoped she didn't. 'Well, I shall certainly be telling Amy she's not ready to start practising on her own yet—especially before taking the exam for the music scholarship to Upland House—but perhaps I could talk to Giles at the weekend and suggest that your sister should stop attending Amy's practices, since she seems to dislike it so much.'

'Oh, would you? That would be a real help . . . it's a bit awkward for me at the moment. But I wouldn't want Giles to be cross with Amy, or . . . or anything.' Isobel's voice trailed away uncertainly.

'Well,' said Valerie briskly, 'Amy wrote to ask me to speak to Giles, so she can hardly complain if I do so, can she?'

'I suppose not,' Isobel was doubtful.

Valerie thought she sounded wretched—not at all like her usual bright, outgoing self. She decided to keep an eye on Lorna Cartwright.

*D*aniel started work on Lorna's portrait. She chose to be painted wearing a simple low-cut dress of black silk, which showed off her white skin, impressive cleavage and fair hair to striking effect. She had bought it in Paris the year before on her way to visit her parents; it had been incredibly expensive and Lorna thought it had been worth every centime. She knew she looked stunning in it and Giles's reaction when she had given him and Isobel a dress parade had certainly confirmed this. Daniel also expressed admiration for both the dress and her appearance, but somehow she felt faintly dissatisfied with his response. His enthusiasm seemed tainted with an undercurrent of mockery and his spoken compliments were not enough for Lorna; she craved for homage.

Artist and model had clashed about the background. Lorna had wanted to be painted in the drawing-room of Glendrochatt, but although Giles had readily given permission—without reference to Isobel—Daniel had refused, point-blank, to agree. One picture entitled *The Mistress of Glendrochatt* was enough, he decided, and much as Lorna might crave to claim that position—even if spelt with a small 'm', Daniel thought wryly—he had no intention of abetting her ambitions, so Lorna posed in one of the heavy Chippendale-style dining-room chairs, set against the dark-red velvet of the stage curtains. As the portrait was not a commission and Daniel was not charging Lorna a fee, she could hardly insist. She knew Daniel wanted to exhibit the finished picture and had every intention of offering to buy it if she liked it enough. She had already decided to present it to Giles and Isobel to hang at Glendrochatt. She thought Isobel would find it difficult to refuse such a gift, however much acceptance went against the grain.

Lorna found the sittings frustrating. She had looked forward to her solo sessions with Daniel and was contemplating making a pass at him, but he seemed unreceptive. For his part, Daniel found the physical attraction he had originally felt for Lorna had disappeared as completely as if a light had been switched off.

From a professional point of view, he thought the formality of Lorna's appearance would make an admirable contrast to his portrait of Isobel, but although he was extremely pleased with how both pictures were going, and knew he was working at his very best, he feared Lorna wasn't going to like his vision of her.

What he did not know was that Lorna had gone into the theatre one night and secretly uncovered his half-finished portrait of Isobel. She had looked at it with amazement and felt sick with jealousy.

$\mathcal{T}$he first backcloth was nearly finished now, though there was still some fine detail to be added, and Daniel had already started on the second, commissioned by Lord Dunbarnock. It was an altogether simpler and less detailed proposition, designed to be used in conjunction with the original one and hung in front of it when an indoor set was required; through a large cut-out, arched and pointed like a Gothic window, the winding river and snow-capped hills on the first backcloth could be viewed, as though in the distance. Isobel thought it looked like the background in an early Italian painting and Daniel had been pleased when she told him this. 'Good. That's just the effect I wanted,' he said.

$\mathcal{H}$ave a lovely time.' Isobel, brittle as barley sugar, felt she might snap with resentment as she waved Giles, Amy and Lorna off at four o'clock on Friday afternoon. She couldn't help thinking that Lorna, while making it plain she intended to relish every moment of the trip herself, was trying to make her feel a neglectful wife, an uninterested mother of talented Amy, an over-obsessive parent to Edward and a manhunter who was setting her cap at a younger man.

She watched Giles's car disappear down the drive and walked slowly back into the house.

Daniel was in the kitchen, having a mug of coffee with Joss and Mick. All three men shot her a commiserating look. They were united in their distrust of Lorna.

'Any hope of you giving me a sitting now?' asked Daniel.

'Oh, Daniel, Edward will be back from school soon. I don't think there's time today.'

'I'll give Edward his tea,' offered Joss. 'You go and get your picture done. Do you good to have a rest.'

She looked from one to the other and, although she was deeply touched by their concern, the anxiety she read in their expressions did nothing to make her feel very sanguine about the effect Lorna's presence would have on Giles.

'Please come,' said Daniel, smiling at her persuasively. 'I want to get it finished. I'll let you see it soon.'

'Well . . . all right.' Isobel decided an hour of Daniel's company was just the medicine she needed and, having made a token show of reluctance, gave in with a clear conscience—sauce for the gander could be sauce for the goose too, she thought, the memory of Lorna's expression as she had settled so smugly into the front seat of the car beside Giles filling her with resentment. It occurred to her that while she welcomed the chance to sit for Daniel this afternoon, she was in no hurry for him to finish the portrait.

'Thanks, Joss,' she said. 'You know what a star you are. Come and give me a shout if Ed wants me or you get fed up' and she followed Daniel down to the theatre.

Joss and Mick looked at each other.

'Do Giles good to get a fright.' Mick grinned. 'I hope Izzy gives him one.'

'Yeah. Just so long as no one gets too badly hurt in the process,' said Joss doubtfully.

Twenty-four

I never thanked you for the bluebells,' said Daniel after he had settled Isobel on the rug at the edge of the stage and started to paint.

'They were meant to be my thank you to you—for cheering me up so much that awful evening. For listening but not asking questions. For liking my children and being so nice to both of them. For making me laugh.'

'All part of the service,' he said lightly. 'I'd do it again any time—you only have to lift your little finger and I'll be right there, twisting round it.' He added, 'I think you know that, don't you?'

'Perhaps,' she replied, looking down and plaiting the fringe of the rug with great concentration.

'Besides,' Daniel went on, 'you don't have to thank me for anything. But I do have to thank you—because you have done something for me.'

She did glance up then, as he had hoped she would, her head tilted slightly, unknowingly taking up just the pose he wanted. Her eyes looked enormous. 'Meaning?'

'Meaning that you have taught me to feel again.'

'But you may get hurt,' she said.

'Probably. I'll face that when it happens. But you made me see that one has to take that risk—that it's not good enough to carry protection around all the time like a snail. I've thought a lot about what you said.'

'Wow!' she said. 'How very unnerving.'

'My responsibility, though, not yours. Don't worry, it's a conscious decision.'

'I hope you won't regret it.' Her voice was sober.

'I promise I won't,' he said. 'It will have been worth it.' And he added deliberately, 'No matter what.'

They were both silent for a while, their thoughts running on separate but parallel lines. Then Isobel laughed suddenly, her face lighting up in the way he had come to love.

'Don't you go and get all serious on me, will you? You sound ominously as if you think you've had a conversion experience or something—like one of those *born-again* people about religion.'

'Perhaps I have.' He grinned. 'I wouldn't know. I've never had one before.'

'I mistrust the scary zeal of the convert,' she said darkly.

'No zeal, I promise. Cross my heart.' He laughed back at her. He thought that when he was with her everything he looked at or listened to—even his thoughts—seemed clearer and brighter, as though she had the power to retune all his senses.

'Do you believe in God?' she asked suddenly.

He considered. 'Ye-es,' he said, after a moment. 'I think I do. Perhaps not in a conventional way. My ideas wouldn't fit any one particular faith and I have a barrel-load of doubts.'

'Me too,' she agreed, 'but I think they're important, don't you? It's total conviction that terrifies me; people who think their way has to be the right one with no room for adjustment, like Fee's mother-in-law, for instance, who's sure God is one hundred per cent on her side and that she'll zoom straight to heaven on a first-class ticket when the time comes; fundamentalists and one-remedy fanatics.'

'Do you think it's possible to be a zealot and still have a sense of the ridiculous?' he asked, thinking how much he loved her brand of wry humour and self-mockery.

'Someone once told me that unless you can laugh about your religion you're not on comfortable terms with the Almighty,' she said. 'I liked that. A bit like the way one always teases the people one loves best, I suppose.'

'Please keep teasing me then.' Daniel cocked an eyebrow at her.

'Oh, I will,' she promised. 'I will.'

Both of them were aware that they might be about to cross dangerous new boundaries in their relationship.

The time skimmed by and what Isobel had intended to be only an hour's sitting stretched on.

It was a shock to them both when Joss came in with Edward. 'How ya doing, you two?' he asked. 'Here's a chap who's had his bath and wants his mum to read him a story.'

'Hello, Ed, darling. Oh, Joss, I'd no idea it was so late. I'm so sorry. This modelling business makes one lose all sense of time!'

'I dare say that depends who the artist is,' said Joss drily. 'Still, no worry,' he added, although for once he felt a little uneasy. 'Me and Mick'll be off now, if that's OK by you. Mind how you go.' He had been on the point of suggesting that Daniel might like to meet them later at the Drochatt Arms, but changed his mind. Daniel knew where to find them if he wanted.

Isobel read Edward an extra long story out of an extremely boring book about prehistoric monsters and then, at his request, read him the same chapter all over again rather than move on to the next one. How strange it was, she reflected, that one could read aloud—rather well, too, she prided herself, as she invented different voices for the various deadly dull monster characters—and at the same time have a completely separate train of thought thundering through one's head like an express train.

'Hath the long-legged thpider lady gone?' asked Edward as she tucked him into bed.

'Well, she's gone with Daddy and Amy to do music.'

'Will she come back?'

'Yes, darling, but not until Wednesday.'

'How long ith Wednethday?'

'Quite a long time.'

'I like it when she'th gone,' stated Edward.

So do I, thought Isobel, oh, so do I.

$\mathcal{I}$t occurred to her that she could now offer Mick and Joss, who had originally volunteered to sleep in the house and look after Edward and the dogs while she and Giles were away, the chance to have the weekend off after all. She wondered whether Daniel was intending to work over the Bank Holiday; he had said nothing about his plans for the weekend. As she came downstairs she had no idea whether or not he intended to stay at Glendrochatt at all. The thought that he might be going off somewhere suddenly seemed unwelcome.

Daniel was sprawled on the sofa in the kitchen watching television with Flapper curled up beside him. Wotan lay under the table watching him disapprovingly.

Daniel had changed out of his old painting clothes; he got to his feet as Isobel came in. 'Is it OK with you for me to stay here this weekend?' he asked diffidently, as though he had read her thoughts. 'I could easily go away if it's not convenient.'

'Please stay,' said Isobel. 'Edward and I would like to have you with us.'

She made a cheese soufflé for them both while Daniel chatted to her, telling her stories of his travelling days when he had wandered round the world painting, stopping or moving on as the mood took him; and of the excitement when, after two years of wandering, he had come back to England and his first London exhibition had been a huge success.

He was a good storyteller and made his adventures sound hilarious, but she sensed an inner loneliness in him. 'You clearly had nothing particular at home to draw you back. Were you ever tempted to settle anywhere abroad?' she asked.

'Not really,' he said. 'I don't think it would have helped. I'd still have been stuck with myself if I'd tried to put down roots anywhere else. I might take off again some day. It suits me to be footloose.'

'And fancy free?' she asked—but at that moment the telephone rang.

It was Giles, to say they had arrived safely at the Broughtons', although it had been a long drive with bad Friday night traffic. He didn't ask Isobel how she was or tell her that he loved her as he usually did when he was away from her; she thought how surprisingly easy it is to pick up an atmosphere from a disembodied voice on the telephone. Giles sounded so cool and unlike himself that if she had been on her own she would have given way to misery. Then she spoke to Amy.

Amy, who was usually bursting with chat, sounded very constrained. Isobel felt absolutely certain that Lorna was in the room with them both.

*I*sobel had arranged for Edward to go to play with Mungo on Saturday and drove him over to the Fortescues in the morning.

Fiona was surprised to see her, having expected Joss. She looked at Isobel with concern when she heard of the change of plan. 'Why don't you stay here for lunch too?' she suggested. 'Duncan's gone fishing, Emily's got Tara Duff-Farquharson for the day and there's loads of cottage pie. I'd love it.'

But Isobel said she had to get back to Glendrochatt. 'It seems such a good chance to get lots of odds and ends done while Giles and Amy are out of the way,' she said unconvincingly. 'Besides, I promised Daniel I'd give him another sitting.'

'Oh, Izzy,' said Fiona on an impulse. 'Do be careful.'

'Why should I be careful?' Isobel did not pretend to misunderstand. 'Giles chose to have Lorna instead of me.'

'I thought you just said you wouldn't go with him because of Edward?'

'Umm . . . but it was also because I didn't want to leave Lorna at home to make trouble with Mick and Joss—and anyway Ed's terrified of her. I certainly didn't expect Giles to take her with him and Amy.'

'Sounds as if you've been hoist with your own petard.'

'Maybe,' said Isobel, sticking her chin out and looking defiant, 'but I don't see why I shouldn't make the best of it. Don't look so stuffy, Fee. I'm only enjoying some company. Yes, I do like Daniel, but I've no intention of letting things get out of hand.'

'One never has,' said Fiona.

Isobel and Daniel had a picnic lunch in the garden.

Scotland in May can be cold and bleak, but the fine spell was still holding. The banks of azaleas that grew right down to the edge of the loch were at their best, making not only the whole slope but the water itself look as if it was on fire, so many yellows and oranges were reflected in it. She took Daniel to her favourite haunts on the estate. They walked—and they talked.

They discussed his ambitions as an artist and how much he was enjoying working on the two portraits, hoping to exhibit them the following year at the Royal Portrait Society's annual exhibition in the Mall Gallery; if they were accepted it might prove an important turning point in his career. They talked about her hopes and fears for her children; about whether Amy should be encouraged to become a professional musician or whether, as Flavia had hinted, it might prove too tough a life; about Isobel's own career as an actress, which had never really taken off; about the uncertainties of Edward's future.

'I feel we're in a lull at the moment,' she said as they followed the course of the burn up the hill behind the house. 'That fit was a set-back, but we're in as good a phase with Ed at the moment as we've ever been in and I know it can't last. It's great to have his Review over for this year, but he can only stay at Greenyfordham for one more year anyway. Then we'll have to start all the battling for the right placement again. It's funny about your link with the Camphill schools because—though part of me dreads the thought of him boarding anywhere—that's definitely our top choice. The people there are all so lovely, so dedicated. I like their whole approach and what they stand for.'

'I can still quote some of it,' said Daniel. '*Do I fail to see the other person's spiritual and human potential because it appears he has none? Or am I inhibited by some blindness in myself that does not allow me to recognise the other's potential?* That makes one think a bit, doesn't it?'

'It certainly does,' Isobel agreed. 'And we need to try to find the right niche for Ed for the future—his own world—in case anything ever happened to us. Also, it wouldn't be fair for Amy to be saddled with all the responsibility for Ed one day. It isn't as if she had brothers and sisters to share it with.'

'Did you not want any more children—after you'd had Edward?'

'Oh, yes, desperately. We don't know why Ed is as he is but we'd both have been prepared to take the risk again. Only I was very ill when the twins were born and I can't have any more children now. It's been a sadness.'

'Camphill is a way of life, a whole way of thinking,' said Daniel, feeling it would be better to get back to a safer subject. 'It gets under your skin . . . but it must be a great anxiety trying to decide what's best for Edward.'

'Um. But even if it's what *we* want, will we get the green light from the Council? That's always a worry. God, it's hot! Let's stop for a bit.'

They had come to stepping stones across the burn, a place where the children liked to come. Isobel flopped down on the bank under the shade of a gnarled rowan tree. In autumn its scarlet berries would be a bonfire of colour, and Isobel always picked them and made batches of rowanberry jelly to eat with grouse.

Daniel sat on a boulder and looked down at her. 'Do you actually know anyone with a child at any of the Camphill schools?' he asked, lighting a cigarette.

'I've a friend who has a handicapped son of sixteen at the one near Aberdeen where we'd like Ed to go. She says they're fantastic—they cope with the most difficult children and honour them all. I must say I dread the onset of puberty for Ed. That obviously brings a whole new set of problems.'

Daniel grinned. 'What's professionally known as "Inappropriate Public Behaviour" I seem to remember?' he suggested, puffing smoke at the midges that hovered around them.

'Exactly.' Isobel giggled. 'My pal says some of the advice can be hilarious. She once asked one of the helpers what to do when her son started to get sexual urges and was told . . .' Isobel gave a snort of laughter and imitated a foreign accent: ' "Oh, vell, ve try to make ze children identify zeir emotions with somsing beautiful. Ve say, Look at zat lovverley sonset." But as my pal said: "There you are in Perth High Street in the pouring rain, your son's gazing at women's underclothes in a shop window, he's got a jumbo erection and is masturbating away for Scotland—and where's the bloody sunset?" '

'Tricky,' said Daniel.

'I suppose in your case your career was a foregone conclusion, but you're so brilliant with Ed. Did you ever consider working with handicapped children yourself?' she asked curiously.

'I thought about it, yes. I still do occasionally,' he admitted. 'What you were telling me about the art therapy—that was interesting. I wouldn't want to give up my own commissioned painting completely, but that made me wonder if I could ever use any skills I may have in some other way as well.'

'There's more to you than meets the eye, Daniel Hoffman.'

'Tell me more about Glendrochatt,' he said, not wanting to be lured back to the subject of his own past. 'Is there a ghost? This sort of house ought to have one.'

'We're supposed to have the statutory Grey Lady—she's always been known in the family as Green Jean.'

'Sounds very politically correct . . . so not really grey at all?'

'Well, I've never actually seen her myself,' admitted Isobel, 'but my father has. She disappeared into a wall at the end of the passage. She tends to nick things, which is a bit of a bore. Then, after you've searched for days and turned the house upside down, she'll put them back somewhere quite obvious like the hall table.'

'That sounds pretty human to me,' objected Daniel.

'Oh, don't say that. You have to keep on the right side of Jean.'

Daniel could see she was half serious. 'Tell me more,' he said. So she told him about the Grant family history, about Giles's father's love for his self-destructive wife and how he'd hoped that giving her the theatre to make her happy would cure her depression.

'I once asked Lady Fortescue what my mother-in-law was really like,' Isobel continued, giving a snort of laughter. 'She gave that sweet smile that signals her total disapproval, crimped her mouth at the edges like a piecrust and said that if she'd been a horse she wouldn't have bought her—Fee always says she was lucky her ma-in-law didn't run her hands down her legs and look at her teeth when she got engaged to Duncan. Old Violet didn't mean to be funny, but doesn't that give you a telling vision of foam-flecked nostrils and a wildly rolling eye?' She added soberly, 'I find it hard to forgive Atalanta for what she did to Giles, but I really loved my father-in-law. It was a frightful shock when he dropped dead of a heart attack.'

'What was he like?'

'Very handsome, very elegant—imagine an immensely long pair of tartan trews with monogrammed slippers at one end and terrifying beetle eyebrows at the other—but hidden in the middle, the kindest heart you can think of. Lots of people found him remote and thought him arrogant, but he was always divine to me and we used to talk about everything under the sun. He said the saddest thing once: Giles and I were going to America, for a month and I asked him if he'd be lonely here without us. He said yes, but that he'd survive because he'd had so many years of practice. I could have cried. He adored Giles but found it hard to show his feelings. Funny, but the week before he died he suddenly thanked me for being a bridge between them both and helping them to get close. It wasn't at all a typical utterance and I was terribly touched. I've often wondered if he had some sort of presentiment that he was going to die. I've never told anyone that before, not even Giles,' she said. 'I feel if we can make a success of this theatre venture I will be doing it partly for him—and I think Giles will partly be doing it for his mother.'

'This whole place means a lot to you, doesn't it?' Daniel asked.

'Yes,' she said. 'I've dug my roots in deep.'

Daniel, so rootless himself, felt hollow with loneliness.

*D*espite his brave words of the day before he couldn't help wondering what he might be letting himself in for by getting so involved, not just with this woman, whom he found so entrancing, but with the whole family, whose way of life was so very different from his own. The answer that presented itself seemed bleak.

They did not talk about Isobel's marriage, but the subject hovered over them like the threat of thunder on a hot summer's day.

Twenty-five

Valerie Benson delivered Amy home in the middle of the morning on Monday. She had picked her up early from the Broughtons in order to avoid the build-up of Bank Holiday traffic and they had stopped at a Little Chef for a second breakfast.

Usually Amy came back from Suzuki events on a high, music almost visibly sparkling out of her—Daniel's portrayal of Amy in the backcloth, with notes flying round her like an aura, had captured her essence wonderfully well—but one look at her face this morning told Isobel a story she did not want to know.

'Hi, darling. Have you had a lovely time? How did it all go?'

'It was OK,' said Amy, unresponsive to Isobel's welcoming hug, and she went straight off to look for Edward. Normally she would have rushed to greet her mother, her feet leaving the ground as she wrapped herself round her.

Isobel looked at Valerie, a question in her eyes. 'How kind of you to bring her back, Val. Can I give you a cup of coffee?'

Valerie hesitated. She had half hoped to be able to drop off Amy without seeing Isobel. 'Well, just a quick one. Thank you.' She followed Isobel into the house.

'I take it the course has not been a success?' Isobel put two cups of coffee on the kitchen table.

'There was nothing wrong with the *course*.' Valerie was not sure either what to say or how to start to say it, which was most unlike her.

'Go on, tell me,' insisted Isobel. 'Amy didn't do well because she didn't like my sister being there instead of me. That's what you're going to say, isn't it?'

'I wouldn't go as far as to say Amy didn't do well. I didn't sit in on any of her individual lessons, of course, because I was taking classes at the same time myself, but Amy's one of my star pupils and I happen to know Brian Cotterell who was teaching her, so I asked him what he thought. He said she was very musical—good technique, sightreading excellent—but he thought she lacked *enthusiasm*. . . .' Valerie looked at Isobel. '*Amy* . . . to lack enthusiasm! I said to him, "We can't be talking about the same child!" She's always made music with such verve—such . . . such joy.' Valerie looked nonplussed. 'She's not happy, Isobel. You'll have to do something about it.' She added in her forthright way, 'I think you need to do something for your own sake too. Your sister acts as if she's in charge of your child *and* your husband. Most people assumed she was Giles's wife and she did nothing to put them right.'

'Did you try to talk to Giles?'

'I did try, yes, but I never managed to see him alone. It's a very busy schedule as you know, but Lorna was always with him whenever I had a free moment. I shall be very upset if Amy's chances of a scholarship are affected by this.' She looked challengingly at Isobel.

You'll be upset, thought Isobel. What about *me*? Aloud she said, 'If I try to talk to Giles about letting Lorna get so involved with Amy's music it looks as if I'm being petty and jealous, but I can see I'll have to have a go at him. He's so perceptive as a rule that I'm amazed he doesn't realise quite how much Amy hates it.'

It was on the tip of Valerie's tongue to say that love made one blind, but she bit back the words in time. 'Oh, well,' she said, 'you'll just have to put him straight. I shall certainly speak my mind when he next brings Amy for a lesson—whether your sister comes with him or not.' She heaved herself out of the chair and gave Isobel an unexpected goodbye kiss. 'Your husband is a delightful man,' she added. 'But they all need to be shown who's boss sometimes. You hang on to him, my dear.' Isobel thought she sounded as if she was talking about an unruly dog.

*A*t Gattersburn Park Country House Hotel, on Tuesday morning, Giles and Lorna lay in a huge Jacobean four-poster bed. There were linen sheets on the bed, flowers on the antique dressing-table, the heavy oak furniture gleamed and smelt of beeswax, and the casement windows looked over a topiary garden with yew trees cut in the shape of chessmen. There was even a selection of books on each bedside table as there would be in a private house: old cloth-back copies of P. G. Wodehouse and Agatha Christie, as well as glossy new photographic books of Hadrian's Wall, famous English gardens and chateaux of the Loire. It was all very tasteful. A bogus ancestral portrait, the varnish much cracked but the frame in excellent condition, gazed down at them from the wall with impersonal aloofness.

Giles, propped up on one elbow, ran his other hand lazily along Lorna's shoulder, down the inside of her arm and up again. He traced the hollows round her collarbone with one finger, then drew loops up and down her throat as though he were carefully practising joined-up writing. He looked down at her. 'Breakfast now, or a little later on?' he asked.

'A little later,' said Lorna, stretching like a cat and then starting to do a little stroking too.

*T*he weekend had gone entirely to Lorna's plan. The Broughtons had been friendly and welcoming, and Lorna had behaved impeccably in front of them, stressing how upsetting it was for Giles that Isobel had to stay behind because of Edward—not to mention the disappointment for Isobel herself, said Lorna, wide blue eyes full of touching sympathy. 'It's so sweet of them both to think of asking me to come instead. Such a treat for me and typical of their generosity,' she had said earnestly to Linda Broughton. 'I only hope I can be enough of a help to Giles as a talent scout to thank them both.'

The Broughtons thought Isobel's sister charming, absolutely charming—and *so* elegant—although they agreed that Amy seemed to have grown much less attractive than when they'd spent a night at Glendrochatt the previous autumn: so rude to her aunt and such a sulky expression. A difficult age, perhaps—and of course there is that handicapped twin at home, isn't there? Perhaps one should make allowances, said the Broughtons—not making them—but if a child of theirs had been so unappreciative of all the trouble her father was taking over her music they wouldn't have stood for it.

Early on Saturday morning Giles, Amy and Lorna had set off for the girls' boarding school, which had offered its music wing as a venue for the course during the half-term break. Lorna had loved it all: the involvement and the interest, the fun of meeting the parents and all the young musicians. Her fingers had itched to smack Amy for being so sullen and insolent, but she hadn't really minded. It suited Lorna very well for Giles to be annoyed with his precious little daughter. 'Please don't worry on my account,' she had said to Giles, when he apologised to her for Amy's ungracious attitude. 'I do think Amy's a bit spoilt at the moment, but then she's always been used to getting so much attention. I'm sure it'll come out in the wash.'

Giles had seen his daughter in a very unfavourable light and Amy had been as defiant as she dared. After the first day was over she had felt worn out with disappointment at her own poor performance and by many other turbulent emotions, which she did not really understand. The discovery that she had left behind the threadbare old rabbit that had accompanied her to bed every night of her life was the last straw.

'Don't be such a baby, Amy,' said Lorna, who had taken it on herself to come upstairs to turn out Amy's light and found her squirrelling frantically through her suitcase, possessions thrown all over the room. 'What a mess! Pick up your clothes. You're nearly eleven, much too big to make a fuss about a rabbit.'

'He must be somewhere. Mummy always packs him.'

'Well, perhaps you'll remember to pack him yourself next time. I was doing all my own packing when I was your age.'

'Where's Daddy?'

'Daddy's busy. There's a dinner party and Mr and Mrs Broughton have asked friends in specially to meet him.'

'Please ask him to come up,' said Amy, turning her face away and not kissing Lorna goodnight.

Lorna had gone down and told Giles, 'Amy's exhausted, so I've tucked her down. She's practically out for the count. I should think she'll be asleep already.'

'I'll just go and pop in on her all the same,' said Giles, but at that moment the Broughtons' first guests arrived and he got waylaid. He had gone up to check on her as soon as dinner was over but by then she had cried herself to sleep.

$\mathcal{T}$he weekend had finished on Sunday evening with all the children playing together; the smallest ones in the front row—some of them as young as four—played the tune of *'Twinkle, Twinkle Little Star'* on their tiny fiddles, while the older children played more complicated harmonies. It was a lovely ending to two days of music making. Lorna had thought it enchanting and had fantasised about what it would be like to have a budding little virtuoso of her own.

She and Giles had spent the following day exploring the lovely Northumbrian countryside and had found an attractive-looking pub in a small village, which served lunches. They had ordered fried scampi and a bottle of chilled Sauvignon Blanc.

'Oh, Giles, I am enjoying myself,' said Lorna. 'You always were the best company. I haven't had such fun for years. It was wonderful of you to let me come, although I feel a bit guilty about Izzy.'

'She could have come if she'd really wanted. Ed seemed perfectly all right again and we've often left him with Joss and Mick before.'

'I know, but that's just why I feel so guilty,' Lorna insisted. 'If there are repercussions I shall feel it's partly my fault. I have to say I think it's quite brave of you to leave her, given the circumstances.'

'What circumstances?'

Lorna hesitated. 'Oh, nothing really. I shouldn't have said that. Forget it.'

'You'd better tell me what you mean.'

Lorna gazed out of the window. 'I'd really rather not,' she said with a show of reluctance.

'Oh, come on.'

'I may be wrong, of course . . . it's just that Daniel and Izzy seem so . . . well . . .' She let the sentence trail away and looked out of the window.

'You mean you think Daniel has fallen for Izz? I know. I thought so too. But she's just flattered and he'll get over it.'

'Oh, Giles, I think it may have gone much further than that.'

'What exactly are you suggesting?'

Lorna covered her face with her hands. 'I'm afraid they're having an affair,' she whispered. 'Oh, Giles, I'm so sorry.'

'I don't believe you.'

'Perhaps it's better that you shouldn't.'

'Don't give me that!'

Giles sounded so angry that Lorna almost regretted having started the conversation, but once having embarked on it, and with the precious two days alone together still to come, she ploughed on: 'You won't want to hear this but perhaps you ought to know. I left the theatre early the other night and Isobel and Daniel were together in Edward's bedroom. I saw them. Let's just say they were very wrapped up in each other.'

'Oh, come off it, Lorna.' Giles's own suspicions of that evening were confirmed, but they were a still a long way from what Lorna was insinuating. 'You're forgetting that Edward was there too. Izzy, of all people, would never be having it off with Daniel in Ed's room. It's inconceivable.'

'Perhaps.' Lorna loaded her second barrel, and took aim. 'But I'm afraid there have been other times. I've also seen Izzy leaving Daniel's bedroom when they've thought there was no one else in the house.' She made it sound as if this was no isolated occurrence. 'I think it's time you got Daniel to show you the portrait of Izz,' she went on. 'I think it tells its own story.'

'You mean he's actually shown it to you?' Giles, frustrated that Daniel had still not let him look at it, felt outraged that he should not be the first person to see it.

'I don't think he really meant me to see it,' said Lorna, and added less truthfully, 'It happened to be uncovered one day when I was having a sitting . . . but you must judge for yourself. Perhaps I'm imagining things.'

Giles felt as if he'd been kicked in the stomach. Deep down he suspected he was being manipulated, but doubts still niggled, adding their poison to his own guilty feelings and making a powerful cocktail of resentment, suspicion, the wish to punish Isobel and an urgent need for self-justification. 'Let's not allow fruitless speculation to spoil our jaunt,' he said. Isobel would have recognised the dangerous glitter in his eyes and known that Giles's reckless demon had taken him over. 'We'll deal with the situation when we get home. Have you ever been round Alnwick?'

'No,' said Lorna. 'But I've always wanted to go.'

'Then let's.' Giles gave her his most brilliant smile. They had a thoroughly enjoyable afternoon together. Giles was the most amusing and stimulating companion with whom to go sightseeing: he had an eye for noticing the small details that might easily be missed, possessed a fund of architectural knowledge and was invariably full of the sort of offbeat little anecdotes that add seasoning to history.

When they eventually arrived at Gattersburn Park, an imposing mansion recently converted into a luxury hotel, Lorna had gone to check in while Giles parked the car. She came back across the dark panelled hall to meet him as he came in. 'Something rather awkward has cropped up,' she said.

'Don't say they've messed up the reservation. I had written confirmation from them.'

'But they haven't changed the room and they're denying all knowledge of my call telling them about the alteration. They've only got the double room in the name of Mr and Mrs Grant. What d'you want to do about it?'

Giles knew with absolute inner certainty that Lorna had never made that call, but his demon was in charge.

'Perhaps we should just enjoy it for old times' sake, Giles?' she asked softly.

They stared at each other.

'Why not?' said Giles. 'As you say, for old times' sake.'

Twenty-six

With the arrival of June, the first proper month of summer, the weather broke. Cloud descended, wrapping the hills in a grey shroud of gloom and making them invisible from the house, while driving drizzle across the loch blotted out the view of the low ground. The weather matched Isobel's mood: she felt she could no longer see in what direction her life was going.

Giles and Lorna had not returned on the Wednesday. Giles telephoned to say they had been disappointed by the performance of the cellist, but there was a string quartet of young musicians who were giving a concert at Newcastle University on Saturday who'd had interesting reviews—it seemed a pity not to go to hear them while he was in the area. Didn't Isobel think so?

'Good idea—why not? Go for it,' she said brightly and, 'Yes, we're all absolutely *fine* here, in great form. Of course. Don't hurry home.' As she put down the telephone she felt shaky. This can't be happening, she thought, wondering how she could reconcile her acute misery about Giles and Lorna with her growing attraction to Daniel. Which had come first? Old riddles about chickens and eggs floated through her mind—to which, of course, she found no answer.

It was a relief to be able to go down to the office and chat to Sheila Shepherd, as she had always enjoyed doing in the past, without the feel of Lorna's breath on her neck. It was good to think about plans for the months ahead, both for the Arts Centre and the family, without knowing that everything, no matter how personal, would be discussed with Lorna and that her sister's influence would be brought to bear on any decision that was taken. It made Isobel realise what an increasing tension this had become—but also how pointless any project to do with Glendrochatt or the children seemed without Giles to share it with. Isobel felt like a boat adrift.

'Isobel! How are you the day? It's so good to see you. You've become quite a stranger.' Sheila beamed at her. 'I was just away for my cuppy when I heard your step. Will we be having one together now?' Isobel said that would be lovely and wondered what Sheila really thought of the new situation in her office.

I must make some plans of my own, she thought. I used to be able to take decisions so easily. Why does everything have to be so much more complicated now? It seemed as if the comforting black and white of her former opinions had blended into a blur of many varying shades of grey.

She took two small practical decisions and felt better for having done so. The first was to let Joss and Mick go off for a holiday as soon as possible, because in July the annual migration of southerners up to Scotland would start, and with it would come the usual stream of friends and relations wanting to stay at Glendrochatt. It sometimes got a bit too hectic for comfort, coinciding as it did with the school holidays and all the children's ploys, but on the whole Giles and Isobel both welcomed the invasion and loved dispensing hospitality. Then there would be the opening concert and the start of their first season. Mick and Joss needed a break before that.

Isobel's second decision was to stick to a plan, which she had been on the verge of cancelling: a promise to go to Prague for a week with her parents. The trip had been booked months before and she had originally been looking forward to it, but recently she had felt so threatened at the idea of leaving her husband and her sister alone together that she had contemplated suggesting to her parents that Lorna might like to go in her place. Now she felt that such caution had already been rendered pointless by her own refusal to go to Northumberland. If there was anything going on between Giles and Lorna—and she was sure there was—then it had already taken place. Let them get on with it, she thought. Events will have to take their course.

On Thursday afternoon there was a telephone call from Mrs Baird, Amy's headmistress. Amy had been involved in a fight and had not only scratched the face of another child quite badly, but pulled out a sizeable chunk of her hair. Isobel felt herself go weak at the knees and sat down on the arm of the kitchen sofa where she had picked up the telephone.

'Oh, God, how awful. Whatever can have come over her? Who was the other child?'

'Tara Duff-Farquharson.'

Isobel groaned. Mrs Baird said, 'As far as I can make out there were no other children involved in the actual quarrel and I can't find out what caused such an attack from either Tara or Amy, but physically Tara certainly came off much worse and is quite badly shocked. I'm having to send her home early and I think in the circumstances Amy should be sent home too. I feel I ought to suspend Amy for a week but I should welcome your guidance. She's not the Amy we know at the moment and various members of the staff have commented on how difficult she's been lately— especially since the half-term break. Perhaps we could talk about this some time? Anyway, can you possibly come and fetch her?'

'I'll get in the car straight away. I should be with you in half an hour. I am *so* sorry.'

'Trouble?' asked Joss, looking at her expression.

'Definitely trouble. Amy's just savaged Tara Duff-Farquharson.'

'Well, bully for Amy,' said Joss cheerfully, winking at her. 'Hope Amy came off best.'

'Apparently she most certainly did,' said Isobel with a reluctant laugh. 'Oh, Joss, I do love you.'

$\mathcal{W}$hen she got to the school, Isobel agreed with Mrs Baird that she should try to get the truth out of Amy and would ring Mrs Baird back when she discovered what had triggered the trouble. It was agreed that she should keep Amy off school the following day, to make a point to the other children, but that, providing some understandable explanation was forthcoming, she could return the following week, having been dealt with at home as her parents saw fit. Isobel found herself unwilling to tell Mrs Baird that Giles was away, which she knew was ridiculous because he often had to go away on business.

Amy was completely uncommunicative on the way home and Isobel, most unusually, failed to get anything out of her at all. 'We just had a fight,' was all Amy would say, shrugging her shoulders with a defiant, don't-care gesture.

'Amy, darling, I simply can't help you if you won't talk to me. This is so unlike you. There has to be a reason for your behaviour. Mrs Baird says it was a really vicious scrap and that one of the teachers had to rescue Tara, but you haven't got a mark on you of any kind. Please tell me what happened to make you do this.' But Amy's mouth remained tightly zipped. Isobel thought of asking her if such naughtiness had anything to do with anxiety about Giles and Lorna, but was afraid of putting ideas into her daughter's head that might not already be there.

'Well, I'm sorry, darling,' she said when they got home. 'You really leave me no option but to send you straight up to bed. I'll come and see you later. You know I'll listen to your side of things if you change your mind. It's up to you.'

Amy walked upstairs with her head in the air, a lonely, unhappy little figure, and Isobel watched her go with a heavy heart.

Daniel, coming over from the theatre in search of a cup of tea, found her still in the hall five minutes later, sitting on the bottom step of the stairs, her head in her hands. 'Isobel, you don't half look weighed down with cares. What's up?' he asked. He longed to take her in his arms as he had done when he'd found her crying in Edward's room.

Isobel told him about Amy.

'Bet some of the other kids at school know the score,' said Daniel. 'Have you asked Fiona to pump Emily about it?'

'Of course! How feeble of me. Why didn't I think of that?'

'A little question of the wood and the trees? Easy for an outsider to see.'

'I don't think of you as an outsider,' she said, jumping up. 'I'll ring Fee at once.' As she went towards the kitchen she stopped and gave him a quick kiss on the cheek. 'Thanks, Daniel.' He watched her go, all defences down, his heart in his eyes, though she did not see it.

Joss, who walked through the front door with Edward a minute later after helping him off the school bus, looked at Daniel and raised an eyebrow. 'Hi there, Daniel, you look like that guy Oliver Twist. You hungry or something?' he asked.

'Only for the unobtainable,' said Daniel lightly.

'Better stay hungry then, mate,' said Joss.

Grizelda Murray was doing the school run, so Isobel caught Fiona just before Emily got home. Fiona was deeply sympathetic. 'Poor *you*,' she said. 'I'll talk to Emily as soon as she's home and get back to you.'

When Fiona rang, Isobel was sitting at the kitchen table having tea with Mick, Joss and Daniel. Edward sat in front of the television looking at a Walt Disney video and eating scrambled bantam's eggs. Six new bantams, including a magnificent cockerel, had been delivered the week before with love and apologies from Flavia and Brillo. Edward had been enchanted.

Isobel rushed to answer the telephone. 'Ah . . . now that would explain things,' she said, after Fiona had told her Emily's version of events. 'Thanks, Fee, but oh, dear, I suppose I'll have to ring up Jolly Jilly Duff-Farquharson and grovel to her anyway.'

'I think you'll find her very understanding,' said Fiona. 'She's not half as bad as you seem to think. I like her.'

'Don't tell me,' Isobel groaned. 'I don't want to know. You're going to say that under that team-spirited, who's-for-hockey, head-girl exterior there beats the heart of a lovely, warm, generous woman.'

'Something like that.' Fiona laughed. 'Good luck anyway. Mind you ring me with any stop-press news.'

Isobel went upstairs.

Amy was lying face down on the bed. Isobel sat beside her. 'I think I know what the trouble was, darling,' she said softly. 'Emily told Fee what happened. It was all about Edward, wasn't it?'

Amy sat up. She looked terribly white. 'Oh, Mum,' she wailed. 'Why did God make Ed like he is? It's so unfair.'

'I find it difficult too,' Isobel agreed sadly, wishing she could hand her stormy little daughter a plate of comforting, pink-iced certainties. 'But the truth is, I don't know, darling. I certainly can't think God *wants* children to be like Ed and I think He loves Ed just as he is—and that's all we can any of us do. I'm afraid there are no easy answers.' She stroked Amy's tousled hair back from her face. 'When I was your age, Grandpa used to tell me that we have to learn that life *isn't* fair, then try to be as fair as we can to other people. But it's awfully difficult. Would you like to tell me what happened?'

Amy sat up, her chin on her knees, and relived the afternoon's events.

*W*hy were you crying like that in RE, Amy?' Christopher Murray had asked. Girls cried at the most peculiar things in his opinion, but not usually Amy Grant, who was almost as good as a boy. He was bored stiff with RE himself, though he quite liked pretty Miss Preston who took it.

'I *wasn't* crying,' Amy said, although she had been.

'Yes, you were,' said Tara. 'I saw you too and I know why you were crying. It's because you've got a funny brother like the crippled boy in that Bible story Miss Preston was reading us.'

Amy had been quite unprepared herself for the effect the story had on her. She only knew that it made her think of Edward and she had suddenly felt overwhelmed with anguish. The fact that this had been apparent to someone else was unbearable. 'Edward's not *funny*,' she said fiercely, glaring at Tara, 'and anyway, you don't know him.'

'Yes, I do and he is. I saw him the other day at the Fortescues'. He's a weirdo: he looks weird, he sounds weird and he is weird.' Tara made her mouth lopsided, pulled a crooked face and squinted. 'But Mummy says we all have to be specially nice to him because he's *handicapped* and not like other people,' she added self-righteously.

'Shut up! Shut up! Shut up!' Amy had shouted, clenching her fingers. 'You don't know anything about anything.'

'Your brother is a weirdo, a weirdo, a weirdo,' sang Tara, who had a few scores of her own to settle with popular, confident Amy—at which moment Amy had launched herself at Tara like a Cruise Missile.

$\mathcal{I}$t was so scary, Mummy,' said Amy now. 'I really didn't mean to hurt Tara but I thought I was going to burst. Just for a minute it was wonderful when I hit her—and then I couldn't stop and it was awful. Now I hate her because she made me do it.'

'Oh, darling, I expect I'd have punched her too if I'd been your age and I'd probably have felt like it even now, but it's not the right thing to do and hating doesn't solve anything. You'll have to say you're sorry.'

'What about Tara? How could she say such beastly things about Ed?' asked Amy. '*She* should say sorry too.'

'Yes, she should. But that's up to her and her mum to work

out. I don't suppose she feels too good about it really and anyway you obviously gave her the most awful bashing.' Isobel looked at Amy's intense face and trembled for what the future might have in store for this passionate, talented, deeply loyal child. She said: 'Amy, I think you should realise that people who aren't used to Ed can find him quite . . . threatening at first. You're going to have to learn to cope with it now, because it will get more difficult, not less.'

'Threatening? Ed wouldn't hurt *anybody*.'

'*We* know that, because we love him and he's special, but he *is* very different and people are often afraid of what they don't understand. They don't know how to react.'

'None of my other friends call Edward a weirdo.'

'Most of your other friends have known him for ever. Tara's new up here—sometimes it's hard to break in and make friends. She may feel you all gang up against her.'

'Tara wants Emily to be her best friend instead of mine,' muttered Amy.

Isobel sighed. 'Ah, well, you'll have to work that one out between you, but not by fighting. Listen, Amy, Tara was horrid to taunt you about Ed, but the way to deal with people like that is to try to make them understand, not to wallop them. Did you know that Aunt Lorna's afraid of Ed too? She doesn't know how to behave with him either and it makes her jumpy, and although I know she can't help it I still find that hard to cope with myself sometimes and so does she. Does it help to know that?'

Amy swallowed. 'When will Dad be coming home?' she asked in a very small voice.

'Soon,' said Isobel, thinking she wouldn't have minded landing a few well-aimed punches on her errant husband. Why isn't he here to help me with all this? she thought furiously. It was all very well to preach forgiveness to Amy, but she had a smouldering fuse burning away inside herself that was far from comfortable.

'I think I'm going to be sick,' said Amy suddenly, making a dash for the basin.

Isobel held her head while she retched and heaved, and eventually brought up the contents of her stomach. 'There, that's all your rage gone away down the plughole,' Isobel said, wishing she could as easily get rid of her own angry lump, now permanently lodged somewhere in her chest. 'You'll feel much better now, darling.'

She sponged Amy's face, and put her in her own and Giles's big bed—always considered a treat when the children were ill. 'I'll get your book for you. Have a nice read and go into a different world. That's what I try to do when I'm miserable.'

'D'you think Daniel would come and visit me? He tells brilliant stories.'

'I'm sure he would. I'll go and ask him.' Isobel wondered— not without satisfaction—what Giles would make of this request by his daughter.

In the end Isobel did not have to ring the Duff-Farquharsons. Jolly Jilly got in an apology first, and said that Tara had told her all about it and was very ashamed of herself.

'How is Tara?' Isobel asked, having apologised profusely for her own daughter's wild-cat behaviour.

'A bit shaken, but she'll mend. Perhaps she's learnt something. Let's try to get the children together on neutral territory when things have simmered down a bit, before the Pony Club hop, anyway.'

Jilly Duff-Farquharson could not have been nicer or more generous, Isobel admitted to Daniel afterwards, but added darkly, 'That still doesn't mean I have to like her, or fall in with all her jolly, well-organised plans.' Daniel gave her a very amused look.

He had gone to sit with Amy and Isobel had been much cheered, when she went to suggest that Amy might come down to supper in her dressing-gown, to hear shrieks of mirth coming from her bedroom. Daniel was regaling Amy with tales of the various fights he'd been in himself as a boy.

'Amy and I've got a plan, if you agree,' said Daniel. 'Since she's been banned from school tomorrow I think she should do something educational. I've never been to Edinburgh. How about me driving you both there for the day and taking you out to lunch, and then you could take me sightseeing?'

'Say yes, Mum,' begged Amy.

'Sounds more like a treat than a punishment,' objected Isobel. 'You don't deserve it.'

'I won't do it again and I *will* say I'm sorry,' wheedled Amy.

'Hm!' Isobel tried to look disapproving, but of course she agreed.

*T*hey had a brilliant day. They sang songs at the tops of their voices in the car and Amy tried out her latest crop of school jokes on Daniel, who obligingly pretended not to know the punchline answers. He also provided her with some new ones in delightfully dubious taste. 'For goodness sake, Daniel! What are you trying to do?' asked Isobel. 'I don't want her suspended from school *again*.'

They started the culture blitz with Holyroodhouse, where Amy gloried ghoulishly in the brass plaque marking the spot of Rizzio's murder. She had been reading Alison Uttley's *A Traveller in Time* and was deeply into anything to do with Mary, Queen of Scots—though she thought it very disappointing not to catch a glimpse of her drifting through a wall. 'Mum never lets me stay on in Edinburgh at night and do any of the Ghost Walks,' she grumbled to Daniel. 'It's so bóring.'

'You'd be a screaming wreck if you really saw one,' teased Isobel. 'I know you, you'd be in our bed half the night for weeks afterwards.' As they walked back to Daniel's car she said, 'Oh, now there's a bit of history in the making for you both. That building over there, which used to be the headquarters of Scottish & Newcastle Breweries, is about to be pulled down to make way for our brand-new Scottish Parliament. You'll be able to tell your grandchildren that you remember how it used to be in the old days.'

Daniel winked at Amy. 'I think Mum rather fancies herself as a guide to the city,' he said. 'Perhaps she could get a job with the Tourist Board if the concerts don't work out.'

'Next time I'm in Holyrood in a few weeks' time you won't recognise me,' Isobel told them. 'I shall be all dolled up in my glad-rags because Giles is on duty at the Royal Garden Party this year.'

'What sort of duty?'

'Well, like his dad before him, he's an Archer,' she explained. 'Officially they're the Queen's Bodyguard and take it in turns to attend her at State dos when she's in Scotland—though a fat lot of use they'd be in an emergency because they carry bows but not arrows on ceremonial occasions. Giles fancies himself no end in the kit.' She giggled. 'He and Duncan Fortescue and various others have real archery practice sometimes, which they take frightfully seriously and they're unbelievably competitive over their scores. It's hilarious: like little boys playing at Robin Hood.'

Isobel decided they would drive to the St James Shopping Centre next. 'Parking in Edinburgh can be a nightmare,' she said, 'but we could leave your car in the multi-storey there and take a taxi to stop ourselves being utterly flaked at the end of the day.'

On the way across the Esplanade, below the castle, Amy pointed out the Witches Well to Daniel. 'Three hundred women were burnt to death here,' she told him, eyes round with horror. 'People thought they were all witches. Imagine that!'

'I'd rather not. I like women too much—especially entrancing white witches who cast irresistible spells over one' and he looked at Isobel.

'Do you actually know any?' Amy was impressed.

'I do know one, actually, but they're pretty rare,' he said.

'Come on, you two, buck up. We've got a lot to see.' Isobel walked on hurriedly and refused to allow her eye to be caught.

She could feel her heart pounding—although she knew this was not because of the uphill climb to the castle—and she felt both guilty and elated.

They visited the great banqueting hall and Isobel's special favourite, the little chapel of St Margaret. 'I always like coming in here,' she said. 'Isn't it lovely? Come on, Amy, tell us what you know about it.'

'Margaret was old Malc's queen and got sainted up after she snuffed it because she did Good Works for the poor.'

'Sounds just like Mrs Duff-Farquharson,' said Daniel.

They went down to the dungeons next to inspect Mons Meg, the famously huge fifteenth-century cannon made of long metal bars hooped together. 'We can't go home and not tell Ed we visited Meg,' said Isobel. 'But what a relief not to have him with us. He's fixated on that wretched gun; we can never get him past it, can we, Amy? He knows far more about it than I do but he always has to ask the same questions twenty times.'

'I think guns are boring.' Amy made a face. 'Let's look at the crown jewels. Me and Emily love them.'

'If Daniel's with us in August, darling, we'll have to bring him to the Tattoo,' Isobel said to Amy, hoping very much that he would be. After they had exhausted the delights of the castle they climbed down the two incredibly steep flights of steps, Amy happily jumping and counting, to Johnston Terrace and then they cut through to the Grassmarket to have a restorative pizza.

After lunch Amy had wanted to go to the nearby joke shop, beloved of all local children, but Isobel refused. 'This is meant to be a strictly educational day.'

'Daniel would love it and Daddy always lets us. Pleeease, Mum.'

'Absolutely not.'

'I'll bet you'll want to spend *hours* in that boring old deli you're so hooked on,' complained Amy. 'It's not fair!'

'Ah,' said Daniel, 'but then your mum hasn't just left one of her friends half bald and had a go at gouging her eyes out . . . as far as we know, that is,' he added, grinning.

Amy giggled, but decided it was not a propitious moment to push her luck with her mother.

'Still, you're right, darling,' admitted Isobel. 'I'm glad you reminded me. I wouldn't half mind just popping in quickly to V and C to stock up with a few goodies. Leith Walk's on our way home anyway and I swear I won't be long.' Amy looked disbelieving. 'You'll love it Daniel,' said Isobel. 'Cheeses to die for. A sniff of Valvona and Crolla's like getting an instant fix of sunny Italy in the middle of our grey and windy city.'

'A very beautiful city, though,' said Daniel. He insisted they had to go to the Scottish National Gallery before they went home and was shocked to hear that Isobel had never taken Amy there before. 'But we'll only look at five pictures,' he announced.

'Why only *five*?'

'Because that's all my artist grandmother used to let me see when she first started to take me round picture galleries. Then you will come away hungry for more.'

He was right. Amy had not wanted to leave.

*T*hat night, before they went their separate ways to bed, the urge to compete with Giles and play with a few dangerous flames of her own overcame Isobel. She let Daniel kiss her goodnight— and was deeply disturbed by it. 'Oh,' she said rather accusingly, when he eventually lifted his mouth from hers, 'so you're a good kisser as well as a good artist, Daniel Hoffman. There's no end to your talents.'

They stood by the window in the drawing-room in the fading summer light. Then she placed her hands on his chest and leant her forehead against him. 'I can feel your heart beating through your shirt.'

'I'm not surprised.' said Daniel. 'It's had quite a day.'

Twenty-seven

Giles and Lorna returned on Sunday. They walked into the kitchen at Glendrochatt as everyone was finishing lunch. There was instant, wary silence.

'Hi there, all,' said Giles, sounding more insouciant than he felt. Edward, who seldom greeted anyone voluntarily, didn't even look up, but this time Amy also remained glued to her chair, although she stopped eating. The three men at the table nodded a guarded hello. Isobel got slowly to her feet, looking from her husband to her sister.

Lorna had always possessed a rather feline beauty, but the sleek, satisfied look of a recently fed cat was very marked—a cheetah perhaps, thought Isobel, eyeing her sister's long elegant legs. There was an unmistakable gloss about her—if she had been an animal Isobel imagined you would have said her coat was in wonderful condition. Two black combs with diamanté tops held back her shining tawny hair and she had acquired a light suntan which was very becoming. A Hermès silk scarf, which Isobel had not seen before, was knotted elegantly round her neck.

Lorna swooped to kiss her younger sister with a great show of affectionate concern: 'Little Izz—how've you *beeeen?*' she asked. Isobel felt herself go rigid.

'And how are the children?' Lorna went on as though they were not present. 'You look tired, Izzy. I do hope there've been no more dramas with Edward and that it hasn't been too much for you, coping here all on your own.' Joss sent her an absolutely killer look, Mick raised his eyebrows, but Daniel's expression was inscrutable.

'I'm fine, thanks,' said Isobel.

'Well, we've had a *lovely* time—we're longing to tell you all about it. Shame you couldn't go, Izz. You missed a really interesting concert last night and I adored the music weekend. It's all given me lots of new ideas for things we might do here. Thank you for lending me your husband.'

'Glad you enjoyed yourself—and it *was* only a loan,' said Isobel drily. Lorna smiled her Mona Lisa smile.

Giles, on the other hand looked extremely uneasy. 'So how's my Little One,' he asked, flicking Isobel's nose and kissing her in a casual way that she found insulting.

She had meant to play it all very cool, but instead heard herself saying tartly, 'What's all this *little* business with you both? Do you think I've become like Mrs Pepperpot in one of her shrinking fits or something?'

For a week Giles had been allowing himself the luxury of resentment, feeding the prickly plant assiduously and letting it grow, but the sight of Isobel and the hurt vulnerability behind her indignant expression turned his heart over. Suddenly all his suspicions seemed what indeed he hoped they were: a fabrication of Lorna's. A rush of remorse and love welled up in him. He gave Isobel a smiling, questioning look, then held out both hands in a spontaneous gesture of appeasement—to be met with a wall of stone.

'I take it you've had lunch? Who wants coffee?' Isobel went to put the kettle on, pointedly ignoring his outstretched hands.

Giles's smile faded, to be replaced by something much less pleasant. All right then, he thought furiously, his pride smarting from such a public rebuff, so be it; if you don't want my humble pie then let's keep going as we are. We'll see which of us cracks first.

'You look like a sulky little boy, Giles,' said Isobel, looking over her shoulder at him and raising her eyebrows derisively, knowing exactly where to place the needle, 'caught with his spoon in the jam pot perhaps?'

'A bit of sweetness is a nice change, sometimes,' said Giles, silky smooth, and added, looking at Daniel, 'And how did the artist's modelling sessions go while I've been away?'

It was not a good start to the homecoming.

That night, Isobel forced herself to talk to Giles about the children. She not only told him about Edward and the spider pictures, but also about the recent difficulties with Amy: about Amy's hidden anguish over Edward's handicaps, which had triggered the fight with Tara, and finally about Amy's resentment of her aunt. The part about Edward was easier than she expected, but the part about Amy's music was not. She was tempted to shirk it and her courage nearly failed, but for her daughter's sake knew she had to say something. She tried to be brief and to sound as impartial as possible—which wasn't very successful.

'And Valerie agrees,' she finished. 'So it's not just me, Giles. We both think you should stop Lorna from coming to Amy's practices.' Giles listened, deadpan. Isobel, who had always thought she could read every nuance in his expression, realised with surprise that this time she had no idea how he was going to react.

'All right,' said Giles unexpectedly, after a silence—disconcerting her. He had come to the same conclusion himself and would have much preferred to take the initiative, but devotion to Amy came first. He was secretly very ashamed of the way he had ruined her weekend and very aware, too, that the magic of their special bond was hideously at risk. The same could be said of his relationship with his wife, but that was more complicated.

'Then I'll see it doesn't arise again,' he said coolly and then, seeing how surprised Isobel looked, added with a mocking look, 'Satisfied?'

He did not let her see how shaken he was by the significance of Edward's new horror of spiders or about Amy's flaming defence of her twin—such a contrast to his own shabby behaviour of the last week, he felt. Self-dislike scorched Giles, leaving him feeling as emotionally raw as if a layer of his skin had blistered away. He determined to do some serious thinking, not only about his son but about his own attitude towards him—but he wasn't ready to discuss this with his wife yet.

Isobel had wondered what she would feel if Giles attempted to make love to her, as he would normally have done after an absence, but she need neither have feared nor hoped. They might have been two strangers in bed together.

*O*n Monday morning, while Isobel was out and Lorna safely in the office, Giles went down to the theatre.

Daniel was standing on a plank between the two trestles working on Lord Dunbarnock's backcloth. He was immediately aware who had entered but did not turn round.

'Oh, you *are* getting on,' said Giles. 'I do like that. Have you anyone in mind to go inside the frame?'

Daniel had painted a pale grey interior, with mouldings picked out in a slightly darker shade. He was working on a *trompe l'oeil* picture frame over the fireplace. 'Just an idea—I wondered if you'd like to have portraits of some of your sponsors on the wall? I know Lord Dunbarnock appears in miniature in the other backcloth along with all of you, but I thought it might be fun to put him over the fireplace here as well, since this is his gift? But it's entirely up to you, of course.' He didn't say he had discussed it with Isobel.

'Excellent idea,' Giles agreed. 'Perhaps the others should be Violet Fortescue and old McMichael? They're our biggest bene-factors.'

'Fine.' The two men were being studiously polite, but the ten-sion in the air was like static electricity. 'I can work from pho-tographs. I could go and take pictures or they can let me have existing ones. Would you organise that for me?'

'Yes, I'll certainly do that.' Giles jotted down a note on the little leather-bound memo pad he always carried with him. 'And now,' he said, 'it's portraits I've actually come to talk about. I think it's time you let me see Isobel's.' If Giles expected opposi-tion, he was disappointed.

'I thought that's what you'd come for. Yes, I'll show you,' said Daniel easily. 'It's pretty nearly finished now. I could make small adjustments if necessary—little details—but I have to say I'm very pleased with it.' He climbed down. He had no intention of letting Giles think he was nervous and he took his time, putting away his brushes and moving some paint pots. He collected an easel from the back of the stage, set it up, then went and fetched the large canvas, still covered, and placed it carefully on the pegs of the frame. 'Right, then,' he said, pointing to a spot on the floor. 'You want to stand about there' and he flipped back the covering.

Giles stood with his hands in his pockets and looked at the picture of his wife. Daniel watched his face and could see a small muscle in the corner of his eye flickering, though otherwise he was completely still.

In the portrait Isobel was sitting on the steps of Glendrochatt, one elbow on her knee, her chin resting in her hand. Her gaze engaged directly with the onlooker; she was not exactly smiling, but looked lit-up—on the point of laughter. It was an intimate, loving look. Flapper sat on a step below her, so real it would have come as no surprise if she had suddenly leapt, yelping, out of the canvas and gone chasing after a rabbit. Isobel was wearing a bright-blue open-necked shirt, jeans and a pair of black espadrilles. An open book lay beside her and a half-finished cup of coffee.

On the bottom step, as though it had just fallen out of the pocket of her jeans, lay a curiously shaped coin. The front door above her was open, giving a glimpse of the interior of the hall, where a violin could be seen lying on a chair together with some sheet music. The picture was oval and in an outer ring surrounding the central figure were five roundels. Each showed a different view of Isobel, as though she had been glimpsed through a window: curled up reading in a chair, laughing with her hair blowing in the wind, sleeping under a rowan tree by the burn and cooking in the kitchen with a tea towel tucked into her belt. In the top one she was standing outside the door of the theatre in evening dress, as though she was going to a grand ball, a tartan sash knotted on one shoulder.

The picture was, quite simply, stunning.

'Well?' asked Daniel eventually—and there was a challenge in his tone. There was another long silence while Giles continued to gaze at the portrait. Then he turned to face the younger man. 'I asked you to paint my wife. I didn't ask you to steal her.'

Twenty-eight

Giles and Daniel confronted each other. Daniel felt outraged by Giles's comment.

In view of Giles's own recent defection—so careless about something so enviably precious, he thought angrily—and considering the hurt he knew Isobel was suffering, Daniel felt he'd been amazingly forbearing himself. All right, he thought, so I've kissed your wife once—something I'd been longing to do for weeks—but I've been scrupulous in not pressing her to go further. What made this harder to bear was the knowledge that he knew he might well have been successful if he'd tried—he had felt Isobel's response to him. He was torn between two conflicting emotions and saw no way of reconciling them: the longing to see Isobel happy again and the desire to have her to himself.

'You can't steal what is given to you,' he said, consciously baiting Giles. 'I painted what I saw, as I told you I would. When you first suggested I might try my hand at painting Isobel you said you'd only want the portrait if I managed to capture *your* vision of her and I told you then that whether I achieved what you wanted or not, it would be a commission and you'd have to pay me. I take that back. If you don't want the portrait I'll happily keep it myself and there would be no charge.'

His words whipped into Giles. The trouble was that Daniel

had captured his vision only too well. All that Giles loved best in Isobel was there to be seen: her openness, her brightness and her special look—that quick, amused, loving glance, which he had always thought of as belonging especially to him—had apparently also been given to someone else. Despite Daniel's words, Lorna's trouble-making and his own gnawing suspicions, in his heart of hearts Giles still doubted that they'd actually slept together . . . yet. But that there was some spark between them he didn't doubt. Could Daniel be a serious threat? A few weeks ago he would have laughed at the idea, now he wasn't sure. He cursed his own folly. He cursed his own vanity. He had never seriously considered for one moment that he might lose Isobel's love; now he wondered uncomfortably if she would be capable of embarking on an affair that was purely light-hearted? The thought that her feelings for Daniel might be serious was terribly threatening and the realisation that she might also be badly hurt herself seemed suddenly un-bearable. I have been inexcusably reckless, thought Giles.

To complicate matters further, apart from admiring Daniel's work as an artist—and he was very pleased with what had been done in the theatre—Giles had grown to like and respect him during the last month, but he wished profoundly that this weren't so. It would have been much easier if he'd been able to indulge himself in a satisfying hate.

And now there was the portrait. It frightened him to bits. The painting was much too strong to be to be considered chocolate-boxy, thought Giles, and it was a much better picture than just a good likeness, for it had captured the essence of the sitter to a quite remarkable degree. He knew he could not possibly part with it. 'It's wonderful,' he said abruptly. 'I know it. You must know it too. I'd be crazy not to keep it. It has to hang at Glendrochatt; I couldn't bear it to be anywhere else.'

'Thank you,' said Daniel, not knowing what else to say.

'The small pictures round the edge,' Giles went on, 'they're brilliant too. Did you take lots of photographs of Isobel apart from the actual sittings with her?'

'I did take some, but mostly I've used quick sketches I'd done—as I did for you in the backcloth—all except for the glamour one at the top, that is.' He laughed. 'I asked Isobel if she'd put on a grand dress for me one evening, but she said her hair was a mess and she couldn't be bothered to fiddle with it. So she let me borrow the dress and the jewellery to paint and produced a photograph of herself wearing it.'

'I thought so. I took that photograph myself last year before we went to the Black Watch Ball. I keep it on my dressing-table always.'

Giles felt relieved. He would have hated the thought of Isobel dressing up especially for Daniel while he himself was away. I'm a dog in the manger, he thought, and I've got myself into a serious mess. Aloud he said, 'Tell me something. Has Izzy seen it?'

'No,' said Daniel, appreciating Giles's honesty and generosity despite himself. 'No one's seen it yet. I always keep it covered when I'm not working on it—and I lock it away in the green-room with all my painting kit when I'm not in the theatre. But it was your idea, your commission. I thought you should be the first to see it.'

Something in Giles's expression—as if an idea had suddenly hit him between the eyes—told Daniel a story. Of course! he thought, of course, I might have guessed. Lorna has a set of keys. She's looked at the portrait and talked to Giles about it already. Aloud he said, 'I'd like Isobel to see it now, though.'

'Perhaps we should show it to her together?' suggested Giles.

'Yeah, OK,' Daniel agreed, although he longed to show it to her by himself.

'What about Lorna's portrait? How's that going?'

'Well on the way. I'm pleased with that too, but I'm not sure how much she'll like it herself.'

'Why's that?'

Daniel hesitated. He knew the answer very well, but did not know how to express it to Giles. 'Let's just say my "vision", as you call it, of Lorna may not coincide with her own,' he said drily.

'But you don't have that worry over Izzy?'

'I don't think Isobel has a particular vision of herself. In fact, she really seems to have no idea of her impact at all—it's part of her charm.'

'I don't need you to tell me what my wife's charm is,' said Giles. Having achieved a temporary truce, all his animosity rushed back.

'No?' Daniel had a derisive look in his eye. 'I thought perhaps you did,' he said pointedly.

They were standing eyeing each other when the side door opened and Lorna came in.

*T*he week in Northumberland had been a long-standing dream come true for Lorna, but now that they were back at Glendrochatt everything seemed more complicated. She had revelled in her moment of jubilation when she and Giles had first walked in on the family at lunch; now she found herself unsure what to aim for next. Her original goal had been to entice Giles into having an affair with her; to prove to him, to Isobel and, most important of all, to herself, that if she set her sights on him again he would not, this time, be able to resist her. This she had triumphantly achieved. Lorna had gloried in having Giles completely to herself, but it was like an addiction: she craved for more and more attention, and dreaded having to share him with anyone else, even, thought Lorna, with his children—or perhaps especially with them. Lorna cringed at the thought of the children. If forced to choose between her and them she had little doubt that his family would win with Giles every time. So where does that leave me now? Lorna asked herself.

She had lain awake in the flat on Sunday night, her body aching for Giles's touch, her mind filled with unwelcome questions, which drilled remorselessly into her brain.

A *ménage à trois*, though the idea had been titillating to start with, had no long-term appeal. She could not—*would* not—live much longer on Isobel's territory and feel herself a humiliating second in every way. But on the other hand if she took herself off to Edinburgh, bought a flat there and went into business with Daphne Crawford and Ruby McQueen, would life as Giles's mistress be fulfilling enough? I might end up as a sad old also-ran, thought Lorna with horror, always waiting for the telephone to ring, never doing anything in case Giles might choose to drop in on me. And what was the alternative? Had she any realistic hope of becoming Giles's wife and—here was an issue that Lorna hardly dared to let herself contemplate—if it came to it, would she really be capable of trying to oust the sister whom she had always resented but persuaded herself that she loved? I could have been close to Isobel if only she'd been different, if only she'd needed me more, thought Lorna, her demon of self-pity welling up inside her, but Isobel has always had everything I've ever wanted, without even trying. Now that she had proved a point with her long-awaited victory over her sister, ought she to remove herself from the scene while she felt herself to be in the ascendancy? Her head told her this would be a clever thing to do, but her heart cried out for Giles.

Lorna had tossed and turned.

The morning had not started well for her. Giles had been unsatisfactorily evasive about his movements for the day; she had a panicky sense that he was already trying to distance himself from her now that he was home. Without his presence the office seemed dreary and unappealing. Instead of treating Sheila Shepherd with her usual condescending affability, she had been positively disagreeable to her, complaining about a letter Sheila had written to the opera group clarifying arrangements. 'You really should have left that until my return,' Lorna said with quite unwarranted sharpness. 'I prefer to do all the correspondence about the festival myself.'

Lorna, who considered herself superior in every way to kind, accommodating Sheila, expected an apology, but this time she had read Sheila wrong. 'You may prefer it, Mrs Cartwright,' she said with a quiet reproof in her voice that Lorna had not bargained for, 'but you were not here, were you? Nor did any of us know when you might be back. I discussed it with Isobel and she felt we should send them a letter straight away—but I'll mention it to Giles if you like.'

That was the last thing Lorna wanted her to do. 'Oh, well, never mind. I suppose it can't be helped,' she said ungraciously. After dealing with some telephone enquiries she suddenly felt such a desperate need to be with Giles and see what he was doing that on the flimsiest of pretexts she went to look for him.

Joss, who was tackling a huge pile of ironing in the kitchen, had told her where she would find him. He gave her a quizzical look and an insinuating grin that was hard to bear. Lorna had some scores to settle with Joss and was constantly on the lookout for the right opportunity to do so. The sight of this huge hulk of a man ironing Amy's knickers filled her with distaste.

She had not been expecting to find Isobel's portrait on display in the theatre.

'Oh, hi Lorna . . . come and look at Izzy's portrait,' said Giles, giving her a look that was not at all the highly charged exchange of intimacy for which she had come in search. 'I know you told me you'd seen this already, but now that it's actually finished it would be interesting to hear what you think.'

Self-possessed Lorna, who prided herself on being able to disguise her feelings, felt herself turn slowly scarlet under Daniel's ironic gaze, the flush starting at her neck and creeping treacherously upwards. Daniel must be aware of her illicit prying.

She gazed at the image of her sister, a sick feeling in her stomach, then said with an attempt at lightness, 'Yes, I did catch a glimpse of it one day—I think you must have forgotten to cover it Daniel—but of course I didn't get a chance to study it in detail.' Neither Giles nor Daniel said anything, but their silence was disconcerting. She went on slowly, 'It makes a very pretty picture, of course—very charming, *very* flattering—but if I'm honest I think perhaps it tells one more about the artist than the sitter.'

The minute the words were out of her mouth she knew she had made a mistake.

'And what does it tell you?' asked Giles.

'It tells me that Daniel fancies himself in love with Isobel,' Lorna replied defiantly, a reckless Gadarene urge making her rush over a clifftop.

'Yes, so you hinted to me the other day,' said Giles. 'Well, Daniel? Is she right?'

'I hope she's wrong in calling the picture *pretty*.' Daniel looked at Lorna with a disdain that shrivelled her up. 'But yeah, she's right about one thing. I do love Isobel. I can't help it. But Izzy's so honest herself that I'd never dream of insulting her with flattery. Luckily there's no need for that anyway. And just for the record, Giles, your wife is not in love with me. I only wish she were.' And he walked out of the theatre, leaving Lorna and Giles together.

Twenty-nine

Lorna went and linked her arm through Giles's and leant her cheek against his shoulder. 'Oh, Giles,' she said, 'I'm missing you so much I just had to come and find you. It was awful without you last night. I could hardly bear it. Did you miss me too?'

Giles did not respond.

'I'm so relieved you've seen the portrait at last,' she went on, 'though it's probably difficult for you to face it. The moment I saw it, all my suspicions about Daniel and Izzy were confirmed. I don't think Daniel was being quite truthful with you about Izzy's feelings, do you? Now that you've seen it for yourself, I'm sure you see what I meant, don't you?'

'Oh, yes,' he said. 'I see all right. But I don't think you were quite truthful with me either, Lorna. You deliberately went and looked at it without Daniel knowing, didn't you?'

There was a fraction of a second when Lorna nearly admitted the truth in the hope that perhaps Giles might respect her for doing so, but in one of those hairline decisions that can never afterwards be altered she denied it.

Without a word, Giles disengaged his arm from hers and walked forward to replace the cover over the portrait.

He felt desperate to find Isobel as soon as possible, to tell her how much he loved her, how much he was already regretting his own hurtful and destructive stupidity of the last week, to discover what her feelings for Daniel really were—something in between Lorna's jealous accusation and Daniel's generous denial, he suspected. At all costs he needed to set the record between them straight before Isobel discovered that Lorna had seen the picture first.

He did not know that he was already too late.

Isobel, who had promised to stop at a newsagent's in Blairalder on her way back from the school run to get cigarettes for Daniel— much as she disapproved of him smoking—had gone straight to the theatre on arrival home to give them to him. She did not know that she had missed Daniel's exit by seconds, but on hearing voices she paused in the doorway and was shattered by what she saw: not Daniel at all, but Giles and Lorna, not only standing arm in arm, but studying *her* portrait together. She turned round at once and walked away as fast as possible, her canvas shoes making no sound on the flagstones, but her heart thumping so loudly she was amazed they didn't hear it. Flapper, ever responsive to Isobel's state of mind, cast anxious looks at her mistress and pattered along at heel instead of roaring on ahead.

When they got back to the house the telephone was ringing. Isobel picked it up. 'Hello?'

A woman's voice, asked, 'Is Daniel Hoffman there by any chance?'

'I'm not quite sure where he is at the moment. He'll be somewhere around but it might take me a few minutes to find him. Shall I ask him to call you back?'

'Oh, yes please. I've tried his mobile but . . .' the voice sounded amused ' . . . as usual it doesn't appear to be switched on and I particularly didn't want to leave this message on his mechanical answering service.'

'Who shall I say it is and does he know your number?' Isobel was full of curiosity. Daniel never seemed to have telephone calls.

'It's his mother speaking. He knows my number.'

'Oh, goodness . . . well, how . . . how very nice to talk to you.' Isobel was uncomfortably aware that she sounded astonished. 'I'm Isobel Grant. Daniel's painting the most fantastic scenery for our theatre here in Scotland,' she explained, deciding that Daniel's mother wouldn't have the faintest idea what her son's commitments were, let alone to whom she was speaking.

'Ah, then it's you whose portrait he's been painting—the one he's so pleased with?'

'Well . . . yes, he has been painting me.' Isobel was even more surprised. She had not imagined that Daniel was in touch with his mother at all. Everyone seems to know more about my portrait than me, she thought. Aloud she said, 'I'll go and look for Daniel. Is there any message?'

'Just ask him to ring me as soon as possible. Say there's something he really needs to know.'

'I'll look for him right away.'

She realised that she would have gone looking for Daniel anyhow. She needed to talk to him. Had he shown the portrait to Giles and Lorna? If so, I've got a big bone to pick with you, Daniel Hoffman, thought Isobel.

Mick was on the garden tractor mowing the grass in front of the house. 'Any idea where Daniel is?' she asked.

'Yeah, just seen him charging off up the hill looking like a combustion engine that's about to explode,' answered Mick, grinning. 'I doubt if you'll catch him up. Want me to go after him for you?'

'No, thanks,' said Isobel. 'I need to see him myself.'

Mick made no comment but he watched her go up the track by the burn and wondered what could be so pressing that she needed to set off quite so fast herself.

She found Daniel sitting by the pool with the stepping stones, below the little waterfall where she had taken him the week before. She had thought he might be there. 'Daniel?'

He looked up, surprised, and there was no mistaking the pleasure in his face the moment he saw her.

Isobel tossed him the packet of cigarettes she had bought and stood looking at him, hands thrust deep in the pockets of her jeans, her eyes full of questions.

Flapper leapt blissfully into the shallow run below the pool and started trying to catch the silver threads of water in her mouth as they cascaded over the stones. She was convinced that one day she would be able to present Isobel with a marvellously precious and unusual offering—a canine equivalent of trying to catch a falling star—rather than the frisbee-like dried cowpats or half-dead rabbits that were her standard love tokens.

Isobel was out of breath from hurling herself up hill and her always vivid colouring was even brighter than usual. Daniel thought she looked stormy and unhappy. He also thought she was the most dear and desirable woman he had ever encountered.

'You showed Giles my picture without me,' she said.

'I did. I had so much wanted to be with you when you first saw it, but I suppose he's shown it to you now? Did you . . . did you like it, Izzy?' he asked. He hardly dared to scan her face for a reaction and yet was quite unable to look away.

'I don't know because I didn't look. Giles appeared to be discussing it with Lorna and I certainly wasn't prepared to be last in line to see it. I think you might both have waited for me to be there too, Daniel.' She sounded belligerent but there was a telltale tremble in her voice. 'You may think me very petty but I can't bear it that Lorna has seen it before me,' she burst out.

Daniel was silent. He lit a cigarette and blew smoke rings into the air to give himself time before replying. It struck him that it would be very easy to score a few points off Giles and it was extremely tempting to do so.

When at last he spoke he said: 'You're not being fair to either Giles or me. He came and asked to see your picture this morning—as he had every right to do because I'd told him it was pretty-well finished—so I set it up on the easel for him to look at. We talked about it, then he suggested we should show it to you together as soon as you came in. Lorna wasn't there at that moment.' He thought it was ironic that in his desire to save her from hurt he should be defending Giles to Isobel. I suppose this is what *really* loving someone lets you in for, he thought wryly. How very inconvenient, what an unfair con.

'Well, she sure as hell was there when I came in,' flashed Isobel. 'I went to the theatre to give you your beastly fags and they were standing arm in arm in front of it. They didn't see me, though. I fled.'

'Giles wasn't exactly welcoming to Lorna when she turned up,' he said.

'And did they approve of the picture?'

'Yes—and no.'

'What's that supposed to mean?'

'I think Giles is actually very pleased with it—in a way. He seems to think I've captured you on canvas all right, but . . .' He laughed ruefully and gave her the amused look she had grown to love. 'Let's say he appears to have problems with the fact that I've managed to do so and seen a look he didn't think was on public view.'

'Oh.' Isobel was disconcerted, not knowing whether to be pleased or sorry. 'What about Lorna? I bet she had something to say?'

'Too blooming right, she did. She made some routinely bitchy criticisms in general that got up my nose a bit—she really is insanely jealous of you, Izzy—then she made one helluva shrewd comment.'

'Which was?'

'She said it revealed as much about me as about you. She said it showed I was in love with you.'

'God! And what did you say to that?'

'I said she was absolutely right,' said Daniel quietly.

'You said you loved me in front of Giles? Whatever possessed you to do that? What on earth did he say?'

'I didn't wait to find out.' He grinned at her. 'I zoomed up here like a mad hornet before he swatted me.' Then he added seriously, 'But I also told him I knew you weren't in love with me—if that's any comfort to you—any more than he's really in love with Lorna.' He gave her a disconcertingly penetrating look. 'As you very well know if you're really honest with yourself.'

'Oh, Daniel.' She looked very bothered. 'I don't know what I feel any more. My world's gone all topsy-turvy. I can't get my balance back.'

He looked at her with great sadness. 'Me too,' he said. 'A couple of months ago I'd happily have done one of two things— or rather I'd probably have tried to do both. I'd have done everything in my power to get you into bed with me, then I'd have run away from you. You've changed all that.'

'You've had enough hurts in your life. It makes me squirm that I had the unbelievable nerve to preach at you about it. What an odious prig you must have thought me. Now I can't bear the idea that I might hurt you myself . . .' She stopped suddenly. 'Talking of hurts, I quite forgot. I came to give you a message but seeing you put it right out of my head. You'll never guess who rang.'

'Who?'

'Only your mother, that's who.'

'Oh, yes? And what did she want?'

'I thought you'd be stunned.' She was rather disappointed at his reaction. 'I didn't think you ever spoke to her.'

'I never told you that. So, what was the message, then?'

'No message, but she wants you to ring her. She said it was urgent.'

'She always does—proper old drama queen, my mum.'

'Will you ring her, though?' she persisted, thinking how very little she really knew about him despite his growing importance to her—his dangerous, insidious importance.

'Of course.' He got up, stubbing out his cigarette and burying it under a stone. He came over to her and took her face in his hands, looking mockingly down at her. 'Disappointed?' he asked. 'You thought I might refuse to have anything to do with her. We may not be close, but I keep tabs on her from time to time. I like to know what she's up to just for the record. You're bursting with curiosity about her, aren't you?'

'Yes,' she admitted, laughing back at him, miseries about Giles and Lorna, umbrage about her portrait, thoughts about her children all blown temporarily out of her head by the strength of her feeling for him at this particular moment. 'Yes, Mr Mystery, I'm bursting all right. Let's go and find out about it, but . . . kiss me first.' And she put her arms round his neck.

Thirty

When Daniel and Isobel got back to the house, a good half-hour later, Giles was lurking about in the hall trying—and failing—to look simultaneously busy and casual.

He gave his wife a brilliant smile, the one she had always loved so much but had not received lately. 'Hello, you two. Where on earth have you been? I've been waiting for you to get back, darling, because—guess what—it's look-at-the-picture time this morning and I've already been allowed a preview.'

'Yes. Daniel told me.' Isobel had no intention of making things easy.

'So let's go down to the theatre now. It'd be nice if we were all three together when you see it for the first time, don't you think, Izz?'

'Especially since you've had a chance to discuss it with Lorna first.'

Giles raised his eyebrows at Daniel; somehow he had not expected Daniel to have told Isobel this—though he supposed he could hardly blame him.

Daniel looked impassive. Inwardly he felt excruciatingly uncomfortable.

'No, it wasn't Daniel who told me that,' said Isobel, correctly interpreting her husband's questioning look and eyeing him in a very unfriendly way. 'I've been down to the theatre once already this morning. You and Lorna looked as if you were enjoying the preview together very much—cosy for you both. I didn't like to intrude.'

'Oh, Izz, it really wasn't like that. I'm sorry Lorna saw it first but I can explain.'

'You always, always can,' Isobel told him, 'but this time I don't want to hear.'

'But you must want to see your portrait?'

'Of course I do, but now that you've had your special little private viewing, Daniel can show it to me any old time. It surely doesn't matter whether you're there or not.' It was the most hurtful thing she could think of to say and she could tell from Giles's face that it had achieved its purpose, but it brought her no satisfaction.

'I think I'll leave you two to your discussions,' said Daniel, not prepared to act the gooseberry while his patrons played verbal games with rapiers. 'I've got to go and ring my mother. But I hope you'll take a look, Isobel. I'd like to know what you think' and he walked away to do his telephoning in the privacy of his car. It is complicated to want to bang a married couple's heads together to bring them to their senses if you have just been kissing one of them.

Husband and wife watched him go, neither sure what their next move should be. Isobel had been dying to see the picture for weeks; now she could have wept with disappointment. What should have been a lovely moment of shared excitement between them all seemed horribly tarnished—by herself as well as Giles, she thought miserably. She was uncomfortably aware of having behaved shabbily in front of both men.

Giles saw the uncertainty in her face, guessed her thoughts and made up his mind first. 'Please come, Izzy,' he said, not trying to switch on the charm this time. 'Come for Daniel's sake as well as mine if you like. We have much sorting out to do, you and I, but this is not the moment. Let's just go and look. I think we may have a remarkable heirloom for Glendrochatt and our family, and you of all people need to see it.'

'Oh, OK, then.' Isobel shrugged. 'Might as well, I suppose.' She knew she sounded grudging. She was far from prepared to wipe any slates clean yet—and disconcerted to discover that she wasn't even sure she wanted to—but she couldn't help thinking that whatever her husband's other failings might be, meanness of spirit had never been one of them.

They walked down to the Old Steading together, but not casually hand in hand, fingers interlaced, as, even after twelve years of marriage, they often did. There was sufficient width for two people to walk comfortably side by side down the flagged path, which led from the house to the theatre, but this walk was not comfortable in any way and the emotional distance between Giles and Isobel seemed like a chasm.

Giles knew he was being weighed in a balance and measured against Daniel—and wondered if looking at her portrait, painted with such acute insight, might tip the scales too heavily in Daniel's favour for recovery to be possible.

Isobel knew that her feeling for Daniel, which had started as a spontaneous liking and then expanded into an enjoyable flirtation, was now dangerously close to tipping over into something far more serious.

The difference between them was that Giles had suddenly, if belatedly, realised all that he stood to lose by his own reckless unfaithfulness, while Isobel—inflamed by resentment of her husband and sister—had not. Giles thought he would have to play his cards with all his gambler's flair and intuition if he were to win his wife back, but was too experienced a poker player to disclose his hand too soon. And what of Lorna? wondered Giles with a sinking heart. He felt terribly guilty about her, sorry for her and afraid for her—but even more afraid for himself. Lorna might do anything.

$\mathcal{M}$ick and Joss were in the theatre when Giles and Isobel walked in. Mick was mending a fuse and Joss was sweeping the floor. It was a relief to both Grants to find them there.

'Hi there,' said Giles. 'We've got permission from Daniel to look at his new work of art. Izzy's going to confront her own image for the first time. Come and share the moment with us' and he went to the easel and folded back the cover.

They all four stood back and looked. Giles had half hoped that a second viewing might affect him less, but he found himself stunned all over again by what he saw.

Mick let out a long whistle. 'Well, what do you know! Hasn't he just got her to the life?'

'Hey, Izzy,' said Joss admiringly. 'You could step out of that frame. I hardly know which is the real you. That's some picture you've got yourself there, Giles.'

They looked at Isobel to see what her reaction was.

'Do I really look like that?' she asked, feeling dangerously close to tears.

'Yes,' said Giles. 'You really do. It does you justice, little Izz— and that's saying something.' A few weeks ago she would have given anything to hear him say this.

'Even better of Flapper, though.' Mick grinned, winking at her and they all laughed, relieved to have the tension broken.

At that moment Daniel came in. Isobel knew at once that something was wrong. His face had a shut-in look.

'Oh, Daniel—the picture—I don't know what to say.' She went and held out her hands to him, then changed her mind and let them fall.

'Do you like it?' he asked and his eyes searched her face.

'*Like it*? It's amazing. I can't believe it's me. I *love* it. You must have known I would.'

Daniel was acutely conscious of the scrutiny of three watchful pairs of eyes. 'Then that's all that matters,' he said, smiling at her.

'And you've put Edward in for me.'

'Yes,' he said. 'Thought you'd like that.'

Giles stood watching them. 'Edward?' he asked, puzzled. 'Where's Edward?'

'The 'crookit bawbee' on the steps. I told Daniel that Edward is my crooked sixpence,' said Isobel with a catch in her voice, still looking at Daniel.

Giles had never heard Isobel say this about Edward. A horribly familiar feeling from his past swept over him: a feeling of desolating exclusion. He was a small boy again, longing to please his adored mother and unable to break into the glass bubble of indifference that seemed to surround her. He would never have believed that any of his feelings about his mother could in any way resemble how he felt about Isobel. 'Thank you for explaining the symbolism to me,' he said drily. 'I suppose the violin represents Amy. Do I feature in the picture too, by any chance?'

'Well, it's your house, your wife and your children that are represented,' said Daniel.

'Isn't that enough for you?' asked Isobel.

'It ought to be.' said Giles. 'But no, not at the moment. It's not nearly enough.'

'I came to tell you both that I have to go away,' said Daniel. 'I'm sorry because I'd hoped to finish the other backcloth this week. It's done except for finishing Lord Dunbarnock's portrait, but I'm afraid it'll have to wait. I will have it ready before the opening concert, but something unexpected has cropped up.'

'What's happened?' asked Isobel. 'Is it about your mother?' She desperately did not want Daniel to go away.

'Not really, but she wanted to save me from reading in the press that a friend has died suddenly. Do you remember me telling you about Carl Goldsmith, Izzy, the chap I went to stay with on Iona?'

'Your grandmother's old friend, the one who was your guru?'

'I suppose you could call him that. He was on a lecture tour in the States and collapsed suddenly. His daughter, who lives out there, got hold of my mother. Apparently he was in the advanced stages of cancer, but I had no idea. I must go to his funeral. My mother seems to think I may be one of his executors or something.' He pulled a wry face. 'An unlikely choice if so. I've no idea what would be involved.'

Isobel couldn't help thinking that Daniel's mother must care for him more than he liked to admit if she had wanted to save him from the shock of unexpectedly reading bad news. 'Oh, poor Daniel. I'm so sorry.' She thought he looked shattered. If they had been alone she would have put her arms round him.

Daniel looked at Giles. 'Is this OK with you?' he asked rather formally. 'I'm quite well ahead with everything.'

'My dear chap, of course. What can we do to help? Can we take you to a train or the airport?'

'No, thanks. It's very kind but I'll just trust to my old banger and head off this afternoon.'

'I'll do you some sandwiches,' said kind-hearted Joss.

$\mathcal{L}$orna, who couldn't settle to anything in the office and felt impelled to go and see where everyone was, found them all standing round the portrait. She was expecting Giles back in the office but he had not come. She had been filled with dread by his aloofness since their return and especially by his coldness earlier that morning. A mixture of anxiety and disbelief kept her in a state of restlessness that was at odds with her outward composure. They all looked round as she came in.

'Goodness, still here admiring Daniel's handiwork?' she asked. 'So, are you pleased, then, Izzy? You certainly should be.'

'Well, yes. I'm thrilled,' answered Isobel. 'But I gather you didn't like it much.'

Lorna raised her eyebrows. 'On the contrary, I think it's charming—most decorative.' She managed to make this as nearly an insult as possible. 'What I'd like to know now is when my portrait is going to be unveiled? I can't let my little sister steal all the limelight, can I? I think the two Forsyth sisters ought to be seen together.' She smiled brightly at them all, but it sounded more like a threat than a joke.

'OK, then,' said Daniel, surprising her. 'Why not? Yours is nearly finished too. Give me a hand, will you, Mick? Could you get the other easel?' Together they brought the second canvas down from the stage and set it up on the other side. As Daniel uncovered it there was an expression on his face that made Isobel intensely uneasy.

The two portraits could hardly have been more of a contrast: the one informal and natural, giving the viewer the feeling he or she might have dropped in unannounced and caught the sitter at a relaxed and happy moment; the other carefully posed and contrived—a wonderful piece of eye-catching window dressing. Lorna looked stunningly beautiful; her picture would have drawn attention in any crowded gallery. But the discontent, the unhappiness, the emptiness and the venom were all there—Lorna's face gazed out of the canvas with the concentrated stillness of a cobra about to strike. It was a deeply disturbing picture.

There was an uncomfortable silence. Isobel found herself catching Giles's eye with acute anxiety—one of those shared moments that had been so conspicuously missing between them of late. Joss and Mick looked from the painting to their boots and back again, and shuffled their enormous feet. Only Daniel looked directly at Lorna.

Isobel darted a look at her sister and was amazed by what she saw. Lorna looked triumphant. She really has no idea what the rest of us can see, thought Isobel. She thinks it's wonderful.

Lorna felt a surge of pleasure and renewed confidence. She even indulged in a little pity for her sister. Giles, who loves beauty and elegance so much, can't fail to make the comparison between us, she thought. He is bound to feel some divided loyalty, but I need not have worried after all. I must be a little patient and perhaps not be too available for a while. She smiled condescendingly at Daniel. 'Thank you, Daniel, well done,' she said, as though she were a schoolmistress handing out good marks for an essay. 'I think you have quite a future ahead of you and, of course, now that I've seen it, I hope you will let me buy the portrait?'

'I'm very relieved you like it.' he said with an irony that was quite lost on Lorna, but he did not answer her question. 'The figure is finished but there are a few details of the background that I need to work on before it's complete. I'll leave it here for the time being if I may, and also all my painting things,' he said, addressing Giles. 'Will you excuse me if I get on my way now?'

'Of course.' said Giles. 'We'll look after everything for you. Ring us and let us know how things go. Good journey. I'm sorry about your friend.'

Isobel followed Daniel out of the theatre and, after a moment's hesitation, Giles let them go and stayed behind.

*I*sobel and Daniel stood by his car. 'How long do you think you'll be gone?' she asked. 'I might be away when you get back. I told you I'm going to see my parents. Will you have to go to the States?'

'I've no idea. Possibly. I don't want to leave you, Izzy.'

'I don't want you to go.'

'I'll ring you and let you know what I'm doing.'

She gave him a watery smile. 'I'll believe that when it happens! Where will you be staying tonight?'

'I'll go to my mother's house first. I don't go a bundle on her latest man, but at least he won't show me the door.' He handed her a piece of paper. 'Here's the address.'

'Oh, Daniel, you're not as detached from her as you like to pretend. Be kind to her. She must love you really.'

'In her way, perhaps. Not very reliable, but better than nothing, I suppose. You've shown me that. You want everyone to be loved, don't you?' he asked.

'She did want to tell you about Carl herself.'

He smiled down at her, but his face was sad. 'Yes, she did do that. What haunts me is that I didn't pick up on Carl's illness when I was with him on Iona. All I did was bang on about my own problems—of whom you were the chief one, I may say.' He kissed her very gently. 'I *will* see you again, Izz.'

He sounded as though he were making a solemn promise— but more to himself than to her, she thought. There was something about the way he said it that filled her with anxiety. They would see each other again—but for how long and what then?

'Drive your old rattle-bones carefully,' she said. 'Don't break down again. I won't be there to rescue you this time.'

She stood and watched until the car was lost to view and Daniel, looking more in his driving mirror than at the way ahead, could see her slight figure standing in front of the house until he went through the gates at the bottom of the drive, turned out on to the road and headed south.

Thirty-one

After Daniel's departure life returned to as near a routine as ever prevailed at Glendrochatt: children's ploys, school runs, social life with friends, the running of the estate and the festival events—all these went on as usual. But under the outward normality everyone felt as if they were existing in a strange kind of limbo.

Giles knew it was not only with his wife that he needed to work things out. He was horribly conscious that a magic had gone missing from his relationship with his daughter too. He felt as if he had been under a myopic spell, which had suddenly been lifted, leaving his original vision miraculously restored, but also enabling him to see with awful clarity the damage he had been busily engaged in creating.

He did not tell Isobel that he had telephoned Valerie Benson to discuss Amy's performance at the Northumbrian weekend and been given the benefit of some of her famously unvarnished home truths. 'Yes, she gave a very disappointing account of herself altogether,' she had said. 'But it wasn't Amy who was the cause of the problem, it was your tiresome sister-in-law—and, of course, yourself,' she had added crushingly. 'Still, I don't worry too much. Provided things can be sorted out at home it shouldn't affect her chances of a scholarship. And Amy needs to learn that you have to give of your best regardless of your personal feelings, as I shall certainly tell her at her next lesson.' I bet you will, you old harridan, thought Giles, both chastened and amused by this barbed homily, and left in no doubt as to who the arch criminal was in Mrs Benson's beady view. He found himself longing to regale Isobel with this latest Valerie-ism, something they usually enjoyed together. He made a date for Amy's next lesson the following week, definitely not to be unaccompanied by her aunt, he promised meekly.

When Giles joined Amy for her practice the following morning—and he was well aware that, untypically, she had already started playing without him—he went and put his arm round her shoulder. 'I think I owe you an apology, darling,' he said. 'Valerie tells me it puts you off, having Aunt Lorna to help us with your playing, so we'll go back to just you and me, shall we?'

'*I* told you I hated her coming, *and* I told Mum too, but you wouldn't take any notice.' Amy tilted her chin in a way Giles thought was reminiscent of her mother. He had been expecting a rapturous reaction but it was clear that his daughter was still deeply offended with him and not prepared to be appeased quite so speedily; privately he respected her for this.

'Well, I got that wrong, then,' he admitted. 'We all get things wrong sometimes, even you, little Miss Know-it-all. And I'm sorry the weekend went so badly for you. I know that was my fault too.' He went on with a touch of asperity, 'So, let's not waste any more time over that. We'll start again now. Let me hear you play the Fiocco, which gave you such trouble on the course, and then we'll move on to the first movement of the Vivaldi.'

Amy gave him a challenging look—and played like a dream.

*L*ater Giles told Lorna, as tactfully as he could—and Giles could be very, very tactful if he chose—that Valerie Benson had suggested it might be wiser for her not to sit in on Amy's practice sessions at the moment. He didn't tell her it was from Isobel that he had first heard this, nor that it had become patently obvious to him anyway how much Amy resented her aunt's presence.

'So, much as I value your judgement, I think we'll go a bit easy on your involvement with Amy's music,' he said.

Lorna had raised her eyebrows but seemed to accept the verdict. 'I do think Valerie's a bit of a troublemaker though. I didn't much care for her attitude to me at the weekend, but you're so wonderfully generous-minded to everyone, Giles, you probably didn't even notice. It's clear she dislikes anyone else having any influence with you and of course that panders to Amy's possessiveness of you too. She must have complained to Valerie about me and I don't think you should let her get away with that. It's for you to say what happens. I can see Valerie's given Amy a wonderful start with her music, but I do wonder if she's really the right teacher for her now that she's moved on a stage. Daphne Crawford was telling me only the other day that she knows of a marvellous man in Edinburgh who teaches violin with amazing results. I think you should consider a change for Amy.' As she did not want to risk a confrontation with Giles at the moment she did not, however, press the matter. 'I wouldn't be able to come and help you with Amy next week anyway,' she went on, 'because as you know I'm going to spend a few days with Daphne talking about possible future plans. Sheila ought to be able to cope without me for a bit because though we shall be hectic after the opening concert, there isn't *that* much to do at the moment.'

Giles felt extremely relieved that Lorna hadn't made more of an issue of the situation, because he had also decided that in the next few days he must make it clear to her that their brief affair was over. He dreaded doing so.

Lorna smiled very sweetly at Giles. She was biding her time.

*E*dward was totally occupied with the new bantams Flavia had given him, of whom the star attraction was Mrs Silkie, a shiny black lady with whom he was deeply in love. Mrs Silkie wore a feather hat that would have done credit to the mother of a bride and laid beautiful ivory-coloured eggs. Much to everyone's relief the demise of Pecker and Claws had ceased to be mentioned at regular five-minute intervals, but Edward's new obsession was rapidly becoming equally trying. He also enquired with maddening repetition when the 'painting man with pictures on his arm' would be back. Isobel would have liked to know this too. She wondered what Daniel was going through and waited for the telephone call he had promised. He was constantly in her mind.

Mick and Joss went off for a ten-day holiday in Africa, which advertised itself as providing 'the adventure of a lifetime'—enough thrills and spills to satisfy the most daring holidaymaker. Too many spills and you might come home satisfied but in a wooden box, suggested Giles. 'Nah, no worries,' said Mick. 'It'll all be a doddle.' Everyone missed them both and, without Joss's unobtrusive, invaluable help both with the children and in every part of her domestic life, Isobel was extremely busy, which perhaps was just as well as it left her less time to brood about the future—though it made her realise more than ever how much she had come to rely on Joss.

While they were away, Lorna chose to have one of her periodic attempts to drip poison on the two New Zealanders. She was determined to get rid of them and tackled Isobel directly. 'I know you're not going to like this, Izzy,' she said, reminding Isobel of her old nickname of *'The Prefect'*, 'but I really think you ought to suggest that those two should move on elsewhere when they come back from their holiday. There's no need to spell out anything specific, just say you think they've been here long enough and you are making other arrangements.' She had reverted to telling Isobel how she thought she should run every aspect of her life, as though Isobel was still the schoolgirl sister and her years of successful marriage and motherhood had never happened.

'Like what?'

'Well, Daphne knows of a very reliable agency, or you could advertise in *The Lady* for a married couple. It needn't be any sort of burden for you. I'd deal with all the correspondence, vet the applicants and make a short list of possibles for you.'

Like hell you will! thought Isobel, who could have strangled her sister for looking so smug and yet felt an unwilling pity for her too.

'And when they come back, am I supposed to say, "You've been utterly marvellous for a year, identified with all our projects, done everything we've asked and more, adored our children—one of whom is exceptionally difficult—and despite the fact that we all love you and you suit us to a T we want you to push off now because you don't get on with my sister?" '

'Oh, Izzy! You always overreact so dreadfully. Look . . . I can see how convenient they are from your point of view, especially Joss, but you're so naïve—you always were—and it makes you blind to a very obvious hazard.'

'Such as?' Isobel was well aware what Lorna wished to insinuate and what her motives were in trying to besmirch the two young men who had become her implacable foes, but she had no intension of allowing her sister to shelter behind vague innuendos.

'Such as the fact that you let Joss do . . . well . . . really very intimate things for Edward. Also Amy flits about in front of him with nothing on but her towel when he's bathing Edward, which I don't think he should do anyway. I saw her only the other night, chatting away in the nursery bathroom practically starkers. I sent her packing, of course, and let Joss see what I thought.'

'Don't be silly, Lorna. Joss is gay. He can't be a threat to Ed *and* Amy—unless you're suggesting Joss is a paedophile?' There was a furious glitter in Isobel's eyes.

'N-no, of course not. Well, not exactly.' Lorna was a little thrown by such directness. 'I just think it's all . . . unsuitable.'

'Well, thank you. I'll pass your concerns on to Giles,' said Isobel dangerously. 'And I take it that if Edward needs any particularly intimate attention if I'm not here—like shooting diazepam up his bum, for instance—you'll volunteer to do it for him instead?'

Lorna flushed angrily. 'That's revolting, Izzy. You're impossible.'

'It's a fact of our lives. Look, Lorna,' said Isobel, trying to be calm, 'of course one has to be incredibly careful who looks after one's children and we were very watchful to start with—I'm not a fool. But I'd trust Joss with the children more than anyone else I know, other than Giles, that is. Joss really adores Amy and Edward. In fact, he loves us all. Be very, very careful what you say.' She didn't add that the person she would never trust with her children was Lorna herself. Normally she would automatically have relayed this conversation to Giles, but now she felt miserably inhibited from doing so in case he misinterpreted her motives. Why does Lorna have to infect everything with unpleasantness? she wondered. But Amy's growing up. I suppose I shall have to tell her to be more circumspect, she decided, not because of Joss, but in general; and she thought how sad it was that in order to provide one's children with necessary self-protection, one inevitably had to chip away at their childish innocence and innate trust. She didn't tell Lorna that Joss himself had recently suggested that perhaps the time had come for Amy and Emily Fortescue to be a little less uninhibited in their attitude to nudity in public.

*I*sobel and Giles treated each other with an arid politeness that was quite foreign to them both and utterly lacking in intimacy. There was no catching of each other's eyes, either in amusement or sympathy; no private moments of delight—not even of irritation—no pillow-talk; no sex.

Isobel was unaware how closely Giles was observing her, having decided that any attempt to reinstate himself in his wife's good graces would be counter-productive unless the timing was absolutely right.

One Saturday Isobel and Fiona Fortescue took Amy and Emily to the cinema in Perth. They had promised the girls as a special treat that they would have supper afterwards at *Paco's*, opposite the City Hall, and Edward and Mungo had been left in the care of Caro, latest in the line of Fiona's Australian mother's helps. Giles had announced that he didn't want supper but would put a 'piece' in his pocket, take the boat out and try for a trout. He took his rod down from the pegs in the long passage by the back door and set off, landing net clipped to the strap of his fishing bag.

From the window of her flat, Lorna watched him striding off down the path, the devoted Wotan at his side. She let him get a start, then took a short cut through the rhododendrons so that she met him, apparently by chance. 'Oh, Giles, how lovely. Are you going on the loch? Can I come too?'

It would have been so normal and easy to have said yes, but Giles knew that if he did, Lorna would be guaranteed to make sure that Isobel knew about it later and, no matter how innocent the outing had turned out to be, the worst construction would be put on it. He said, 'I don't think it would be a good idea, Lorna. I've been wanting to talk to you. Please don't think I didn't enjoy our week together; you know I did. We had a lovely time, but we shouldn't have had it—either of us—and now it's over. I can't betray Izzy again.'

'You don't think it's somehow evened things out?' asked Lorna. 'You once betrayed me too.'

'No, I didn't,' said Giles. 'I know you've always implied that, but you know equally well it wasn't like that. We had a student affair and very lucky I was too. It was terrific while it lasted, but I never told you I loved you, not once. I never asked you to marry me. I never made you any promises before you went away. It was you who chose to go travelling and said we needed space and you were right. As soon as you returned I came and told you how I'd met Izzy and what had happened. Be truthful, Lorna.'

But of course it was the truth of all this that really rankled and the person with whom Lorna had always found it most difficult to be honest was herself.

She took a lightning decision. 'I completely understand,' she said unexpectedly. 'Our week together was wonderful for me too, but now we're back here with Izzy and we can't seize every little moment when her back's turned. That wouldn't make either of us happy.'

She smiled up at Giles and he felt a huge sensation of relief. He had not thought for a moment that she would prove so easy. Perhaps he had been maligning her after all? 'That's generous of you, Lorna. You are also a stunningly beautiful woman and any-one who loves you will be lucky.'

'Well, catch some fish,' she said brightly. 'Tight lines!' And she watched him go down to the loch with the feeling of having played her cards very well.

$\mathscr{L}$orna took herself to Edinburgh a few days later with her mind full of ideas. Going into partnership with the serious and well-qualified Daphne was a distinct possibility. Daphne's talent for manipulating bones—and Lorna's for manipulating people and timetables—might be a brilliant combination. If Ruby McQueen was less to her personal taste, then at least she was no sort of threat either. Lorna had no doubt that she would easily be able to dom-inate the droopy Ruby, whose appearance suggested she had been young in the sixties and not got round to changing her dress style since. Her long greying hair hung like an uneven hem round a face of nebulous sweetness that must once have been extremely pretty; her goodwill was both as genuine and as transparent as her flowing Indian cotton skirts—and equally likely to trip her up, thought Lorna scornfully. A little less preoccupation with circle dancing and a brisker attitude to accounts and appointment sys-tems would not come amiss for a start, but all the same, Ruby could have her uses—a bulging address book and friendship with

Grizelda Murray being two of them. Grizelda had a lot of useful contacts.

It was peaceful without Lorna's disturbing presence at Glendrochatt. Isobel hoped she would stay away as long as possible.

Thirty-two

Daniel rang Glendrochatt from the States. He desperately longed to talk to Isobel and picked a time when he thought there was a good chance she might answer the telephone. However, it was Joss who picked up the receiver in the kitchen. At least it wasn't Lorna, thought Daniel thankfully.

'Hi there, Joss. Could I speak to Isobel? I'm ringing from New York.'

'Sure, I'll give her a yell. She can't be far away,' said Joss, but then Giles's voice had cut in and, after telling him what had happened, where he was and that as yet he had no way of knowing when he would be back in Scotland, Daniel felt unable to ask for Isobel again. Giles guessed his dilemma but did not feel like facilitating an intimate chat between Daniel and his wife.

'Give my love to Isobel and the kids,' said Daniel, unable to think of any reason for prolonging the call further.

'I will. See you some time, then.' Giles rang off.

Daniel, achingly homesick for somewhere that could never be his home, visualised everything at Glendrochatt so clearly that his artist's eye could even conjure up the pattern of the elegant faded rugs in the hall, see in detail the Meissen figures of the monkey band in the drawingroom, imagine the tattered pile of Edward's dinosaur books on the kitchen sofa, and Amy's school blazer and satchel flung higgledy-piggledy over a chair. He could smell wisteria from the garden, woodsmoke, dog beds and old leather chairs in the nursery, and with his inner ear he could hear the music that was nearly always being played somewhere in the house.

Long after he had rung off, he sat by the telephone in the drab apartment of Carl's oncologist daughter Eva, who had a heart of gold, teeth like tombstones and the kind of skin that looks faintly grubby even when you know it to be clinically clean. She smelt faintly of camphor, possibly as a precaution against moth, thought Daniel. He admired her intellect, liked her kindness and ached for a laughing young woman with a bright complexion who made frivolous jokes on subjects about which she actually felt extremely seriously—and who was another man's wife.

Carl had left him the cottage on Iona and a request that he should act as his literary executor; both were unexpected and both seemed unwelcome. Daniel was filled with desolation and a disconcerting anger against Carl—partly for landing him with property and responsibilities, and not being there to listen to his objections to them, but especially for dying before Daniel had told him how much he valued him. Eva's generoushearted acknowledgement that Carl had always regarded Daniel as the son he had never had himself made him feel worse than ever.

'My father really loved you, Daniel. He often told me so.' She beamed toothily. Guiltily he declined her suggestion to cook him a meal—one sampling of her culinary efforts had been more than enough—called an old friend from his art college days, and decided to go out and get seriously drunk. Anything, anything to take his mind off Glendrochatt.

*G*iles and Amy, armed with their fiddles, attended the June Pony Club hop as planned, but with Mick and Joss away Isobel chose to stay at home with Edward. It was a perfectly legitimate excuse but she could easily have gone if she'd really wanted. Mrs Johnstone would have come in, or Edward could have stayed with the

Fortescues, but a chance remark of Grizelda Murray's had alerted Isobel to the fact that Lorna had carefully been planting landmines at strategic intervals. Isobel had no intention of exposing herself publicly to the speculation about the state of her marriage that was obviously circulating.

'Oh, Izz.' Fiona looked very distressed. 'I know Dismal Daphers has been filling Grizelda up with untrue gossip—Grizelda's a fool—but don't you see? If you give in to it you're letting Lorna score a bull's-eye.' But Isobel was adamant. Giles, not unaware of the rumours himself and very anxious to scotch them, had tried to persuade her to go, but on meeting a wall of apparent indifference from his wife had been needled into saying, 'Don't you think it's time you stopped sulking?'

The minute the words were out he regretted them, but it was too late. After that, nothing would have prevailed on Isobel to change her mind.

Because Giles had to go straight to the party from a meeting in Edinburgh, Isobel was to drop Amy at the Duff-Farquharsons, who had offered to take her along with them. She arrived at their house with considerable trepidation, but Jolly Jilly—no surprise to learn she had been in charge of organising the food for the party, thought Isobel—gave her an effusive welcome and shouted for her husband to come down and meet her. General Duff-Farquharson, who bore a strong resemblance to a capercaillie, was the owner of several chins and a voice as fruity as his nickname; but he was friendliness itself. Clearly no malice had been borne about his daughter's injuries and hatchets were firmly interred. He was one of those huge men who Isobel suspected would be astonishingly light on his feet when dancing reels; he was already resplendent in his kilt, ready for any action that might be required of a supervising father, from rescuing wilting wallflowers to dragooning any reluctant small boys on to the dance floor.

'Plum's always absolutely splendid with the young,' confided Jilly proudly. 'You need have no worries about Amy.' The absolute splendidness of both the Duff-Farquharsons made Isobel feel quite limp. She handed over her contribution of fruit salad and meringues, but turned down the offer to stay for a drink because Edward, at his most withdrawn and uncooperative, had refused to say hello or get out of the car; Isobel hadn't known whether to be relieved or sorry.

'Suck and swallow, Ed,' she hissed urgently as she made her farewells, not wishing the Duff-Farquharsons to spy the trickle of saliva escaping from the corner of his mouth as they beamed at him through the car window and waved goodbye. Edward did not look up, but sat glued to a book about lepidoptera, his pebble glasses almost touching the glossy illustrated pages; lepidoptera was—suitably perhaps—his latest buzz word and one of which everyone at home was heartily sick. It was amazing how he could manage to introduce it into the most unlikely conversations.

Isobel went home to watch a video on sharks, which she had sat through many times before, and felt forlorn. She wished desperately that her son could be twirling away with the other little boys of his age, dashing the 'White Sergeant' and hurling through 'The Duke of Perth' to the lively playing of his father and his twin. She had answered Edward's endless questions about piscatorial predators—about which he knew far more than she did—but her thoughts were about Daniel.

It was midnight when Giles and Amy got in. The party had been FAN-TAS-TIC said Amy, yawning hugely. She had danced every dance for which she wasn't actually playing in the band, and she and Emily and Tara had succeeded in tripping up four boys during 'Strip-the-Willow', which was really cool.

'So was it all right between you and Tara?' asked Isobel, who had worried whether Amy and Tara would get through the evening without any further upset.

Amy looked amazed. 'Oh, Mum, of course. I like Tara now. Didn't I tell you?'

'No,' said Isobel. 'You didn't.'

Giles tried to put his arms round her. 'So how has my love been?' he asked, thinking she looked wretched.

Isobel shook him off. 'Fine,' she replied brightly. 'Edward and I had an absolutely scintillating evening. How was Jolly Jilly?'

'Delightful,' said Giles, 'if you have a penchant for overblown peonies.' But there was no answering glimmer from his wife.

$\mathcal{I}$t had been a relief to have Lorna out of the way. All the family found her return depressing, but when Mick and Joss got back the atmosphere lightened immediately. Everyone—except Lorna—was overjoyed to see them looking larger, more bronzed and fitter than ever. The adventure holiday had been an unqualified success. They had bungie-jumped from bridges, rafted down rapids, abseiled down vertical rockfaces, encountered wild animals and generally had a thoroughly relaxing holiday, they said. They were extremely scornful about the weediness of some of the other participants of the tour for whom Isobel felt considerable sympathy.

Edward, who had been longing to see his beloved Joss and had driven Isobel crazy by asking at least every ten minutes exactly what time he would be back, was quite unable even to give him a greeting when the great moment arrived. Joss and Mick might have been invisible for all the notice he took as they walked through the door.

Joss was quite unperturbed. 'He'll talk when he's good and ready,' he said peaceably and added with a grin, 'I'd better make the most of his silence, though. It won't last.'

'Oh, Joss,' said Isobel. 'I do love you. You always make everything seem so *easy*.'

'No point in making life harder than it has to be,' said Joss and Isobel had felt abashed.

Mick and Joss had come back laden with presents for everyone. Amy was enchanted with a T-shirt covered in huge black lion's pad marks, but as Edward had expected to be brought something live—a scorpion or tarantula at least, if not a python—he was less impressed. However, as Joss pointed out, the hens might not have welcomed the arrival of a python quite so happily. Quite soon

Edward was filling Joss in with the latest stop-press news of Mrs Silkie. Mrs Silkie was nesting, he said, and there was the excitement of wondering when her eggs would hatch. Once this idea had lodged in Edward's head he could think of little else.

Lorna had come back from Edinburgh at her most glamorous, but uninformative about her plans. To Isobel's relief she announced that she would be going away again shortly—'If that's all right with you, Izzy?' she asked sweetly. The thought of leaving Lorna loose at Glendrochatt to commandeer her husband, upset her children and cause havoc with her staff had begun to seem like the height of folly to Isobel, and she had contemplated telling her parents she couldn't go to them after all, except that she badly needed time to sort herself out away from home. She knew she could not resolve her differences with Giles until she had seen Daniel again.

If anyone had told me two months ago that I could be in this state I would not have believed them, she thought painfully.

*B*efore Isobel left, Giles tried for a reconciliation.

'And did you sleep with Lorna during your little Northumbrian idyll?' asked Isobel, who knew the answer perfectly well.

'Yes,' Giles admitted. 'Yes, I did. No excuses, Izz, and it won't happen again, I promise. I'll tell you about it if you're ready to hear but I might just ask you first, have you slept with Daniel?'

'No,' said Isobel, but Giles could also read the words 'not yet' in an invisible 'thinks' bubble over her head. They parted with nothing solved between them.

*L*orna returned again to Glendrochatt before Isobel. She had given no indication when she might be back and Giles, who had gone for a couple of days' fishing on the Lochy with Duncan Fortescue, was considerably disconcerted to arrive home and see her red VW parked outside the back door. His heart sank. From his point of view the timing could not have been worse, leaving it horribly easy for anyone so minded to imagine that he and Lorna were making the most of Isobel's absence.

Lorna gave him an affectionate greeting, but no more so, he reassured himself, than any loving sister might give her brother-in-law. Then again, Lorna wasn't a very loving sister.

'So good to be with you again, Giles,' she said.

'Lovely to see you too,' said Giles automatically and then, to be on the safe side, 'Lorna, please don't think I'm being presumptuous, but you do understand that things are over between us, don't you? I did mean what I said the other day.'

'But of course.' Lorna opened her blue eyes very wide and looked at him with studied innocence. 'Dear Giles,' she said slightly mockingly, though teasing was not normally her style, 'you made yourself quite clear. I admired you for it.'

'It's just that I wouldn't want anyone to get the wrong idea about us.' Giles, who had always fancied himself as being urbane and subtle, felt he was being extraordinarily heavy-handed.

'No indeed,' said Lorna.

She behaved with unexceptionable propriety, giving Sheila Shepherd a pleasant greeting and treating Mick and Joss, if not with friendliness, at least without open hostility. For their part they looked as if the live scorpion Edward had so badly wanted had suddenly materialised in the Glendrochatt kitchen. Joss would have liked to take off one of his size eleven flip-flops and swat her with it.

'Will Lorna be joining you for dinner?' he asked Giles when they were all four having tea with Edward, Amy having gone to stay with Emily for the night.

'Thank you, Joss; that would be very nice,' said Lorna graciously before Giles could answer. Joss raised an eyebrow at Giles, who turned down the corners of his mouth and gave an almost imperceptible little shrug, which Lorna saw.

'I'll leave something out for you both then,' said Joss. 'Me and Mick are going for a dram with Bruce and Angus.'

———

$\mathcal{D}$uring supper Lorna told Giles about her plans to go into partnership with Daphne and Ruby. 'I wouldn't leave you here until October, when the festival will be well under way,' she said, 'and I could always come over and give you a hand if anything special cropped up. But I realise I have to make my own life. You've both made me see that in your different ways. I've put my name down with various estate agents and eventually I shall look for a house in Edinburgh, but meanwhile I've taken over the lease of a flat in Moray Place from a friend of Daphne's who's going abroad for six months.'

'You have been busy.' Relief flooded over Giles.

'I have, haven't I?' said Lorna, smooth as polyester. 'I always like to crack on once I've put my mind to something.'

After supper she suggested they should play duets. 'Not for too long, though,' she said. 'I could do with an early night.'

Giles wasn't sure this was a good idea and decided he would call a definite halt if it looked as though Lorna had any schemes afoot, but after they had played enjoyably together for an hour or so Lorna said she was tired and must go over to the flat. Giles kissed her goodnight as casually as if she'd been a maiden aunt, saw her out and took the dogs for a run. They hadn't been so easy together for ages and he felt it boded well for the remaining weeks left before Flavia's Gala concert when Isobel and Lorna would still have to work together. At least my part of the mess is sorted out, he thought thankfully. He shut the dogs in the nursery and locked up. Before he went to bed he looked in on Edward, although there was not much to be seen but a hump of duvet from which a tremendous snoring was issuing. Nobody in the family liked sharing a room with Edward, who bubbled like a volcano all night.

Giles went into his dressing-room, where earlier in the day he had dumped his overnight bag, but he couldn't be bothered to unpack it now. He flung his clothes on the single bed, which

even in his and Isobel's state of armed neutrality he had not resorted to sleeping in, then had a long relaxing bath in the vast
bathroom that lay between his dressing-room and their bedroom.
The bathroom could be freezing in winter, but tonight the temperature was perfect. The windows were wide open but the curtains were not even swaying, so unusually still was it. Giles did
not bother to turn on the light—the half-light of midsummer
evenings almost lasts until dawn in Scotland and if, as on this
night, there is a moon as well it never gets really dark. It was
certainly peaceful but somehow everything and everywhere
seemed echoing and hollow without Isobel. We have to get things
right, thought Giles, fool that I am. Lorna, Daniel, they can both
go hang. I should never forgive myself if I lost Izzy.

He went into their bedroom, full of resolution but also anxiety,
acutely conscious of her absence and got into bed.

But the bed was already occupied and as he climbed between
the sheets a pair of arms twined round his neck, a naked body
slid against him and a mouth opened to his.

'Oh, darling!' whispered Giles. 'You're back.'

For one mad, impossible moment he thought it was Isobel—
and then he knew it wasn't.

He wrenched himself free, almost spitting Lorna out as if she
were choking him. 'What the hell are you doing here?' he asked
furiously.

She gave a cry of anguish. 'Don't, Giles, don't. Please don't
push me off. We're so good together, you know that. I love you
so much. Have Izzy too, if you must—if she still wants you, that
is—but don't send me away. I can't bear it. I'd do anything for
you.' She was shouting now.

She tried to clutch at his hand but he snatched it away, hitting
the bedside light, which landed on the floor with a resounding
crash. All the books fell off the bedside table. 'I told you it was
over and you agreed. Stop it, Lorna.'

'I never agreed,' she said passionately. 'And I never, never will.
I let you have your little attack of conscience to get it out of your

system and because I knew you had to come to your senses again soon. If you make love to me you'll know we can't do without each other. Please, Giles, please.'

Somehow he managed to hold her away from him, astonished at how strong she was, horrified by her desperation. Then she gave a terrible yell and seemed to freeze, turned to alabaster by the moon. The door, which was always left ajar at night in case the children called, was now wide open.

Standing at the end of the bed, gazing at them both, thumb in mouth, was Edward.

Thirty-three

Giles leapt out of bed, reached for his dressing-gown and was beside Edward in a second, appalled that his son should have witnessed such a scene.

Lorna looked for a brief moment as mesmerised as a rabbit under the eye of a stoat. Then she quickly pulled the sheet under her chin and gazed back at Edward with something frighteningly close to hatred in her eyes. 'You horrible little boy,' she hissed. 'How dare you spy on us!'

'Lorna! There's no call for that,' said Giles sharply. 'What is it, Ed? Have you had a dream?'

'Henth,' said Edward.

'What about the hens?'

'Chipping.'

'What are you talking about?'

'Eggth—chipping,' said Edward. 'Mithith Thilkie. Eggth.'

Giles looked at him. 'Edward, it's the middle of the night. Don't tell me you've come to ask if we can go and check whether that bloody hen of yours has hatched her eggs?'

Edward beamed at him as though he had at last guessed the answer to a particularly amusing riddle, as indeed, from his point of view, Giles had. The two long dimples his mother loved to see appeared like cracks down his cheeks. He nodded delightedly, looking like the drawing Daniel had given Isobel, which was framed now and hanging by her side of the bed—the side where Lorna was presently lying.

'Certainly not!' said Giles trying to sound stern, but feeling close to hysterical laughter. 'I never heard such nonsense. We don't go and look at hens until the morning.'

'When will it be morning?'

'Not for a very long time. You go straight back to bed and I don't want to hear another sound from you, or I shall be really cross.'

'Aren't you going to punish him?' asked Lorna in a shaking voice.'

'*Punish him*? Of course not. We must have woken him up. Hardly surprising, given the racket you've just made. If he wakes in the night he never has the faintest clue what time it is.'

'He can tell the time perfectly well. I've heard Izzy practising with him.'

'Oh, Lorna.' Giles was genuinely exasperated. 'It doesn't *mean* anything to him. Surely you must have understood that by now?'

'I understand he's a spiteful, nasty little boy and very spoilt.' Lorna was beside herself.

Giles gave her a look of horrified dislike. 'I am going to take Edward back to his own bed now,' he said icily. 'I suggest you go back to yours immediately—and stay in it.' He propelled Edward out of the room without a backward glance at her.

Five minutes later, when he came back, Lorna had gone. Once tucked back in bed and told very firmly not to get out again, Edward went to sleep almost immediately, but neither Giles nor Lorna slept at all.

The same question had occurred to them both: would Edward be able to tell Isobel what he had seen and if he could, would he do so? Lorna hoped desperately that he could and would—it seemed her only hope. She did not think Isobel would easily forgive Giles if she believed he'd been making love to Lorna in her own bed, in full view of her child, and surely that is what, with a little help, she would believe?

Giles hoped desperately that Edward couldn't and wouldn't, although he was absolutely clear that he must tell Isobel exactly what had occurred at the first possible opportunity. He was equally clear that it was imperative he should send Lorna away from Glendrochatt and decided it would be his only chance of salvaging his marriage.

I had no idea, thought Giles with a sense of revelation, what a cauldron of emotion bubbles beneath Lorna's controlled exterior. It's frightening and pathetic. Lorna is a deeply sad person but I have never thought of her like that before. How obtuse I have been.

Lorna did not appear at breakfast in the big kitchen, but then she often got her own coffee and toast in the flat before going over to the office. Outwardly all was normal. Edward went off as usual on the Greenyfordham bus and Fiona had promised to drop Amy back that afternoon after school. Isobel was due home the following day and a fax to Giles from New York announced that Daniel also hoped to return to Glendrochatt, though he was not sure of the timing.

Giles couldn't help wondering if Daniel and Isobel had been in touch with each other. Isobel had telephoned home from her parents' house in France, and spoken to Amy and Edward, but had managed to avoid talking to her husband by quickly handing the telephone to her mother so that she could have a lovely chat to the grandchildren, as she often liked to do. 'Have a word with Granny first, darling,' Isobel had said brightly when Amy told her Giles was waiting to speak to her.

'Are you the live granny or the dead granny?' Edward had asked with interest when it was his turn.

'I'm the live one, darling,' Isobel's mother had said, much amused.

Isobel had rung again from the hotel in Prague. 'Give my love to Daddy and Mick and Joss and Aunt Lorna,' she had said to Amy, lumping them all conveniently together, thought Giles, when Amy passed on this message. 'Tell them I'm having a lovely time and Prague is as magic as everyone told me. Granny and Grandpa send lots of hugs.' She had asked Edward about the welfare of the hens and the 'speedy lady with the long ears'—his private name for Flapper—but only his heavy breathing told her he was there because this time he hadn't been in a conversational mood.

It all sounded so normal it was impossible to get an idea whether any emotional turbulence might be going on at either end of the telephone line.

Amy had to practise as soon as Fiona dropped her home because she had missed her morning session. Giles thought she seemed unusually subdued and her playing reflected it. It crossed his mind to wonder whether Edward had said anything to her about the previous night, but he realised there had been no chance for them to be alone together.

He felt awful himself and had a splitting headache. 'Anything the matter, Amy?' he asked. 'Are you OK?'

She gave him a startled look. 'I'm fine,' she insisted, but he was sure she wasn't telling the truth. 'Why? Didn't I get that bit right?' She sounded belligerent.

'Yes, it was lovely, particularly the opening bars, but let's remember to start with a down bow. We'll move on to the next bit now.'

He thought perhaps she was just tired. She and Emily had probably chatted away to each other for half the night, He cut the practice short for both their sakes. 'Go and have your tea with Ed. I'll come and see you both later. Perhaps I could read to you in bed when you've done your homework.'

He decided to swallow some paracetamol before he coped with any more family life.

Amy found Edward in the kitchen. Joss was scrambling eggs. Lorna was sitting at the table having a cup of tea and trying to make conversation to Edward. She was getting absolutely no response.

'Toast or bread, Amy?' asked Joss.

'I'm not hungry, thanks.'

'Suit yourself,' said Joss cheerfully. He didn't believe in pressing children to eat if they didn't feel like it, bribing them with too much choice or making mealtimes into a battlefield. But he too thought Amy looked very wan—missing her mother, perhaps. Good job Isobel would get back tomorrow, thought Joss. He wished Lorna would go away; in place of her normal aloofness she seemed thoroughly jumpy and ill at ease. She didn't usually attend children's tea and he couldn't understand why she was focusing so much attention on Edward all of a sudden. She always made him nervous anyway. Amy didn't look too thrilled to see her aunt either, he noted.

'When will Mum be back?' asked Edward for the umpteenth time.

'Tomorrow,' said Joss patiently, also for the umpteenth time. 'She'll be here to tuck you into your bed tomorrow night. Not tonight, Ed, but tomorrow.'

'So will there be a long-legged black spider in Daddy's bed again tonight?' asked Edward.

The effect of this question was dramatic. Lorna choked and went scarlet. She spilt tea down her immaculate ice-blue T-shirt, Amy went deathly white.

'You ask a lot of silly questions, Edward,' said Joss sharply. 'Get on with your tea.'

Lorna rushed out of the room.

———

It was unfortunate timing that Giles had asked Lord Dunbarnock, Lady Fortescue and Mr McMichael to dinner that night to discuss fund-raising events. Even for informal supper Violet Fortescue wore her tremendous pearl choker, which had so many strings that it gave her the elongated look of an African tribeswoman whose throat has become stretched by the constant wearing of neck rings.

It was an uncomfortable meal, with Lorna hectically over-playing the hostess role and Giles burningly aware of an open hostility to himself from Joss and Mick that was most unusual. They did not explain it, but they didn't need to. Giles wondered exactly what had been said and by whom.

Joss came into the dining-room halfway through the main course to announce that Amy had just been sick. Neil Dunbarnock looked as panic-stricken as if he'd found himself in contact with bubonic plague, and only a super-human effort of will prevented him from bolting out of the house and speeding straight to the doctor's surgery in his nineteen-thirties open touring Alvis. Could the child's germ be catching? What was the kitchen hygiene like at Glendrochatt? Bacillus E coli could lurk dangerously in many a crevice waiting to pounce on the unwary. He pushed the remains of the Chicken Paprika nervously to the side of his plate, thoughts of salmonella floating alarmingly through his mind.

Lady Fortescue treated Joss to a glance straight from the North Pole and said, 'Oh, dear. How unfortunate,' in a voice of frosted sweetness like a lemon sorbet, and deftly turned the conversation to more pleasant and appropriate topics. She was astonished that Giles should actually go upstairs in the middle of dinner to see Amy. What did one employ staff for? she asked herself, even such unsuitable ones as the extraordinary man who acted as general factotum to the Grants. In Lady Fortescue's opinion Joss would have been better employed shearing sheep or mending motorways.

It took all Giles's conscious effort to thaw her glacial disapproval. Mr McMichael got dreadfully garrulous after a second glass of port and lingered droningly on, long after Lady Fortescue and Lord Dunbarnock had departed. Giles thought he might never be able to shift him again and feared he would become a fixture at Glendrochatt as though set up by a taxidermist. When he finally managed to ease his guest out of the front door and insert him in his car, Giles felt completely wrung-out.

$\mathcal{T}$he following morning Amy appeared to have recovered. She played brilliantly at her practice and Giles judged that she was perfectly all right to go to school. It was a relief. Things were bad enough already without Isobel coming home to find anything wrong with either of the children. He drove Amy to the garage at Blairalder where Grizelda Murray picked her up. There was no school for Edward because it was a staff training day at Greenyfordham, so he pottered about happily about near Mick, who was working in the courtyard of the Old Steading.

Lorna, going down to check that all was in order there before Daniel's return, found Edward sitting on the step outside the theatre playing with his bag of serpents and dinosaurs. She looked at him with distaste, unhappily ashamed of her revulsion and quite unable to overcome it.

Inside the theatre the two portraits still stood on their easels on either side of the stage exactly where Daniel had left them when he had been called away so unexpectedly. Drawn as if by a magnet, Lorna went to look at hers, needing to be reassured of her own physical beauty, craving a boost of confidence as an addict might require a shot of 'Speed'. What she saw affected her like a high-voltage electric shock.

Someone had daubed paint all over the portrait. There were open tins all around and one of Daniel's largest brushes, used for the stage scenery, lay on the floor, bristles gunged up with paint. The face of the portrait was completely unrecognisable, a running blotch of clashing colours. A pool had formed underneath the picture as red, orange and black had dripped down it on to the floor. Lorna did not doubt for a moment who was responsible. She whisked out of the door, got hold of Edward by the scruff of the neck and yanked him to his feet. Then she took him by the shoulders and shook him, like a terrier with a rat. 'What have you done to my picture, you wicked boy?' she shouted.

Mick, coming round the corner with a wheelbarrow, heard the commotion and could hardly believe his eyes. 'Leave him alone!' he yelled urgently, dropping the barrow and breaking into a run. Lorna let Edward go so suddenly he sprawled on the ground. She was shivering all over and her breath came in gasps as though she had been competing in a hundred-metre sprint. 'What the bleeding hell d'you think you're doing?' demanded Mick, picking Edward up and setting him gently down beside his bag of toys. He turned furiously to Lorna, but before he could speak she grabbed at him, her nails digging into his brawny arm.

'Come and look,' she shrieked, almost dragging him inside the door. 'Look what that child has done. My portrait is completely ruined.' Then she started to scream hysterically.

Joss and Giles arrived almost simultaneously. 'What the hell's going on?' They gazed from Lorna to the picture in disbelief.

'Stop it,' said Giles, but Lorna, quite unable to stop, screamed on. 'Stop it this minute, Lorna.' Giles dealt her a swift slap across the face. There was sudden complete silence.

'Oh, God, I'm sorry,' said Giles. 'What have I done?'

'Only what I've been dying to do for weeks, mate,' said Mick, with a shaky attempt at a grin. 'She seems to think Edward's been redecorating her picture for her and she doesn't much care for the result. I thought she was going to kill him for a moment.'

'Edward?' Giles was stunned. 'You must be mad, Lorna. Edward would never do that. He couldn't manage it even if he wanted to.'

'Then who did?' asked Lorna, one hand held to her stinging cheek. 'Tell me that. Of course he did it and *you know why.*'

'Don't be absurd,' said Giles scornfully. 'If you think Edward capable of deliberately sabotaging your bloody picture just because he witnessed your failed attempt to try to seduce me in my own bed . . . ' Giles broke off suddenly. 'Where *is* Edward?' he asked.

'In the yard with his monster bag,' said Mick, who had exchanged an enlightened look with Joss during this speech. Perhaps hostility to Giles was out of order?

Giles strode to the door. 'Ed? Ed?'

But Edward had vanished like a puff of wind.

$\mathcal{T}$hey called and shouted for him all round the theatre. They separated and went searching round the house and garden. They looked in the castle where he had gone after the hen drama and they looked in the hen-run. There was no sign of him.

'I'm sure he's only hiding,' said Lorna, starting to feel panicky.

'Of course he's fucking hiding,' said Mick. 'Wouldn't you be hiding if you'd just been terrified out of your wits?'

'It wasn't my fault that . . .' began Lorna, but Giles cut her short.

'It doesn't matter whose fault it was. What we have to do is *find* him.' They decided to be systematic. Each of the three men would take a specific area and they would meet back at the house in forty minutes.

'Where shall I look?' asked Lorna desperately.

'Anywhere. Everywhere. We must just keep looking and calling,' said Giles. 'He can't have gone far.' But he sounded more as if he were trying to reassure himself than because he believed it.

'Don't *you* call out to him, Lorna.' Mick scorched her with the contempt in his voice. After the scene he'd just witnessed he was certain that the sound of Lorna calling would send Edward into a state of panic, which would be completely counter-productive. They really had no idea how far he might go or what he might do. Edward's abilities and reactions could never be judged by other people's standards.

After forty minutes' intensive searching and still no trace, grim possibilities started to occur to them. The woods? The old quarry? The loch? . . . *The Loch?*

'Go to the office, Lorna,' said Giles urgently. 'Tell Sheila what's happened and for God's sake stay by the telephone. I've got my mobile on me. Tell Sheila to get hold of Bruce and Angus, and anyone else on the estate she can find, and get them here. If we haven't found him in an hour I'm going to ring the police.' Lorna went without a word.

'He can't possibly be far,' said Giles again, unable to believe that Edward could disappear from under their noses in so short a time. 'Joss, try the house again. Check all the cupboards and the cellar, and keep checking the hen-run. Mick, you go up the burn. I'm going down to the loch to look in the boathouse. Meet again in an hour. Ring me if you find him.'

Giles was off down the path to the loch like a bullet.

*D*aniel, having driven through what remained of the night straight from Heathrow, turned the old Volvo in at the gates of Glendrochatt and felt like a homing pigeon nearing its loft—only it wasn't his own loft, he thought ruefully. He was more like a bird that has found delightful and unexpected shelter after being blown off course by an overpowering gale.

It had started to pour with rain and he was surprised to see a gang of men without waterproof clothing standing deep in consultation near the bottom of the drive, getting drenched. There were two of the foresters, old Mr Burnett who lived on the estate and who'd been Hector Grant's factor for years, Alec the shepherd, the Johnstone brothers, Mick, Joss and Giles. Must be another leak in a pipe, thought Daniel, who had grown used to the unreliability of the temperamental Glendrochatt water supply. Pity. He felt like a bath. He wound down his window, getting all the water he could want straight in his face. 'Hi there!' he called out cheerfully and then, seeing their faces, 'Hey, anything wrong?'

Giles came over. 'Daniel. We've lost Edward. Bit of a drama. Lorna lost her temper with him and he's vanished.'

'I'll come and join the search at once.'

'No,' said Giles. 'No. There's something better you could do. We need Amy. Those two have an extraordinary rapport and she might have an idea. If I ring the school, could you possibly go and get her?'

'Of course.'

'D'you know where it is?'

'Yeah. I've collected her before.' Daniel was already turning the car round as Giles started to dial the school number.

Mrs Baird was waiting with Amy on the school steps. Daniel opened the car door. 'Hop in,' he said.

'Oh, Daniel. What's happened to Ed?'

'I don't know, Amy. Daddy just said he'd gone missing, like after Flavia's dog got the chickens, I suppose.' Daniel guessed it was much more serious this time, but thought this might reassure her. 'I gather he had a bit of a barney with your Aunt Lorna or something. I expect they'll have found him by the time we get home.'

'Was it . . . was she furious about the picture?' asked Amy in a strangled voice. 'Did she think Ed did it?'

'Did what? What picture?'

'Yours. The one of Aunt Lorna.'

'Oh, Amy, I've no idea. I've only just got back.' He suddenly remembered his arrival at Glendrochatt and Lorna's anger when Edward had upset the paint. 'Why, what's happened to it?' he asked, keeping his voice casual.

'I wrecked it,' said Amy. 'Early this morning. On purpose.'

'What did you do that for?' Daniel took a quick look at her. Tears were pouring down her face.

'Because, because . . .' Amy twisted her hands and struggled to speak. 'Because I hate Aunt Lorna. Because Emily heard her mum telling her daddy that Aunt Lorna is trying to take Daddy away from Mummy, and lots of people at school have four parents and because . . .' Amy's voice sank to a whisper. 'At tea yesterday Ed asked if there was going to be a spider in Daddy's bed again last night,' she said.

The bitch, thought Daniel angrily, the significance of this utterance entirely obvious to him. The bloody bitch. How could she? Then it seemed as though in his head he was seeing a hand, with a finger wavering in the wind like a weather vane, and slowly the finger turned and pointed at himself.

'Oh, Daniel,' said Amy. 'It was your picture too. I'm so, so sorry.'

'Look Amy, it doesn't matter a hoot about the picture, and no one's going to part your Dad and Mum.'

'Promise?'

'I promise,' said Daniel, speaking strictly for himself, on two counts. 'Anyway, what did you do to it?' he asked.

'I got your big brush and opened all your pots of paint for the scenery and sloshed them all over her face. If Aunt Lorna thought Ed did it she must be mad. He could never have opened the tins, never. It was quite difficult,' she added and Daniel thought he detected a touch of pride despite her woebegone appearance.

'It must have given you one hell of a kick.' Daniel envisaged the scene. 'But I hate to tell you, Amy, you won't really have ruined it. I'll be able to clean it because the theatre paints are water-based and they won't bond to the oil ones I used for the portrait. So bad luck. Bet you don't know whether to be pleased or sorry.'

She gave him a doubtful look. 'I don't mind about Aunt Lorna but I mind about you. I never thought about you when I did it.'

'Thanks,' said Daniel.

'You're not very angry with me?'

'Of course not, cross my heart. Now think hard, Amy. Where is Edward? That's what matters.'

'With Mrs Silkie?'

'Surely they'll have looked in the hen house? First place one would think of.'

'But Mrs Silkie isn't in the hen house,' said Amy. 'That's why Edward's been able to visit her on his own. We didn't tell anyone because we thought they'd shut her in again. She's nesting out all by herself in a secret place that only Ed and I know about.'

$\mathcal{G}$iles did not immediately see Isobel when she arrived home after driving herself back from Edinburgh airport, because he was on the telephone to the police and had his back to the door. She walked into the kitchen and was astonished to find it full of men, all totally sodden and all looking grim. No one said anything and she listened with horror as Giles told the sergeant at Blairalder police station what had happened.

'He's been missing for three hours now,' she heard him say. 'Yes, we've had everyone on the estate searching. Not a sign, no. With a normal child one might not be quite so worried, but this is Edward . . . well you've known him all his life. I don't need to explain to you. Oh, will you really? Thank you so much, Sergeant Morris. See you shortly, then.' He turned round.

'Oh, Izz, thank God you're home. You heard?'

'Yes,' she said, very white. 'Tell me properly—everything.'

But at that moment there was a shriek. 'Mummy! Mummy! Mummy!' Amy erupted into the room and hurled herself at her mother. 'Look!' she said.

Standing in the doorway behind her was Daniel, a small, limp, wet figure in his arms.

For a moment nobody dared to speak or move. Edward appeared completely lifeless. Then, 'He's OK,' said Daniel uncertainly. 'At least I think so. He's breathing, but he won't speak.'

Isobel flew to him. She touched Edward's face with one finger as though it was something very fragile. 'Ed? It's Mum. Everything's all right darling. I'm here.'

She looked at Giles, then back to Edward. Giles came and stood behind her, his hands on her shoulders, and looked down at his son, a muscle in his face twitching. 'Hospital or Dr Nichol?' he asked.

'Try Dr Nichol first. If he's not there we'll have to take him to the Infirmary, but I'd better get his wet things off quick. Can you carry him straight upstairs, Daniel?'

There would be time for explanations later. Amy followed them up.

It took only moments to get Edward out of his sopping clothes and into a hot bath, and Giles came up almost immediately to say that by great good luck Dr Nichol had been at the surgery and would come at once. They put Edward on Giles's and Isobel's big bed, and Amy curled up beside him. Edward was completely silent. He didn't appear to know who any of them were.

Daniel looked at the close family circle centred round the un-responsive little figure on the bed. None of them noticed when he slipped away quietly and went downstairs.

In the kitchen Joss was ringing the police station to say Edward had been found. Giles himself would telephone Sergeant Morris later on, he said.

Lorna was standing by the window. 'Do you think I should go up to them?' she asked Daniel.

'You keep away,' said Mick fiercely, casting her a menacing look.

Daniel saw her wince. 'I don't think they need either you or me just at the moment, Lorna,' he said and felt an unwilling wave of pity for her. We're two outsiders looking in through a lighted window, he thought.

'I don't think he had another seizure,' said Dr Nichol, 'al-though we'll give him the diazepam all the same. His chest is clear so far, but we'll have to keep a very careful eye on that. We don't want pneumonia again.' He gave Isobel and Giles a compassionate look. He was extremely fond of them both and admired how they coped with Edward in their very different ways. 'I'm afraid you may be in for a bit of a difficult time. He's gone right back into himself, hasn't he? His way of coping with shock.'

'But will he be OK again?'

'I think so. I hope so. It may take a bit of time. I don't really know. I'll write to Dr Connor and we'll get her advice. I expect she'll want to see him.'

'We'd got so far with him, further than we ever dreamt.' Tears streamed down Isobel's face. 'I can't bear to start the fight all over again,' she whispered. 'I don't think I can do it.'

Giles held her close. 'Yes, you can, Izz,' he said. 'You can do anything. We'll do it together.'

'I'll look in tomorrow.' Dr Nichol himself felt choked up. 'He's tough, that one, a survivor. He'll come round. I'll see myself out.'

$\mathcal{B}$ oth Giles and Isobel had been profuse in their thanks to Daniel. 'It was entirely due to Amy,' said Daniel truthfully. 'Giles's instinct to get her was spot on. She's the star.'

He thought he would never forget the moment when they had found Edward in the wood, deep in a hollow under the roots of a densely leafed shrub, curled tight as a hibernating mouse, gone to ground, totally silent. Mrs Silkie, normally a vociferous lady, had been silent too, guarding her secret eggs against intruders.

The searchers must have walked right past Edward several times.

$\mathcal{L}$ orna had rung Daphne and gone to Edinburgh that night.

'Thank you for all the help you have given us, but you are leaving us straight away to start your partnership with Daphne, aren't you, Lorna?' Giles had asked her, his face expressionless, his voice even. She had looked at him for a long moment in silence, then her eyes had dropped and she had gone to the flat to pack her things.

'Oh, Giles,' said Isobel doubtfully. 'I'm not sure you can really do that.'

'I just have,' said Giles.

————

*T*wo days later Edward appeared to have recovered physically from his ordeal, but had still not spoken. He played with his bag of monsters, rolled up endless little bits of torn-off paper and lined them up, or just sat with his thumb in his mouth, rocking gently to and fro. Joss's patience and gentleness with him was touching. Isobel had told him that the spider lady had gone and thought there had been some faint flicker of reaction in his blank, inward-looking eyes. He was to see Dr Connor the following week, but Giles and Isobel felt cautiously optimistic about the long-term outlook.

They began to be cautiously optimistic about the future of their own relationship too. There were some things that were still too painful to talk about, hurts that could not be ignored but could not be healed in a hurry either, but they both knew that their priorities had been given a sharp shake-up and that they were lucky to have a priceless second chance to try to get their marriage right.

Daniel stayed on for three days, working flat out to finish the backcloth. Then he suddenly announced that he was off.

'But you will be coming back soon, won't you?' asked Isobel.

'I don't think so,' said Daniel quietly. 'But I've had a wonderful two months. Let me know how Ed gets on.'

Isobel and Giles stood together on the steps of Glendrochatt and waved him goodbye, as they had done for so many departing guests.

'Sad, Izzy?' asked Giles gently, feeling his own throat constrict at the look of pain on her face.

'Yes,' she replied, tears not far away. 'I have no right to mind, no right at all. Daniel once told me how he's always shied away from letting himself love anyone, but I thought he loved me. It's very wrong of me, but—oh, Giles—I can't help being hurt that he can just whisk away like this.'

'He's going *because* he loves you,' said Giles. 'I know that even if you don't.'

$\mathcal{D}$aniel went from Glendrochatt to Iona and spent the night in the cottage. The house seemed full of Carl's presence. On a still, grey day with a fine drizzle falling, he took Carl's ashes to St Columba's Bay as had been requested in his will.

The stones on the beach, speckled like oyster-catchers' eggs, looked dull without enough light to bring out their colours and the rocks above the bay loomed very black. Daniel saw a round dark head bob up about twenty yards out to sea, disappear and re-emerge, to the right, but closer in. Daniel and the seal watched each other with equal curiosity. Then it disappeared and when he saw it again it was much further away.

He scattered the ashes on the edge of the water, where the tide would take them out to sea. In his head he heard Carl's warning voice: 'Real loving can be very costly,' the old man had said.

'You were right, as usual,' said Daniel aloud, to Carl, 'but maybe it's worth it. I'll let you know some time.'

Thirty-four

At the beginning of July the usual flock of summer visitors started to arrive at Glendrochatt like migrating birds, so that the Grants were seldom on their own—perhaps, in the circumstances, a good thing.

Mrs Johnstone spent a great deal of time making up beds and complaining about the number of what she sniffily called 'all those one-nighters' who used up a great many clean sheets and caused a lot of laundry. Joss and Isobel felt as if they were constantly planning and preparing meals for an army, but Isobel suddenly realised that she had started to enjoy entertaining their friends at Glendrochatt again, a pleasure that had been missing of late, when Lorna's disturbing presence hovered like a dark shadow over the house.

Early in the school holidays Isobel and Fiona went into Edinburgh with all the children and, while the Fortescues' invaluable Caro took them to the zoo, Isobel, egged on by Fiona, had her hair completely restyled and cut really short.

'Oh, Fee, I feel quite naked.' Isobel put her hands behind her bare neck and gazed doubtfully at her reflection.

'You look absolutely fantastic,' said Fiona firmly. 'I love the way your hair curls round your face. Can't think why you haven't had it short before.' They met the children for lunch, and Amy and Emily were wildly enthusiastic about Isobel's appearance. 'Brill, Mum!' breathed Amy. 'Can I have mine done too?'

'Jeepers! It makes you look *years* younger!' said nineteen-year-old Caro admiringly.

Isobel pulled a wry face. She hadn't thought, at thirty-three, that she looked all that old before. 'Glad you approve,' she said. Edward, his thumb jammed tightly in his mouth, gazed at his mother, expressionless, and said nothing. 'Do you like my hair too, darling?' asked Isobel rashly, but Edward turned his head away, lurched off and wouldn't look at her. Isobel tried to pretend she didn't mind, but could have kicked herself for adding to Edward's insecurities at this particular time and felt increasingly nervous about what Giles's reaction might be.

When they eventually got home, after an exhausting and argumentative afternoon buying new shoes for the children and trying to reach some compromise between what Amy and Emily considered trendy and their mothers thought was practical, Giles looked at his wife in astonishment. 'Izz! Your lovely hair! What *have* you done?'

'It's my new image. What do you think?'

'I loved it as it was before.'

'Well, you had a funny way of showing it,' said Isobel tartly, a spark of challenge in her eye.

Giles laughed at her expression. 'Oh, well, I expect I'll get used to it in time,' he teased, walking round her appraisingly as if she were an exhibit in an art gallery.

'I don't want you to get used to it. If you ever get used to me I shall change it again immediately to something even more drastic,' she threatened, half serious, then added anxiously, 'Don't you really like it, Giles?'

He was touched by her vulnerable expression. 'You look absolutely irresistible,' he assured her and kissed her to prove it.

————

$\mathcal{I}$t was a huge relief to hear from Lorna that she had decided to return to South Africa for a visit—she said she had unexpectedly discovered that she still had affairs to settle up there and anyway wanted to see various friends again. It seemed a face-saving solution for everybody, and both Giles and Isobel desperately hoped she would decide to stay out there for good.

Giles also received a letter from Daniel. After he read it he tossed it across to Isobel, acutely aware that she had been unable to take her eyes off it since she caught sight of the handwriting on the envelope. Daniel's letter was curiously formal, almost stilted. He thanked Giles for giving him two such interesting commissions, hoped the festival would be a great success and said how much he'd enjoyed his time at Glendrochatt. He sent his love to the family and enquired especially after Edward.

'Good heavens,' said Giles, 'would you believe it? He's actually got an address for once. What can have got into him? That's a real turn-up for the books.' Isobel read the letter with what she hoped was an outward show of nonchalance, though it did not deceive Giles who was watching her face. Daniel said that he'd rented a house near the Camphill community in the south of England where he had been brought up; he was considering buying it, building on a studio and settling there for good, but had not yet made up his mind what to do with Carl's cottage on Iona. Later, when Giles had gone off to the estate office, Isobel reread the letter several times, searching for clues to any secret messages that might be hidden between the lines, and did not know whether to be disappointed or relieved when she could not find any. She was half tempted to keep the letter and store it away for future furtive perusals, but after an inward struggle she put it back on Giles's desk.

$\mathcal{A}$t the beginning of September news came through of two major changes that would be facing the Grant family in a year's time.

The Council had agreed to fund Edward for a place at the Camphill school near Aberdeen when he reached the age of twelve and could no longer stay at Greenyfordham. The thought of Edward going to boarding school made Isobel sick with anxiety, but Dr Connor had convinced her it would be the right decision for him. He had started to talk again and was slowly beginning to regain some of the ground he had lost, but it was a difficult and anxious struggle. Amy would be going away the following September too. She had won the coveted music scholarship to Upland House. Amy herself was enchanted, Valerie was delighted, but though Giles felt extremely proud of his daughter he knew he would find it very hard to watch this particular little songbird spread her wings.

'Oh, darling, it will be the end of an era and it really scares me,' Isobel told him. 'Only one more year as the four of us are now.'

'Then we must make the most of it,' Giles answered soberly and put out his hand to her.

Mick and Joss announced that they had decided to go travelling again once the Old Steading season finished at the end of November, though they vowed they would be back. No one could imagine life at Glendrochatt without them and the whole family dreaded their departure.

Final arrangements for the Gala concert filled everyone's minds. The tickets had all sold out weeks ago, the programmes were printed and the revamped theatre, with Daniel's backcloth in place, looked wonderful.

The day before the concert the weather was ominously grey and drizzly—not at all what Giles and Isobel were hoping for. Flavia and Megan Davies, who were staying with Flavia's uncle and aunt, came over to Glendrochatt to practise. Megan, a bubbly, excitable Welsh girl who'd been at the Guildhall with Flavia, went down to the theatre with Giles before lunch while Flavia stayed to gossip with Isobel. Giles left Megan down there, telling her to ask Angus, who was busy putting up signs for the car park, if there was anything she wanted. Megan came rushing back to the house in a frightful panic. 'Please come quick and stop your helper chap from touching my harp,' she gasped breathlessly to Isobel. 'He says he's going to throw it on the trailer. He wouldn't listen when I begged him not to touch it. He said not to worry it would be 'just fine', but he'll absolutely wreck it.'

Isobel shrieked with laughter. 'He doesn't mean *your* harp,' she said. 'A haap—with a long "a"—is what they call a tarpaulin up here. It's short for "Haappen it may rain". He's got a whole lot of chairs in the trailer, which mustn't get wet, so he only means he's going to chuck a cover over them in case the heavens open.' Megan felt so faint with relief that she had to sit down.

Isobel filled Flavia in about all the other dramas that had happened since the Forbeses' fateful visit in May—to everyone's relief Brillo had been firmly left behind this time.

'Alistair and I were really worried about you and Giles,' said Flavia. 'We both thought Lorna was out for the kill, but I couldn't help wondering about you and Daniel Hoffman too. Even in the short time we met him anyone could see he was head over heels in love with you, and you . . . well, you kept talking about him so much, Izz—always a dangerous give-away. Alistair couldn't see it, but I could.'

'Was it so obvious?' asked Isobel wonderingly. 'I hardly knew it myself then, but yes, there was something special between us.' She added seriously, 'Thank God I shall never know what it might have turned into. It's a bit of an irony that in a funny way Lorna saved us all by causing that awful drama with Edward, but I reckon we've paid a high price. Giles and I are slowly finding our way back together, but it's sometimes a bit like walking in the dark with only a torch.'

'Walking in the dark can be very exciting,' suggested Flavia. 'And I'm sure there's a special star up there to guide you both. It can't be easy, but keep slogging on, Izzy. We've always thought you and Giles had something unique going between you.' Flavia gave Isobel an encouraging hug and vowed to herself that she would do her best to give a very special performance for Giles and Isobel the next day, both to launch their new venture and as an offering for their marriage.

$\mathcal{W}$ith the help of Fiona and one or two other local friends—including Jilly Duff-Farquharson who proved to be a dab hand at crumpling wire-netting, soaking 'Oases' and whose secateurs, attached to her belt by a special sort of lanyard, never went missing as everyone else's seemed to do—Isobel went wild with decorations and Glendrochatt was filled with flowers. 'I don't want the house to lose its family character and suddenly look all "corporate",' Isobel told her team of helpers. 'I just want it to look its ravishing best and smell delicious, but perhaps we could do something a bit more formal in the theatre.' They put two huge arrangements of lilies, carnations and autumn foliage on pedestals at either side of the stage and the effect against the dark-red curtains was stunning.

Flavia asked if Amy, who had been allowed a day off school, would like to sit in and listen as she and Megan rehearsed, although nobody else was to be allowed to disturb them. 'She might pick up a thing or two,' suggested Flavia, 'and I'll explain what we're aiming for.'

'Wonderful idea.' Giles was pleased that Flavia was taking Amy's potential seriously.

'You'll have to keep really quiet, darling, sit like a little mouse at the back and not interrupt,' warned Isobel.

'Of course,' said Amy.

To everyone's relief, the grey pall had lifted by Saturday morning. Fears that guests might be soaked before they even reached the theatre, that cars would get bogged down in the field, and that the bar and gallery would be swamped in dripping umbrellas and coats, began to recede.

At seven o'clock the family were ready. Edward had been sent to spend the night with Mungo at the Fortescues'; Caro, having pronounced herself to be tone-deaf and said she'd rather hear a pig being stuck any day than have to listen to a classical concert, had cheerfully agreed to look after the two boys. Isobel, who had been braced for a battle with her daughter over clothes, was surprised and relieved when Amy meekly agreed to wear her tartan taffeta skirt and frilly white shirt rather than the bottom-hugging lycra miniskirt in which she fancied herself.

The audience started to arrive early and it was clear that Perthshire Society was turning up for the event not only in force but dressed to kill. As Fiona whispered to Isobel, Grizelda Murray's grey crochet tube, which looked like the result of an unfortunate cross between chain-mail armour and a very old floorcloth, was a killer, but Flavia's deceptively simple shocking-pink silk shift was absolutely to die for. Lorn Dunbarnock, resplendent in his kilt, flowing hair and whiskers freshly shampooed and conditioned for the occasion and smelling discreetly of 'Extract of Limes' with a slight undertone of Dettox, had a moment of pure panic, which nearly sent him hurtling straight home when he spotted the lilies in the flower arrangements. Could he sense a sneeze coming on? He'd never actually had an attack of hay fever or asthma, but one never knew when long-expected disasters might suddenly strike and the sight of all that virulent-looking brown pollen was threatening in the extreme. He felt in his sporran for the antihistamine pills he always carried with him.

When everyone was finally seated Giles stood up to welcome his guests. He made a graceful speech, thanking all the festival's generous sponsors, the committee and everyone who had worked to get the renovated theatre ready; to warm applause, he mentioned the debt they all owed to his father; he paid a tribute to his mother, the original inspiration for the theatre, which resulted in some nervously polite clapping—though Lady Fortescue looked as if she'd unexpectedly bitten on a clove in an apple pie but was too well-bred to spit it out in public—and most of all he wanted to pay tribute to his own personal inspiration: his wife Isobel (terrific cheers and stamping, in response to which Isobel turned pink with pleasure).

'Now,' said Giles, 'on to the really exciting part of the evening . . .' and he went on to introduce Flavia and Megan.

The two musicians delighted everyone with their performance—or almost everyone: Lady Fortescue managed to remain as resistant to Flavia's magic as if she had sprayed herself with a high-factor anticharm protection before risking exposure to its dangerous rays—but most people were enchanted not only by the quality of Flavia's and Megan's playing but by their youth, looks and personalities. 'A notable partnership—let us hear them again as soon as possible,' one professional critic, not normally noted for his enthusiasm, wrote the following week.

The programme was a clever mix of lollipops for the ultra-conservative members of the audience, with some more challenging pieces for the musically adventurous. Their final rendering of the 'Hindu Song' from Rimsky-Korsakov's opera *Sadko* was greeted by tumultuous applause and as the performers came back on stage for the fourth time to cries of 'encore', Flavia stepped forward to make an announcement.

'I'm so glad you seem to have enjoyed our concert,' she said, 'because Megan and I have certainly loved playing for all of you. I'm enormously looking forward to taking my series of master classes for young flautists this week and hope some of you will come along to listen—and perhaps spot future stars in the making—but now, to celebrate a wonderful occasion, as a thank you to a terrific audience and as a special surprise for Giles and Isobel, Megan and I are going to be joined by an extremely talented young musician who is genuinely home-grown. Ladies and gentlemen, Amy Grant is going to join us to play an arrangement we have made for flute, harp and violin of traditional Hebridean melodies.

With a theatrical flourish Flavia held out her hand as, to Giles's and Isobel's astonishment, Amy, looking as composed as a true professional, got up from her seat beside them in the front row and walked up on to the stage.

For a moment Giles felt a terrible twinge of jealousy. It was the first time anything had happened in Amy's musical life in which he had had no direct input and he struggled between pride and resentment. Pride won. Then Isobel slipped her hand into his and Giles's fingers closed tightly over hers. A feeling of overwhelming pleasure and gratitude flooded through Isobel as Amy started to play with the two established artists. How lucky I am, she thought. Perhaps I have never truly appreciated the full extent of Amy's talent before, or the dedication that Giles has put into encouraging her. Individually we've both put great exertions into our children's progress, but now it's time for us to make a joint effort for them both in their very different ways.

They learnt later that Amy had actually been practising for weeks and it had all been a carefully prepared and well-kept secret between Flavia, Valerie and, of course, Amy herself. Far from sitting listening at the back like a quiet mouse, Amy had actually been rehearsing with the two musicians. It seemed a perfect ending to the opening concert of Glendrochatt's new centre.

During the tremendous champagne supper that followed the performance the renovations to the Old Steading Theatre were voted a huge success, the backcloth was pronounced a witty delight and Daniel's portrait of Isobel, now hanging in the drawing-room, was a sensation. Everybody talked about it. There was general disappointment that the artist had not been able to be present to receive congratulations in person, and several people expressed interest in getting him to paint their own likenesses for posterity and asked for his address. There were a lot of enquiries about Lorna, too, and much surprise that she was absent. Giles and Isobel explained about her unexpected trip to South Africa but said guardedly they thought she might possibly attend some of the other festival events later on—and privately hoped this would not be so.

After an interminable speech from Mr McMichael and an extremely good and short one from Lord Dunbarnock, Giles and Isobel once more stood on the steps of floodlit Glendrochatt and watched the last concert goers depart. It was well after midnight and the guests had seemed unwilling to leave.

'Oh, darling, what a triumph—and all due to your vision,' said Isobel. 'Don't you feel proud of our house and our daughter?'

'Very proud,' said Giles. 'Proud of my son too, but proudest of all of my wife.'

'What a beginning to our new venture and what an end to an extraordinary summer.' Isobel rubbed her cheek against the sleeve of Giles's velvet jacket. 'We had a lucky escape, didn't we, darling? We so nearly lost each other. Don't let's ever, ever do that again.'

'We won't,' said Giles. 'We'll keep our footing now, no matter what.'

'No matter what,' echoed Isobel, and they turned and walked back into the house with their arms round each other.

EPILOGUE

On a day in early October Lorna lay on the sofa in her drawing-room gazing at her portrait as though it exerted a magnetic pull on her. She simply couldn't stop looking at it.

Daniel had cleaned it and removed all traces of Amy's attack. No one would now guess that there had ever been anything wrong. He had finally agreed to sell the picture to Lorna, for an exorbitant sum, on condition that it could be exhibited in London the following year. She was pleased, though amazed that he could bear to part with it himself. He had sent it up to her flat in Moray Place, where it was waiting for her when she got home from her trip to Capetown.

And I am still just as beautiful as ever, she thought with satisfaction, although I am a different person now. I am two people. She put her hands on the almost imperceptible bulge below her waistline. It was just over four months since her week in Northumberland and for the first time that morning she had felt the baby quicken.

She had not broken the news of her pregnancy to any of her family yet. It was enough, so far, to hug the pleasure of it to herself. How it would affect Giles and Isobel remained to be seen, but affect them it certainly would. Lorna would make sure of that.

Life is full of uncertainties, thought Lorna, for all of us—but she looked forward to the future with renewed hope.